THE TWISTED ROAD
A Barrister Perris Novel
Book One

A. B. Michaels

HISTORIUM PRESS

Copyright © 2026 by A.B. Michaels
All rights reserved.

No part of this publication may be reproduced, distributed, or transmitted in any form or by any means, including photocopying, recording, or other electronic or mechanical methods, without the prior written permission of the publisher, except in the case of brief quotations embodied in critical reviews and certain other noncommercial uses permitted by copyright law.

Cover Design by Tara Mayberry
www.TeaberryCreative.com

Paperback ISBN: 978-1-964700-76-2
Ebook ISBN: 978-1-964700-77-9

Published by Historium Press U.S.A.
2026

Other Titles by A.B. Michaels

"Barrister Perris"
Historical Mystery Series

The Twisted Road
*Smok*e (coming in 2026)

A Golden City/Barrister Perris Novella
Affair at the Majestic

"The Golden City"
Historical Fiction Series

The Art of Love
The Depth of Beauty
The Promise
The Price of Compassion
Josephine's Daughter
The Madness of Mrs. Whittaker

"Sinner's Grove Suspense"

Sinner's Grove
The Lair
The Jade Hunters

Dedication

To those whose moral compass points unerringly and consistently true north. You are rare, indeed.

If you do not change direction, you may end up where you are heading.

Lao Tzu

Chapter One

Bloody Tuesday

**San Francisco
Turk Street Car Barn
May 7, 1907**

Nineteen years old, with the long, skinny limbs of a colt, Jimmy Walsh crouched behind a lamppost and shivered in the early morning fog. He dropped the brick he'd been clutching and hesitated before picking it up again. "This ain't right," he said, just loud enough for his nearest comrade in arms to hear. "It's like waitin' for Beelzebub to unleash his hounds of hell." Several yards away, the wooden barn that housed the city's electric trolley cars remained shuttered, but the sounds inside, muted through the mist, told him the show was about to begin.

Toke Griffin, a rock in one meaty hand, took a drag of his cheroot with the other. The smoke mixed with the fog, obscuring his leathered face. Two decades older than Jimmy, he was a union man from way back. This strike was nothing new. "Yeah, well them mutts are takin' our jobs and we got to stop 'em any way we can." He tossed the rock a few times and caught it. "They're scabs and rotten to the core. We got to let them know it." The gas-powered streetlight above Jimmy hissed, letting off sparks and a sulfurous belch. Toke barked in appreciation. "Even the damn lamp's on our side."

"Shut the hell up!" Another hiss—this one from a fellow striker, positioned behind one of the barbed wire barriers the scabs had set up to protect the cars. "You'll give us away."

Toke continued to grouse but lowered his voice. "Hell, you think they don't know we're out here? They're chompin' at the bit same as us." He tossed his rock again. "But we got right on our side, just like old Davey and Goliath. You wait and see."

Jimmy tried to swallow but couldn't get passed his Adam's apple. Lord, he wished he had some water or somethin' else to calm the jitters taking over his body. Even his lucky red flannel shirt was no help. Why didn't he keep the grub his mother had given him as he'd left that morning? She'd been up before him, knowing he had to go and not even trying to talk him out of it. "You keep your head down," she warned as she handed him the bag with bread and cheese and a slice of apple cake in it. She'd even put in a mason jar full of cider.

"Sure, sure, Ma," he'd told her, "Don't worry about it. I'll be fine." Giving her a peck on the cheek, he'd headed out, but once around the corner, he'd ditched the bag, thinking it would look squirrelly bringing a lunch sack to a riot. *What a damn fool.*

It shouldn't have come to this. It'd been over a year since the earthquake and fire had torn up the city, and the roads were still a tangled, busted-up mess. It was tricky driving the streetcars, and there were fewer drivers to boot. All the union wanted was an eight hour day and three bucks a shift. But United Railroads kept bickering with the city over repairs and used that excuse to refuse the union's demands. What else could the carmen do but strike? Then the company brought in the Farleymen to drive the cars—four hundred of them! It stunk to high heaven and Toke had the right of it: they had to stop the scabs from taking their jobs.

The crowd outside the barricade was growing. Jimmy saw groups of Poles and Italians and Irish, even Chinese. They weren't members of his union, but they were workingmen all the same, showing their support. That was labor for you, sticking together to get the job done. But there were also women and kids pouring out onto the street, like it was a parade or something! Thank God Ma had stayed home; he hoped his cousin was smart enough to keep her distance, too. This kind of ruckus was no place for females.

But damn if there weren't plenty of ladies mixed in with everybody else, a lot of them young and fired up, itchin' for a fight just like the men. He'd never admit it, but deep down, part of him admired their courage. Like Toke said, they were sticking up for what was right.

He was chewing on those thoughts when the big wooden doors on the barn began to slide open with a screech and the streetcars lumbered out, each driven by a scab, and each protected by several men with clubs and a guard with a rifle. The clock in the tower above the car barn soon started chiming the hour, but it was nearly drowned out by all the people screaming insults as they surged through an opening where the cars were supposed to leave the yard.

The strikers rushed by Jimmy, shoving him out of the way and already throwing whatever they'd been carrying—rocks and bricks and bottles—toward the scabs. Some strikers on the roofs pushed iron girders they must have got from construction sites; the beams hit the cars with a sickening clang.

Jimmy started to throw his brick, but stopped when he got a look at the second car and who was guarding it. Damnation, it was Emmett Barnes! That sonofabitch used to be a union man—not to mention Jimmy's best friend—and now he was a hired gun for the Farleymen! He watched Emmett shoot his rifle into the air a few times, and his shots were answered by rooftop union men protecting the strikers on the ground. He couldn't see Emmett's face too well, but he bet his ex-friend wasn't happy, especially since his shots hadn't stopped the crowd from swarming around his car. Jimmy wasn't part of that crowd; he couldn't make himself move—like he was paralyzed or something—as he watched it all unfold.

A brick sailed through the air and hit Emmett in the face; he dropped down, and Jimmy couldn't see him anymore. He glanced to his left and saw a man taking photographs of everybody. "Quit takin' pictures!" Jimmy yelled at him. "Get out of the way—you're gonna get hurt!"

More and more people began pushing Jimmy from behind, determined to stop the cars from running. He turned back to Emmett's car and saw ... and saw the rifle pointed toward the crowd from another angle. No, pointed right at *him*. Emmett? It couldn't be. He wouldn't do that, would he? He wouldn't—

Jimmy Walsh started to put his head down like his ma had told him, but he wasn't fast enough. He heard the crack of the rifle and felt the thump of the bullet hitting his skull. Then he felt nothing at all.

Chapter Two

A Tainted Case

A barrister's duty is to champion his client and seek justice in a court of law; when the client is guilty as sin, it complicates matters.

Jonathan Henry Perris rose to give his closing argument in the matter of the state of California vs. Horace Baxter. He faced the twelve men sitting in judgment before him.

"Gentlemen of the jury, you have already heard the facts of the case. My client, unfortunately, did shift money in relatively small amounts, from his firm's accounts payable to his own savings account, over the course of several months. Those deposits did indeed line up chronologically with the amounts later deemed missing from the company's ledger. It's notable that Mr. Baxter, being the mathematical expert that he is, was precise in his recording, which speaks to his intent, as you shall see.

"That is the 'what' of this case and we shall stipulate that for the record. But the 'why' of Mr. Baxter's actions is crucial and so, if you will indulge me, I would like to frame it within the context of the world in which each of us lives ... a world comprised of three lives: one public, one private, and one *secret*."

The prosecuting attorney looked comically befuddled. "Objection. What relevance does this have to the case before the court, Your Honor? Who cares why the defendant broke the law? The fact is, he broke it."

Judge Cormer cocked his head toward Jonathan. "Mr. Perris?"

"I believe motive has much bearing on this case, your Honor. I will make my point as succinctly as possible, but you will see the relevance, I assure you."

The judge scratched his beard. "Overruled, then. Proceed, Mr. Perris but do make it succinct."

Jonathan turned back to his audience. "For example, I have come to know the public lives of many of you sitting here today. You are, generally speaking—" he said this with the hint of a smile, "— a reputable lot: a banker, a woolens merchant, a sheep rancher, to name a few. I too have a public persona. I am an immigrant, of course, but a respectable one, I hope. I am a trial attorney—what we would call a 'barrister' in England." He extended his arms as if to display himself to the jury. He was wearing an impeccably tailored gray wool suit. "I bathe, I shave, and I dress suitably for my profession.

"But, like you, I also have a private life. I am not married and those who visit my abode might notice the lack of a woman's touch." He kept his rueful smile in place. "I indulge in perhaps more than the occasional whiskey, and I keep erratic hours because, unlike many of you, I have no one waiting for me."

His tone began to harden. "Were I a fly on the wall in your homes, what would I witness, I wonder? Perhaps a perfect illustration of domestic bliss ..." He leveled his gaze on specific members as he spoke. "... or perhaps not. My guess is that one or more of you enjoy your own favorite spirits to help you relax after a long day. Perhaps you drink too much, and your better half doesn't like it. Maybe you get a thrill out of playing the ponies and you become despondent when you lose more money than you can afford. Maybe your temper runs hot, and your colleagues, not to mention your family members, have borne the brunt of it."

Some individuals were becoming restive; a few looked decidedly uncomfortable, no doubt wondering where Jonathan was headed.

Certainly, Jonathan's legal counterpart wondered. "Really, Your Honor? Is any of this relevant in the slightest to the matter at hand?"

Jonathan caught Judge Cormer's warning look and forged ahead. "Ah, but then there is the secret life that many if not all of us lead." His voice dropped. "Perhaps you find pleasure with those you shouldn't be seen with ... maybe an addiction has you in its grip. Or perhaps you've done something so nefarious and so perverse that no one, *no* one must ever learn about it." He leaned toward the jury box. "What if I, for example, were a murderer? What if one of *you* were? None of us would ever know it because it's a *secret*." Jonathan let the last word linger.

"My client, Horace Baxter, led three lives, too. To the public he was an experienced adjustor for a respected insurance firm, in charge of determining the amount of payout for a given claim and reimbursing clients for their loss. His private life was relatively tame, with a harried wife and three boisterous young children, whom he adores."

Jonathan now grew animated, as if to let the jurors in on salacious gossip. "But his *secret* life involved a woman. Not in the sense you would imagine. Not a voluptuous siren who would turn the head of any man. No, gentlemen. She was his much younger sister, a dear sweet girl, naïve in the ways of the world, whom he had protected his entire life. She had been led astray and become, of all things, an *opium* eater. She was not married and could not hold a job. The only way to pay for her habit was to prostitute herself."

Jonathan glanced at his client. Horace Baxter was a hefty, florid man who was now slumped and staring at the table in front of him: a man mortified beyond the pale.

Days before, Jonathan had railed against the man who had lied to him and professed his innocence until discovery had proved him guilty on all counts. Only then had he explained his true reason for "cooking" the company books.

Jonathan sorely regretted taking the case, which he had done at the request of a colleague to whom he owed a favor. He wanted to believe he'd ignored his own instincts about the defendant, but in truth, he hadn't picked up any warning signs until it was too late. He should have known better.

"You have ruined any chance for me to establish reasonable doubt," he'd admonished his client. "For God's sake, man, with so much on the line, you don't keep such a secret from your attorney!" Jonathan had advised Baxter to throw himself on the mercy of the court by exposing all, but adhering to such a strategy didn't make it any easier to stomach.

Jonathan now continued his argument. "Imagine yourself in Mr. Baxter's shoes, gentlemen. Someone immeasurably close to you follows the wrong path and no matter how much you entreat them, harangue them, threaten them, cajole them, you cannot break the chain of dependence, a chain that has brought shame to your family—*secretly*—but at any moment could become public knowledge and lead to societal rejection and possibly the loss of your employment, resulting in economic ruin for you and your loved ones. It's a conundrum, is it not?"

He singled out the banker, who flinched slightly under Jonathan's gaze. "You have one recourse left, which is to find a discreet sanitarium where your beloved little sister can get help. Such a place costs money that you do not have. So, you devise a plan to obtain that money knowing in your heart that it's wrong to embezzle but rationalizing that it's a small amount compared to the company's vast book of business, and that you will find a way, somehow, to pay it all back. You are so intent on doing that, moreover, that you keep precise records. Your plan is to, over time, replenish the account, claim a 'slight miscalculation' in the monies due and return those amounts to each client.

"The time comes when you have enough set aside to pay for the treatment, and you are about to send your sister away when a curious and astute co-worker finds something amiss." Jonathan shrugged at the end of his tale. "And so you, like Mr. Baxter, might very well find yourself here today.

"I humbly ask you to consider the "why" of this case, gentlemen, in light of your own secrets, and show mercy on this man who did the wrong thing for the right reason. That is all."

—⋅✦⋅✦⋅—

Ten days later, Jonathan returned to the central jail to have a final word with his client. Although Horace Baxter was found guilty, the jury had taken pity on him and recommended time served, along with a modest fine and of course, the return of the stolen monies. Baxter would have to find a new job, but at least he wouldn't rot in a prison cell.

"You gonna break open the bubbly after getting your man out of jail?" The desk sergeant wanted to chat, but Jonathan was in no mood for it. He had a few parting words for his client and the sooner said the better. "That's a capital idea, but I'm afraid more mundane duty calls. Have you got Mr. Baxter's personal effects? I'll take them to him."

The sergeant handed Jonathan the bag and waved him through. "Well, don't be modest. The state had him dead to rights, but you got him off light as a feather. You're a silver-tongued devil, you are."

Jonathan ignored the compliment as he made his way down the hall. "That's not always a good thing," he muttered.

Horace Baxter was pacing his cell, waiting to be let out, when Jonathan arrived, asking the guard if he could have a few moments of privacy with his client.

"Thank God this day has arrived," Baxter said once the guard left. He donned his coat, buttoning it over his ample girth. "I'm ready."

"Well, I'm not," Jonathan said. "Sit down."

"What?" Baxter frowned. "Is something wrong?"

Jonathan fought to keep his words—and his actions—under control. "You might say that. I've been in contact with your so-called sister."

Baxter swallowed. "So ... you've seen Franny? How ... how did you—"

"Imagine my surprise when I called on your long-suffering wife to ask about your sister's welfare, only to find out it's *her* sister—sweet, young Francine— who's taken to a life of prostitution because of her addiction. And when I found that not so sweet young girl, plying her trade on Stockton Street, it turns out she's disappointed as hell that you aren't going to get her the help she so desperately needs. So disappointed, in fact, that she let slip who was responsible for her predicament in the first place."

The desperate look on Baxter's face spoke volumes. "Wh—what did she say?"

"You know what she said. And you know the only reason she doesn't share that information with her sister is that it would destroy your family."

"You don't understand. I mean ... how tempting it was. I ... I couldn't help myself." He hung his head, apparently bewildered by his own fall from grace.

"You couldn't keep your pants buttoned around your wife's sister—a member of your own family? And you did nothing when she began to escape her guilt through opiates?" Jonathan's disgust was palpable. "You are a pathetic excuse for a human being, Mr. Baxter. You are the worst kind of bounder because you're self-indulgent and you're weak. The only reason I'm not exposing you is the same reason Francine suffers in silence." Jonathan leaned in and lowered his voice. "But heed my words: if you go near that young woman again, I will personally see to it that you pay the price—and believe me, that price is much too high, even for a mathematical charlatan like you."

"What's going to happen to her?" Baxter whispered.

Jonathan rose to his full height. "That is no longer your concern. You focus on keeping your family fed, within the boundaries of the law."

The two men said nothing more as Jonathan escorted Baxter out of the jail and into a waiting hansom cab.

Good riddance.

It was nearly noon and given his frame of mind, returning to his law office held no appeal. Jonathan considered inviting the woman he'd been seeing to an impromptu lunch, but quickly tabled the idea. Not only was Lena difficult to reach, but in truth he was in no mood to be sociable. Instead, he headed to a nearby watering hole and ordered one of the whiskeys he'd told the jury about. He thought about Francine and what she must have been like before she was betrayed by a brother-in-law she had no doubt looked up to and trusted. Tomorrow he'd find a way to help the young prostitute conquer her demons, but right now, more than anything, he needed to mask the bitter taste of setting a guilty man free.

Chapter Three

The Gift

"You're positively barmy," Jonathan's fellow barristers had told him months before when he tried his last case in London's Old Bailey. They were probably right—he *had* been a bit crazy to leave a successful law practice in England for an American city that had just been decimated by earthquake and fire. But in fact, the timing couldn't have been better because San Francisco was in dire need of legal help as it started to rebuild.

The offices of Jonathan Perris and Associates took up half the top floor of a three-story building on Montgomery Street in the heart of the Golden City's financial district. The suite itself was without charm, but it had survived the earthquake nearly intact, which rendered it prime real estate. Since he abhorred driving, Jonathan considered himself fortunate that his commute entailed little more than a brisk walk along Hayes to Market Street, where he could take a cable car to work—at least when the cars were running. The carmen's strike was about to enter its third month, with no sign of resolution between the warring factions. Service was spotty at best.

Besides Jonathan, the firm consisted of Cordelia Hammersmith and Oliver Bean, two junior attorneys fresh from law school. Cordelia, a young widow, never talked about her earlier life, and Oliver seemed to lack much life experience at all, but they each possessed exceptional intellect. A newly hired private investigator rounded out the team, all held together by the "glue" that was his office manager, Althea. She was a handsome, sturdy woman in her mid-forties whose husband, a lineman on the railroad, had lost a leg in a freak accident and been laid off. He now took care of their four children, leaving her the unlikely breadwinner. She took pride in her work, running the office no doubt as efficiently as she would have her home. Both she and Jonathan were usually the first to arrive, and he often had to insist she leave before him. The strike, however, was taking its toll.

The Twisted Road

A few days after he'd put the Horace Baxter debacle to rest, Althea arrived later than usual, looking harried as she carried her familiar market basket to the small kitchen in the back.

"Good morning, Althea. I trust all is well with your family?" Jonathan delivered the standard greeting as he followed her, a habit born of the knowledge that she often brought in pastries, baked by her husband. He allowed her a stipend for that purpose, which not so coincidentally helped her out at home.

"Yes, all is well on the home front, although I tell you I'm none too happy with the state of affairs out there on the street." She lit the small stove, filled a kettle with water, and set it to boil.

"You're referring to the strike, I take it?"

"I surely am. I tell you, it rankles me no end. Most of us have to ride the streetcar from clear across town to get to our jobs—if we're lucky enough to have jobs—and what do the union drivers do? They shut the whole place down. Not a streetcar running to save your life until the scabs come in, half of whom don't know a car from a horse's behind. You take your life in your hands when you ride, not to mention the grief you get for crossing the picket line."

Althea had a point. With a downtown built on mud flats and shifting sand dunes, cursed with fog and wind, the city was further hampered by dozens of hills, seven of which were imposing enough to have names. Not everyone could easily walk to work. The damaged streets plus the ongoing streetcar troubles added far too much insult to injury. "It's all right to take a Hansom," he offered.

Althea waved him away. "I'll not be spending my wages—or yours—taking a fancy coach every time I turn around. I've got two feet, even if they are tired old dogs. I was lucky enough to hitch a ride part way on my neighbor's produce cart; otherwise, I'd still be looking for a strike wagon or trudging over the hill to get here and these hot cross buns would be your lunch instead of your morning pick-me-up."

"I'm glad you caught a ride," Jonathan said, transferring the pastries she'd brought to a plate. "I've heard the strike could linger for quite some time. What's your guess?"

Althea had filled a teapot and set it to steep. In deference to Jonathan's English roots, she alternated between making tea and coffee; this morning it was Earl Grey.

"I don't know. The drivers deserve a fair wage, but repairing all those torn-up roads doesn't come cheap. Both sides are dug in, and the papers keep fanning the flames with their claptrap about that young guard caught in the middle of the riot. I wouldn't be surprised if we had another Bloody Tuesday on our hands once the jury decides his fate."

"God forbid." Last month, the clash between strikers and scabs had gotten out of control. By the time the melee was quelled by police, dozens had been injured, two strikers were shot dead, and one of the guards, a young man named Emmett Barnes, was on trial for murder. Some considered him a hired killer, while others dubbed him a hero for protecting those who were trying to keep the city moving. The legal proceedings had begun and the public, evenly split between cries of "Hang him!" and "Let him go!" was on edge. Agitators on both sides were spoiling for a fight.

"Promise me that when the verdict comes in, you'll immediately get off the street, and make sure Cordelia and Oliver do the same," Jonathan cautioned.

Althea huffed. "As if I could tell that young lady anything. She's got a mind of her own, that one has. Now, Oliver you might make headway with. He's a reasonable soul, but he can be just as stubborn in his own quiet way. Honestly, Mr. P., you couldn't have picked two more opposite types to help you try your cases."

"I'm well aware of that," he replied with a grin. "They often bring wildly different perspectives to the matter at hand, which is at best enlightening, and at worst, entertaining."

Althea sent Jonathan a pointed look. "As for getting off the street? I'd tell you to take your own advice, but I doubt you'd pay me any mind, either."

Jonathan blew gently on the mug of tea she'd given him; the scent of bergamot was comforting. He reached for a bun. "Your doubts are misplaced, Althea; I live in fear of crossing you." He could hear her chuckling as he made his way to his private office. At the front of the suite, his colleagues had begun to arrive. It promised to be a productive day.

Sometime later Althea knocked on Jonathan's door with several letters in hand.

"A Lord Burnham called to invite you to lunch. He says he wants to thank you for your work on the Horace Baxter case. And these just came." She handed him four envelopes, three of which she'd opened. "Word's getting around. You're the one they want."

Jonathan skimmed the requests for his services. "Excellent. If they're lucky, *we're* the ones they're going to get. Check Cordelia and Oliver's schedules and set up some preliminary meetings, if you would, Althea."

Normally, the prospect of more business would have buoyed Jonathan's spirits, but it was the last missive, whose return address he recognized, that deflated him. Althea noticed his change in demeanor.

"I thought it might be personal," she said. "Bad news?"

He glanced at the letter, which he hadn't yet opened. "This? It's nothing," he lied as he casually placed it inside his coat.

It was not nothing.

At midnight, the partitioned three-story Victorian Jonathan had rented off Alamo Square was quiet as a morgue. He shared a common wall with the Bhandaris, a family of Nepalese immigrants, who were no doubt enjoying the sleep of the innocent.

Jonathan, however, was still awake, having tried diligently through work and bourbon to avoid reading the letter he'd been handed earlier that day. *This is daft*, he thought. He'd known it was coming well before Althea gave it to him … and he'd sensed what was in it without any warning from its sender.

It was the bloody *cadou* at work, the strange extra sense inherited from his mother that she had called, in her native tongue, a "gift."

Gift, my arse. The sense, more than mere intuition or a lucky guess, was a kind of "pre-knowing." Sometimes it was heralded by little sparks in his line of vision, but sometimes there was no warning at all, and it blind-sided him. It was maddeningly unreliable. It certainly hadn't helped him with the Horace Baxter case; he'd felt no inkling about Baxter's hidden agenda, no warning about his perfidy. If the *cadou* was so useful, why hadn't it steered him away from that mess?

"You must accept that you were born under a lucky sign," his mother had told him when they'd quarreled about it. "Let me teach you how to use it and it will serve you well, just as it has served me."

But he'd refused to be taught. To his logical mind, the so-called gift was far more of a curse—the first half of his life, lived with his reckless mother, was evidence of that.

During the decade he'd practiced law in London, he'd only had to deal with his peculiar inheritance a handful of times. But those episodes, as now, had disrupted his concentration in a myriad of ways with no positive results to show for them.

In short, the *cadou* was a hindrance, not a boon. He didn't need it, didn't want it, in fact loathed the only tangible trait passed down from the woman who bore him.

Perhaps he should have learned more about it in order to destroy it.

One thing he *couldn't* do was ignore it. So, with a sigh of resignation, he opened the letter and read:

> *Dear Mr. Perris,*
>
> *It has been eighteen months since you hired my firm, Jackson, Tilson and Benchley, to locate Miss Esme Marie Serafin, a female now age fifty-eight, of Romanian heritage. Since that time, we have tracked down every lead you initially provided and pursued any subsequent trails related to those leads. We have searched both within and outside of the United Kingdom. As you can see from the attached report, all avenues have led to dead ends. The trail, we are sorry to say, has grown cold.*
>
> *We very much appreciate your confidence in our firm, and we wish we could have produced results for*

you, but it was not meant to be. In light of that, I am enclosing half of your original retainer, the rest having gone for expenses, as I'm sure you can appreciate.

Good luck with your search, Mr. Perris, and if we can be of service in any other matter, please do not hesitate to contact us.

Sincerely,
Aloysius Jackson
Jackson, Tilson and Benchley
Discreet Inquiries

"Well, that's that," he said to the room, as if it, too, wanted to hear what had become of his mother. "I have done what I can do."

He waited in the quiet, knowing what came next. The *cadou*, mollified for the moment, left a whisper in its wake.

Keep looking, it seemed to say. *Use my gift to find me.*

Jonathan filed the letter with the agency's other correspondence and took a moment to gather his resolve. "No, it's too late," he announced to the night. "You left nearly twenty years ago, Esmé. You obviously don't want to be found."

Silence answered him, but an echo of the *cadou* remained.

Chapter Four

A Fateful Lunch

The following Friday, it took nearly two hours for Jonathan to make his way across town to the Cliff House, where Lord George Burnham, in San Francisco on business, had invited him for lunch. Much of Jonathan's time was spent trying to hail a hansom cab. The strike had snarled up public transportation to the point that private conveyances were in high demand. He was moments away from hauling out his Landaulet from the garage—a proposition he dreaded—when a cab finally showed up, its horse snorting and prancing from all the activity.

"Four dollars one way," the cabbie said, not even bothering to sound apologetic. The fare was more than twice what the lunch would cost, but the driver knew he could get that and more from the next foot-weary pedestrian. Jonathan climbed aboard.

Perched on a headland above the Pacific Ocean, the opulent seven-story restaurant was built to resemble what some considered a French chateau and others called a "Gingerbread Palace." Miraculously, it had withstood the earthquake and resultant firestorm with only minor damage. The property's leaseholder, John Tait, was so thrilled to have escaped costly repairs that he instigated a major renovation of his own. Exterior improvements were in full swing, and the "new and improved" Cliff House would soon boast an even more dramatic oceanside experience for guests.

The food was decent, offered in a series of public dining rooms and private parlors. But the reason for making the journey had more to do with the views than the cuisine. Jonathan never tired of the biting sea air and infinite horizon; it reminded him that the world remained full of possibilities. It was too bad the experience was marred by dining with the man who'd sent Horace Baxter his way.

Lord Burnham, a baron, was already seated when Jonathan arrived, but he stood up, greeting Jonathan with the usual, "Glad you could make it, old man," even though he was at least twenty-five years older. To Burnham, every male in his social class was an "old man"; it was the password to an exclusive club.

Though he used a walking stick, the baron was about Jonathan's height and in excellent physical shape for his age. His light brown hair was still thick, only just beginning to lose its color, and he hadn't let himself go to seed like so many others in his privileged position. Jonathan suspected the stick was more for status than utility.

Burnham was a bit of a popinjay, yes, but he was well connected. The previous year, he'd introduced Jonathan to several Golden City power brokers who were in London on business. Members of the city's vaunted "Committee of Fifty," they'd been directed by the mayor to oversee the rebuilding of San Francisco from the ground up. Housing and transportation, food procurement and banking, health and welfare — every function of the city had to be dealt with as the new skyline began to rise. Reconstruction on such a massive scale required endless legal maneuvering; based on Jonathan's impressive record—augmented no doubt by his patrician demeanor—they'd offered him more than enough legal work to launch his stateside practice.

Burnham had thus done Jonathan a considerable favor, but such largess usually came with strings. The baron apparently knew Baxter from his work in the insurance field, and he'd asked Jonathan to represent the man. Given the unsavory outcome of the case, Jonathan felt he'd more than repaid his debt. But he suspected the day's invitation wasn't simply a gesture of appreciation. Burnham expected more.

"Thank you for inviting me," Jonathan said.

"We Brits have got to stick together, what? Especially when we're out in the hinterlands. I enjoy the food at the Palace, mind you, but it's a bit more private out here, wouldn't you say?" Burnham had been smoking a cigar and stubbed it out after clapping Jonathan on the back. "Hope you don't mind—I took the liberty of ordering lunch for us. No sense wasting time, eh?"

They took their seats and shortly thereafter a clear broth with sorel mushrooms was served, followed by a poached salmon and squab *en crout*. Jonathan had grown up eating birds and fish, but the seasonings had been much less subtle, and certainly pastry had not been part of the menu. He dug in.

The first part of the meal was spent in idle chatter. Was Jonathan enjoying himself and the work he'd undertaken for the Committee of Fifty?

"Very much," he answered benignly. "The Committee has done wonders in helping to get the city back on its feet."

"No doubt. No doubt," Burnham said. "At least that scoundrel of a mayor did one thing right before they send him off in chains, what?"

Jonathan smiled but said nothing. Like every other institution he'd ever dealt with, from Parliament to London's East End gangs, San Francisco's city government was rife with corruption. Just a few weeks earlier, the mayor, Eugene Schmitz, had been convicted of graft and was headed to prison. The Board of Supervisors should have been frog-marched right alongside him, but every guilty member had turned state's witness and been granted immunity from the crime of taking bribes.

There were no heroes at City Hall.

Getting no rise from Jonathan, Burnham pressed on. "When I heard you took on the case of that murderous doctor, I knew I could count on you to help out my colleague. And by God you did it. Good for you, old man. Show these provincials what a true barrister can do with the law."

Jonathan could feel his blood pressure rising. "Actually, the case regarding Dr. Justice relied in the end on his own testimony, which, had he listened to me, he would never have put forth. I'm just glad he didn't listen to me."

"Oh, you're much too modest," the baron said, already sipping his second glass of white wine. "I hear you did the legwork to paint a sympathetic portrait of the man—a capital way to sway a jury if ever there was one. Of course, you did much the same with Baxter, although it sounds like he'd actually stepped over the line, poor sod. Brilliant strategy on your part."

Jonathan's jaw tightened at the baron's obsequiousness. *Get on with it, man. What do you want?*

About halfway through the meal, Burnham showed his true colors. "You're no doubt privy to the enormous cost of the city's reconstruction," he began.

"Certainly, it's been costly," Jonathan agreed. "Some estimates put it at five hundred million. Staggering. Here it is a year later, and the rebuilding is finally ramping up to full speed."

"Yes, quite." Burnham perused the stem of his glass before finishing off its contents. He signaled the waiter for another refill before adding, "I'm sure you're also aware of the extensive payout the Royal Commonwealth has been forced to undertake."

Yes, Jonathan was all too aware. Burnham was the major stockholder of the Royal Commonwealth Assurance Company, one of the many insurers from Britain and Europe that had underwritten San Francisco's pre-earthquake building boom. Since the catastrophe, that company was required to make good on all the losses it had contracted to protect. "It's a bit of bad luck all around," he said.

Burnham seemed to choose his next words carefully. "The fact is … the Royal doesn't feel it should have to pay one hundred percent of the claims, given that the damage was caused by an act of God, which the earthquake certainly was."

In that moment, Jonathan's misgivings about Lord Burnham were confirmed in spades. "I'm not sure I understand," he said. "Even if your policies expressly excluded such disasters, the overwhelming damage throughout the city was caused by the fire, which virtually all policies cover, exclusions or no."

Burnham's self-confident façade was beginning to waver; Jonathan saw the signs of strain around his mouth as he tried to bolster his point of view. "Yes, but since the fire stemmed from the earthquake, it logically falls under that exclusion and is therefore exempt from coverage."

Jonathan paused before exposing what he felt was the root of the problem. "I don't think you'll be able to sustain that argument, Lord Burnham. Between us, are you going to have problems fulfilling your financial obligations?"

The baron played nervously with the knife next to his plate. After a few moments he looked up. "Candidly, yes," he said. "And I am looking to you for some help in the matter."

Here it comes, Jonathan thought. "How do you think I may assist you...*this* time?"

"You have the ear of James Phelan, who heads the finance subcommittee of the Committee of Fifty. I would like you to have him contact the companies we are underwriting, primarily United Railroads, who owns the streetcars, and explain to them that despite the exclusion, we are prepared to pay sixty percent."

Only sixty percent? That was never going to happen. "You know as well as I do that most companies, notably Lloyd's, are waiving exemptions and paying one hundred percent," Jonathan replied. "And even those who aren't as generous are negotiating down to seventy-five. Frankly, I wouldn't be surprised if many of those didn't end up in court. So, sixty just isn't tenable under the circumstances. Have you tried contacting United directly to see if you can work something out? I have met Mr. Calhoun on several occasions, and he seems quite reasonable."

"My God, man, you think I haven't tried that already? That crook you think is reasonable nearly bit my head off!" He sounded ready to crack but caught himself in time and lowered his voice. "Calhoun's on shaky ground himself with that bribery indictment hanging over his head, not to mention the bloody streetcar strike."

"You have a point," Jonathan admitted. "He probably has little room to negotiate, even if he were so inclined."

"Precisely. Which is why if some relief can't be orchestrated on this side of the pond, you'll have to use your influence on the other."

Jonathan paused in the act of drinking the beer he'd ordered. "What are you talking about?"

"You know bloody well what I'm talking about. A group led by the Duke of Strickland is blocking a bill in the Commons that would enable Her Majesty's Exchequer to offer financial alleviation to companies who find themselves in extraordinary circumstances, such as Royal Commonwealth."

"Why are they blocking it?"

The Twisted Road

Burnham waved his hand dismissively. "They believe companies like mine should rise and fall on their merits, no matter the particulars. They feel that no entity, no matter how beneficial to the public good, is too big to fail. They're completely short-sighted and provincial in their thinking."

"Yet ... Lloyd's of London must have a bigger book of business than Royal Commonwealth and is honoring its commitments in full."

Burnham frowned his displeasure but followed it with a shrewd look. "Be that as it may ... are you saying, given your connections, that you won't help them see the error of their ways?"

"To be honest, I don't believe I would have the influence you ascribe to me, and frankly, I'm not sure they're in error."

"And you won't plead my case to Phelan or anyone else on the Committee of Fifty?"

Jonathan looked directly at Lord Burnham. He didn't think it was possible, but he almost felt sorry for the man. It must be frustrating as hell to see your livelihood and possibly your reputation sliding away and not be able to do anything about it. But he stopped short of true sympathy as he realized why Burnham had done him such a favor so many months before. It wasn't to help a colleague like Baxter out of a future legal jam—it was to help Burnham himself in case he got caught in a catastrophic financial position. His tone remained steady. "Unfortunately, I don't believe there's anything more I can do for you, Lord Burnham."

Burnham took a deep swallow of his third glass of wine. "Well then, you leave me no choice."

"No choice?"

"I have heard that you have, shall we say, quite an active 'social life.' I'm referring to the little matter of your latest skirt."

"Excuse me?"

"You heard me. The woman you're currently sleeping with."

What? How on earth did Lord Burnham know about Lena? "I don't know what you're implying, but—"

Burnham's *bon homie* was gone, replaced by the ruthless demeanor of a cornered animal. "Let's not quibble with *faux* outrage, shall we? It's known that you've been seeing the charming and rather worldly Magdalena von Mendelssohn. I understand she's quite beautiful."

Where was this going? Jonathan slowly nodded. "And what is that to you?"

"You are to see her this evening. *The Pirates of Penzance* at the Orpheum Theater followed by dinner, yes?"

"Where are you getting this information?"

"That doesn't matter. What matters is that I think there are two questions you'll want to ask her."

"What are those?"

"The first is 'Darling Lena, what is your real name?' And the second is, 'Who was the last man you bedded back in London?' Once you know the answers, you'll no doubt want to make sure no one else does. Perhaps then we can speak again about what you can and can't do for me."

It took a few moments for Jonathan to fully digest Burnham's implication. Then it was a matter of deciding whether or not to smash the baron's face into the bread pudding he had ordered for dessert. In another life he wouldn't have thought twice about it. But now … now he refrained, choosing instead to rise from the table and calmly place his napkin beside his half-eaten fruit plate.

"Lord Burnham, thank you once again for recommending me to the Committee of Fifty, even though I now fully understand why you did so. I truly do enjoy the work and the people I am getting to know here. Having said that, I believe I have already repaid my debt to you. Moreover, I now count you among the most despicable men I've ever met, and believe me, there is quite a bit of competition for that coterie. Once I find the answers to the questions you've proposed, I will contact you. And I promise, you will not be happy with what I have to say."

Burnham smiled complacently. "We will see about that."

Jonathan left the Cliff House with no visible sign of agitation, but inside he was seething. Who had he been seeing for the last several weeks and how had he walked into what was obviously a trap? Once again, the *cadou* had failed him.

Left jab. Jab. Jab.
Push him back,
Right hook. *Now.*

As soon as he punched, Jonathan instinctively shifted his stance so that as the man's head snapped back, he could kick his opponent in the groin. Anticipating it, the man grabbed Jonathan's foot and promptly tossed him on his butt.

"How many times I gotta tell you? Marquess of Queensberry, Jonnie boy." Seamus "Mick" McGregor, the ex-fighter and owner of Mick's Boxing Gym, reached down to help his pupil up. "You already know how to brawl; I'm tryin' to show you how to beat the bejesus out of your opponent in a civilized fashion. That's what you asked me to do, ain't it?"

"Sorry, Mick. I wasn't thinking."

"Damn right, you wasn't thinkin'. Now you gonna get your head outta your ass or what?"

Jonathan shook off the rebuke. "Yes, yes. Let's go again."

Several rounds later, with little progress to show for it, Mick called it for the day. It was a good thing he did; Jonathan was sore and sweat-soaked, and more than ready to get cleaned up. It was a slow afternoon, and he was the only one in the old-fashioned shower cage, grimacing as the stilettos of hot water struck his legs, torso and arms. The "needle shower" was aptly named.

Does Burnham know something or is he bluffing? The question dogged Jonathan to the point that instead of returning to his office after lunch, he'd gone directly to Mick's, two blocks over on Sansome. A few rounds in the ring should have dissipated the poisonous energy roiling within him, but it wasn't enough. His mind kept returning to the woman he'd been seeing. If she was truly connected to his past, she'd done a masterful job of hiding it. But to what end?

Before his session with Mick, he'd called Althea to let her know he wouldn't be in the office until later, if at all, but Cordelia had picked up the telephone.

"You gave Althea the afternoon off," she reminded him. "It's a holiday weekend, remember?"

Of course, how stupid of him. How could he have forgotten America's Independence Day? Flags were flying everywhere, and the fireworks set off in his neighborhood last night had gone on forever. It was another sign of how distracted he'd become.

He made light of his answer. "Yes, that's right—the little matter of Britain giving you colonial upstarts the old heave ho. So, what are you doing there, may I ask? Didn't I give you time off, too?"

"Yes, you did, but I've been assembling the facts of the Letterman case and considering some motions. I'm going to show the judge what an absolute scoundrel our client's husband is. I will not let him get away with blaming her for the divorce."

That brought a smile, a welcome distraction this time. Cordelia was so vigorous when proving her case that he'd mentally dubbed her "The Hammer." She was a very attractive young woman who could have gone through life relying on her physical attributes alone. Instead, she chose to focus on her intelligence, logic, and sheer grit; he'd hired her because of it. "I have the utmost confidence in you," he replied, "but please, don't stay too late, especially if you're by yourself. And take a cab home; the streetcars can't be trusted." He imagined Cordelia rolling those intense, dark eyes of hers; she was a native of the Golden City and knew her way around much better than he. Still, it paid to be cautious.

He finished dressing and was gathering his belongings when Mick stuck his head into the locker room. "Gonna be a little after-hours action tonight, just so you know."

Jonathan shrugged on his coat. "I've got a social engagement, I'm afraid."

"Well, it's not startin' 'til well after midnight. The usual, plus a few new players ... in case you're interested."

"Thanks, Mick—and thanks for taking me under your wing."

"Well, I'm still bettin' on Tommy Burns, but you're no slouch. You got a lotta juice in those punches—you just gotta put 'em where they'll do the most good."

"Sage advice," Jonathan said. He was hardly a match for the world heavyweight champion, but he did like to get physical; it was a superior way to let off steam—as long as he kept it under some semblance of control.

Outside the gym he was lucky enough to hail a cab almost immediately and called up to the driver, "Alamo Square, if you please." Heading home, he hoped to relax a bit before the evening began—an evening he already knew would end badly.

Chapter Five

Deception

Magdalena Regina von Mendelssohn was a wealthy, beautiful, and entrancing young socialite from Vienna who had occasionally and enthusiastically shared Jonathan's bed for the past several weeks. He had met her at a house party given by the banker Grayson Daniel, who assumed Magdalena and Jonathan must have a lot in common because they shared an English accent. Hers, she later explained, came from her time spent in a "horrendously dictatorial" boarding school in Oxford. The only positive outcome of that experience, she claimed, was the realization that she had an affinity for art.

Now free to spend her inheritance—her wealthy parents having tragically died in a carriage accident outside of Salzburg—she was in the midst of a self-directed world tour, in which she hoped to "find out where I belong." Naturally, she and Jonathan had struck up a conversation and discovered they did indeed have some overlapping interests, not the least of which was a healthy physical attraction to one another.

Lena, as she liked to be called, preferred to be picked up in the elegant lobby of the *Auberge Pacifique*, a chic hotel in Pacific Heights known for its European clientele. Despite her modern sensibilities, she was discreet when it came to her reputation. "It wouldn't do to bring a man up to my room," she demurred the first time such an invitation was warranted. Instead, they had gone to Jonathan's abode. He was fine with the decision. In truth, he loved his neighborhood, with its mix of immigrants, home-grown and transplanted San Franciscans living in surprising harmony.

Unfortunately, others of his social standing, including Lena, weren't so impressed. Her coolness toward his surroundings was the first of several warning signs that their relationship was not destined to last. But since she hadn't indicated her stay was anything other than a prolonged stop on her worldwide itinerary, Jonathan hadn't been concerned.

Until now.

Per their last conversation, he was to pick Lena up in front of her hotel and head to the theater on Fillmore, after which they would enjoy a late supper and perhaps other amusements. Based on Burnham's salacious innuendos, however, Jonathan's first reaction had been to forgo the night's entertainment and confront her immediately. But he'd reconsidered, deciding to wait until she had relaxed enough to be completely honest with him.

Lena was waiting outside as Jonathan's cab pulled up. She looked smashing, as always, her long, honey-gold hair coiffed into a hairstyle worthy of a royal. She was nearly as tall as he, and the gown she'd chosen, in a burnished red, melted over her slender curves. It was elegant yet flirted with the boundaries of propriety and she had draped a silky shawl over her shoulders to tease the viewer. A day earlier he would have enjoyed the subtle quickening her beauty elicited, along with the anticipation of where the evening would lead. Tonight, however, his body's response was negligible. Although he'd been forced to playact on many occasions throughout his life, he did not enjoy it.

"You look beautiful," he said as he helped her into the cab. "But then, you always do."

She smiled enigmatically, a gesture he now realized she used often. "And you are always most kind," she murmured.

The Pirates of Penzance was a comic opera known for its silly plot and boisterous choruses, best suited to a mind unencumbered by worries—or perhaps designed to distract from them. It failed to deliver on either count.

Lena appeared to enjoy the show but did glance at Jonathan more than once. "We can leave any time," she whispered.

He took her hand in his. "No, I'm fine. Just some work-related matters swimming around in my head."

It was nearly eleven by the time they left the theater, choosing to walk to Antonio's, the Italian bistro where Jonathan had made a reservation. If Lena had any inkling that all was not right between them, she did not show it; in fact, she was slightly more chatty than usual. "I find it amusing that although it is an entirely British satire,

The Pirates of Penzance actually premiered in New York City. Do you not find that comical?"

Jonathan shrugged. "I believe it had to do with copyright matters," he said absently. "Gilbert and Sullivan wanted to help secure the American rights, but in the end were unsuccessful."

Lena tapped his arm lightly. "Ever the barrister, I see. Well, let's enjoy the rest of the evening, shall we?"

I doubt that's going to happen, he thought.

Out of habit, Jonathan had secured a private booth in the back of the long restaurant, and this evening he was glad of it. They talked of inconsequential things through a green salad and veal piccata, but during the tiramisu, Lena once again noted his pensive behavior. "Penny for your thoughts?" she asked.

He could no longer put it off. "I'm wondering what your real name is."

The look on her face told him everything: far from being shocked or bewildered, she hesitated. He could almost see the wheels turning in her lovely head. "What … what are you implying?"

"I think you know. I have learned that you are not who you claim to be, and I'm wondering when I'm to meet the real Lena … or whoever you are."

She stared at him for the longest time before letting go of a small sigh. "Sybil. Sybil West." She smiled and offered her hand as if to make a joke of it. "It's a pleasure to meet you."

When Jonathan continued to gaze at her, she placed her hands in her lap.

"I'm waiting," he said.

The fidgeting began. The rearranging of the cutlery. The sip of coffee, the dabbing of the lips with the napkin. Finally, she met his eyes. "I thought you might know my real name, so I came up with another one."

"And another identity, apparently. I assume you are not from Austria nor the product of a horrific boarding school in Oxford." She shook her head. Burnham was right about the alias, so he was probably right about the rest of her past. But Jonathan wanted to hear it from her directly. She owed him that much. "Why would I have known you?"

Another hesitation. "I knew your brother."

Like an anchor, her words pulled him into the depths. He realized how light he'd felt since moving from London. After Burnham's initial recommendation of him, his connections here in the Golden City had been of his own making—no strings had been attached. Few people actually knew who Jonathan's brother was, only that "Barrister Perris," as they'd dubbed Jonathan, came from what they considered a rather pretentious English background. Now the weight of that background was nearly immobilizing.

"I'd known he had a mistress," he said, betraying no emotion, "but nothing more than that. You are she?"

She straightened her spine, schooling her features into an expression of dignity, almost defiance. Her countenance revealed that she felt herself to be above the connotations of that word, but she couldn't deny that it applied to her. "No longer," she said primly.

Jonathan nodded. "I would imagine that at least is true. I've read the duke is now openly courting an earl's daughter ... and you have been sharing my bed instead. The question is why? Did someone put you up to it? Lord Burnham, perhaps?"

Her eyes flashed and he took a small measure of comfort in knowing she had a few standards left when it came to sleeping with men. "No one forced me, *certainly* not him. I admit that my aim in the beginning was to strike back at your brother. We'd been together for over two years, and I'd hoped, well ..." She shrugged slightly. "But someone betrayed my trust and the man I thought I might spend the rest of my life with washed his hands of me. It was ... painful, to say the least."

"I'm sure it was. And I know very well that anger can make a person do things they might otherwise find repugnant." *Much like I feel now.* "But it seems like quite an elaborate charade for a spot of emotional revenge."

Sybil responded with "Hell hath no fury, haven't you heard?" But her attempt at levity failed again and she tried a different approach. "It may have started out as revenge, but then ... then I got to know you.

You look very much like him, you know, but you are altogether different men. You make love differently, for one thing. You're at once more passionate and yet you possess a deep reservoir of something quite . . . I don't know, *dark* might be the word. It's intoxicating. I know it must have to do with your upbringing—"

"That is neither here nor there," he interrupted. "The question is, are you going to use this interlude to embarrass my brother or me? I caution that if you do, it will harm your reputation far more than it will his or mine. That may not be fair, but that is the way of it."

Sybil had begun to tear up, but was her emotion real? He gave her no comforting words and she continued her *mea culpa*.

"You're right, of course. It's no more than I deserve." She seemed awash in retrospection. "From the beginning it was all so very complicated. There were too many moving parts, despite the goal." She smiled then, gracious in defeat. "I was encouraged to keep at it, you see, but deep inside I never felt I could pull it off, with him, or with you. And I was right."

Jonathan frowned. "What do you mean 'pull it off'? That might apply to me, perhaps, but why my brother? It sounds like a campaign. And who encouraged you?"

Lena/Sybil looked nonplussed. "Oh, well, a poor choice of words, I suppose." After a moment she added, "I did care for him, you know … and you, too."

Her rationalization sounded weak. "What will you do now?" he asked.

"I suppose that depends on you," she ventured, her eyes imbued with a desperate kind of hope.

You must be joking. But he was never one for abject cruelty; he preferred a more subtle retaliation when required. He reached across the table for her hand. "Lena—or rather, Sybil—you know the answer already. Even if this gambit of yours hadn't come to light, we were not destined for each other."

"I know that," she said wistfully. "I just wish…"

"If wishes were horses, beggars would ride," Jonathan rejoined without heat. He removed his hand. "Will you return to England?"

On this matter Sybil was clear. "Not right away. Your brother salved his conscience by deeding me a property—in Oxford, by the way—which I promptly sold. So, I have funds to take the Grand Tour that I have been prattling on about." She sent him a wan smile. "Are you sure you don't want to see the world with me?"

Her soft cajoling grated on him. "Thank you for the offer, but I am content here for now." He signaled the waiter, who brought the check. It was just after midnight and past time for them to part company. He was beginning to feel more than a little antipathy toward her.

"The Auberge isn't where you're staying, is it?" he asked as they waited for a cab.

"No."

"Then may I take you home—to where you really live?"

Sybil reached over and touched Jonathan's chest. "Does the evening have to end?"

Is there anything worse than feeling anger? Pity, maybe. If she wasn't a woman, he might have verbally sliced her for degrading herself so. Instead, he took her hand and kissed it. "Come now, you know you never cared for my neighborhood. Where can I drop you?"

With a wisp of a smile, she said, "Let me retain this one last charade, won't you?" The hansom cab pulled up, its horse snorting in the cool night air. She called up to the driver, perched above and behind the cab. "The *Auberge Pacifique,* please."

Jonathan helped her into the carriage and climbed in after her.

She looked over her shoulder. "It's not necessary."

"It is," he said. "We'll end this as it began."

They said nothing on the way to the hotel. When they arrived, a uniformed doorman, complete with military-style epaulets and cap, walked over to help her alight, leaving them no privacy for tearful good-byes—not that there would have been any.

"Send me a postcard now and again," Jonathan said, waving away her attempts to pay the driver. "If it's any consolation, my brother has excellent taste."

"A gentleman to the end," she said, and quickly turned to enter the hotel, her posture elegant and self-assured as always. He'd detected the catch in her voice, however, and decided, for his own self-respect, that her regret was real.

Still ... it didn't pass muster that Lena/Sybil would have planned the entire escapade, much less paid for it, by herself. A woman scorned, and all that, but she must have had some help. How else would Lord Burnham have known about her? The thought crossed his mind that she might have financed her revenge in part on her back. Burnham was decades older, but he had money ... at least for now. Or perhaps he'd hired her, not for himself, but to put Jonathan in an untenable position vis à vis his brother. He could imagine the headline: "Prominent Brothers Sharing Mistresses? What's next—Wives?"

He signaled the driver to park on the other side of the street and wait; it took several minutes but his patience was rewarded. Sybil stepped outside again and hailed another cab. She was wearing a darker coat and had donned a matching hat with veil. Where had she gotten them if she didn't have a room at the hotel? His curiosity got the better of him.

"Follow them," he instructed.

Jonathan's cab trailed discreetly behind while Sybil traveled east across downtown. Her driver maneuvered onto Washington toward the water before heading up Kearny to Pacific. There, at the corner, her cab stopped in front of a large clapboard rooming house affectionately known to residents of the Barbary Coast as "Aunt Susie's."

Jonathan had passed it many times on his way to Mick's gym. It was in fact a well-known brothel whose rooms were rented out in four-hour increments. Sybil, still veiled, exited the cab and walked inside.

Jonathan felt the anger he'd tamped down earlier begin to resurface. Is *that* how she'd been financing her ruse? My God, it couldn't be! He tapped loudly on the roof and his driver pulled over.

"How much?" Jonathan asked.

"For the ride or for Aunt Susie's?" The cabbie smirked as he quieted his horse. Receiving nothing but a glare for his attempt at humor, he mumbled the price of the trip. Grim-faced, Jonathan paid for it and sent the cabbie on his way.

For several minutes he stood outside, staring at the edifice. It simply didn't make sense. How could a woman as beautiful, clever and sophisticated as Sybil—a woman who had been consort to a powerful member of the aristocracy in London—stoop to earning her keep by working in a low-rent bordello? What had happened to her? For that matter, what had happened to Jonathan? With all his experience, why hadn't he picked up on such a grift? Why hadn't his wretched *cadou* warned him of her duplicity? Perhaps he was getting soft after all, not paying enough attention to where he was and, more importantly, *who* he was.

Long-buried memories welled up in him, turning his insides rank. If his brother had harmed her in some way, he would make sure the man paid far more than the deed to a piddling house in Oxford.

But no. She did not strike him as a victim, even at the end. She seemed to be well aware of the game she'd been playing. Perhaps turning tricks was something she enjoyed; perhaps that was a game, too.

He thought about following her into Aunt Susie's and confronting her. But to what end? No matter how she explained herself, it would no doubt be a lie. They had no future, so making a scene would solve nothing. After considering his options, he made the decision to let it go. He'd let *her* go. She was smart enough to know he'd been right about whose reputation would suffer. Tomorrow he would contact Lord Burnham and call his bluff. Did the man really want to be caught up in a lewd but short-lived scandal? The upper crust would titter, but it didn't tolerate snitches, no matter the transgression. For his tattling, Burnham would become a social pariah, which was not the way to dig himself out of his current financial predicament.

Still, Jonathan's hostile energy continued to flow, and he checked his watch. Mick's after-hours game of Faro was just getting started. It was illegal, yes, but indulged in by those on all rungs of the city's social ladder. Tolerated by the beat cops, it too was an enterprise in which informants paid dearly. It was also a game Jonathan enjoyed immensely. Perhaps he'd salvage something of the evening yet.

He pulled his coat collar up against the frigid night and headed toward Sansome, just a few blocks away.

Chapter Six

Arrested

The young woman lay sprawled next to the sagging cathouse bed in a position rarely if ever assumed in her line of work. Her throat, no doubt flawless only hours before, was now split nearly from ear to ear, jagged and lined with the dark stain of bruises. The victim's lacy chemise, probably once a pristine white, was now pale pink, having soaked up some of the blood. It appeared that someone had tried to sop up the rest of the bodily fluids surrounding the body.

Notebook in hand, Detective Alan Hennessey grit his teeth in disgust. He needed to make an identification but hated bringing a civilian in to do it. Sergeant Roland Jansome, whose precinct it was, had no such qualms. He soon returned, gripping the arm of a much older soiled dove.

"I don't wanna look! I don't wanna look!" she wailed, bracing her skinny legs against any forward movement.

"Come on, Wilma," Jansome said, "She don't look familiar, so we need you to identify her. Her face ain't messed up too bad. Won't take but a minute."

"It's gonna be Birdie, the new gal, I just know it. This was her time in the room. I can't do it!"

"Sure, you can," Jansome coaxed. "Just a little closer now."

Wilma sniffed, inching her way forward, clinging now to the officer's arm as if approaching a cliff leading to an abyss. As soon as she got close enough, she leaned timidly forward, letting out a gasp when she saw the body. "That ain't Birdie." She looked back at Jansome and repeated. "No sir, that ain't Birdie at all."

"Who is it, then?" Hennessey asked.

"I ain't got a clue," Wilma swore. "No sir, never seen her before. All I know is, that ain't Birdie, thank the Lord." She made the sign of the Cross across her weary breasts and sniffed again, her hand shaking as she pulled her ratty shawl tighter against the cold in the room. "Can I go now?"

"Yeah, you can get your fix now, darlin'," Jansome said. "Thanks for your help."

A young investigator was taking photographs of the crime scene, the powder flashing menacingly in a nearby pan to illuminate the corpse.

Wilma stopped at the doorway and turned around. "Hey, that ain't right takin' pitchers like that—give 'er some respect!"

"It's a new thing, Wilma," Jansome said. "The photographs help us figure out who did this. You want us to find the killer, don't you?"

Wilma huffed. "Course, I do. But just so you know, that ain't no workin' gal." Her eyes went big with fear. "Hey…"

Jansome looked at her. "What?"

"Nothin, just … you don't think it's another one of them Jack the Ripper types, do ya?"

"God, I hope not," he said. "But you best stick to customers you know 'til we sort this mess out."

After instructing Jansome to line up more potential witnesses, Detective Hennessey turned back to the body. There was no outward evidence that she'd had sexual relations; they'd have to confirm that through an autopsy. But there were defensive wounds. The combined stink of blood, sweat and other effluents, not quite masked by the scent of a cloying perfume, pretty much told the tale.

A deputy checked the pockets of a dark coat still slung over a chair, then moved to a chest of drawers and found a small purse. Aside from a few dollars, he pulled a hat check token from a local hotel. "Swanky," he murmured. There were also two skeleton keys, one of which fit the door of the room they were now in. A bill from a modiste for some clothing alterations was made out to "M v. M" and there was a ticket stub from a local theater.

"Looks like she went to the Orpheum tonight," the deputy said. "I heard that *Pirates* show is pretty funny." The last item was a calling card. "Maybe she went with him." He handed Hennessey the card, who read it and barked, "Sergeant!"

Jansome returned, took the card from Hennessey and read it. "Damn it all to hell," he muttered.

The card read:

The Twisted Road

Jonathan Perris, Esquire
Attorney at Law

Six inches long with a weighted ivory handle, the blade sliced through the thick air of the cellar with amazing speed, flipping end over end until it hit the shoulder of a straw man Jonathan had constructed and dubbed "Mr. Bilge." The moan came not from the painted hay bale but from "Bonnie Jonnie" himself.

"Buggers," he muttered. "Getting soft." He selected another knife from the case and adjusted his grip. Pulling back with more force, he let go and watched with satisfaction as Mr. Bilge took a direct hit to the heart. "That's more like it."

After the faro game and its aftermath, his adrenalin still flowing, Jonathan had returned home and headed straight to his cellar, doffing his coat and practicing the skills he'd perfected at the age of ten. Knife-throwing soothed him; he much preferred a blade to a gun.

After a few more hits—one to the neck, one to the gut—Jonathan's energy began to ebb. His last throw had reopened the cut over his eye; he could feel it dripping onto his shirt. *Enough of this,* he thought, rubbing his knuckle. *Mick would not be pleased with my form tonight.*

His thoughts lingered on the woman whom he now knew to be Sybil. *She'll be all right,* he told himself, heading up to bed. *She'll regroup, find herself a rich nabob, and live happily ever after.*

It was almost five in the morning, and he'd just drifted off to sleep when he was awakened by a loud banging on his front door. *It's not even light outside; is there no end to this regrettable night?* The pounding continued as he headed down the stairs.

Perhaps it was one of his neighbors in distress. "I'll be there!" he called out and quickened his pace.

The door offered a small glass portal and he checked to see who might need his help. Seeing a police officer's uniform, his heart sped up. Two coppers stood on his landing, and he let them in.

"Officers," he said. "What is it? What's going on?"

The elder beat cop glanced at the younger before inquiring, "Mr. Jonathan Henry Perris?" At Jonathan's nod, he continued. "You are under arrest for the murder of Miss"—he glanced at his note—"Miss Magdalena von Mendelssohn. Please just come along nicely. We don't want no trouble."

Lena? Did he mean Sybil? *Dead*? "I'm sorry," he said. "I was just with her this evening. Are you saying she's dead?"

The younger cop snickered. "Yeah, that's usually what 'murdered' means." He pulled out a set of handcuffs. "Turn around."

"There's no need. I'll come peaceably. Just let me get my jacket."

"Sorry. Gotta cuff ya," the older man said. "Where's your coat? I'll get it for you."

Jonathan remembered he'd left it on its usual peg in the cellar. Mr. Bilge might be difficult to explain. He held out his hands. "Never mind. Just ... let's get this over with."

"Suit yourself." The older cop shut the front door while his partner shackled Jonathan.

"You're in a heap of trouble, mister," the younger officer said almost gleefully. "A shit heap of trouble."

Chapter Seven

Unexpected Help

During the next several hours, Jonathan was grilled by Detective Hennessey, a middle-aged, barrel-chested Irishman with sharp blue eyes who clearly didn't like the English, especially those who sounded like dues-paying members of the upper crust.

Jonathan knew the drill; he'd certainly coached his clients often enough. Answer the questions truthfully but succinctly. Offer no more information than the question requires. Never elaborate if a one- or two-word answer will suffice. And *never* offer information that your questioner hasn't asked about, especially details that might "complicate" your case. To that end, Jonathan didn't volunteer the fact that Lena Mendelssohn was really Sybil West. As far as the law was concerned, at this moment she was merely a socialite he'd squired around town, nothing more.

And that's all she *had* been to him—at least until his lunch with Lord Burnham.

After the detective finished his interrogation, no doubt frustrated at the dearth of information he'd gleaned, Jonathan spent the next several hours contemplating his frigid holding cell and the events that had led him to it. He regretted not bringing his jacket and wrapped himself in the cell's moth-eaten wool blanket. High on the wall, next to a narrow window only now beginning to share a glimpse of dawn, a kerosene lamp hung morosely from its iron hook. Its rancid fumes, along with the chill, brought back memories, both benign and dark. He'd sat in rooms just like this one countless times over the past decade, albeit not as a prisoner. How quickly one's circumstances could change.

He'd been told little of why he was under arrest. Each time he'd asked the deputies for details, they'd brushed him off; at one point one of them said with disdain, "You oughta know - you were there." The only facts he'd ascertained were that Lena—*Sybil*, he reminded himself—had been stabbed and left in a room at Aunt Susie's, apparently after a tryst with a man everyone assumed was Jonathan.

They'd discovered her name using a hat check stub from the *Auberge Pacifique*. Apparently, she'd become chums with the concierge.

What did he know about her, beyond what little he'd shared with the investigator? The Lena he'd known was young, beautiful, intelligent and well spoken; that much was obvious. She was a skilled but fastidious lover, a fact he had *not* shared. He had no illusions that he was or had been her only partner and had taken precautions because of it.

He did know that she was an art aficionado. They had attended two or three gallery exhibitions together, and even though he now questioned her claim to have attended art school in Europe, she was quite knowledgeable about the latest painters, movements and styles. Indeed, during her time here in the Golden City she was—or so she'd told him—attending a class given by the miniaturist Rosa Hooper at the Art Institute on Nob Hill.

What else? She seemed to be up on events transpiring in Europe, although they rarely dug into complex issues. She wrote well, as evidenced by the charming notes she'd sent him on more than one occasion. And she dearly loved spring flowers "because they remind me of my childhood at our country estate outside Vienna." Another lie.

Melancholy filled him, not for the loss of a deep love, not even for the awkward position in which he now found himself. But what a horrifying way for a young woman to die. Sybil had dubious morals, yes, but that didn't justify what had happened to her. By her own admission, she'd thrown her lot in with someone of substance she hoped would do right by her. Whether for good reason or no, Jonathan's brother had cast her aside, leading her down the path that had ended with her murder. Who wanted her dead?

Certainly not Jonathan. Admittedly, when he'd followed her to the cathouse, he'd been in a foul mood. Thank God, he'd not followed her inside. Once he'd made peace with the situation and walked away, he'd assumed he'd never see her again.

But whom had she met? His thoughts turned to Lord Burnham and his earlier supposition. Did the man have a hand in it? If he hadn't orchestrated her attempted ruse with Jonathan, he'd at least been aware of it. But Burnham was focused on blackmail—a crime that only succeeds if the parties involved are worried about or threatening exposure. That can only happen if they're alive. Jonathan hadn't even had time to report back to the baron his reaction to the ugly truth Sybil had revealed.

A persistent thought intruded: what of his own brother? Apparently, Malcolm had recently begun seeing someone who fit perfectly into his social sphere; they seemed to be making the London society columns with regularity. Could he have wanted to permanently discard his former mistress to avoid a messy scandal? That possibility didn't bear thinking about. His own brother, for God's sake!

It was mid-morning when the guard rapped on Jonathan's cell to let him know a "so-called attorney" named Miss Cordelia Hammersmith was there to see him.

What in the hell? How had Cordelia learned of his predicament so soon? But he kept his ire in check—he must remain calm at all costs. "She is indeed a member of my law firm. By all means, let her in."

Petite with hair the color of dark chocolate, Cordelia was dressed in a severe-looking suit of forest green, almost mannish in style, save for the lacy white collar. The ensemble downplayed her femininity but could not erase it. As always, she looked professional—until she made a move *completely* out of character. With a sharp intake of breath and a determined expression, she hurried over to Jonathan and, rising on her toes, threw her arms around him as if they were long-lost lovers. "I will be your alibi," she whispered quickly in his ear. "I can say you were with me." Jonathan reacted instinctively to her embrace by circling her small waist before regaining his senses, taking her firmly by the arms and setting her back from him. The look he gave her was unequivocal. "Absolutely not," he retorted. "You were nowhere near me last night and I'll not have you sacrifice your reputation on my behalf."

He had hired Cordelia as a clerk straight out of law school because of her legal acumen; it had come, however, inside a prickly personality that at times she found difficult to rein in, even with her employer. Now, however, he almost laughed with relief at the glare she sent him. *That* was the Cordelia he knew.

"But there is no way you murdered that woman," she insisted, "and unless you can prove where you were…"

"Thank you for your vote of confidence. But it's not like you to assume an outcome without knowing all the facts. Let's wait until they're at hand before we determine what remedies are needed."

"How can you be so … so *British* at a time like this?" She proceeded to pace the narrow confines of the cell. "Tell me everything."

Jonathan watched her with amusement, if mirth could even be called for in his present situation. His eyebrows rose. "Everything?"

Cordelia had the decency to look sheepish. "Well, perhaps not *everything*—certainly you can leave out details that aren't pertinent."

There's no question about that, he thought. *The fewer details the better.* "Thank you. Well, Miss von Mendelssohn and I attended a performance of *The Pirates of Penzance*, had a late supper at Antonio's, and I dropped her off at her hotel a little after midnight."

"She lives in a hotel? Haven't you been seeing each other for a while?"

"It's been several weeks, yes. I met her while we were preparing for the Tom Justice trial."

"If she was here that long, why didn't she rent a house or apartment? It's awfully expensive to rent a hotel room."

Jonathan hesitated. If by some miracle he could get by without revealing all he now knew about Sybil, perhaps he could contain what would otherwise be a lurid addition to the scandal sheets, both here and in London. "I don't know. Perhaps she felt she was simply passing through."

Cordelia snorted. "Well, she certainly lingered with you long enough."

Jonathan merely raised his eyebrows again. *Draw your own conclusions.*

It took Cordelia a moment to absorb the implications of her comment, at which point a blush began to wend its way up her neck. It lasted as long as it took her to take her next breath. "Well, it's odd, that's all. And how did she end up in a cathouse, for goodness' sake? She wasn't—"

"No." Jonathan shut down that line of inquiry immediately. "She was not." Whatever she was, he'd never accept that Sybil was a common doxie. But who was she, really? "Now I have a question for you. How did you learn of my predicament so quickly?"

"Oh, my neighbor's son is a sergeant in this precinct," she said. "He was on duty when the call came in and helped investigate the scene. He knows I work for you, so he told his mother to tell me, and…"

"Did he give you any details about what they found?"

She scowled. "Why, is there some incriminating evidence I should know about?"

"Of course not, at least as far as I'm concerned."

"Well, that's not exactly true, is it?" Her look was censorious. "They found the ticket stub for tonight's performance and your calling card."

"Those wouldn't necessarily go hand in hand."

"Except that you did take her to the theater tonight. Then there's the matter of the cab ride."

"The cab ride?"

"You remember—when you dropped her off at her hotel and then followed her to Aunt Susie's? Apparently, you weren't very happy when you paid the cabbie." Cordelia rattled off the events with a hint of sarcasm.

Jonathan could only shake his head. "How on earth do they know all that?"

She shrugged. "As soon as word of the murder got out, your driver stepped up to report a 'suspicious customer' who followed a woman to Aunt Susie's. His description fit you to a T."

It did look dodgy. "Well, I did stop in front of the building, but I went on from there. I absolutely did not enter Aunt Susie's."

"All right. Where did you go?"

To an illegal faro game—but you won't hear that from me. "I … went for a walk," he said. "By myself."

"A walk? In that neighborhood? I'm sorry, but a jury is not going to buy that."

"Miss Hammersmith ... I haven't yet hired you to defend me."

That prompted another glare, but it was tempered by an emotion he couldn't define. He imagined it was the fear that if he went down, she'd be out of a job. There weren't a lot of attorneys in San Francisco willing to take a chance on a cheeky female subordinate, no matter how brilliant. He motioned for her to sit on the bunk and pulled up the cell's only chair to face her. "In this country, I am innocent until proven guilty, and aside from the fact that I was seeing the poor woman, there is nothing to connect me to her death."

"But there is," she said quietly, all her bravado gone.

It was his turn to frown. "What could there possibly be?"

She set her questioning eyes on his. "They've already interviewed several of the girls. It seems a man about your size visited Aunt Susie's more than once ... and he had an English accent. 'Like a real gent,' one of them said."

"Well, it wasn't me," he snapped. "Put me in an identity parade."

Cordelia looked incredulous. "If you mean a line-up—No! That's the last thing you want! They said he always wore a black coat and hat and spoke very little. Being the early part of the month and a payday, it was apparently quite busy, so no one's a hundred percent sure if they saw him that night. Once one of them hears your voice, they'll peg you for that 'gent' whether it was really you or not. And there's one more thing."

Jonathan wasn't sure he wanted to hear it. "What?"

"They examined her hands and nails; turns out she put up a fight before whoever it was did her in." She pointed to the cut over Jonathan's eye. "That looks fresh." Then she reached for one of his hands and turned it over. His knuckles were bruised. "And this? When did this happen?"

"Last night."

"On your so-called 'walk'?"

"That's right."

"On the Coast? After midnight? What—you just happened to run into a wall in the dark?"

"Something like that."

The Twisted Road

Taking a deep breath, Cordelia rose and straightened her skirt. "I will see about having you released on bail," she said formally, as if she really were his counsel. "It may take some time, but I'll figure something out."

"You don't have to—"

Yet another glare, this one well-deserved. "I'll be in touch." She called down the hallway through the bars. "Guard?"

After Cordelia left, Jonathan sat on the bunk feeling somewhat hollow. *She doesn't believe me,* he thought as the emptiness inside of him began to fill with a niggling sense of dread. *But why would she? She really knows very little about me.*

He began to pace the cell himself; it seemed to shrink with each pass. But he calmed his nerves by planning the first interview he'd set up after he was free. He hoped Lord Burnham hadn't fled to places unknown. If he had, Jonathan would hunt him down. *I deserve some answers,* he thought, *and by God, I'm going to get them.*

Chapter Eight

Battle Plan

What does he not want us to know?

Like a too-friendly neighbor, the question made itself at home at the forefront of Cordelia's brain and wouldn't leave. She was extremely vexed about it. How was she supposed to focus on her own cases when her boss was busy getting arrested for murder?

As she headed to the office, she found it intriguing that her first question wasn't "Did he do it?" Despite having no evidence to bolster her belief—and in fact some rather glaring details pointing to his guilt—she simply couldn't accept that Jonathan Perris had committed murder. Since she'd begun working for him, first as a law clerk and now as a junior associate, he'd been even-tempered, patient, supportive, and, aside from an annoying streak of over-protectiveness, completely professional. True, she didn't know much about his personal life, but he hobnobbed with the top tier of San Francisco society, and they seemed to have no problem with him. Violence wasn't part of his nature—with some people you just *knew*.

Unfortunately, a person's gut feeling carried no weight in a court of law. She had to come up with an alternative theory based on the evidence, and the defendant wasn't exactly forthcoming with the facts she needed to build it. Well, she'd save him in spite of his stubbornness ... as soon as she learned the pesky *why*.

She reached Montgomery Street and headed upstairs to the Jonathan Perris Esquire and Associates law offices. The building wasn't impressive, either inside or out, but to Cordelia, it was heaven —a place where her intellect was appreciated and she could fight for justice, all while bringing home her very own paycheck. She didn't have to depend on a soul—well, except for her boss, who was now in a royal mess.

After starting the process to secure Jonathan's bail, Cordelia had summoned her colleagues to the office for an "emergency meeting." To her surprise and delight, all had readily agreed to be there, despite the holiday weekend.

The Twisted Road

Althea was the first to arrive. A comforting mother hen to all of them, she administered the barnyard, handling the countless small but necessary tasks that any office needs to be productive. She was middle-aged, but still young enough for "girl talk" — a pastime Cordelia loved but hadn't had the time to indulge in for several years. Today, however, they had more important things to discuss.

"What's so important you called everybody in on a weekend?" Althea asked, making a beeline to her natural habitat, the kitchen. "Not that I'm complaining, mind you. Cliff and the boys have been supposedly "testing" leftover firecrackers all morning, and my ears are still ringing."

Moments later their new investigator, Dove, whom Cordelia had known since childhood, popped his head in the door. "Did I hear someone say testing? If so, I'm available to sample anything you might have brought in your magic basket." Althea had indeed brought some leftover blueberry pie, and Cordelia swallowed her frustration at having to pass on what was undoubtedly a scrumptious treat. Why was she the only one at the firm who had to watch her weight? The temptation was never-ending.

Althea paused, teapot in hand. "Lordy, where's Mr. P.? He's usually the first one here."

At that moment, Oliver Bean, the other junior associate, arrived. "Thank God," Cordelia said. "Everyone, please—we need to meet in the boardroom right this minute."

With puzzled looks, they all took seats around the conference table. Cordelia stood at the head, inhaled sharply and announced, "Mr. Perris is currently sitting in jail at the Vallejo Street Precinct. He's obviously been in a fight, but that's the least of his problems. He's there because he's been accused of murdering a prostitute. And the worst of it is, he won't spill the beans about where he was when the crime took place."

After a moment of shocked silence, Althea spoke up. "That is the most ridiculous twaddle I ever heard of. Mr. P. killing a woman? No way, no how."

"I agree. I simply can't imagine it." The news left Oliver completely befuddled, as if Cordelia had announced that Martians had landed and wished to hire their firm.

Dove liked to sketch cartoons during meetings, but Cordelia knew he did that to help focus on the matter at hand. In this case he was the only one to face reality. "From what you say, it doesn't look good, especially the part about him having gotten into a scrape. We need to find out what that was all about, even though it sounds like he wants to keep it under his hat."

"Maybe somebody attacked him," Althea said.

Dove shrugged. "Then we need to find the punk who did it." He proceeded to draw a hog-faced brute.

If there were such a punk, Cordelia already felt sorry for him. Unlike her employer, Dove was well acquainted with violence. It crossed her mind that after this, Jonathan might think San Francisco was too rough and tumble for his upper-class sensibilities. Imagine being beaten up *and* accused of a crime you didn't commit! The notion of his departure dampened her spirits, but she shook it off, stepping onto the small fruit box she employed to reach higher on the large blackboard that dominated one wall of the room. She quickly wrote the words "Bail," "Cab Driver," "Magdalena von Mendelssohn," "Aunt Susie's," and "Midnight to Three a.m." before turning to the group.

"The victim, Magdalena von Mendelssohn—"

"Wait, isn't she the woman Mr. P.'s been seeing for the past several weeks?" Althea asked.

"That's not good," Dove said.

"And what was she doing in a house of ill repute?" That query from Oliver.

Cordelia tamped down her irritation. "Yes, I know it looks bad, but things aren't always what they seem. Mr. Perris insists she was not a prostitute and for now we have to believe him." She put an "O" next to the victim's name and the phrase "cab driver."

"Oliver, I'd like you to see what you can find out about Miss Mendelssohn ... what hotel she was staying at, who she might have been traveling with, her family background, and so on. Supposedly she was a guest at the *Auberge Pacifique* Hotel, but that place is pricey so maybe she stayed somewhere else as well. Sergeant

Jansome at the Vallejo Street station might be able to slip a few details to you if you tell him I was asking. Also, please get the name of the cab driver who apparently gave Mr. Perris a ride that night. Our tight-lipped employer is adamant that he didn't go inside the bordello, and we want the driver to corroborate under oath that he did not see him enter the building."

Even though Cordelia had no right to give him orders, Oliver was such a gentle soul that he didn't balk as she would have in his place. "I will get right on it," he said.

Putting a "D" next to "Aunt Susie's," she turned to Dove, who was putting the finishing touches on his comical sketch. "Dove, you already know where I'm sending you; the area around Aunt Susie's should be familiar territory. Something happened between midnight and three a.m. Hopefully somebody saw something unusual that we can use."

"Will do," he said.

"I'm in the process of posting bail. It's going to be high, given the charge, so I'm hoping the Firestones will help us out."

"And me?" Althea asked.

"The most important job of all: fielding any calls, from friends or foe, like the newspapers. Art Sussman from the *Bulletin* will be on our tail as soon as he gets wind of it. And you know the D. A.'s office is itching to bring us all down a notch after Mr. Perris got Tom Justice acquitted. So, I would say 'obfuscate,' Althea; we need you to obfuscate."

"It's a good thing I know what that word means," Althea muttered.

Cordelia stepped down and wiped the chalk off her hands. "We have our work cut out for us," she said. "Let's get to it."

Chapter Nine

A Trip to the Coast

Cordie certainly knew Dove well; he *was* an expert on the area near the waterfront known as the Barbary Coast. The neighborhood got its name from the sixteenth century's pirate-infested North African shores because it hosted debauchery in all its forms. As a young soldier, Dove had found plenty of trouble inside the Coast's dance halls, gambling houses, saloons and bordellos; it was a near miracle he had only a facial scar to show for his misadventures. Later, as a Pinkerton agent, he was often pegged to pursue quarry who had run to ground there. "Dove will know where their hidey holes are," his colleagues bragged, and he usually proved them right.

Hopefully he could deliver for Cordie, too.

During the day, the heart of the Coast, Pacific Street, looked innocent enough. In fact, since the earthquake and fire, that street and others had been hastily reconstructed to attract a higher-class clientele. Aside from the garish signs, the entertainment venues seemed almost respectable. The bars were relatively quiet, their true purpose only hinted at by the occasional strains of honky-tonk wafting through an open door. Brothels like Aunt Susie's looked like proper boarding houses where unmarried schoolteachers or librarians might live. And the burlesque theaters? Those were now called "resorts" and catered to the average working man looking for a little spice in his life.

Bad things still happened, of course, especially when the sun went down and the bright lights popped; the socialite's vicious murder was proof of that. But overall, violence had dropped dramatically from pre-quake days and the merchants of sin wanted to keep it that way. It made sense for the police to button up the case quickly by pinning it on someone the victim knew—someone like Jonathan Perris.

But it didn't feel right. Dove would bet his last dollar that his boss was a straight shooter—even though, he thought with a grin, the one thing he knew for certain was that the man didn't like guns at all. Of course, that didn't signify in this case, because the victim was slashed,

The Twisted Road

not shot. Regardless of method, Dove couldn't picture Jonathan Perris as a killer of women. Something else was going on.

He began his canvass with a leisurely stroll west on Pacific to the cable car line on Mason. If Perris had been heading home, that's the line he would have used. Along the way, Dove stopped by several familiar haunts like Pinkie's, One-Eyed Jack's and the Empire Saloon. He knew most of the proprietors; at this hour they were usually checking inventory and setting up for the night to come.

Lips Williams was wiping down the bar when Dove sat down and ordered a beer. Lips was a muscular Jamaican who ran the Stealth Lounge, a Black-and-Tan music club near Taylor Street. He sounded like a college professor and played a soul-wrenching trumpet.

"Any sort of ruckus happen on the street last night?" Dove asked.

"No, indeed, nothing out of the ordinary," Lips reported. "We all heard about the unpleasantness at Aunt Susie's, so several of us compared notes afterward. Aside from the usual drunkards, no scurrilous characters made an appearance."

"What? No one vile or contemptuous showed up? No degenerates? No reprobates? You must be losing your touch."

Lips smiled but quickly turned serious. "We heard the crime was quite nasty. I certainly hope they apprehend whoever committed it. It's not good for business to have such madmen out and about."

Dove suppressed a grin; Lips was known as a master of understatement.

Leaving the Stealth Lounge, he changed direction, heading east toward the waterfront. In each establishment he encountered the same refrain. Aside from a few drunken brawls, quickly taken care of by bouncers, it had apparently been a quiet night.

That left the alleys, where from experience, Dove knew the worst atrocities often took place. Stick-ups, beat downs, rapes, and worst of all, murders usually happened where the general public dare not go ...

... unless for some reason they didn't want to be seen.

Dove turned down Sansome and walked by Mick's Gym, where he knew the occasional after-hours faro game took place. There was no set schedule, and Mick kept a tight lid when they did happen. He'd never admit to hosting the game, nor would any of the players—some of whom were city mucky-mucks. When beat cops did catch wind of a session, they played deaf and dumb—for a small fee—so it was nearly impossible to pry such information loose. Still, Dove knew that Jonathan worked out at the gym. Maybe Mick had let him in on some late-night action.

He headed down the alley and saw an old buzzard of a man straightening up his poor excuse for a shanty. Since the quake, thousands of average folks had lost their homes, but it had been much worse for those who were already on the edge. Dove recognized Jorrie Parks by his wild mane of still-curly steel gray hair. Sad sacks like him had had to scramble just to find a place out of the cold that wasn't filled with rubble. He'd known Jorrie for years, had even tried to get him help a while back. But the bum seemed disinterested in reclaiming a decent life, content to eke out a living by scrounging and panhandling.

"Here, Jorrie, let me help you with that," Dove said, stepping up to catch the long end of a piece of wood.

Jorrie peered up with gin-soaked eyes, not quite sure if he knew the stranger, but apparently glad for the help anyway. "Thank ye kindly," he said as they worked together to shore up his lean-to.

"Say, Jorrie, remember me? I've met you quite a few times."

Jorrie squinted at him and frowned. "You the law?"

"Not anymore," Dove said, "but I do need something and thought you might be able to help me."

Though half pickled, the old man was still sharp enough to be wary. "Help you what?"

"Just a little information." He pointed to the back door of Mick's almost directly across the alley. "About a faro game last night."

Jorrie had begun to shake his head before Dove even finished his sentence. "I don't know nothin' about that, no sir." He resumed fiddling with his shack.

Dove stuck his hands in his pockets to seem as innocuous as possible. "Well, here's the deal, Jorrie. I happen to know there was a game last night," he lied. "I also know that you park yourself here because sometimes the winners come out and they're so happy they send a few bucks your way. Am I right?"

Jorrie couldn't look at him. "Mebbe. Mebbe not."

"Look, I'm not askin' for names, but a man's life may hang in the balance, and you'd want to help him out, wouldn't you?"

Jorrie shrugged. "Depends on the man, I guess. Some of thems is real bastards." He rubbed his arm as he said it.

"Was there a bastard here last night?"

The old man looked again at Dove and his eyes registered. "Hey, I know you."

"Yeah, we go way back, we surely do. So, did someone give you a bad time last night?"

"I can't rightly say," he hedged. "I don't wanna get Mick or anybody else in trouble, see?"

Dove nodded. "I get it. But sometimes, even though you don't really see anything, you probably have dreams about it, yeah? And you could tell me what you dreamed about. It could be worth your while."

He patted his jacket and waited while Jorrie processed the offer. After a few moments the old man nodded.

"Yeah, I dreamed I was sittin' here counting up the change I'd gotten from a few fellas after they left. Then a bit later a man come out, pissed as all hell. I was just standin' there and he says, 'What are you looking at, you old fart?' and kicks the side of my house here. Then he starts walking down the alley and stops halfway, up against another door, before looking back at me. I turn away like I don't see him, even though I know he's still in the alley. Turns out he's waitin'."

"What's he waitin' for?"

"Well, a little bit of time goes by, and another man comes out, a bit older than the first one, nice lookin' gent, and sees me. He's like you — he helps me shore up the side of my house and then he reaches into his jacket, pulls out his wallet and hands me a ten-dollar bill. Ten dollars! He says, 'Here you go, maybe this will help you get a better roof,' in a real smooth, hoity-toity way, like he was the King of England or somethin'."

"Go on," Dove said.

"Now, this is just a dream," Jorrie reminded him.

Dove sent him a smile. "Of course."

"So, I says to him, real quiet like, 'Mister, there's a guy halfway down the alley might be waitin' for somebody—mebbe it's you,' and damned if he doesn't lean toward me and smiles real big and says, 'How delightful,' and starts walking right toward him!"

"Then what happened ... in your dream, that is."

"Well, I starts to hear a lot of fists flyin' and heads crackin' and bodies slammin', and pretty soon the first guy is lyin' in a heap, groaning, and the smooth talker says"—here Jorrie affected a high-class British accent that was pretty accurate— "'Two weeks ago I won your car and tonight it was three months' salary, Randall. What's it going to be next, the deed to your house? My God, man, forget your problem with me—-focus on your gambling habit.'"

"Jorrie," Dove said, "you have quite a way with accents, you know that? You sounded like a perfect English gentleman, there."

Jorrie puffed out his sunken chest with pride. "I do have a good ear."

Dove pulled out two dollars and handed them over. "Well, I can't afford a ten spot like the man in your dream, but I do appreciate hearing about him."

"Any time," Jorrie said with a grin displaying about half the teeth he was no doubt born with.

Dove left the old vagrant to his housecleaning and walked leisurely around the corner to the front door of Mick's Gym. Then he went inside to talk to Mick.

Chapter Ten

The Search Begins

Jonathan awoke Sunday morning with a dry mouth, a scratchy beard and a crick in his neck, but those were nothing compared to the thrum of unease that pulsed through him once he fully registered where he was.

After Cordelia's visit the previous day, he hadn't heard from her or anyone else. But what did he expect? She was merely an employee; perhaps she'd learned something that had convinced her he was capable of such a heinous crime. Even if he'd been willing to explain where he'd been, there was no one who knew him—or liked him—well enough to risk their reputation or livelihood by corroborating his story. The notion that he had no one in his corner shouldn't have unnerved him since so much of his life had been spent with that understanding. But it *was* unsettling because he hadn't felt quite so vulnerable in a long time.

For God's sake, stop this self-pity. The authorities had nothing with which they could truly pin him to the crime. In fact, they should drop everything and arrest George Burnham before he skipped town. The man had to be involved in this mess somehow. But given Jonathan's current circumstances, his accusations would have been soundly rejected, and rightly so. The police didn't go around arresting people just because an accused murderer said they ought to.

It was late afternoon before the guard walked up to his cell and unlocked it.

"You're free to go," he said.

In light of the mental gyrations he'd been going through, Jonathan was taken aback. "What?"

"Do I have to spell it out to ya? Your bail's been posted, not to mention a couple of witnesses came forward to vouch for your whereabouts last night."

Jonathan frowned but said nothing. *If Cordelia fed them that story about us being together, I will throttle her!*

When he followed the guard down the hall to the sergeant's desk, Dove Rebane, the investigator he'd hired on Cordelia's recommendation, was waiting for him.

"Dove! What's this—"

Dove jumped up, his eyes imploring Jonathan to be quiet. "Sorry, boss, I know you didn't want anyone to find out you'd been taking private boxing lessons with Seamus McGregor after hours, but that's the way it goes. Mick and your sparring partner—you know, Randall Carpenter, the assistant DA.?—have already been deposed and put you in the clear."

"Put me in the clear?"

"Yeah. They've testified you were boxing at the gym at the time of the murder, so you're no longer a suspect."

"Wait a minute. The guard mentioned something about bail."

"Yeah, Cordie handled that through the Firestones. Took her a while to track them down and get the paperwork expedited. She didn't know about your alibi; she was just working her little ass off to get you out of the cooler. But it should be just a formality at this point. Come on, let's get you home and cleaned up. You don't wear so well in a jail cell."

Jonathan realized the less said the better, so he gathered the few belongings they'd confiscated and followed Dove out the station door.

"Alamo Square?" Dove asked.

"Yes, indeed." Jonathan was still reeling from the abrupt change of events. He waited until they'd caught a cab before addressing Dove again. "What in the bloody hell did you just pull off?"

Dove leaned back in his seat. "Not just me," he said. "First off, I'm dying to know: why in the hell do you need boxing lessons? You pulverized that Carpenter buffoon. Mick and I had to go to his house because he was too sore to get out of bed. He's going to have a crooked nose, thanks to you."

"All the more reason why testifying on my behalf should be the *last* thing he'd do."

"*Au contraire*. Mick about blew his top when I told him Carpenter attacked you in the alley. He threatened to expose the whole nasty business, faro game and all, if Carpenter didn't buy into the story. It was Mick's idea about the boxing lessons, by the way. 'Always tell as much truth as you can,' he said. He's got a point. So, no one finds out about the faro game, and your alibi sticks. The only downside is you having to admit you're learning how to fight—which, as I said, is nuts, but helpful in this case."

"So... how did you even know that Carpenter attacked me?"

Dove tapped his temple. "I have my sources ... sometimes they tell me their dreams." He smiled and left it at that.

Several minutes later they reached Jonathan's home near the square. He hopped out of the conveyance and turned back to Dove, extending his hand. "I trusted Cordelia's judgment in hiring you and she did not disappoint me. You haven't, either. Thank you."

He saw that Dove was about to make a wisecrack but refrained at the last minute. They locked eyes and shook hands. "You're welcome," he said.

Jonathan started to enter his front gate but turned back. "Dove, this isn't over. We need to find out who killed the woman you know as Magdalena Mendelssohn. And I think I know where to start, first thing tomorrow morning."

Dove gave a small salute. "At your service."

Jonathan entered his small foyer and looked around. It was tidy and quiet—even the grandfather clock he'd brought over from England, a gift from his late father, had stopped ticking. As he wound the clock, he made a mental priority list: Find something to eat. Take a hot bath. Get a good night's sleep.

His plan was interrupted by a timid knock on the front door. This time the visitor was Mrs. Bhandari, holding a bowl covered with a faded cloth. She was a small, plump woman dressed in her native garb —a skirt, blouse and sash that Jonathan had learned was called a *ghalek*.

"You look like you have trouble," she said. "I bring you some *kwati dal*. Good bean stew. You eat and feel better."

Hers was a simple, neighborly act of kindness, but his reaction to it caught him by surprise. His eyes began to water and he covered his embarrassment with a glib apology for the disturbance two nights earlier. She waved away his excuses. "People make mistake all the time. They see someone and think one way, then learn it very much a different way. Eat and feel better—and take bath." She smiled at him and went down the steps, her mission accomplished.

"I will," he called after her. "And thank you!"

The stew was delicious, as was the bath, although despite its warmth, he couldn't shake the cold reality that whoever killed Sybil was still at large. Was it truly Burnham? Was he in on her scheme and lost his temper because she backed out? If so, why meet at Aunt Susie's? And if he was the culprit, was he resting easy thinking Jonathan would take the fall? When it became obvious that Jonathan was out of jail, what would Burnham do next?

Dressed in his robe, Jonathan set about checking the back door as well as all the windows. A small horizontal casement had been left slightly ajar in the laundry room off the kitchen. Vesta, the woman who cleaned his house each week, had probably left it open to let the linens dry, but Burnham would not fit through it and there were no signs that anyone else had entered his home … yet. He secured the window and added "Increase security" to his list.

Afterward, he called the Palace Hotel to see if Burnham was still in residence. The man had checked out, but he'd left a forwarding address in Sausalito. Good. At least he hadn't yet left the country, which meant there was still time to track the bugger down.

He pondered how best to approach the investigation. Assuming Burnham was the killer, it wouldn't be enough to simply confront him. The man could easily deny all and point the finger back at Jonathan. That might lead to a closer look at Jonathan's alibi, which would not be good. No, Burnham needed to be squeezed in an evidentiary pincer movement, in which facts pointing to his guilt rendered his lies meaningless. Jonathan was sure his colleagues could help in gathering those facts.

Yet, proving Burnham's guilt would require revealing the man's motive, which would in turn expose Jonathan and more importantly, Jonathan's brother, to unwanted scrutiny and no doubt public ridicule. It amazed him that fellow Brits as well as Americans felt no compunction about mocking Jonathan, yet were equally envious of him, simply because he seemed to be a member of the privileged class. He was not above using that impression, whenever necessary, to achieve his goals, but it was a double-edged sword; there were those here and back in London who would love nothing better than to smear him and his family in the press. Indeed, wasn't that precisely what Burnham had threatened to do?

So, was it possible to track the events of Sybil West's—not Lena Mendelssohn's—last days and determine that Burnham was perhaps nothing more than an angry lover? Burnham wouldn't be quick to reveal his financial machinations unless he had to; after all, he was beholden to the same upper crust for his own status. Jonathan would present the "spurned lover" theory to his team, but he saw no need to reveal more. He'd direct them to see what they could discover about Sybil's last days while he went after the quarry himself. Hopefully it would be enough.

Early the next morning, Jonathan headed to the office and waited impatiently for his staff to arrive. As always, Althea was prompt; she had brought a cinnamon Bundt cake "to celebrate you getting out of the calaboose." Dove was next, followed quickly by Cordelia and surprisingly, Oliver Bean, who wasn't known for his punctuality.

"It's good to see you, sir," Bean said. "We all figured it must be some terrible mistake." Earnest, humble and keenly empathetic, Jonathan's youngest employee was an old soul encased in a very tall, extremely thin body; he was the perfect foil for Cordelia, who was decidedly smaller, but much more of a force to be reckoned with. They each brought a unique perspective to their work, and, as Althea had lamented, were often at odds with each other, presenting opposing but valid views. Jonathan liked their contrasting styles—they made for creative brainstorming sessions, which is what he hoped would happen now.

While everyone settled, Althea brewed coffee and brought it in along with the sliced cake. He asked her to sit down as well.

"I want to thank each of you for coming to my aid in the past few days. I assure you I rarely find myself on the wrong side of the law and it was heartening to know I had supporters on the outside looking out for my welfare." He looked directly at Cordelia. "Miss Hammersmith, thank you for working so diligently to post bail for me, and for … for your willingness to provide me with an alibi." He saw her begin to blush and turned his attention to Dove. "Dovydas— Dove—I truly appreciate your creative "solution" to the rather thorny problem of proving my whereabouts without having to expose matters that, well, need not be exposed. You are quite a jack of all trades, and we are lucky to have you as part of our team."

Dove paused in his usual scribblings to acknowledge the compliment with a nod.

"And Oliver." Jonathan pointed to the list that Cordelia had left on the board. "I am sorry for your no doubt fruitless search into the background of Miss Mendelssohn. It was destined for failure, as you shall soon see. Althea, what can I say? You are our Mother Goose." He gestured to the table and its contents. "You feed us and keep us organized and provide a haven in what can sometimes be a chaotic world. For that I am eternally grateful."

His office manager beamed, as he knew she would.

Cordelia raised her hand. *Of course, she has something to say.* "Yes, Miss Hammersmith?"

"Why did you use the word "rarely" when it comes to being on the wrong side of the law? Have there been other times you've gotten in trouble?"

How much time do you have? he thought, but merely smiled. "That, I'm afraid, is a discussion for another time. For now, I thank you all and yet must ask even more of you. The woman you know as Magdalena Mendelssohn did not deserve her fate, and I am enlisting your aid to help me find whoever killed her."

The group looked baffled.

"Wouldn't that be a job for the police?" Oliver asked.

"Normally, yes," Jonathan said. "But there are extenuating circumstances that the authorities aren't aware of, and I would like to see if we can make progress without involving them."

That excuse sounded weak even to him and he could tell Cordelia was about to argue, but Dove jumped in.

"Where do we start?" he asked.

Good man, Dove. "We start with the fact that Miss Mendelssohn was, to my chagrin, an imposter, which I was made aware of the day of her murder. Her real name was Sybil West. I have reason to believe she was connected somehow to an acquaintance of mine, a Lord Burnham, who is here in San Francisco on business. Frankly, he's at the top of my suspect list—indeed he's the *only* one on it at the moment. I'm heading out to speak to him now."

Cordelia scowled. "Is it a good idea to confront someone you think might be a killer? Maybe you should take Dove with you."

Jonathan smiled briefly. "I assure you I'm capable of playing my cards close to the vest, Miss Hammersmith; I don't think I'll need a bodyguard quite yet."

By her expression Cordelia wasn't placated by his answer. "Well, then what *would* you have us do?" she asked.

"You said that several of the women at Aunt Susie's made reference to a man with an English accent. That man most certainly was not me. Who was he—old, young, husky, slender? I understand he wore a coat and hat, but can the women recall any details at all about his appearance? How often did he use the bordello? Did he meet the same paramour each time or were others intimately familiar with him? Perhaps someone knows more than she was willing to share with the police."

"So, you're thinking it could be this Lord Burnham you mentioned?" Oliver queried.

"Possibly. A spurned lover, perhaps. The baron is similar to me in height and build, but of course that doesn't narrow the field by much."

"Is that all?" Cordelia pressed. "Do you have anything else?"

She really can be quite irritating at times. "Yes, I do. Miss West, or Miss Mendelssohn as I knew her, was an aspiring artist. She said she'd been taking a class at the San Francisco Art Institute on Nob Hill. I believe it was taught by a miniaturist by the name of Rosa Hooper. Whether she lied about that endeavor, I don't know, but assuming she was telling the truth, perhaps a fellow classmate can cast some light on Sybil's activities."

"What about her living quarters?" Oliver asked. "I found no record of her as Magdalena Mendelssohn."

"It's a good question," Jonathan said. "I confess I always dropped her off at the *Auberge Pacifique,* which, I'm rather ashamed to admit, she led me to believe was her place of residence. It was not. She may have stayed at a lesser hotel, or even a rooming house, under her real name. I simply don't know."

"And the police," said Dove, "are probably running around in circles trying to find out about a woman who doesn't exist."

"Precisely," Cordelia chimed in, "which is why we should tell them who she really is."

She's like a dog with a bone, Jonathan thought. *For once, can't she just trust me?* Yet given the events of the past two days, why would Cordelia or any of them trust him? Were he in their shoes, he certainly wouldn't. He would have to appeal to the gentler side of their natures. "Under normal circumstances I would agree with you, Miss Hammersmith, but ... if you would be so kind ... I have my reasons for taking this a bit farther before bringing the authorities back into it. Hopefully in a day or two we'll know more and be able to set them on a more productive course."

"I suppose if it's just for a day or two," Cordelia muttered.

"Sounds like a plan to me," Althea said, beginning to clear the table. Jonathan started to speak but she held up a hand. "I know, Mr. P. My job is to obfuscate, obfuscate, obfuscate."

Jonathan's puzzled look elicited a chuckle from Cordelia.

"You are the best, Althea," she said.

Perhaps I've missed something, but there's no time for it now. "I must be going," he said. "I will leave it to you to determine how best to ferret out the information we seek."

With that, he hurried out of the room.

He had a killer to catch.

Chapter Eleven

Working Women

*A*nother pesky "why," Cordelia thought as she headed out to interview the artist Rosa Hooper. She'd pried out of Dove why Jonathan stayed mum the night of the murder. Illegal gambling *and* getting into a fistfight—much less a donnybrook that he'd apparently won? That didn't sound like the Jonathan Perris she knew. And now wanting to keep their investigation from the police? What was he hiding this time? Men. Who could understand them? She'd give it a few days and then insist on bringing in the authorities. *Whether he likes it or not, it's the right thing to do*, she told herself as she rode the private cable car up Nob Hill.

At the top of California Street, the San Francisco Institute of Art was a mere shadow of its former self. A year earlier it had been housed in the overpowering Victorian mansion built by millionaire Mark Hopkins. Along with the rest of the Big Four railroad barons, he had built an estate on the steep hill towering nearly four hundred feet above the waters of the bay—hence the need for the cable car. The poor tycoon hadn't even lived to see it finished, and his forty-room monstrosity had eventually been donated to the Institute (by his widow's gold-digger second husband, no less) for "instruction in and illustration of the fine arts, music, and literature." The estate had held that role for a dozen years until the earthquake and fire destroyed everything. Now, a much smaller, plain vanilla structure had taken its place, and art students were once again learning their craft, albeit in far less pretentious surroundings.

Probably for the best, Cordelia mused. *Art appreciation shouldn't just be for the rich.*

Once she reached the summit, Cordelia found her way to the Institute's administrative wing and from there was directed to the office of Rosa Hooper Plotner, a former San Francisco debutante who had made a name for herself by painting miniatures of well-heeled patrons. After studying with William Keith of the San Francisco Art League, she'd honed her skills abroad, won several awards and was now teaching at the Institute while raising her young son. She looked like a garden variety society matron except for her hands. They told a different story—that of a working artist with muscular palms and paint-stained fingers. *How steady and focused she must be to paint such tiny, intricate portraits,* Cordelia thought. *Who says women are flighty!*

It was just after lunch and the artist was between classes, looking over some sketches. Cordelia introduced herself and explained that she had some questions about a student under Rosa's tutelage.

The art instructor was perplexed as she glanced down at her daily calendar. "I am supposed to meet with a Detective Hennessy later today and you arrive at my office beforehand. What is this all about?"

"Ma'am, do you have a student by the name of Sybil West?"

Rosa shook her head. "I don't know anyone by that name. Is there a reason I should?"

"How about a Lena Mendelssohn?"

"Yes, she's in my afternoon workshop." The woman pulled a sketch from the pile she'd been perusing. "She's showing quite a bit of promise." She checked the timepiece pinned to her bodice. "Class begins in about forty minutes if you'd care to wait for her."

Cordelia paused before sharing the bad news. "I'm afraid Lena won't be showing up today. She has … has passed away."

Rosa's shock was genuine. "My God, how terrible! Is that why the police are showing up? What on earth happened?"

"She was found in a rather compromising position, and we believe she was murdered. My firm is investigating her death along with law enforcement and we thought perhaps you'd be able to shed some light on her activities here. For example, whom she may have associated with at the Institute."

Rosa seemed to ponder the question as she looked out the window. When she turned around, it was as if she'd made up her mind about something. "We have a group within the school known as the 'Incendiaries.' Pretentious, I know, but most of our students are young and idealistic. They want to make a statement with their work." She smiled grimly. "They want to change the world."

I know the feeling, Cordelia thought. *But it's easier said than done.* "So, it isn't just a social club?"

Rosa shrugged. "For all I know it is, but they seem rather serious about discussing political issues; it often spills over into class. They're quite in favor of the streetcar union's strike, for example."

"And Lena was part of this group?"

"Yes, she usually set her easel next to one or two of the members, and I would often see them together around the campus. She was new to the Institute but was quickly accepted by them."

Cordelia had brought out her notebook. "Can you give me the names of some of the students that Lena considered friends? They might be able to help us pin down the events that led to her death."

Rosa agreed and wrote down several. As she handed the list to Cordelia, she said, "I added one more person you might want to interview. I doubt she's a member of the Incendiaries, but she is certainly a provocative individual in her own right. I did see them together more than once." Rosa said the latter with a hint of derision.

Reading the name, Cordelia looked up in surprise. "Alma de Bretteville? Isn't she the—"

Rosa nodded as if she knew the rest of the question. "Yes, and whatever else you may think of her, one fact is inescapable. She knows *everybody*. And much as I might hate to admit it"— she held up another sketch—"she's a damn fine artist to boot."

Alma de Bretteville. Some might add "The Notorious" to her name. Cordelia had read about her exploits and was intrigued by the notion that she might somehow play a role in the case.

She rose to leave, list in hand, when Rosa stopped her. "Miss Hammersmith, if I may ask, who is the Sybil West you referred to earlier? Was she a friend of Lena's?"

It pained her to lie, but since her boss wanted to keep Lena's true identity hidden—at least for the next few days—Cordelia figured discretion was called for. But that applied to the artist as well. "No, she's just a name we ran across. Probably nobody. But Mrs. Plotner ... although I would never advise you to lie to an officer of the law, I would caution you that, unlike our conversation, whatever you share with the authorities may end up on the front page of tomorrow's newspapers. And I would hate to see the Institute's name leaked to the press and therefore associated with what appears to be a dastardly crime—especially since there's no known connection to the school at this point." She held up the list of names. "This will help us tremendously, but you can rest assured our inquiries will remain discreet."

Rosa's eyes had grown wide at Cordelia's words, but she seemed to understand their implication. "I will choose my replies carefully," she said. As Cordelia got up to leave, they shook hands and Rosa added, "Best of luck," followed by a muttered, "If Alma's involved, you're going to need it."

Dove had a devilish streak in him—no doubt about it. Which is why he asked Oliver Bean to accompany him to Aunt Susie's. From the first time they'd met, he'd pegged the fresh-out-of-university Oliver as overly naive—the kind of idealistic young man who needed a dose of real life to help him grow up. Truth be told, Dove was looking forward to watching the young attorney squirm.

Having set up an appointment, they made it to the brothel late in the morning, a perfect time because the prostitutes were up and getting ready for customers who weren't yet knocking on the door.

"I'll interview the madam and you see what you can glean from the working girls," he said to his young colleague as they hopped off the hansom cab.

"If you're sure," Oliver said.

Dove smiled. "Absolutely."

In the velvet-swaddled front parlor, half a dozen hookers sat passing the time, like factory workers on a lunch break. One read a fashion magazine while another laid out cards on a low table for what looked like a game of Solitaire. Another rubbed a sweet-smelling lotion on her arms and legs, while still another brushed her long, straggly blond hair. They all looked up when Dove and Oliver came in, but none were enthusiastic about starting their work shift early.

"Hello, my loves," Dove announced. "Where might I find Aunt Susie this fine morning?"

The hair brusher nodded toward a curtain leading to another room; Dove winked at the group and patted Oliver on the shoulder as if to give him courage. "Honey lambs, this is Oliver. Be kind to him, won't you?"

Oliver paid him no mind. "Ladies," he said cheerfully to the assembled group, "I'm honored to make your acquaintance. I don't believe I've been in the presence of so much exquisite femininity in one room before. Do you mind?" He gestured to the middle seat of the davenport and once given permission, settled himself comfortably between the two women sitting there. "I confess, I'm here to ask a few questions about the unfortunate incident of the other night—in an unofficial capacity, of course, nothing to do with the authorities—but what I *really* want to know is, what do your johns do for you that make them your favorites?" He wiggled his eyebrows. "I'm hoping to pick up a few pointers."

The last thing Dove did before heading through the curtain was to pick his jaw off the floor as the sound of bawdy laughter filled the air.

Aunt Susie, a former prostitute who'd worked her way up the management ranks, was making entries into a ledger when Dove politely knocked on the door frame. Although she was probably pushing fifty, the woman had kept herself in very good shape. She was dressed modestly and her dark-brown hair, woven with streaks of gray, was set in a respectable bun. Her surroundings were equally benign: a bookcase filled halfway with popular titles, a color scheme of cream and peach for the curtains and rugs, and an ornate but well-constructed walnut desk. The only sign that she was not a middle-class matron was the lit cheroot resting in a tray next to a glass of something that looked suspiciously like whiskey.

She regarded him with a critical eye. "Mr. Rebane, I take it. You've got exactly fifteen minutes before I boot you and your charming cohort out of here. We've got a business to run." She gestured to the chair in front of her desk and continued to peruse him. "You're better lookin' than most of the clients and the coppers around here, I'll give you that. Now, what is it you want to know that I haven't already told the police?"

Dove took his seat, pulled out his notebook and got right to the point. "How many rooms have you got here, Aunt Susie?"

"Fifteen, give or take."

"Give or take?"

"Well, we convert some parlors if there's a big demand. You know, paydays, holidays, and so forth."

"And you rent them out in four-hour increments to the girls, is that correct?"

"That's right."

"I understand you told the police the room was supposed to be occupied by a young woman, new to the house, named 'Birdie,' but Birdie wasn't around the night of the murder, and she hasn't been back since. Do I have that right?"

"You do, but that's old news. Tell me what you really want to know."

Dove pointed to her ledger. "You're obviously a sharp businesswoman, so why not tell the police Birdie's real name and everything you know about her? Why not tell them her comings and goings, her schedule, and so on, so they can track her down?"

Aunt Susie hesitated, bristling. "What makes you think her name isn't Birdie?"

"The same reason your real name isn't 'Aunt Susie.' If it were, you'd be a lot grayer, because this place has been Aunt Susie's since before my grandddad used to take me for ice cream and have me sit outside slurping it while he paid his respects to his 'dear old auntie.'"

'Aunt Susie' grinned and held up her glass. "Maude Shaeffer," she said, "just between us."

"Of course. Nice to meet you, Maude. Point is, 'Birdie' is a common nickname for short prostitutes with skinny legs. So, who is she, really?"

Maude shook her head. "The damn thing is, I don't know. This young woman comes in about four months ago during a slow period. Pretty little thing with big blue eyes and curly dark hair, almost to her waist, and says she'd like to rent the room between eleven p.m and three a.m. every night. Says her name is 'B.' She asks what I charge, I tell her, and she says she'll take it. She comes back the next day and pays me double what I asked for—*double*—and pays for four months in advance. What am I gonna say to that, I ask you? That covers a lot of quiet nights."

Dove leaned forward. "I take it she got the name 'Birdie' from you. So, what was her story? What kind of customers did she entertain?"

Maude took a drag of her tobacco. "That's just it. She rarely used the room! Didn't live here. Maybe once or twice a week she'd come in, sometimes followed by a smooth-talkin' gent, all dressed in black. Other times the john would come in by himself and she'd show up later, or not at all."

"What about the man? What'd he look like?"

"Six feet, give or take—slightly shorter than you, I'd say. Always wore black, had dark hair, and the beginnings of a beard, I think. Sometimes another woman came in, bundled up in a long coat and veiled hat. When they hide like that, we figure they're fat cats going for kink, so we look the other way. But we knew it wasn't Birdie playin' dress up because the lady was a lot taller, and her hair was different—not nearly as long and much lighter."

"Like the murder victim."

"I'd bet money it's one and the same. But she never said a word to anyone, just went straight to the room."

"Did the gent follow as usual?"

"It was busy that night, so I'm not sure if he came in before or after or even at all. Not sure if any of the girls paid attention, either. I only gave Birdie one key, but they're easy enough to duplicate. I'll tell you one thing, though."

"What?"

"That man might be a killer, but he sure did know his way around the ladies—both Birdie and the mystery woman liked his style. They got pretty vocal at times."

"They ever call out his name?"

"Not that I heard. Just a lot of oohing and ahhing. 'Kitten' this and 'baby' that. Typical sweet talk."

Dove checked his notes to make sure he covered all angles. "Did Birdie pay you in cash?"

"Yeah, but she handed it over in a bank envelope. It was Crocker, same as my bank."

"Could you tell which branch?"

"The return address said 'C Street.' And before you ask, no, I don't know where she lives or how she earned the money; all I know is she didn't earn it on her back working here."

"And you said there's been no sign of her since the murder."

Maude jerkily stubbed out her cheroot. "She probably knows I'd give her what for if she showed her face again. My God, if she had anything to do with that killing, I can't guarantee there wouldn't be another murder to report."

Dove rose and returned his notebook to his pocket. "Can't say as I blame you. I think my fifteen minutes are up, so I'll see if I can get my partner out of your ladies' hair and we'll be on our way. Thanks for your time … Maude."

The latest 'Aunt Susie' grinned. "Go on with you."

Dove returned to the parlor to find the doxies eagerly gathered around Oliver as he demonstrated a somewhat awkward version of Three Card Monte.

"You see, that's how it's done," he explained to them, flipping over one of the cards. "So, never think you can outsmart a card shark—they'll let you win until you've bet too much money." He glanced at Dove and rose from the couch. "It's been a thoroughly delightful time, ladies," he said, executing a slight bow. "Thank you for sharing your insights with me, and remember, you may lose your money and other unmentionables, but your inner virtue can never be taken from you."

The ladies swarmed around Oliver, chirping and giving him hugs.

"What, nothing for me?" Dove asked, his arms outstretched.

The scraggly blond said it all: "You're only as good as your coin, mister, but this man—" she gave Oliver another squeeze—"is worth his weight in gold."

They were halfway to the street corner before Dove asked, "Just out of curiosity, where'd you learn Three Card Monte?"

"From Mr. Perris," Oliver said. "It's quite astonishing what our employer knows. He's full of surprises."

"He's not the only one," Dove muttered as they headed back to the office.

Chapter Twelve

A Broken Man

The Palace Hotel had given Lord Burnham's forwarding address as an estate in the Oakland Hills known as Vista Bellissima. It was the West Coast retreat of the British Ambassador James Bryce, accessed by a series of electric streetcars bookending a ferry ride from the center of San Francisco.

Jonathan arrived at the residence in the early afternoon. Several minutes after he knocked, a staid-looking butler answered the oversized double doors. Before Jonathan could speak, the man said, "I'm afraid the ambassador is not in residence and will not be returning for several weeks." He began to shut the door, but Jonathan smoothly stopped his attempt.

"I'm actually here to see Lord Burnham," he said. "I understand he's a guest of the ambassador." He handed the butler his card. "I'm sure he will see me. We're old friends."

With pursed lips the butler glanced at the card and then (rather reluctantly, it seemed) opened the door wider to allow Jonathan to enter. Once inside, the servant gestured to where a bank of large windows offered a spectacular view of the Golden City across the bay. "Lord Burnham is rather under the weather today and is recuperating out on the terrace. If you'll excuse me, I will check to see if he is receiving visitors."

While he waited, Jonathan took in the trappings of Ambassador Bryce, the well-heeled British diplomat. Why stay in hot, muggy Washington D.C. when one could rusticate in luxury on America's scenic west coast? No doubt Lord Burnham had helped pave the way for the man's appointment, which granted him access to an opulent retreat when necessary. *If you're going to hide out after committing murder, you may as well do it in style.*

In a few moments the butler returned and ushered Jonathan out to the back terrace, which spanned the length of the prairie-style home. The architect had cleverly cantilevered the upper floor over the outdoor space so that the view of the cityscape from within would not be marred by patio furniture. Yet outside, an equally enthralling atmosphere existed; protected by the overhang of the upper floor, the terrace was a veritable fern garden. One felt embraced by lush greenery, with the promise of hidden delights made by a path leading down the hill.

Unfortunately, the beauty of the surroundings seemed to be lost on Burnham, who looked as if he had come down with consumption. He sat with a blanket draped across his knees even though the slight breeze was neither too cool nor overly warm. When he looked up at Jonathan, his eyes were red-rimmed yet hostile. He did not look like a man who had exacted revenge or solved a problem.

"Come here to gloat, have you?" he snarled.

The man's demeanor was unexpected. "What do you mean?" Jonathan asked.

"You know damn well what I mean. You think you're no longer vulnerable. That the matter we discussed will now go away. But you are dead wrong. I will personally make sure your nightmare is just beginning."

The baron was not making sense. "I'm not sure what you're referring to," Jonathan began quietly, "but I can assure you, removing Sybil West from the picture was no way to solve anyone's problems— not yours, nor those you perceive to be mine."

"Then why—" Burnham's tone was fierce, but he stopped himself as he looked up to see the butler standing at the terrace edge in watchful silence. "My *friend* and I have no need of your services at the moment, Corning. I will call out if I need you."

"Very good, my lord," the butler said, and disappeared into the house.

The anger inside of Jonathan once again started to churn. How *dare* this man sound affronted after setting Jonathan up! "I told you I would contact you after Sybil and I talked. Was the blackmail simply a ruse to set me up? Did you think I would take the fall while you solved whatever little embarrassment you thought Sybil represented for you? What—did she tell you she wasn't interested in seeking revenge on my brother after all? Or worse yet, did she tell you she was no longer going to share your bed?"

Burnham surged out of his chair and lunged for Jonathan, his strength nearly overwhelming as he clasped his hands around Jonathan's throat. "How dare you speak of her like that!" he raged. "You are not worthy of the ground she walked upon!"

Caught off guard, Jonathan reached up to pry Burnham's hands away. He pushed the older man as hard as he could, causing Burnham to stagger back and almost fall. At the last minute the man righted himself and reached for the walking stick he'd propped next to his chair. He raised it high, ready to strike. Lunging forward, his aim was off, and Jonathan easily sidestepped him. Once again Burnham went tumbling, this time falling into a heap, sobbing with frustration.

"You think I killed her," Jonathan said incredulously.

"Well, didn't you? You found out she was deceiving you—and I, I was the one who told you! My God, if I had known…" Burnham was now lost in a filthy bog of self-recrimination and didn't even respond when Jonathan reached down to help him up.

"Lord Burnham, I swear to you I did not kill Sybil West. In fact, I came here to confront you, assuming *you* killed her."

At that, Burnham looked at Jonathan, equally befuddled. "Why on earth would I kill her?"

"I don't know. I thought perhaps because she was about to thwart your plan to compromise me. Or perhaps in your own way, you loved her. She was your mistress, she spurned you, and—"

Burnham shook his head. "No, no. *no*. You have it all wrong. I loved her, yes, but not the way you think. My God man, she was my daughter!"

Chapter Thirteen

Troubled History Revealed

The next few hours were difficult for Jonathan but excruciating for George Burnham. Over whiskey and a cold supper provided by the butler, Burnham unleashed his inner turmoil, no doubt feeling at last that he could express his anguish openly.

"I couldn't keep my dick in my pants, you see," he explained morosely. "The daughter of one of my business partners was a vixen; she offered herself to me and I obliged. She was scarcely out of the schoolroom, and, just my luck, she got with child. Once Sybil was born, her mother dumped the babe on me and took off for parts unknown. She could not stand the staid life staring her in the face; I think I was a means to an end for her."

"So, you raised Sybil? Why then did she not have the name 'Burnham'?"

"Raise her? My God, man, I didn't even acknowledge her—admitting my mistake would have ruined me. Besides, I was already engaged to be married. So, I foisted the infant onto a childhood friend—a vicar, and his wife. He had a lovely little parish on the coast, in Kent. They had no children of their own and were grateful to have her. My wife, meanwhile, had a devil of a time conceiving—we lost five before they could take root. And when she finally managed to hold on to one, she died giving birth. My legitimate heir, a little boy, died right along with her. That makes me the end of the line." Burnham paused to wipe his face. "Poetic justice, wouldn't you say?"

Jonathan knew from experience that one cannot ascribe cause and effect to every event, especially when it comes to families. Sometimes one is lucky, and sometimes that luck is nowhere to be found; it has nothing to do with the type of person you were heading into the experience. "Perhaps," he hedged. "But sometimes things happen over which we have no control."

"I suppose you're right," he conceded. "Still, I've often wondered if things would have turned out differently if I'd had the courage to claim Sybil and raise her as my own flesh and blood. But who's to say she would have turned out any better?"

"You talk as if she did something wrong. She is the victim in all of this."

"On the face of it, yes, but I must tell you, she most definitely took after her mother. She was hell to raise, according to my friend, and he should know, eh? Always a wild child, always defying her natural station in life."

The notion of one having a "natural station" didn't sit well with Jonathan. It smacked of social caste—a stricture from which one cannot escape, no matter how hard one tries to overcome it. "It sounds like she wanted more than the life of a vicar's daughter; is that such a terrible thing?"

"It's one thing to want to better yourself, I suppose, but she wanted much more than that. She wanted to be on top of the heap, no matter what it took to get there. And the damnable thing was, she grew up to have the means by which to do it. You know what I'm talking about. Your brother knows. She was a beauty, again like her mother, and charming and yes, manipulative, too. When she grew old enough and learned that she was my so-called 'ward,' she learned how to manage me as well."

"Did she know you were her natural father?"

"She never admitted as much, nor did I, but I suspect she knew. She never approached me carnally, thank God, but somehow, she knew I would do anything for her. I gave her a locket once, for her fifteenth birthday, with a place inside for her to put pictures of her husband and her children one day. I even had her name engraved on the back. But it wasn't to her taste. The next year she convinced me that I would have a jolly good time taking her shopping, and by Jove, the bill at the end of the day was staggering. Once she left the schoolroom, she talked me into subsidizing her move to London. She wanted to try her hand at art; what a fool I was to indulge her."

"How so?"

"She loved fashion and frippery, so I assumed she'd tire easily of the bohemian life. The last thing she'd want was to be shackled to a starving artist or to be one herself." He chuckled lugubriously. "It wouldn't be long, I thought, before she came to me for help in entering the business world. She was sharp and literate. I told her she could become a secretary and meet a decent young man, a civil servant, perhaps, with whom she could build a life."

Or maybe she could have aimed higher and become an attorney, like Cordelia, Jonathan thought. *The world is opening up for bright young women.* "But that didn't happen, I take it."

"No, she melted into that sordid world. I don't want to think about how she made her way in it. I sent money periodically, but it was never enough. A few years back she did seem to come around, although not in the manner I would have preferred. She said she was through with the artistic life and needed blunt to improve her wardrobe. I was skeptical, but she said she had a plan. And indeed, she did. She'd gotten a position at Harrods selling God knows what and somehow put herself in front of your brother. You know what happened next." He'd continued to imbibe after the meal and swallowed the last of his latest drink.

"I don't, really," Jonathan had to admit. "My brother and I are not close."

Burnham fiddled with his glass and took the time to refill it; it was obvious he felt uncomfortable talking about his daughter's personal life. "I believe she thought it would end with a marriage proposal and she would become a duchess." He smiled grimly. "But we both know affairs like that rarely do. Apparently, she sowed the seeds of her own demise by getting caught with another man—whom, I do not know. Your brother sent her packing, as well he should. Not long after, she announced she was leaving for the states—San Francisco, to be precise."

"And that's when you suggested she put herself in front of me."

Burnham looked at him with bloodshot eyes, but there was truth in them. "No, I had nothing to do with it. She'd done her own homework; in fact, she asked me what I thought about her plan to seduce you. I told her it was a fool's errand, that you were a typical cad who would take what you wanted and leave her, just as your brother had. I could see that I had hurt her, but she grew very stubborn and said, 'I won't fail this time.' It seemed like false bravado to me, but she was determined."

Burnham's description of him rang uncomfortably true. As beautiful and charming as Sybil had been, Jonathan had been nowhere close to falling in love with her. He felt the dull ache of regret, but his next words were harsh. "If you thought she was making a mistake, why didn't you stop her?"

"As if I could." Burnham muttered. "No, like any indulgent parent, I gave her funds and contacts to help her get established. She had decided to reinvent herself as Magdalena von Mendelssohn and had even come up with a fraudulent passport from God knows where. She instructed me to leave her messages at the Auberge, even though she had only spent a couple of nights there upon her arrival before moving on."

"Where did she move to?"

"Dammit, I don't know. I should have asked, but I didn't." He took another quaff of whiskey. "We met every week or so for lunch. As usual, she was not forthcoming with any worthwhile information except that which pertained to you. I think she wanted to show me she'd been right, and I'd been wrong. She was certainly attracted to you and no doubt hoped that this time things would work out. But they didn't, did they?" His eyes welled up again, as they had throughout the evening. After a moment he looked at Jonathan. "Do you have children on either side of the blanket, Perris?"

"No."

"Planning on it?"

"I haven't given it much thought."

"Well, take my advice and give it a bloody lot of consideration before you take the plunge. Because, despite your better instincts, despite knowing everything you should *not* do, you will do it and more to make your child happy." He closed his eyes on a painful thought and opened them again. "I should have told her who she was," he lamented. "I should have told her how much I loved her." Heaving a sigh, he sat back heavily, his emotions spent.

Jonathan left shortly thereafter, promising to let Lord Burnham know of any progress determining who had killed the man's daughter.

The Twisted Road

On the way back to the city, he realized that Burnham seemed to have given up on the idea of blackmail. Perhaps it was no longer important; perhaps all that mattered was dealing with the grief a father must feel when their only child is gone.

Chapter Fourteen

An Unusual Request

By late afternoon, Cordelia had returned to the office and finished organizing her notes from the interview with Rosa Hooper. Jonathan hadn't yet come back from his confrontation with Lord Burnham, and to keep from worrying about him, she busied herself with tying up the loose ends of the Letterman case, which she had won to the satisfaction of everyone except Mr. Letterman and his disgruntled attorney. Divorce was never a joyous outcome, but at least Minnie would be getting the best settlement possible.

Althea popped her head into Cordelia's office, coat in hand along with the basket she often carried to and from her home in the Sunset District. "I'm heading out," she announced. "You know what the boss man says."

"I know. 'Do not go home by yourself after dark, Miss Hammersmith,'" she mimicked. "'It is terribly unsafe out there.'"

"Not bad," Althea said. "And he's got a point."

"Point taken," Cordelia said. "Now go on home to your sweet family."

Two hours later, Cordelia was still at it when she heard a knock on the outer door. Thinking her boss might have forgotten his key, she reached for the knob, stopping herself just in time and calling out, "Mr. Perris, is that you?"

"No, ma'am. It's Paul Nuncio. We met a couple weeks ago when I brought some items for Mr. Perris."

Ah, yes. The previous month her boss had been invited to a gentleman's club by one of the young assistant district attorneys who'd lost the Tom Justice case. She'd heard later (not from Jonathan, of course) that it was a set up: the jerk was apparently hoping to win Jonathan's fancy car, a Landaulet, in a game of pool. Jonathan had somehow turned the tables and won the jerk's car instead, so Paul Nuncio, a fellow club member, had brought over the paperwork and keys.

Since Nuncio had been in on the attempted trick, Cordelia figured he was probably a jerk, too. She considered sending him away, but curiosity won out in the end. She opened the door.

It was indeed Paul Nuncio, carrying a briefcase. He was the same young, earnest attorney she recalled—nice-looking but unsure of himself.

"I take it Mr. Perris isn't in?" he asked.

Cordelia set her jaw. "No, he isn't, but I assure you I am more than capable of helping you. Won't you come in?"

She ushered him into the boardroom and sat across the table from him. "What can we do for you?"

"Well, I ... I was hoping to talk privately with Mr. Perris about a possible case."

Be nice, she told herself. "A case? Well, that's splendid. You know of course that our firm would maintain complete confidentiality, should you—"

"Oh, it's not for me," he said. "It's ..." He stopped and rose from his chair. "Perhaps I should come back another time."

"I believe we've had this conversation before, Paul. You are in perfectly good hands with Miss Hammersmith."

Jonathan spoke from the doorway; his suit jacket was draped over his arm, and he held a stack of letters. Obviously, he had let himself in without making a sound. How did he do that?

Inside, Cordelia sighed with relief. Outwardly, she smiled her thanks and turned back to Paul. "You were saying, Mr. Nuncio?"

Paul looked up at Jonathan, who was nonchalantly going through his mail. Apparently, the man now felt secure enough to speak.

"You've probably been following the case of Emmett Barnes, the guard for United Railroads—that's who I work for," he reminded Cordelia.

"Yes, I remember," Cordelia said. "The jury's still out on the Barnes case, I believe."

"It's coming in tomorrow," he said, "and it's going to be 'guilty.'"

Cordelia frowned. "How can you possibly know that?"

Paul looked to Jonathan for help. Her boss simply shrugged and continued reading his mail. "I just know. But here's the thing—the verdict's not right. Or at least it's not fair."

"What do you mean?" she asked. "The case has been presented to a jury of his peers. Although I don't know how you would know this in advance, you're saying they'll find that he did it. What is the issue here?"

"The issue is that, in my opinion, Mr. Barnes has not gotten a fair trial. I ... I overheard something ..."

Jonathan's interest was piqued now. He put his mail down. "Go on," he said.

"When the striker, Jimmie Walsh, was killed, Mr. Calhoun—he's the president of United—was *furious*. He started yelling that the guards weren't supposed to shoot anybody, that they were just there to look intimidating. He said by shooting a striker, all the sympathy was going to shift from the railroad to the union, and that wasn't good for business, or for him."

"But the evidence ..." Jonathan prompted.

Paul hesitated, then pulled a folder from his briefcase and pushed it toward Jonathan, who indicated that Cordelia should look at it instead. "I'll admit, it looks bad. They know the shot came from his rifle, even though he has denied pulling the trigger. But so much about the case is rotten, from the way they handled the jury to the way they presented evidence—or *didn't* present it. The whole thing stinks."

"Who is 'they'?" Cordelia asked.

"Mr. Calhoun and the company attorney he assigned to the case. He told Mr. Reynolds to do whatever it took, short of bribery, to make sure United Railroads lost the case and Emmett Barnes was sent up the river."

"That doesn't make any sense," Cordelia argued. "Why hope for your side to lose?"

"Because then it would look like United wasn't above the law, that our company always does what's right, even if our side loses. What do they care about Emmett Barnes, anyway? They didn't even know him. So, Mr. Reynolds didn't bother to weed out pro-union jurors during *voir dire*. And he didn't even try to build a case for Emmett Barnes's innocence or even let the man speak for himself."

"Why didn't you bring this up during the trial?" Jonathan asked.

Paul squirmed a bit in his seat. "I did ... sort of. I suggested that Mr. Reynolds look deeper into what Emmett Barnes was saying, about being hit with a brick and all, and build a case of reasonable doubt, but he dismissed my concerns. He said, 'We don't have to prove him innocent—they have to prove him guilty.' That may be true, but I know what Mr. Calhoun ordered him to do, and what he did was put on the weakest defense I've ever seen. It's just not right."

"It seems rather late in the process," Cordelia said. "Like shutting the barn door after the horse has bolted."

Paul grew animated, appealing to both Cordelia and Jonathan. "Listen. I know the verdict will be guilty, and if you've been reading the papers, you know there's going to be a lot of controversy about it. There may even be riots. I also know the company isn't going to fund an appeal. But you can. I can get word to Mr. Barnes that you'll take his case."

Did Emmett Barnes really get a fair trial, and if not, would they be able to rectify that? Cordelia began to look through the file. "On what grounds could it be appealed?"

"I don't know. I don't think you could prove witness tampering or other irregularity. But maybe go for a retrial on the basis of new evidence. There must be something you can find to bolster his version of events. I mean, Mr. Reynolds didn't call one witness—not one! Maybe someone saw something. Maybe ...." He took a deep breath. "Look, even if there's nothing new, or you do find something and he's still found guilty a second time, at least he would have gotten his day in court. At least he wouldn't have been railroaded into hanging for something he says he didn't do—and yes, that pun was intended."

Cordelia settled her gaze on the young attorney. "By your own admission, you didn't put all that much effort into getting Mr. Barnes the justice he needed when he needed it most. Why are you so adamant about helping him now, and why come to us?"

Paul looked at Jonathan, who shrugged and said, "Two entirely legitimate questions."

Like a defendant confessing a crime, the man laid bare his motive. "I'm just starting my career. I'm nobody at United Railroads. What I've witnessed goes against every principle I was taught in law school. A man's reputation, his freedom—even his life may hang in the balance. It makes me ashamed of my profession. But honestly, if I want to keep my job—and I do—there's nothing I can do personally to make things right. But from what little I know of you, Mr. Perris—and you, Miss Hammersmith—you'll do what's necessary to see that justice is served, even if it doesn't favor the defendant, and even if it ruffles some feathers along the way. I admire that kind of courage, even if I don't possess it myself."

Hmmm. It took courage for Paul Nuncio to admit he didn't have any. And it really would be a travesty if Emmett Barnes went to jail, or worse, because he hadn't received the best defense possible.

"Well," said Jonathan, "I'll be happy to discuss this with Miss Hammersmith, and —"

"—and we can decide how best to proceed with the appeal, Mr. Nuncio."

Paul looked from one to the other in disbelief. "Does that mean you'll take it on?"

Cordelia caught Jonathan's eyes. *I can handle it; let me show you.* It took but a moment for him to acquiesce. "I imagine that's what it means," he said.

Cordelia smiled at her boss before facing Paul. "Yes, that's what we mean."

Paul was visibly relieved until Jonathan added, "We'll take on the case, but I do ask a favor of you in return."

Paul looked uncertain. "What is it?"

"Should Miss Hammersmith need your services in any way—say, for some help with background information—you are to accommodate her, even if it makes you uncomfortable to do so. Will you be able to do that?" There seemed to be an undercurrent between the two men, as if they were talking about more than just the case. Cordelia made a note to ask her boss about it later.

"I … yes, of course. Yes, I'm sure I can," he said forcefully, as if to talk himself into it.

"Fine, then tell Mr. Barnes we'll be in touch—that is, if he would like us to proceed."

"Oh, he will," Paul said as he rose to leave. "He would be a fool not to take the lifeline you're throwing." He looked at Cordelia and Jonathan soulfully. "Thank you. Thank you so much."

"And Mr. Nuncio—Paul—I recommend that if we win—"

"—*When* we win," Cordelia blurted.

"I stand corrected," Jonathan said with an amused glance at her. "When we win, I recommend that you not use the opportunity to share 'I told you so's' at the United Railroad office, at least if you want to rise high enough in the company to have some influence."

Paul grinned. "Good advice." As he reached the door, his expression turned sober again. "Um, I'm not exactly sure how Emmett will pay for your services. Perhaps his family can raise the money—"

Jonathan nodded in Cordelia's direction. "Miss Hammersmith will attend to that, I'm sure."

Lord, it hadn't crossed my mind, she thought and smiled weakly in assent.

After seeing Paul out, she headed toward her office, but Jonathan stopped her. "You are quite certain you want to tackle this?"

She nodded, an image of Jonathan sitting in that jail cell popping into her head. "I am. If a defendant can't get a fair shake, no matter his guilt or innocence, then our system crumbles. If we have a chance to keep that from happening, we ought to take it."

"You are wise beyond your years. But I must warn you—there will be ramifications beyond the case itself which may not sit well with everyone in this firm."

Cordelia dismissed the idea. "We can handle it. We are made of the sternest stuff."

"I hope you're right," he said. "Sometimes facing public scrutiny, much less censure, can be much more painful than one bargained for."

Cordelia wasn't sure if he was referring to himself and decided she didn't want to know, so she changed the subject. "Dove, Oliver and I picked up leads in the search for the real Sybil West," she said. "How about you—any luck?"

"Let's just say I have had to shift my thinking completely on the matter. Lord Burnham is not our man. We meet in the boardroom tomorrow morning and begin anew." He turned to leave but thought better of it. "Miss Hammersmith, what are you doing here so late?"

Cordelia sighed. *Some things never change.* "I know. It's not safe for a young woman alone at night."

"Precisely. I'm happy to walk with you to catch a cab whenever you're ready."

'It's not—"

"It is," he said, in a tone that left no room to argue.

Chapter Fifteen

New Assignments

The following morning, Cordelia stopped by the courthouse and learned firsthand that Paul Nuncio's prediction about the verdict and the public's reaction to it was true. Shortly after word leaked that Emmett Barnes was found guilty of murder, a throng of strikers and their family members gathered in the fog-shrouded street to celebrate. Hastily made signs read "Hang the Scab High" and "Kill the Killer." The crowd chanted "First Barnes, Now Calhoun" in reference to the United Railroad president's recent indictment for bribery. A group of what looked like University students chimed in, wearing red and carrying their own "Socialists and Workers Unite" placards. Food hawkers showed up offering biscuits, steaming mugs of coffee and ripe peaches suitable for both eating and throwing. A few musicians formed an impromptu band featuring a banjo and a kazoo. The growing horde took pains to impede any streetcars that might come lumbering along the tracks.

It was quite a festive atmosphere until the railroad supporters showed up. Their signs were equally strident, claiming "No Justice for Emmett" and "Protect Yourself—the Law Won't." A fistfight broke out, leading to a large-scale free-for-all. Several photographers had shown up to record the mayhem and an enterprising young reporter had even lugged a Dictaphone outside to record his observations on the spot.

Cordelia spied Freddie Coleman from the *Examiner;* she'd met him while he was covering the murder trial of Dr. Tom Justice. Freddie was a wiry man in his late forties who always seemed to be chewing something. She'd never seen him spit, and he smelled like licorice, so she was pretty sure it was gum.

"Hey, doll," he said when she approached, "watch where you're goin'; it might get as bad as Bloody Tuesday out here, and that was no picnic."

"I believe you," she said, falling in step with him. "You getting some good shots, Freddie? Who do you think is in the right?"

Freddie looked at her as he slung one camera behind him and loaded another. "Both sides got their good points, and both sides are full of baloney. I'm just tryin' to get it all on film and sell some papers. Let the people decide, I say. Now get out of here before you get yourself hurt."

Cordelia squeezed his shoulder. "You take care, yourself," she said before hurrying along. Just as she reached the entrance to her building, the sound of police sirens pierced the air.

"They'll put a stop to that right quick," Althea pronounced when Cordelia entered the office. She must have heard the sirens, too. "Once they all vent their spleens, maybe we can get back to normal around here."

"Doubtful," Jonathan said as he headed to the boardroom. "Good morning, Miss Hammersmith. Care to tell Althea what's on your docket?"

Althea looked from one of them to the other. "What's going on?"

Though Cordelia glared at her boss, he merely smiled.

"Um, I'll explain later," she promised. "We have a meeting to attend." Inside the room she saw Oliver standing at the blackboard finishing a list. Oh, how she envied his six-foot-plus height! No fruit box needed for him. Taking the seat next to Dove, she handed her notes to Jonathan and contemplated Oliver's list, which read: "Long, dark coat," "Not fat," "possibly black hair under a fedora," "about six feet," "scruffy beard," "low voice," "soothing," "Sounds like a Brit," "Name could be 'Lev.'"

"'Lev?' Why haven't we heard that before?" she asked.

"Because Oliver charmed it out of the ladies at Aunt Susie's." Dove's voice held a note of pride.

"One of them heard it through the door one night when it was occupied," Oliver explained. "Apparently whoever was in there with him couldn't control herself and moaned it out loud. Could be his name."

Cordelia glanced at her employer to see if he had any reaction to the notion that the woman he'd been seeing might have slept with another man during their courtship. He was leafing through Cordelia's notes and did not seem fazed in the slightest.

"Possibly," Jonathan said, looking up. "Or it could be, shall we say, a term of endearment."

Dove nodded. "Exactly. It means 'lion' in Ukrainian."

"What?" Cordelia was appalled. "You mean as in 'Oh, you're such a ferocious lover?'" She snorted. "That's ridiculous. Don't tell me a woman has actually…"

Dove shrugged. "Well, there was a young lady in—"

"I think we get the picture," Jonathan interjected. "The takeaway from what you've gathered so far is that such a man, who might possibly be named Lev, may or may not have joined Miss West on the night she was murdered. For all we know at this point, the mystery woman who rented the room may have found out about her competition and done the deed herself. There is much more work to be done, especially since I have eliminated Lord Burnham from consideration."

"Why is he off the list?" Cordelia asked.

"From personal information he shared that exonerated him, as well as the fact that aside from his accent, he doesn't fit the description Oliver has laid out." Jonathan scanned the information they'd all collected and quickly doled out assignments: Oliver was to check with the Crocker Bank branch on C Street to determine the name of the curly-haired young woman who had withdrawn money several months earlier. "It's quite a long shot," he conceded, "but you obviously have a gift for charming information out of individuals. Perhaps you'll get lucky." To Dove he said, "I've noticed you often sketch during meetings. Have you ever taken art lessons?"

Dove snickered. "Not in your life."

"Well, you're about to. I think you're the perfect student to join the Art Institute and look into such extracurricular activities as, say, the—" he looked down at Cordelia's note. "—the Incendiaries."

Dove grinned. "Oh, that's going to be fun."

Cordelia frowned. "What about me?"

Just as Jonathan was about to respond, Althea entered with a message. He read it and motioned for his office manager to stay before turning to Cordelia. "You, Miss Hammersmith, have a new client waiting—one Emmett Barnes, who is thrilled that you are taking his case on appeal."

Althea looked shocked, as did Oliver. "Wait—isn't that the convicted shooter they're all rioting about?"

"The very same. Miss Hammersmith and I have reason to believe that justice was not served, and she is willing to suffer the slings and arrows of outrageous publicity to represent Mr. Barnes in the hope of securing a new trial. Don't be surprised if tomorrow's headlines include variations on 'Shameless Attorneys Defend Convicted Killer—It's All About the Money' or some such drivel. The question is, are the rest of you comfortable with the fallout from that exposure? It won't be pleasant."

To Cordelia's immense relief, none of them balked.

"I suppose you will just have to win the case," Oliver said resolutely. "I'll be happy to help you however I can."

Smiling in spite of herself, Cordelia felt a touch of guilt for always complaining about his tardiness. *Oh, who am I kidding? It's still and always will be annoying!*

"Bring it on," Dove said. Cordelia might have known—he always did enjoy rubbing people the wrong way. And Althea?

Their office manager shrugged. "I'm getting pretty good at obfuscating."

"It looks like you have the blessing of the staff," Jonathan said. "Now, while you are off seeking justice, I'm afraid I will be entering into much more dangerous waters."

Now what? Cordelia's heart sped up. She decidedly did *not* like the thought of anyone close to her in danger. Finding her boss in jail had disturbed her more than she cared to admit; she was sure she'd feel the same way had it been Oliver or Dove.

"Is that such a good idea?" she said. "You just got out of one scrape. Will we have to pull you out of another? Do you need help?"

Jonathan rubbed his chin. "Come to think of it, perhaps I *could* use some assistance this weekend. Are you willing to accompany me, Miss Hammersmith?"

Cordelia swallowed. "Certainly. How should I dress? Should I bring a weapon?"

"I leave the weaponry up to you as well as the dress," he said with a perfectly straight face. "It is a garden party, after all."

That afternoon, Cordelia headed to the jail for her first meeting with Emmett Barnes. The guard, a robust man with the look of an unsuccessful prize fighter, took it upon himself to warn her. "You best keep on your toes because that kid's a powder keg. He gets real frantic, real angry, and then he sinks down into his own personal hell. Back and forth. Back and forth. I think the cell's getting to him. He don't like being confined. Just wait'll they send him to the Big House." He shook his head as he pulled on his large key ring to open the cell door.

"Hey, Killer. Looks like you're getting your last meal early," the jailer said to the prisoner. "Pretty girl to see you. Looks good enough to eat."

"Thank you for your insights," Cordelia said blandly. "I'll call you when I've finished conferring with my client."

A beefy, ginger-haired young man, Emmett had a thick neck and small, close-set eyes that gave the impression he was a dim-witted thug. He'd been sitting on the bed with slumped shoulders and downcast eyes, a little boy suffering through a scolding, but popped his head up at her arrival.

Cordelia extended her hand. "Hello Mr. Barnes. My name is—"

"Cordelia Hammersmith. I know. Paul told me. He said the best he could do was a lady lawyer, but I'll take what I can get."

Cordelia bit down on a sarcastic retort. "Mr. Barnes—may I call you Emmett?"

"Sure," he mumbled.

"Well, Emmett, I suggest you try your very hardest to explain—leaving no detail out, mind you—why you should not be sitting in this cell."

Chapter Sixteen

The Garden Party

Josephine and Edward Firestone were pillars of San Francisco society and had been for many years. It helped that Edward came from old money in Arlington, Virginia, and Josephine from Philadelphia's Main Line, but that didn't account for all of their good fortune. They'd met at Cornell University in New York and moved west for the adventure of it. Three children and untold investment and managerial success later, they had greatly multiplied their financial and social credibility, becoming one of the Golden City's most influential couples.

Jonathan had met them through a business acquaintance, and through them, their only daughter, Katherine. Kit, as she was called, had inherited her parents' independent streak and become a nurse even though it was not considered fashionable for a debutante to have her own career. Aside from her beauty, which was considerable, it was her intelligent willfulness that attracted Jonathan to her. She seemed to enjoy his company as well, but before their relationship could deepen, she asked him to defend a "friend" of hers who'd been accused of murder. In truth she was in love with the man, a young surgeon named Tom Justice.

Jonathan won the case and lost the girl. However, he earned the family's loyalty and gained a friendship of sorts with all of them, including Kit and Tom. Their trust in him had helped get Jonathan released from jail and their affection often earned him an invitation to a Firestone soiree.

Known for their frequent political and social gatherings, the Firestones had special reason to host this particular party, because Kit and Tom had just announced their engagement.

For his part, Jonathan wanted to thank the Firestones for their willingness to post his bail; their belief in him had touched him deeply. On a more practical level, he knew that Josephine would invite the millionaire sugar magnate Adolph Bernard Spreckles (known to friends as "A.B.") and would insist that he bring along his "companion"— one Alma de Bretteville, the woman mentioned by the art instructor as knowing Sybil West.

Jonathan had met Spreckles and the twenty-six-year-old Alma through the Firestones a few months earlier. She was a force of nature with no qualms about interacting with anybody, regardless of their social status. The fact that Alma showed up on Cordelia's list of possible links to Sybil came as no surprise; with luck she'd paint a more detailed picture of "Lena von Mendelssohn," the woman Jonathan had hardly known at all.

There was an additional advantage to attending, especially with Cordelia by his side. A few days earlier, she'd interviewed Emmett in his jail cell and was convinced that he had, in fact, gotten a raw deal in the courtroom.

"The story he tells is strange but compelling," she'd reported. "He swears he was knocked out and couldn't have shot Jim Walsh. Based on the trial notes, his attorney didn't present Emmett's side of the story at all. He was either totally incompetent or intentionally set on seeing Emmett convicted. We can do better."

The word had spread about their firm's involvement and now the newspapers were full of nasty headlines similar to those Jonathan had predicted.

It was all about money, of course. Fremont Older, the publisher of the *San Francisco Bulletin*, and Spreckles didn't support the carmen's strike, but they *hated* United Railroads. The UR president, Patrick Calhoun, wanted to repair the streetcar system with the existing overhead lines, which Spreckles, Older and their allies opposed. They felt the wires were unsightly and should go underground—a very expensive proposition, but one which would benefit their own commercial interests in the long run. Only the city's board of supervisors could grant permission for the overhead repair, which it had, thanks to a suspicious exchange of funds. In the *Bulletin's* opinion section, Older had even accused Calhoun of fomenting the strike to divert attention from his own bribery indictment.

Anyone who supported United Railroads in any way was tarred with the same brush; thus, the paper's editorial pages had savaged

Jonathan's firm for taking up Emmett Barnes's appeal. Since Cordelia was taking the brunt of the acrimony, it would help if those attending the party could see her as more than the latest ammunition in the ongoing battle between the railroad and the union. In fact, she was a very attractive, intelligent professional.

Cordelia certainly looked the part. When he picked her up at her rooming house, he was pleased to see that she had eschewed her normally mannish work attire for a feminine summer frock which she'd accessorized with a delicate straw boater. The hat's black ribbon matched her rich, dark hair, which she wore in a soft, Gibson-girl style, no doubt to give her some height.

"What, no notebook?" he teased.

She patted her matching drawstring bag. "I am never without one; this version is just a wee bit smaller."

Jonathan nodded his approval. If Cordelia matched her genteel appearance with decorum and restraint, others might begin to see what he saw in her—a sharp legal mind and an outstanding example of modern womanhood. All she had to do now was curb her tongue.

If only it were that simple.

Jonathan had jokingly told Cordelia to bring her "weapon of choice" to the garden party. An hour into the soirée, Cordelia wished she *had* brought something—at least a paring knife; if so, she could have flayed the tongues of several guests who seemed to delight in wagging them where she and Jonathan were concerned; in fact, Jonathan himself could use some trimming.

The party had started out well enough. The Firestones lived atop Nob Hill, fairly close to the Art Institute, in a beautiful Queen Anne-style mansion that had been damaged, but not destroyed by the quake and fire. It was surrounded by lovely gardens, both manicured and natural, the type of setting Cordelia had dreamed about as a girl, despaired of ever attaining as a young woman, and was now indifferent to, because it no longer embodied her hopes and dreams. Several dozen guests were now strolling the estate, some of them playing croquet and others badminton. A more sedate group enjoyed a string quartet set up in a gazebo called the Ruby because of its deep red color.

A long banquet table had been laid with all manner of fine picnic fare. Juicy melon wedges and huge strawberries competed with summer vegetables like corn on the cob and crisp asparagus spears. Off to one side a chef discreetly grilled skewers of beef and pork, calamari and shrimp, along with the catch of the day. And the desserts! Tarts and cookies and berry crumbles and every pie imaginable, including Cordelia's all-time favorite, lemon meringue. *I will be good*, she thought. *That pie does not have my name on it.*

She had no quarrel with her escort, either, at least at first. Jonathan looked quite handsome in his light wool suit. San Francisco normally defied the traditional expectations of summer with its cold, dreary temperatures, but today the sun had burned off the usual fog and many of the men, including her boss, had removed their jackets and rolled up their sleeves. Cordelia was partial to a strong pair of male arms, and Jonathan's did not disappoint.

But his attitude toward her negated nearly all of his attractive qualities. Whenever socially powerful guests came up to them—no doubt to meet the fool who was defending a convicted killer—Jonathan would introduce Cordelia as "my esteemed colleague and a superb attorney" or some such drivel. And if any of them asked her a question related to the latest news reports, Jonathan would smoothly interject with some banal response such as "Miss Hammersmith doesn't pay attention to such rubbish; she finished at the top of her class at the University of California and is focused on proving herself in the courtroom. She is quite the asset to our firm." Such a response was usually met with a smirk and some euphemism related to "My, you certainly are ... modern."

After half a dozen such mortifying exchanges, Cordelia had had enough. She firmly took her boss by the arm and practically marched him to a shaded tree set slightly apart from the throng.

"What on earth are you doing?" she hissed.

He frowned. "What do you mean?"

"I mean you're not letting me get a word in edgewise. And you heap on so much praise that everyone you've introduced me to now thinks I am a half-wit that you hired out of some misguided pity."

He had the gall to look amused. "Ladling it on a bit thick, am I?"

"Like my grannie's porridge," Cordelia shot back. "We could barely stuff it down for the lumps in it. But she kept shoveling."

"That is a ridiculous analogy, of course. I simply want the rest of society to know what I know about you. My apologies if you find my praise of you offensive."

Cordelia fumed. He was *not* going to make her feel ungrateful. "Well, you are doing me no favors." She surveyed the crowded field, which seemed to be comprised of "men of substance" palavering with one another and fashion-conscious women conspiring about some unknown topic. It dawned on her what Jonathan was really up to. "You're trying to protect me again, aren't you? You think I might not survive the onslaught of ridicule if I fail to help Emmett Barnes, or perhaps even if I do."

Her employer gazed at her, his gentle expression confirming her accusation. "People can be vicious."

Meeting his eyes, she shook her head slightly. "You think I don't know that? Mr. Perris, there is much you don't know about me. But one thing you *need* to know: I can, and I must fight my own battles. I will not rely on you or anyone else to fight them for me."

He scrutinized her a moment longer before nodding slightly. "All right then. What would you prefer I do?"

"I propose we split up and I get to know these individuals, some of whom may become clients, and others who may turn out to be adversaries. You know what they say: 'Know thy enemies.'"

"'Know thyself,'" he murmured. "I should have known you'd be a student of Sun Tzu."

Cordelia grinned at him. "Yes, you should have, but I won't hold it against you." She checked the timepiece she'd stuck in her small bag. "Shall we meet up again by the dessert table in, say, an hour, and compare notes?"

"Excellent idea," he said. "I do have some contacts to make."

They sauntered back to the edge of the activity and parted company. Despite her protestations, Cordelia felt somewhat bereft as she watched him stroll confidently into the crowd. Within moments he seemed to be swallowed up by several attractive females who flitted about him until a young woman approached him who stood head and shoulders above the rest. Literally. She was at least six feet tall with luxurious dark hair, an angel's perfectly proportioned face, and a figure that any woman would envy—and any man would lust after. She wasted no time in brazenly hugging Jonathan and kissing him exuberantly on the mouth. Cordelia found it disconcerting to witness their affection until she saw the older mustachioed man standing slightly apart with a bemused look. That's when Cordelia recognized the celebrity whom she'd missed the opportunity to meet.

Alma de Bretteville was magnificent.

Chapter Seventeen

The Incomparable Miss de Bretteville

"Jonathan, you young buck, come here and give us a bloomin' hug!" Alma de Bretteville, ravishing as always, took Jonathan's face between her hands and noisily gave him what the Scots might call a *smoorich*. He knew her to be intelligent and insightful, despite the fact that she'd left school at the age of fourteen and her manner was delightfully shameless.

He grinned at her. "Careful, old girl; I'd hate to get on Adolph's bad side so early in our acquaintance."

Alma guffawed and blew a kiss to A.B., whom she referred to as her "sugar daddy." Spreckles held his wine glass up to toast her and resumed his conversation with Fremont Older.

She wasted no time putting Jonathan on the spot regarding the Emmett Barnes appeal. "Pretty gutsy of you to take up that guard's case. A.B. thinks you're crazy, but crazy like a fox. He thinks you put your new gal on it, so if it goes south, you can blame her. Me, I think you're smart to let her show you what she can do." She winked at him. "Mark my words. She's a woman, which means she's gonna do more than just fine. I know Judge Fisher to be a fair man, so we'll see. Me and A.B. got a bet going; I get a new fur coat if you win." She poked Jonathan in the chest. "So, you better win."

Spreckles' insinuation regarding Jonathan's motive for putting Cordelia on the case rankled, but he couldn't help chuckling at the woman who had the mogul by the short hairs. "Your wager is well placed. I wouldn't bet against Cordelia Hammersmith, either."

After a few more minutes of artful chatter, he broached the topic he'd wanted to talk to Alma about. "No doubt you heard about ... Miss Mendelssohn's death. I understand you and she were art students together."

Alma's exquisite eyebrows rose. "Did she tell you that? I knew you two were burning up the sheets, but..."

Jonathan winced. *Is nothing private in this town?* "Ah, no. Your art instructor—"

"Ah yes. Miz Plotner. The miniatures class. Of course, she'd flap her jaw." Alma took Jonathan's arm and commenced the obligatory stroll around the grounds. "Lena and I did chew the fat quite a bit. She was smart as a whip and talented as all get out, poor thing. It didn't take long to figure out she was playin' *some* kind of game, but I sure didn't expect it to end the way it did." She patted Jonathan's arm. "I'm damn sorry you got caught up in it."

Jonathan knew to tread lightly; he wanted to find out what Alma knew without revealing Lena's true identity. "It was shocking, to say the least," he said. "Ironically, we had agreed to part company the very night she was attacked—in a brothel, no less."

"I heard. But there's no way she was a workin' girl. I'm not one to judge, so she could easily have confessed that little peccadillo. We talked mainly about art, and of course she often mentioned 'the handsome young attorney' she was seeing. It was obvious she liked you."

"And I liked her. But I had my own concerns. What game do you imagine she was playing?"

Alma lifted her shoulder. "Who can say? But I could tell from the get-go that she didn't have the deep pockets she wanted others—like you, maybe—to believe she had. She rented some rooms on Fulton and that street's not known for its fancy lodging. In fact, I think she mentioned once that she had a roommate, but I couldn't swear to it."

A roommate? On a street that's lower on the social rung than Jonathan's own? How did poor Lena/Sybil manage two so completely different lives? "Do you know her address, by any chance?"

"Sorry. I only know it was Fulton because she talked about crossing the street to the park every day for her 'morning perambulation.' I mentioned I knew someone who lived on Fulton near Stanyan and she said she was staying a few blocks farther west. Didn't the police find out where she lived?"

The police are stymied because they're looking for a Lena Mendelssohn who never existed. He shook his head. "What about her school chums besides you? Did anyone stand out?"

"She spent a lot of time with some students who think they're gonna change the world through their art. I call 'em the 'Bolshevik Bullshitters' but they call themselves the 'Incendiaries.' A few skinny young men with scraggly beards, living off some pitiful allowance or dead-end job. A few queers—you find a lot of them in the art world—and a smattering of female hangers-on. Lena found them amusing. 'They're always good for a laugh and a free glass of wine,' she said once."

"How can I find out more about them?"

Alma looked at him curiously. "Why? Why not let the police do their jobs and stay the hell out of it? Didn't your stint in the hoosegow teach you anything?"

Jonathan stopped walking to emphasize his point. "Because I came very close to being put on trial for her murder ... and because she didn't deserve to die like that. The police don't seem to be making headway, and by God, someone should pay the price for what they did to her."

Alma gave him a hug. "Sounds like Lena has a true knight in shining armor in you—too bad she's not alive to enjoy it." She paused and added, "Tell you what. You want to find out more about that group, go see Quincy Bass. He teaches a few classes at the Institute, one of which is called 'Art for the Masses,' if you can believe that. Thinks we all ought to like the same thing for the sake of political unity and the state ... he paints wretched pictures of poor tenant farmers rising up and storming the master's house, crap like that. Bass has what A.B. would call 'peculiar inclinations'—meaning he's a sissy boy, which is probably why he sponsors their little club. In fact, they're puttin' on an art exhibit in a few weeks to attract more supporters. Tell him you're interested in supporting his cause and you can probably get him to say or do whatever you want—and not necessarily within reason."

She waggled her eyebrows as she spoke, but Jonathan couldn't bring himself to joke about it. "So, tell me, when is A.B. going to make an honest woman out of you?"

They had come back around to Adolph and Older, who were still engaged in a spirited discussion. Alma sent Jonathan a thousand-watt smile.

"Oh, I'm working on it," she promised. "It's just a matter of time." She disengaged from Jonathan and glided over to Adolph, putting her arm through his. Her sugar daddy continued talking but patted her hand as he spoke. He was the very definition of a self-confident, contented man.

My money's on you, Alma, Jonathan thought. *Spreckles doesn't stand a chance.*

All things considered, Alma had put Jonathan in a better frame of mind, so he decided not to spoil it by confronting Fremont Older about the unfair coverage of Cordelia and the firm. He talked with a few more guests and worked his way over to Kit and Tom in order to congratulate them.

"Looks like the better man won," he said, shaking Tom's hand. Kissing Kit on the cheek, he added, "I'm very happy for the two of you." And the best part was, he meant it.

After a few moments he took his leave, ordering a gin and tonic from a passing waiter and heading toward the dessert table to meet up with Cordelia. He was looking forward to comparing notes with her; perhaps she'd made some worthwhile connections to offset her concerns about everyone thinking her a half-wit. He smiled at the thought of anyone finding her the least bit slow. To know her was to marvel at a bit of lightning, not to mention thunder, trapped in a small but volatile package. He looked for her in the crowd, but when he spotted her, his smile slipped. Something had happened.

Chapter Eighteen

Inconvenient Facts

Making small talk with people simply wasn't one of Cordelia's strong suits. It didn't matter if she had just met them or had known them for years, she invariably ended up arguing over some inconsequential point, such as whether Macy's or Gumps had a better hat selection or, worse yet, which flavor of ice cream was more delicious (they all were, to her dismay). She would much rather tackle headier topics, such as how many angels could dance on the head of a pin (an infinite number or none at all—she still hadn't decided). As a result, attending grand parties like this one felt like a chore, much like washing clothes or peeling potatoes. But if she was ever going to make it as a successful attorney in San Francisco, she was going to have to take a page out of her employer's handbook and "make some contacts."

While Jonathan was off charming Miss de Bretteville, Cordelia found her way to Kit Firestone, who was looking ethereal in a loosely fitted lace dress and sitting in a wheelchair, no doubt to conserve her energy while she recovered from a recent gunshot wound. Her intended, Tom, whom Cordelia had helped defend against murder charges, stood behind Kit, tall and alert like a Praetorian guard. It was apparent to anyone with eyes in their head that those two loved each other without reservation, and Cordelia felt a flash of empathy for Jonathan who, at one point, had entertained the idea of pursuing Katherine. Her boss seemed to have gotten over the loss of that opportunity, however; indeed, he'd had no problem amusing himself with Sybil West until her untimely demise. *His heart was not engaged. That's a good thing.*

"Cordelia!" Kit called out as she approached. She held out her arms for a hug, which Cordelia warmly reciprocated.

"How's the prettiest attorney in the city?" asked Tom, stepping in for his own embrace. Cordelia hadn't remembered him being so light-hearted, which stood to reason, since he'd had a murder charge hanging over his head when she met him. It was wonderful to see them so happy.

"How is business?" Kit asked. "Is Jonathan keeping your shoulder to the wheel?"

"Well, I am busy, but I'm afraid it's of my own making."

"We heard about your latest case," Tom said. "Rather an uphill battle, isn't it? Juries seem to know what they're doing—at least they did in my case, thank God."

Tom was right; overturning verdicts on appeal was no mean feat. In fact, Cordelia wasn't quite sure how she was going to approach it … yet. But what was the alternative when justice hadn't been served? "That may be true, however—"

Katherine understood her perfectly. "Tom, darling, imagine if your jury had ruled the other way; you'd better hope that brave, smart people like Cordelia would be willing to take up your cause, no matter how daunting it seemed to be."

Cordelia grinned. "You are so lucky to have found such an intelligent woman," she told the good doctor. "You'd better keep her."

"Oh, I intend to," he said with a smile, his hand resting lightly on Kit's shoulder. "The sooner I can make her mine, the better."

They were chatting in that lighthearted manner (*not so difficult after all*, Cordelia thought), when Josephine, Katherine's mother, walked up with a well-dressed man whom Cordelia would have considered dignified if not for his overly large mutton chops that connected by way of a bushy moustache. Cordelia could not fathom the male penchant for such melodramatic facial hair. It wouldn't do to comment on it, however.

"Mrs. Firestone, it's so lovely to see you," she said instead. "Thank you for hosting this happy celebration."

Josephine was a petite but formidable woman, still lovely in middle age, and still capable of commanding armies if called upon to do so. "Well, we certainly needed something festive after all we've been through, wouldn't you say?" She leaned in and spoke to Kit in a low tone. "How are you doing, dearest?"

Kit took her mother's hand. "Just fine, Mama. Tom is taking good care of me."

"He'd better," Josephine said, looking up at her future son-in-law with mock severity. She then presented the whiskered man. "Cordelia, I'd like you to meet Douglas Reynolds, an attorney with United Railroads. Poor Douglas was on the losing end of the Emmett Barnes case, although I must say an equal number of parties would have been disappointed had the verdict gone the other way. Douglas, this is Miss Cordelia Hammersmith, who is taking your baton with regard to the appeal."

Cordelia froze. *Is this coincidence or just bad luck? It could be the best or the worst development of the evening, and I haven't even started to mingle!*

Before she could respond, Reynolds offered his hand. "Miss Hammersmith, it's a pleasure to meet you."

She narrowed her eyes, waiting for a veiled but snide remark. She must have waited too long because a curious look came over him. He retained her hand but murmured, "Miss Hammersmith? Are you all right?"

His words broke the spell, and she discreetly took her hand away. "No, I'm fine. I'm just waiting for you to join the chorus of many who seem to feel I'm making a big mistake taking on the case."

Mr. Reynolds smiled at his host, her daughter and her daughter's fiancé. "If you'll excuse us, I think Miss Hammersmith and I might require a private, yet I hope constructive chat." He offered his arm. "Miss Hammersmith, would you care to join me for a stroll?"

Why not? I'd rather be insulted in private any day. "Certainly. Lead on, Mr. Reynolds."

They walked along the perimeter, pausing to watch the croquet game in progress. "I'm terrible at that game," he commented. "My wife loves it, but I never saw the purpose of spending one's time trying to hit a ball through a little gate."

"Ah, then you must feel the same way about golf," Cordelia remarked.

"Oh no, golf is something entirely different. You are trying to get a ball to drop into a little hole." His charming demeanor prompted Cordelia to move past the social niceties.

"I know you had a difficult case," she began. "But I'm sure you did your best." The latter was spiced with sarcasm; she didn't want to betray Paul Nuncio's confidence, but she was now certain that Reynolds had done little to bring about Emmett's acquittal.

Reynolds caught her undertone but took no umbrage. "I know you must feel I provided a lackluster defense, but given the circumstances, I felt it could have been worse. As it is, I think the judge will give him prison time instead of the hangman's noose."

Cordelia frowned. "What do you mean by 'It could have been worse'? The man tells you he's innocent and you do nothing to bolster his case!"

"Honestly, Miss Hammersmith, there wasn't that much to work with—as I'm sure you'll realize soon enough."

Cordelia stopped and faced Reynolds. "You could have at least weeded out the pro-union jury members during *voir dire*."

Reynolds's attitude slipped into mild condescension. "What leads you to believe I didn't? In fact, hardly anyone in the pool was agnostic about the case; for every union sympathizer there was a railroad supporter to match. I did the best with what I had to work with."

Sure, you did. And I'm really six feet tall. But knowing she couldn't disprove his claim, she tried another tack. "Well, what about Emmett himself? Why not let him testify? He seems credible enough."

The lawyer shook his head. "My God, that would have been the worst move of all. Mr. Barnes would have been mediocre on direct and eviscerated during cross. I couldn't chance the whole story coming out."

That stopped Cordelia cold. "The whole story?"

Looking to either side to make sure they weren't close enough to be overheard, Reynolds took Cordelia even farther out of earshot. "I thought for sure that some disgusting little ferret of a reporter would start sniffing around, but Emmett was lucky no one found out."

Cordelia's palms turned damp. *Whatever it is, I'm not going to like it.* "Found out what?"

"That he knew the victim but was furious with him. Jimmy Walsh was Emmett's best friend."

Chapter Nineteen

The Whole Story

Cordelia hadn't been so angry in, well, she couldn't remember when. But Mr. Reynolds's revelations regarding Emmett Barnes's culpability had her practically spitting nails. As soon as she rejoined Jonathan at the dessert table (too upset to even consider a slice of lemon meringue pie), she announced that she had to leave immediately, if not sooner. Her employer looked alarmed and was ready to take her wherever she needed to go, but she held him off.

"You see, this is just what I'm talking about," she explained rather more curtly than she intended. "I have learned something about the Emmett Barnes case, and I must see to it. But you do not have to go with me. I do not need your help. Please, stay and enjoy yourself, and I will explain everything tomorrow."

"Are you sure? You seem quite upset and I would be happy to—"

She caught his arm to stop him. "I know," she replied tersely. "But I can handle this."

She left Jonathan looking bewildered and concerned. After thanking the Firestones once more for their hospitality, she caught a cab and went straight to the jail where Emmett Barnes awaited sentencing and removal to the state prison.

She commenced her tirade as soon as the guard left. "You have not been forthcoming with me, Mr. Barnes." She paced the convict's admittedly cramped cell, finding little outlet for her own agitation. "You have left out critical facts as they relate to your relationship with the victim. Frankly, I am livid and tempted to withdraw from this case."

"Oh, please don't quit on me, Miz Hammersmith," he begged. "I'm real sorry I didn't tell you everything from the beginning. I wanted to explain it all, but I was afraid you'd turn tail and run."

"I have never run from anything in my life, but I won't put up with dishonesty—especially when there is so much at stake. Do you understand me, Mr. Barnes?"

"Yes, yes, I understand. I do. I just didn't think—"

"Spare me the excuses. Now I want to hear your story from the beginning—*again*—and don't leave anything out this time. Are we crystal clear about that?"

"Yes Ma'am."

Cordelia sat down on the solitary chair and pulled out her notebook and a pencil. "Begin."

Emmett took a deep breath. "The story I told you before is true, as far as it goes. I was hired by Mr. Wagner, Mr. Calhoun's second in command. Well, he hired me to protect the scabs—I mean the strike breakers—when the cars rolled out of the barn on that Tuesday. We knew the strikers were going to give us grief, but Mr. Calhoun told us not to hurt nobody if we could help it.

"My pa gave me his 94—that's a Winchester—just before he died and when the doors opened and we rolled out, I held it steady, hopin' it would give the idea that we meant business without having to fire a round."

"Why? Because you're not a good shot?"

"No ma'am. Because I *am* a good shot. That's why the company hired me. Anybody knows you hardly ever have accidents when you know your way around a firearm. They didn't even want us to bring pistols, although some of the guards did. The Railroad didn't want no real trouble. They just wanted us to look tough, is all."

"Then what happened?"

"I was a fool, that's what happened. The yard was crawling with strikers, armed with anything they could get their hands on—bricks and rocks and pipes and two by fours, even rotten fruit. Some had guns of their own. Nobody told *them* to be nice.

"Well, it didn't take but a few minutes for our car to be overrun and I had to use my rifle just to knock people off, like rats off a garbage heap. But there was just too many of them all at once. I shot once or twice in the air, hoping that would scare them, but the mob didn't care and a group jumped on board, one of them wearing a red shirt, I remember that, and someone threw a brick and clipped the side of my head. It hurt like the dickens. I remember dropping my rifle and falling down. Don't know how long I was out of it but at some point, I woke up right back in the thick of things and tried to stand up. Some other scabs had jumped on the car to help fight off the strikers and there were fists flyin' everywhere. I remember blood drippin' down my face; I was dizzy and seein' double and I just knew I was gonna spill my guts, so I dropped to the floor again and started groping around, looking everywhere for my rifle. And I finally spied it clear in the back of the car by the steps along with another red-shirt who laughed and jumped off. So, I grabbed the gun and about that time I heard the sirens and the cops roll in and they started breaking everybody up."

Cordelia reviewed her notes. His story was almost word for word what he'd told her during their first interview. But still he was leaving something vitally important out.

"So why did you kill your best friend?"

The shock of her question caused Emmett to burst into tears. "I didn't kill him —I swear it! I didn't even know anybody had been shot until they told me later at the station!"

"Did you know Jim Walsh was going to be there that day?"

Sure, why not? Jimmy was in the union. Hell, I'd been in the union right along with him, until ..."

"Until what?"

Emmett hesitated. "Until I got mad about something and busted up The Rusty Rail."

"That a local bar?"

"Yeah."

"What were you mad about?"

Emmett started to fidget. It was obvious he knew his story wasn't going to play well. "I ... I was mad at Jimmy for telling his cousin I wasn't good enough for her. She wouldn't go out with me, and I figured Jimmy had a hand in it."

Cordelia sighed "So, you're telling me you thought your friend had talked bad about you, you lost your temper, and you inflicted damage in a bar. That doesn't seem all that uncommon, yet you got kicked out of the union for it?"

Emmett was back to studying the floor. "Well, it wasn't the first time."

My Lord, could it get any worse? "What else did you do?"

"I ... well, I got a problem with the green-eye monster, I admit. And I didn't cotton to anyone takin' a shine to my girl—at least the girl I was hopin' to make mine. So, I got into a scrape or two with a couple members 'cause I thought one of them might be thinking to move in on me, you see?"

"Yes, I see," Cordelia replied in an icy tone. "You were a jealous, insecure, mistrusting fool, which probably drove the girl you wanted away more than anybody else could. She figured you were too much trouble, you were mad as hell, and you took it out on others. Do I have that right?"

Emmett nodded. "I guess Jimmy didn't like what he saw, so he turned her against me, at least that's the way it looked to me. To make things worse, I heard she was seein' somebody else, but Jimmy wouldn't tell me who it was. He acted like I was crazy and denied she was seeing anybody at all!"

"My God, do you blame him? You seemed hell bent on causing harm to whomever she chose to be with other than you!"

Emmett met Cordelia's eyes, his own filled with remorse. "I suppose you're right, but mad as I was, I swear on my mama's grave—she ain't dead, but if she was—that I would never kill Jimmy or anyone like that. I never would." His voice broke. "Never."

Cordelia could see he was hurting so she softened her voice. "But it's been established that it was your rifle, because of the special bullets it uses, that fired the shot. And you shot that rifle. You remember they made prints of your fingertips when you were arrested? Well, they compared that to prints on the murder weapon and they match. You say you dropped your rifle and then found it again. Did it really happen that way, Emmett? I need to know how to explain it in a way that makes sense."

"I *know* it don't make sense, but that's what happened. Yes, I shot my daddy's gun, but only into the air."

"So, your story is, basically, that you lost your rifle, someone picked it up and shot Jimmie Walsh in the head with it, and then returned it to you. The fact that you not only knew Jimmy but had a beef with him played no role in this drama. Is that pretty much it?"

Cordelia's disbelief was evident, and Emmett picked up on it. "I know it sounds far-fetched, but as God is my witness, that's what happened, and I'll swear to all of it in court."

Closing her notebook, Cordelia rapped on the cell to alert the guard. "I'm not going to sugar-coat your situation, Mr. Barnes. The notion that your case could be thrown out due to jury bias is a slim possibility, and even if the judge went along with it, it would only result in a re-trial with possibly more objective jurors. The reality is, no one who looks at this case, especially knowing the connection to the victim you've just admitted to, could conclude, based on your testimony, that what *you* say happened, actually happened." She watched as the young man rubbed his face, like someone just beginning to wake up. "So ... we must bring something new to the table." She continued in a brisk tone, trying not to crush his spirits entirely. "We need some evidence that lends credence to your version of events. Is there anything—*anything*—you can think of that might help us do that?"

Emmett shook his head slowly in a kind of dawning awareness that his conviction had an overwhelming chance of being upheld. Finally, he looked up at her, tears in his eyes. "I'm a goner ain't I?"

Cordelia tried to offer the young man at least a smidgeon of hope, but it rang hollow, and she knew it. Leaving him to his woes, she returned to her boarding house to nurse her own frustration. Why hadn't she done more research before agreeing to represent him? Because her own idealism had blindsided her, that's why. She'd bought Emmett's story and wanted to see that justice was served.

Maybe it had been. Maybe Douglas Reynolds had done the right thing by lying low and hoping the prosecution would fail to prove its case. Then again, if one believed Paul Nuncio—and Cordelia did— then Reynolds had essentially been ordered by his boss to scuttle the case.

Then there was Emmett himself. Other than confessing his strained relationship with Jimmie Walsh, his story hadn't wavered in any significant detail. In Cordelia's albeit limited experience, liars often had a difficult time keeping their stories straight.

As Cordelia saw it, she had two options: one was to withdraw from the case and suffer the consequences, both public and professional. Her worst nightmare would be if Jonathan took the case upon his own shoulders because his word as the head of the firm was on the line.

No, she could not do that to him, which meant she had no option but to continue representing Emmett.

What did that look like? As she'd explained to her client, basing the appeal on jury bias or other irregularity was a long shot at best; the transcript had shown no such mistakes, and she wouldn't feel right about manufacturing a problem where there hadn't been one. She *could* try for defense attorney misconduct, maybe get Paul Nuncio to testify that somehow the case had been poorly tried on purpose.

No, that would be extremely difficult to prove, even *with* Nuncio's testimony, and Nuncio wasn't about to risk losing his job over a little old case of possible injustice.

That left only one other viable option: to proceed as if Emmett Barnes's version of events, no matter how unlikely, did in fact happen. And that meant finding new evidence that would convince the judge, and a subsequent jury, that Emmett was telling the truth. If Emmett couldn't help her find that evidence, she would have to find it herself.

But she couldn't do it alone. That much she knew. Logically she was going to have to recreate the sequence of events leading to the crime, the crime itself, and its aftermath. She was going to have to show how it *could* have happened, according to Emmett's perspective. Unfortunately, there were aspects to the case she simply didn't understand, such as how the prosecution knew for certain it was Emmett's gun that shot Jimmie Walsh, and how he could have done that if fighting at close range.

Adding to her current misery was knowing how she'd pushed her employer away, first railing at him for building her up too much in front of others, and then all but yelling at him that she could handle matters on her own. Jonathan Perris had taken a big chance on her, and this is how she repaid him? What kind of ingrate was she? She wouldn't be surprised if he thought about her rude behavior and decided to let her go. She would be devastated, but could she blame him? The honest answer was no.

She had to do something about it. Her past had taught her that she had only herself to count on, and that had served her well for the last several years. But she was no longer alone; she was now part of a team. That meant not only helping the other members when they needed it, but asking for help when *she* needed it.

And this was one of those times. God help her, she had no stomach for eating crow.

Chapter Twenty

A Reprieve

Monday morning's conference began unexpectedly, with Cordelia sitting quietly for a change instead of fidgeting impatiently for her chance to speak. She looked tired, and she made no move toward Althea's plate of hot cross buns. Those, Jonathan knew, were one of Cordelia's favorites—they had negotiated over the last one several times. Whatever transpired after she left the party apparently hadn't gone well.

Althea, who normally sat in and took notes, glanced at him with eyebrows raised; she too sensed that something was wrong.

Oliver was the first to speak. "So, I wasn't able to find the name of the woman who'd taken money out of the C Street branch of Crocker Bank several months ago. The tellers there said there were too many customers who fit her description, besides which they weren't allowed to give out customers' names to just anybody."

"Losing your touch already, Ollie?" Dove sent Oliver a grin. "Tsk tsk."

Oliver took the ribbing in stride. "A few setbacks make the victories all the sweeter," he said, reaching for a bun.

"Well, it was a long shot," Jonathan said. "I do have something else in mind, something where perhaps you, Althea, would be a help to Oliver. I'll fill you in later on that. Dove, how are you progressing?"

Dove held up a new sketch pad. "Swimmingly. I'm in. Gonna learn how to tear down the evils of capitalism with pen and ink."

"Good." Jonathan turned at last to Cordelia. "And you, Miss Hammersmith? You mentioned you'd have an update this morning."

Cordelia slowly rose from her chair. She was obviously reluctant to speak; he could tell she was preparing for something no one wanted to hear.

"It can't be that bad," he said quietly. "Let's hear it."

She sent him a plaintive look, pulled up her fruit box and began writing words on the board: "Emmett Barnes knew victim," "Emmett was mad at victim," and "Emmett kicked out of union for violent behavior." She then turned to the group. "I have a problem with the Barnes appeal. I learned these facts from Emmett's original attorney, who said that he put on a low-key defense so the truth wouldn't come to light. He was afraid things would go even worse for Emmett if the jury knew his propensity toward violence." She then stepped down, saying nothing, as if waiting for censure.

My God, no wonder she's depressed, Jonathan thought. "How do you propose we solve this problem?" he asked. "Do you want to withdraw from the case?"

The look she gave him was a mixture of apology and regret. "Part of me would love to. I jumped into this quagmire without practicing due diligence. Honestly, it seems insurmountable at this point. But despite it all, Emmett sticks by his story and I gave him my word that I would see it through." She squared her shoulders. "I'm sorry if this puts you all, and the firm, in a bad light, but—"

Jonathan stopped her with a flick of his hand. "To begin with, you were not alone when we were presented with this opportunity. I heard the same story from Paul Nuncio that you did. So, we bear responsibility together. As to whether or not to cut bait, you have made the right decision—the only decision, in my opinion. You gave your word. That, Miss Hammersmith, is what will determine your success or failure in this, or any endeavor." He gave her an encouraging smile. "If it's any consolation, when I spoke to Alma de Bretteville at the Firestones' party, she said the judge is a fair man. How she knows him is beyond me. Furthermore, she expressed her faith in your ability to win your case—you being a woman and all that. So, even though you are the 'face of the case,' and would prefer to do this all on your own, I do insist that you let us help you. We will see it through—all of us, together, as a team."

He assumed the last words would irritate her, but to his surprise, her eyes grew wide and welled with tears. She had never looked so vulnerable.

"Oh, dearie," Althea said and pushed the plate of pastries closer to her. "Have a bun. You deserve it."

Hastily wiping her tears, Cordelia chuckled and reached for one. "I think I need one," she said in a voice swimming in relief.

Dove was perusing Cordelia's written notes. "So, according to Emmett, somebody took his gun and killed Jimmy Walsh. Sounds like we've gotta show how that happened, whether he knew Jimmy or not."

"I think we need to start writing the play," Oliver chimed in.

Dove looked up. "The play?"

"It's what I call recreating the crime in a timeline, so that we know where the major characters were before, during and after the crime took place," Jonathan explained. "'Who was doing what when' sort of thing."

Cordelia, who had tucked her emotions away, agreed. "I have already begun constructing it, which I can present tomorrow. There are several aspects, however—" she glanced at Jonathan— "that I am going to need help with."

Toward the end of the day, Jonathan was putting the finishing touches on a letter to the art professor Alma had mentioned. She'd already sent word that she'd "greased the skids" with Professor Bass by touting Jonathan as "a smart political observer and an eager patron of the arts." While the former was arguably true, the latter certainly was not. But Jonathan had bluffed his way through worse scenarios. As a potential benefactor, he was hoping to learn more about the group sponsored by the professor and its influence, if any, on Sybil. Did they know her true identity or anything about her past connections in London? His work, combined with Dove's, would hopefully yield some decent leads.

He was interrupted in that endeavor by a firm knock on his office door. "Enter," he said.

Cordelia stood at the entrance, looking uncomfortable, as if she'd been sent to the principal's office for the very first time. "I wanted to thank you," she began.

Jonathan leaned back in his chair. "For what, Miss Hammersmith?"

"You had every right to dress me down for blathering on about doing everything on my own, but you didn't scold me in front of the others. It's something I know I'm guilty of and, well, I'm trying to work through it."

Jonathan twitched his lips. "You mean you'll try to refrain from biting my head off the next time I offer to assist you?"

Cordelia smiled briefly. "I make no guarantees, but seriously, thank you. I thought maybe today was going to be my last day. That you would…"

She couldn't finish the sentence. Jonathan quickly rose from his desk and came to her by the door. He placed his hands on her shoulders and insisted she look at him.

"Miss Hammersmith, those things I said about you at the party, while perhaps a bit over the top in your estimation, were completely sincere. I think you are exceptional in so many ways, and that you will be a big part of whatever success this fledgling firm is going to have. We are individuals, yes, but we belong … together. We all do." He kept contact with her a bit longer than he should have before releasing her and didn't know precisely why. But he hoped fervently that she understood what he was trying to say.

She did. "Well, if that's the case, would you mind if you and I called each other by our given names? I seem to be the only one in the office that you refer to by my last name."

"Huh," Jonathan said. "You're right. Your point is well taken. I promise, *Cordelia*, to be better about that in the future."

She smiled. "I'd better get back to work, then."

Jonathan checked his pocket watch. "No, you need to head home. My guess is you didn't get much sleep last night, and you've—we've—got a lot of work ahead of us."

For once she didn't complain.

Chapter Twenty-One

A Potential Benefactor

Two days later, Jonathan paid a visit to Quincy Bass at the San Francisco Institute of Art. The professor's domain was a shrine of sorts; the walls were covered with framed paintings in a singular style, and based on Alma's description, they were all the work of the man himself. Alongside the artwork were various proclamations, certificates and other meaningless accolades from organizations like the Socialist Party of America and the American Federation of Labor. The Ladies' Garment Workers' Union had even named Bass their "Man of the Year." Didn't it make more sense to have a "Woman of the Year"?

"Welcome. Welcome, sir," said Bass, rising from the seat behind his ornate desk. A pale, potbellied man, probably in his early sixties, his head was bald as a robin's egg, but his chin sported a full beard peppered with gray. The lips beneath were plump and shiny; by the look of the chewed-upon pipe resting on a nearby tray, he had what another professor, Sigmund Freud, would call an oral fixation.

Jonathan tamped down his distaste and extended his hand. "It's a pleasure to meet you, Professor," he said, and began with a *mea culpa* he knew Bass would lap up. "I confess my firm is representing Emmett Barnes in his appeal, but as I said in my letter, I'm open to the message you and your students espouse. One never knows where one might find a passion to invest in." He could almost hear the man's lips smacking in anticipation.

"Miss de Bretteville is a delightful young artist who happens to know the city's most influential patrons of the arts. She says you are eager to join the fray and have a bent toward the political. I commend you, sir, for realizing the error of your ways in defending that miscreant, but more importantly, your understanding that creative expression is vital to our cause. I do believe our art can revolutionize the world."

Bass spoke with an affectation that sounded not quite continental. The linguistic artifice was matched by his vapid sloganeering. Alma had summed it up it perfectly: bullshit, indeed. "Yes, well, I've been told that in addition to your own portfolio, you mentor a group of dedicated, ideologically driven students who will soon be putting on a significant art exhibition. Perhaps I might be persuaded to help underwrite the project, if it is indeed of the caliber I've heard about."

"Certainly. Certainly. In fact, I arranged our meeting today to coincide with a workshop I am overseeing with that very group. If you'll follow me, I will introduce you to our aspirants."

Down the hall from the professor's office was a large studio currently inhabited by half a dozen or so young artists, each sitting in front of an easel, drawing their interpretation of a life model posing at the front of the room. The model, a woman, was statuesque with an impressive physique. She was dressed in a generic military uniform whose brass buttons and multicolored stripes signalled discipline, service and valor. With her arm outstretched and wearing a serious expression, she appeared to represent the ideal man or woman, commanding troops no one else could see. The students were sketching in earnest.

Jonathan surveyed the group, wondering which of them Sybil had taken a shine to. A couple of the young men were attractive in a "tortured artist" kind of way, with wiry bodies and disheveled hair. It was difficult to imagine the woman he'd known as Lena being drawn to any of them, but her father had described her love of the bohemian lifestyle, so it was possible. Perhaps she'd found common cause with one of the female students, or even been attracted to the model herself. Were any of them sad that she was gone or, God forbid, reveling in her death?

Professor Bass seemed unaffected by the loss of one of his acolytes. He walked among the art students, murmuring over each one's shoulder, commenting on their work. One of the female students, tall and slender, whose painter's smock didn't quite cover a somber day dress, seemed particularly eager to hear his opinion, nodding as she listened to his critique.

Bass did not touch her, nor any of the other young women, but the males were apparently fair game. One such, a Lord Byron-type with dark curling hair but more muscle, was obviously a favorite. Although he appeared several years older than the others, he was still much younger than the professor, whose hand lingered on his shoulder and discreetly rubbed it. After a moment the younger man looked at Bass with a knowing smile.

The professor moved on, caressing the broad shoulder of his newest protegé, an athletic-looking, blond-haired man. Dove did an admirable job of not flinching when the stubby fingers appeared ready to give him a massage. He murmured something in Dove's ear, causing Dove to nod slightly.

Jonathan suppressed a smile; he couldn't wait to hear his investigator's report on infiltrating the "Incendiaries."

When he had made his rounds, Bass addressed the group. "*Mesdames et messieurs*, I would like to present to you Mr. Jonathan Perris, a successful attorney here in the city who is considering becoming a patron, perhaps even co-sponsoring our art exhibit known as "Ignition." Unlike the upcoming rally in support of the strike, "Ignition" is designed to reach a different audience—a more generous audience, frankly—including many who occupy the same societal orbit as Mr. Perris. His support will greatly enhance the success of our ventures moving forward, so I implore each of you to open your hearts and minds to him so that he can get a true sense of our purpose and the ideals of the revolution."

The young woman in the smock stood up. "Can you really bring more money to our cause, Mr. Perris, or are you just jumping on the latest political bandwagon to drum up more business for yourself?"

Jonathan paused; he hadn't expected the drab bird to have much of a squawk. "Well, I—"

"—As Mr. Perris examines the quality of our paintings, so will he appreciate the depth of our commitment, which will in turn inspire his, I'm sure," Bass said, reprimanding the student with his eyes. Then he turned to the man he'd fondled earlier. "As usual, I will be relying upon you, Lexi, to work closely with Mr. Perris and me to coordinate these efforts. May we ignite the passion of revolution in all who view our work."

With a promise to arrange a follow-up meeting, Jonathan took leave of the school. Although he admired the boldness of the outspoken female, his overall impression was that the students were being indoctrinated into an ideology far more complex than their artwork portrayed. He'd wait to hear Dove's take on the situation.

"You owe me hazard pay," Dove said to Jonathan when they met at the Ringside Bar next to Mick's gym early in the evening. Jonathan had ordered two chicken puddings and a couple of beers, which the two of them were about to devour. "This beer's just a deposit."

Jonathan chuckled. "I don't know. You seemed to be enjoying yourself. I think you've got a new admirer."

"Thank God the one they call 'Lexi' seems to have filled that job opening." Dove shuddered. "Don't know whether he enjoys dancing to Quincy's tune, but he sure knows the steps." He took a bite of the buttery casserole. "The group is a mixed bag, though. Some of them are sincere, like that feisty gal, Nora. You know, the one who tried to nail you on your sincerity? She's all fire and brimstone when it comes to the rights of workers, women and colored folk. I like her spirit. But the other two—Renata and Lucy, I think their names are—don't strike me as all that political. Lucy's a bit of a wallflower who seems like she just wants to belong, and Renata's in it for the relationships."

"Didn't look as though any of them fit the description of 'B,' either."

Dove took a swig from his bottle. "Nope. There could be others who didn't show up for today's workshop, so I'll keep a lookout. Maybe she's a hanger-on—a sister or a girlfriend."

"What about the men?"

"Well, you saw Lexi; even though he seems to attend sporadically, he has the inside track with the old poof. Petro and Simon are content to follow Lexi's political lead, if not his proclivities, and there's Oscar, who seems hell bent on getting Renata in the sack. I don't think he'd care if capitalism ruled the day from here on out as long as he could shag her."

"And the model? She's quite imposing."

"Judith? Untouchable. Mainly because she's a man living as a woman, who sometimes has to earn money presenting as a man. Confusing, but there it is."

"Could have fooled me."

"Yeah, she's a stunner. But the illusion only lasts until she—or is it he?—strips down. Then you're in for a disappointment."

"Think you'll get anything out of them regarding Sybil?"

"I'm working on it. I'm going with Nora to that rally Bass mentioned. Some union types are jawboning, and I volunteered to hand out flyers with her. I have a feeling she's a full bottle ready to spill."

"Good. I'll continue from my end."

The two men discussed their options over a few more beers. Because it was the end of the workday, Jonathan had dispensed with his jacket and rolled up his sleeves. He didn't know Dove well, but he felt comfortable with him, as if he could put away any formality along with his suit and tie. Dove and Cordelia, who'd known each other forever, grew up in a neighborhood filled with immigrant and first-generation families from all over Europe, much like the street off Alamo Square where Jonathan now lived. Dove's people were from Eastern Europe, as were Jonathan's, at least on his mother's side. He felt a certain kinship with Dove because of it—a connection he'd never felt with his own flesh and blood. His mother was to blame for that, he knew; still, it was difficult to forge a bond with a brother you were supposed to be close to yet hadn't grown up with.

His brother Malcolm apparently felt the same way, because neither of them had ever made an honest effort to connect with one another. That's why the decision to emigrate had felt so right—perhaps the only time his *cadou* had told him something that made sense.

Despite the challenges of living in a fire-ravaged city, San Francisco far exceeded Jonathan's expectations. But his contentment was threatened by this sorry mess with Sybil, and he couldn't get beyond the fact that his brother might be at least partly to blame for it. Unwitting or not, Malcolm had pulled Jonathan into the swamp with him, and Jonathan resented him intensely for it. One way or another he was going to find the answer to Sybil's murder, and if his brother was involved in any way, there would be hell to pay, blood ties be damned.

For now, however, it felt good to relax with someone whom Jonathan might, in time, be able to call a friend. He held up his glass. "Another round?" he asked.

"Don't ask me twice," Dove said.

Chapter Twenty-Two

Promising Inquiries

Who was the girl named "B" who had paid for the room at Aunt Susie's, and more to the point, where was she now? No easy answers had come from the art workshop, so Jonathan made it topic number one at the next boardroom session.

Tracing the young woman by her bank withdrawal hadn't led anywhere, so Jonathan had sent Althea and Oliver on a reconnaissance mission to inquire along the stretch of Fulton Avenue Alma had mentioned. The street, which bordered Golden Gate Park, had sustained much less damage than the city's downtown area. It was lined with middle class houses, many of which, as in Jonathan's neighborhood, had been converted into lodgings for both men and women. Althea was happy to play the part of a protective mama, accompanied by her "son" Oliver, who was looking for suitable lodging for her eighteen-year-old daughter who happened to be "busy at her new secretarial job."

Nearly every house that catered to young unmarried women was full. One, sniffed Althea, wasn't fit for anyone who might spend time with Jonathan, no matter what their name was.

"It was a rat trap, it was," she reported. "And the boarders we saw milling about the front parlor could have easily worked at Aunt Susie's."

Oliver demurred. "It wasn't quite like that, but I'll admit the place was in need of repair—"

"And a thorough cleaning from top to bottom," Althea insisted. "In spite of that, they had but one opening—sharing a room with three other women. It didn't strike me as the type of place Miss Mendelssohn, or rather Miss West, would have considered even for a minute."

"No, it doesn't," Jonathan agreed. "I know Sybil had money, albeit not enough to justify staying in an upscale hotel for weeks on end. She would have no doubt preferred her own accommodations, but we all know those are at a premium these days."

"Which begs the question," Cordelia mused, "why would she pick San Francisco to begin with? Truly, who in their right mind would move to the city amidst so much chaos?"

Jonathan had no stomach for suggesting that he himself might have been Sybil's target. Instead, he deflected with a pointed "Who, indeed?" to which Cordelia, realizing her unwitting insult, added, "Present company excluded, of course."

Jonathan smiled at her. "Of course." He turned back to Althea. "No other places had openings, then?"

From Oliver: "There was one other."

"Yes, there was, at Number 477." Althea took over. "It was a nice and tidy house and the lady who ran it—Bernice, her name was—seemed to be on the up and up, although I think she has a hearing problem. 'I run a tight ship,' she told us. 'Only good girls, no men allowed, lights off at ten.' She said she had a lovely room on the first floor that overlooked the garden and that might become available at the end of the month. A young lady named Betsy had rented it back in April and paid up front in cash. Not too long after she moved in, another lady—who was very hoity-toity, Bernice said—became her roommate. She'd only heard the woman's name once, thought it was 'Cintal.' I got her talking about the two renters and she told me they didn't seem to know each other. The lady figured Betsy needed to share the rent because she was a 'Hello Girl'—"

Jonathan frowned. "A 'Hello Girl'?"

"You know, a telephone operator. They don't make all that much to begin with, and they went on strike about the same time the carmen did. Bernice, bless her, felt sorry for the girls, even though she didn't see either of them very often. 'I mind my own business and they mind theirs,' she said. But she hasn't seen either of them since before the Fourth of July even though they're paid up through the end of the month."

"Did she have any idea of what might have happened to them?" Jonathan asked.

"I don't think so," said Oliver. "It sounded like the landlady was waiting for one or both of the women to return to get their things, and if they didn't show up to either pay rent or clear out the room, she would do it for them and gladly rent it out again on August first."

Dove, who had been doodling, perked up. "So, you're saying the room is unoccupied but still furnished?" He glanced at Jonathan with what could only be termed a "meeting of the minds."

"Yes, that's basically what she told us," Althea said. "I have no idea if it's the place we're looking for, but it sounded promising."

Jonathan's wheels were already turning. "Indeed."

The discussion then turned to more mundane cases—the bread and butter legal matters that kept the firm's lights on and its employees fed. With Dove's help, Oliver seemed to have a complicated insurance case well in hand; it was left for Cordelia to report on her latest efforts regarding Emmett Barnes's appeal.

"Miss Hammersmith, I mean Cordelia? What have you got for us today?"

"A field trip," she announced, rising from her chair and reaching for her jacket. "I have arranged for us to go shoot something."

Forty minutes later everyone except Althea stood in a field which formed part of the Russian Hill estate of Aubrey Carlton, a prominent commodities broker and dear friend of the Firestones. Cordelia had telephoned Josephine the day before to see where she might find a convenient private gun range and had received an enthusiastic, "Oh, that would be Aubrey's place. He loves guns more than I love gardening; I'm sure he'd be thrilled to help you. Shall I give him a call?"

They now stood next to a table upon which were placed two seemingly identical rifles and two boxes of ammunition. Next to the table was a ladder, and roughly a hundred yards away, hay bales with targets attached had been set up. Several watermelons were perched on top of the bales. The aforementioned Aubrey Carlton had greeted them with glasses of lemonade and an admonition to be careful. "Miss Hammersmith requested that I set up a means by which you can test the ballistics of two different rifles. I assume at least one of you knows how to do that; if not, I must insist that you not partake in any blood sport in my backyard. The neighbors wouldn't like it, and you know how cranky neighbors can be."

After Carlton left them to it, Cordelia wasted no time explaining why she had set up the demonstration. "To get a new trial, we have to present an alternate theory of the case, one that matches Emmett Barnes's testimony, with evidence to back it up. His conviction was based on the assumption that since Emmett was shooting his rifle during the riot, he must have aimed it at Jimmy Walsh's head and pulled the trigger."

"I'd say that was more than logical," Dove observed dryly.

Oliver Bean had a question. "But how do they know it was Barnes's rifle that killed Walsh? I imagine there were a lot of firearms shooting that day."

"I wondered the same thing," Cordelia said. "It turns out that even though both sides had rifles, there weren't that many of them. On the railroad's side there were six guards, one for each streetcar that left the barn. Emmett was one of those guards. He didn't carry a pistol, but others apparently did."

"And the strikers?" asked Jonathan.

"Most of them used blunt objects, like rocks and bricks and pipes, but they had a few guns, too. Some of them even shot from nearby rooftops. The authorities determined that three Winchesters had been used that day, but only one was able to shoot what I understand is called a "Thirty-Two Winchester Special" bullet. As luck would have it, that was Emmett's rifle, which apparently is different than the most common Winchester, which many refer to as a 'Thirty-Thirty,' because it's built differently somehow. Do I have that right, Dove? I don't know much about guns, but—"

"Yes, you've got it. Each rifle is chambered to use a specific size and type of bullet. The Thirty-Two Winchester Special is a rimfire cartridge that's a bit fatter and has a different primer location than the typical thirty-caliber centerfire cartridge."

"Can you tell much based on the type of wound as to which specific gun was used?" Oliver wanted to know.

Dove, who had been a sniper in the army, warmed to his area of expertise. "For certain you can see the difference between a wound from a shotgun, and a wound from, say, a derringer. But when the bullet calibers are similar, it gets trickier. All else being equal, a Thirty-Two has a bit more power than a Thirty-Thirty, but because the bullet is fatter, it loses power more quickly once it hits a mass. So, a thirty-caliber bullet would have a slightly better chance of going straight through the body than the Thirty-Two." He perused the rifles on the table. "I can demonstrate, if you like."

While Cordelia, Jonathan and Oliver examined the ammunition for each type of gun, Dove expertly loaded one, shot several rounds at the target on the hay bale, and for good measure, shot into the first row of five watermelons lined up front to back on top of the bales. He repeated the process with the second gun and second set of watermelons. Afterward they walked the length of the field to examine the damage caused by the two types of bullets. Dove pointed out that the first two watermelons in each row had been decimated. "You can see that at this range, both calibers can do a hell of a lot of damage. The Thirty-Thirty is optimal at about one hundred and fifty yards, while the Thirty-Two Winchester Special can push to two hundred before its trajectory falls off. Honestly, though, there's not much difference between the two, especially at this distance."

Cordelia couldn't tell one result from the other. "That's a good thing, right? I mean, couldn't we inject some doubt into the mind of the appeals court judge as to which type of rifle shot Walsh?"

"You might be able to get away with predicting similar wound patterns to a Thirty-Thirty, but if they found the spent Thirty-Two Winchester casings near the body, they'd be able to tell which type of cartridge was used, and therefore which gun."

Oliver had brought a copy of the trial transcript and skimmed it. "That's exactly what happened." He showed Cordelia the line where the evidence had been presented.

"But the bullets look so similar!" she said. "All right, maybe someone could have planted the used bullets—"

"They're called 'shell casings,'" Dove corrected, "and frankly, that's a worse cock and bull story than Emmett's claim to have lost his

The Twisted Road

rifle temporarily. You're proposing that someone shot Jim Walsh with a Thirty-Thirty cartridge but then raced down to where the man lay, looked around for the casings, pocketed them, and replaced them with Thirty-Two's. Wouldn't happen in a million years."

Jonathan had been observing quietly. "You said the killer might have 'raced down' from where he shot. That implies Mr. Walsh might have been shot from a higher elevation. I know that in most cases, one can tell by the shape of an entry wound, from which angle the gun was fired."

"You're right," Dove agreed. "You may be on to something. Did they talk about the angle of the shot in the trial?"

Oliver flipped through the notes. "Minimally. An expert testified that the shooter was higher than the victim, that's all."

"And what about distance?" Jonathan continued. "I assume a wound received from, say ten yards, would be much different than one received from many times that distance."

"Yes, no and maybe," Dove replied. "If an individual is shot at close range, you will see evidence of smoke and powder residue that you wouldn't see if he or she had been hit from even a few feet away. Two shots from similar guns and identical distances that are within the guns' effective range would result in something like I just produced. But you would probably see some differences if both the angle and the distance varied marginally from the same gun." He proved his point by climbing the ladder and shooting the still-intact melons from above and then moving the ladder much farther back and repeating the test, using the same gun. They all walked back to see the new results.

"There is a difference," Cordelia said excitedly, feeling some hope for the first time since they'd arrived.

Jonathan posed the question, "Do we know where Mr. Walsh was standing when he was shot?"

Oliver once again scanned the notes. "Well back from the streetcar, it says, although it doesn't give actual yardage. Apparently, he was part of the larger crowd throwing projectiles as the cars came out of the barn."

Cordelia's short-lived excitement dissipated. "What are the chances that Emmett would pick out Jimmy in a crowd like that? There were hundreds out there."

"If you recall, the jury didn't even know the two men knew each other," Jonathan reminded her. "Did the prosecution give any explanation at all as to why Mr. Barnes would have targeted Mr. Walsh?"

"One," Cordelia said gloomily. "He was wearing a red shirt."

"Ah," Jonathan said. "No doubt the same type of shirt worn by the person who rushed Mr. Barnes. He was probably easier to pick out in the crowd. Perhaps they assumed payback on Mr. Barnes's part."

"I think that's the theory they used, but if we can credibly show that the bullet could not have come from where Emmett was standing in the car—for example, coming instead from someone shooting from another angle or farther away, then perhaps—"

"There's just one problem," Oliver said.

"What?" Cordelia almost snapped.

"It seems only one picture was submitted for evidence by the state. If it's the one they put in all the newspapers, Jimmy Walsh is lying down after the police had cleared the area and straightened out his body. You won't be able to see at all where the bullet entered; as I recall there was just some blood next to him on the ground."

"There must have been other photographs taken," Dove said.

Photographs. Freddie Coleman. Cordelia had seen him the morning the verdict came in and he said he'd been there on Bloody Tuesday. If anybody had photographs, it would be him. "You're right," she said, impulsively hugging Dove. "And I know where to find them."

Chapter Twenty-Three

A Disturbing Discovery

After another afternoon posing as a naive art student—a thoroughly enjoyable charade, in his opinion—Dove returned to the office at 10 p.m. He and Jonathan had agreed to find out more about the rooming house where the mysterious Lena/Sybil may have lived; the timing showed his boss wasn't afraid to break a few rules to do it. Good to know.

He made a beeline for the kitchen where Althea often put extra pastries in the breadbox for those working late at night. Unfortunately, there was only one apple fritter left, too small to share. He turned around to see Jonathan in the doorway.

"I'll arm wrestle you for it," Dove said.

Jonathan chose to rummage in the ice box instead. "No, it's yours," he called over his shoulder, emerging with a generous slice of leftover apple pie.

"Damn, I should have thought of that." Dove checked under the sink. "At least there's this." He pulled out an almost-full bottle of Jim Beam. "You gotta love Althea," he said. "She knows how to take care of her chickens."

"It's rather disconcerting that you and I shared the same larcenous thought this morning," Jonathan remarked as they fortified themselves. "But it appears we've been given an opportunity we shouldn't pass up."

Having made short work of the fritter, Dove now savored his whiskey. "I've been thinking about it. Let's say this woman Betsy did bring Sybil on as a roommate. Now Sybil's dead and Betsy disappears, too? That tells me she was somehow involved. Either she knew about it, or…"

"Or she killed Sybil herself. It's quite the misdirection. Most women, unless they're prostitutes, find other locations for their trysts than bordellos. No one has said for certain if *anyone* followed Sybil into the room that night, much less identified a man or a woman. Perhaps Betsy's jealousy got the better of her."

"It's a possibility," Dove agreed. "Sharing a lover with your roommate is a downright stupid idea; it was probably only a matter of time before somebody snapped. What I don't get is what's happened since then. Everyone has been looking for information about Lena Mendelssohn, not Sybil West. This Betsy person could have easily gathered her belongings, told the landlady she was moving out, and left for points unknown. But she never went back. Why?"

Jonathan finished his drink and reached for his coat. "Let's find out."

The two men took a hansom cab to Park Presidio Boulevard and walked the rest of the way. It was a cold night with an emerging moon; the gas streetlights were sporadic, leaving the area filled with unknowable shadows. They passed serpentine rows of tiny shacks (called "cottages" by the press) built to replace the tents that had sprung up throughout that part of town after the quake and fire. Surprisingly, it was quiet save for the desultory barking of a few no doubt scrawny dogs.

Although it had survived the devastation of the previous year, 477 Fulton Avenue was unremarkable—an unassuming clapboard house of no particular architectural style. The front porch offered a weak lamp that bravely shed what light it could, which wasn't much. To the right of the building was a small fenced-off garden, hardly big enough to handle the herbs needed for a decent cook's kitchen. The outer edges were planted with roses, adding some beauty amidst the utility.

Dove stepped warily over the low wall, careful to trample as little as possible. *Someone's going to have bland enough stew as it is; no need to make it worse.* Watching his steps, he was surprised to see Jonathan already at the window; the man hadn't made a sound.

Dove watched as his boss began to open it. In planning their caper, they'd figured it would have to be breached, something Jonathan said he would handle should the need arise. Unfortunately, he raised the window with ease and looked back at Dove.

"Not a good sign." He slid the interior drape to the side and climbed over the sill.

Dove followed suit and took a moment to light the candle stub he'd brought. Two thoughts sprung to mind: the first was that the room was surprisingly large and had been converted into two private areas by means of a blanket strung across a rope. The second was that the room had been thoroughly trashed.

"Someone beat us to it," Jonathan murmured.

Dove nodded. "Maybe we can find something they missed." He found a small dish to set the candle on; it gave off just enough light to ensure they wouldn't bump into something and cause a ruckus.

They set about searching every piece of furniture, clothing and knickknack in sight. Most of the drawers had been left open, their contents scattered on the floor. The top of one dresser held the usual —a small vase of flowers that had long since died; a comb and hairbrush set—while another dresser was covered with a lace doily and displayed a small, framed picture of a young girl with a woman who was probably her mother. The bed linens had been stripped and left in a heap, and the two small wardrobes, set against opposite walls, were open, their clothing hanging in disarray.

Jonathan said nothing, but Dove noticed how methodically he went about his business, feeling every article of clothing for suspicious lumps; searching the few basic tables for unlikely hidden springs. *He knows all the tricks*, thought Dove. *He's done this before.* When Jonathan came to the larger of the two wardrobes, he paused before gently running his hands along the garments, some of which had been sliced, for pockets and other hidden venues.

"Are those Sybil's clothes?" Dove asked softly.

"They are," Jonathan replied, his voice devoid of emotion.

Dove followed the same search protocol but neither of them found anything useful until Jonathan stopped and peered at the long drapes they'd pulled back over the window. After a moment he felt along the backside of one of the panels down to the bottom hem. The first one was empty, but the second one seemed promising enough that Jonathan pulled a knife from his boot (another surprise) and slit the hem. Out dropped a small velvet pouch, which Jonathan opened to find a pair of diamond earrings and a small locket.

"My mother hid jewels in the same manner many years ago," he muttered. "She wanted easy blunt in case she ever had to make a run for it." He replaced the jewelry, put the pouch in his coat pocket and continued on.

Dove heard the bitterness behind the memory but didn't respond; it wasn't the time or the place to dredge up the past, as intriguing as that past sounded. Instead, he finished his own search and looked around to see what, if anything, he'd missed. Under the small writing desk, he spied a waste basket that had tipped over. He picked up several crumpled pieces of paper, which seemed to be versions of a letter that Betsy had been trying to write. Holding one of them up to the meager light, he read, "Mother, please don't hate me for what I did. I had to get away—you know that. And I found—"

Another iteration read, "Dearest Mother, How I miss you, even though what I did is for the best. Will you please think about—"

And finally, an envelope, ink blotched and torn in half, with the address: *Mrs. Evelyn Doyle, 59 Delmar Street, San Francisco, California.*

"Found something," Dove said, and stuffed the papers in his pockets. He looked over to see that Jonathan was standing at a small sink plumbed in the far corner of the room.

"I did, too," Jonathan replied. "Come and see."

The candle stub was by now perilously low, but Dove brought it over to get a better view. In the absence of light, it could have been anything: dirt, mud, even the remnants of gravy poured down the drain. But the light from the candle showed clearly what it was.

Blood.

Chapter Twenty-Four

A Slim Chance

First thing the next morning, Cordelia headed down to Howard Street where her photographer friend Freddie Coleman operated a studio out of his house. Some might consider the severe-looking woman who answered the door to be curt on the way to being rude, but to Cordelia's mind she was simply guarding the gate.

"Mrs. Coleman? I'm Cordelia Hammersmith. Is your husband at home? I made an appointment with him and—"

"Are you here to get some modeling pictures, then? You're kinda short, but you got a nice figure, and your face is very pretty. He doesn't do nudies, though, need to tell you that up front."

Cordelia stopped short of guffawing. *Nudies? As if.* "Ah, no, I'm an attorney, Mrs. Coleman. I know your husband's work from a previous case, and I need to speak to him about some photographs he may have taken."

The woman peered at her for a moment longer before opening the door wide. As Cordelia walked into the house, she said, "Sorry. Those modeling shots help pay the rent, but we got to keep it clean."

"I couldn't agree more." Cordelia smiled with solidarity.

"Fred's finishing up some prints. He won't be but a few minutes."

She left Cordelia to wait in the front parlor. It was small, well-ordered and non-descript, except for the framed photographs that graced every wall. Freddie Coleman might pay the rent taking pictures of aspiring models, but his personal work was truly inspiring. The black-and-white images perfectly caught the essence of the moment captured by his camera—an old man petting his graying dog ... the cry of a child lost in a crowd ... a pair of lovers who cannot contain their joy. She wondered what Josephine Firestone might think of them, and more to the point, who she thought might like to purchase them. More people deserved to see his art.

Cordelia was contemplating one of the photographs when Freddie came from the back of the house, wiping his hands and, as usual, chewing. "I thought I heard you come in. You said you had something important to talk to me about. You got a scoop or something?"

"No," Cordelia said, "but if you can help me in this and keep it under your hat until the time comes, I'll give you an exclusive."

Freddie grinned. "Sounds like a plan. Have a seat."

Over the next several minutes Cordelia explained what she needed and why. "Emmett Barnes didn't get the best defense he could have. I'm just looking to make sure I leave no stone unturned in trying to prove his side of the story."

"So you're sayin' there's a chance a photo's gonna show the angle of the entry wound and that's going to prove your case?" Freddie unwrapped a stick of Black Jack gum and plopped it in his mouth. He offered one to Cordelia, but she declined. Licorice wasn't her favorite flavor. "I dunno. I took a lot of photographs that day. In fact, I was the first camera on the scene when the riot broke out. *The Bulletin* was right on top of it—sent me down to the barn on Turk Street bright and early. I even saw Jimmy Walsh get shot. I was standing near the streetlight on the corner, I remember, and the poor kid wasn't more than seven, eight yards away from me when it happened. Dropped like a stone."

Cordelia's stomach roiled at the thought. One moment Jimmy Walsh was a young man fighting for what he thought was right, and the next he was gone. What if Emmett Barnes really did pull the trigger and she was helping to get him off? *No, she couldn't think that way. The system only works if everyone, no matter their guilt or innocence, gets a chance to prove their case.*

"You all right, doll? You look spooked. Want something to drink?"

"Ah, no thanks. I was just thinking how awful that was for you ... and obviously for him."

Freddie chewed thoughtfully. "Yeah, it was. The only consolation was he went quick. Boom. Left this world."

"Where do you think the shot came from?"

"Hard to say. The guards were shootin' from the cars, but there were shooters on the buildings on either side of the car barn, too, and those were strikers. Their own men were dishin' it out right along with the scabs. Could have been a case of friendly fire, even."

The Twisted Road

"So, what do you think? Can you go through your shots to see if anything might help us out? I can hire ballistics experts who can interpret the wound size and placement if the photograph is clear enough."

More chewing while Freddie considered Cordelia's request. "I thought justice had been done, but if you're telling me there's a chance, even a slim one, that somebody else shot that poor bloke, then sure, I'll see what I can find."

Cordelia rose and shook his hand. "Thanks, Freddie. I'll make it worth your while."

"That's well and good but getting an innocent man out of prison is the most important."

Cordelia left the Colemans' house filled with some semblance of hope. Freddie was a good man and he'd try his best to help. If he found some promising angles, they could begin to build a plausible case that Emmett didn't shoot Jim Walsh; if not, she'd be back to square one. The photographs offered a slight chance, but that was better than no chance at all.

Chapter Twenty-Five

Domestic Trouble

The idea that whoever killed Sybil West tried to wash away the evidence of their guilt in that pathetic little corner sink burrowed its way into Jonathan's imagination and stayed there. Had she been killed by her roommate, Betsy Doyle, and had Betsy run to ground after committing the crime? Had she ransacked the place to make it look like someone else had broken in? Jonathan had to know.

First thing in the morning, he took a cab to 59 Delmar Street and knocked on the door. It was a small, plain dwelling whose only distinguishing feature was a length of black crepe hung over the door frame. No one answered and he was about give up when the door was opened by a hefty man, perhaps in his early fifties, hair thinning and face already showing the mottling common to heavy drinkers. He wore a black band around one of his biceps—a sign denoting a death in the family.

"Hello. Mr. Doyle? I'm sorry to disturb you. My name is Jonathan Perris. I'm an attorney and I've come to see a Miss Betsy Doyle, who—"

"What do you want her for?"

Time to prevaricate, just a little. "I'm afraid that's confidential, but she may be a material witness in a case I'm working on."

The man squinted. "What kind of case?"

Persistent little devil. "I am not at liberty to say, but I believe Miss Doyle will—"

A woman peered around what Jonathan assumed was her husband's broad back. It looked like she was holding a cloth to her face. "Who is it, Jerry?" she asked.

He glanced back at her. "Never you mind. I'll handle it." He turned once more to Jonathan. "First thing, her name ain't Doyle; she's my stepdaughter, not my blood. Second, we haven't seen her in weeks. She got the high falutin' idea that she was better than this place. Good riddance, I say."

"Would you have any idea where I might reach her?"

"I told you we haven't seen her! She rented a place out on Fulton Avenue--that's all I know."

"And your wife—"

"She don't know anything, either. Best you leave now."

The man was about to close the door, when Jonathan said, "It looks like your family has suffered a loss. May I ask if it was a close family member?"

The man scowled, his tone changing rapidly from garden variety rude to outright menacing. "As if you didn't know."

And with that he shut the door in Jonathan's face.

Heading back to the street corner to hail a cab, Jonathan was more perplexed than ever. Why would he know their deceased family member? He noticed that in addition to beefed-up arms, Doyle had calloused hands, possibly those of a dock worker. If Dove could determine the man's schedule, Jonathan could return when he wasn't home. *The wife probably has some information to share and I'm going to find out what it is.*

—✧—

Jonathan had pegged Mr. Doyle's employment: Dove quickly found out that he was a longshoreman who worked the swing shift at the docks. Making his way back to Delmar Street after lunch, Jonathan hoped to catch Mrs. Doyle at a time when she could talk freely. But as he approached her house, she was standing outside the front door, awkwardly trying to lock it. He didn't want to startle her, so he waited at the curb until she turned around. When she did, they made eye contact and his gut took a punch. Not because she was unattractive, but because she was a fine-looking woman whose husband apparently used his fists to win his arguments. Her eyes were beautifully shaped, but one of them was blackened, and she had bruises along her throat which she tried to hide with a stiff collar. She also favored her right arm, which accounted for her difficulty in securing her residence.

In Jonathan's opinion, men who beat their women were the lowest form of scum on earth. He'd wondered more than once if his own mother had left his father because the man abused her. The idea of it haunted him. One thing he *did* know: she had been hurt in many ways by the subsequent men in her life.

He shook off the memories. "Mrs. Doyle—"

"You, again. My husband told you we don't know anything."

"I'm here about your daughter, Betsy, nothing else. Surely you know where I may find her. I mean her no harm, I swear. but I believe she has information I need."

"I've got to get to work."

"I'll walk with you," he said.

"I gotta catch the car up on Masonic."

"I'm headed that way myself."

"Sure, you are." Mrs. Doyle sighed, letting her defiant attitude slip in favor of concern over her daughter's welfare. "I wish to Jesus I *could* tell you where my Betsy is. She left a couple months back."

"May I ask why?"

"It wasn't what Jerry said, about her feelin' she was too good for us. She told me she was a grown woman now, with a real job, and that she had the right to be out on her own. Said she was going to room with one of her friends from the operator job."

"Do you know who that was?"

"She mentioned Ines Somebody. Ines Barreto, I think she said. I never met her."

Jonathan chose his words carefully. "Are you sure about this woman Ines? Could Betsy have made her up to make you feel better about her living arrangement?"

Mrs. Doyle frowned and quickly winced. Her face must be causing her pain. He wanted to cause her husband some pain, too—lots of it. "It could be. I've had my suspicions."

"Your husband said she moved to Fulton Avenue. Did you ever visit her there?"

"No, she just said she lived on Fulton. Never gave us an address. That's what made me think she wasn't tellin' the truth about rooming with that Ines person. I've wondered if she's been shackin' up with someone, but I have no proof of that. I just hope to God it's not true."

"Your husband said she was his stepdaughter. You were married before, I take it?"

"Yes. My first husband died of influenza five years ago."

"I'm sorry for your loss. What was his name, if I may ask?"

"Frank Foster." She looked skeptical. "Why do you need to know that?"

"Just that I can now assume that your daughter's last name is Foster, is that correct?"

"That's right."

Jonathan subtly but unmistakably gestured to Mrs. Doyle's face. "Ma'am, would there have been another reason why your daughter wanted to leave your house?"

He watched her battered face begin to crumble; she opened her mouth as if to confess something, but at the last second, ruthlessly brought her emotions and her expression under control. "I'm sure I don't know what you're talking about. Like I said, I've got nothing more to tell you." She looked up at the street sign. "This is my stop."

Jonathan weighed what he was about to say; there was a fine line between expressing concern and interfering where one wasn't wanted. "Well, if I am able to reach your daughter, I will tell her that you're concerned about her. And my guess, Mrs. Doyle, is that she's equally concerned about you. You do not have to continue in a situation that is … harmful to you."

"You don't know a damn thing about it," she said.

Oh, but I do, he thought. *More than you know.* But he merely tipped his hat and continued walking down the street.

Through one of Dove's many contacts—this one an operator at the Pacific Telephone and Telegraph Company—Jonathan learned that a Miss Ines Barreto, currently on strike, lived with her parents on Nineteenth Street in the Castro District. Jonathan introduced himself and explained that he needed to speak to Miss Barreto about a "matter of utmost importance."

Her mother, no doubt thinking Jonathan was a potential suitor, seemed impressed by his calling card. She called for Ines, handed her the card and practically pushed her onto the front porch. In the name of propriety, the older woman left the door slightly ajar; Jonathan had no doubt she was listening from within.

He removed his hat, and they sat on two wooden chairs overlooking the well-manicured front garden. Ines was a fetching young woman with chestnut hair and big doe eyes. But in addition to her demure white dress, she wore an overskirt of anxiety; the proof of it gave her fingernails the appearance of having been gnawed by a small animal. She was clearly worried about something. He danced around his intention and used his most calming tone, hoping to put her at least partially at ease.

"As I told your mother, I am an attorney here in the city," he began. "I understand you are a telephone operator. Do you enjoy your work?"

She frowned; he could tell she was wondering what her job had to do with him. "Yes. I enjoy it for the most part. But we are—"

"On strike, I know. I find what you ladies are asking for to be completely reasonable under the circumstances."

Her eyes widened. "You do?"

"Yes, indeed. Communication by telephone is fast becoming the only way to do business, not to mention carry on a social conversation when one cannot be in the same room. Women like you must connect hundreds, if not thousands of signals during the course of your day; we rely on you to bring us together through the slimmest of wires, of all things. Without you, we are lost. How exhausting that must be."

He could see her begin to thaw. "Yes, it is. We need them to stop piling on the work and give us more break time."

Smiling, he began to pivot. "Well, I am rooting for you, truly. I, uh, understand you have a colleague by the name of Betsy Foster—"

Caught unaware, Ines froze.

"Miss Barreto?"

"I don't know a Betsy Foster." Her voice held a hint of panic as she began to chew on her right thumbnail.

Time for a more direct approach. "Of course, you do," Jonathan said firmly. "Her mother, Mrs. Doyle, said that you and Betsy had moved together to a place on Fulton Avenue. I know that she no longer lives there. I also know that you never lived there with her. Now, unless she is hiding in the back of this house, can you please tell me how to reach her? I mean her no harm, but I must speak with her about a most urgent matter. I am certain that she can shed light on the last days of a dear friend of mine."

"What friend would that be?"

Ines was clearly stalling for time, but Jonathan stared her down. "You know what friend ... and if you don't, she certainly does." He cocked his head. "Are you in fact hiding her, Miss Barreto? Must I bring the authorities around to—"

"No!" she exclaimed. "I mean, no, she isn't here." She looked back toward the house and spoke up. "Oh yes, Betsy Foster. I know her. She and I work together—or we did until the strike was called."

"But you have never lived together."

"No. We talked about it at one point, but then she ... she made other arrangements."

"With whom?"

She tried to look nonchalant. "I don't know."

"And I imagine you know nothing about a recent murder," he pressed.

Her eyes grew even larger, but she merely shook her head.

She knows, he thought. "You must help me," he insisted. "Otherwise..."

With another glance toward the house, she leaned toward him. "She does not feel safe right now," she whispered.

Jonathan leaned in as well. "Why is that?"

"Something happened," she said. "I do not know the details; she won't tell me. But I do know she is very afraid."

"Then tell me where I can find her. I can get Miss Foster to safety if that is what she needs. She—and you—can trust me on this."

Ines worried the business card her mother had given her, to the point Jonathan wondered if she would begin to chew on it as well.

After a moment, however, she straightened, collecting courage from someplace within herself, and looked at Jonathan without flinching. "Honestly, I don't know where she is; she contacts me when she pleases. The next time I hear from her, I will tell her you were asking about her. If she wants to contact you, she will."

Jonathan rose, bowed slightly and took his leave, knowing Ines's mother was disappointed, but feeling tight with anticipation as he caught a cab back to the office. It was obvious that Ines was protecting Betsy, but from whom? The man she'd dallied with who'd duped her into renting her own lodging and a few nightly hours in a cathouse? Or perhaps her abusive stepfather ... or even the law itself. Betsy could fear being the next murder victim, or she could have found her roommate sharing their lover and killed Sybil in a jealous rage. Perhaps her panic was an act, and she was playing Ines for a fool. But if that were the case, why stick around and draw Ines into the game at all? Why not cut her losses leave for points unknown?

Whatever the cause, it was also apparent that Ines desperately wanted someone to step in and make things better. Someone like Jonathan. He had a feeling he'd be hearing from Betsy Foster in the near future—Ines Barreto was going to insist on it.

His prediction came true sooner than he thought. The following afternoon he received a message, delivered by a skinny, red-haired street urchin, which said *Meet me Tuesday at nine-thirty on the Drum Bridge, Japanese Tea Garden.* It was not signed. Jonathan paid the boy a quarter and asked if the person who sent him required a reply.

"No sir, she just said you'd tip me if I delivered, and she was right."

"Have you shown this to anyone else?"

The boy stammered a bit. "N ... no sir. Just you, sir."

"You'd best be telling the truth," Jonathan warned him. "Bad things could happen if you aren't."

The boy said nothing, merely nodded, turned tail and ran.

A hungry stomach doesn't have much room for loyalty, he thought, and resolved to get to the Japanese Tea Garden early in case someone else decided to join the party.

Chapter Twenty-Six

The Rally

"Why do we strike, you ask? I will explain it in biblical terms: The Lord God put mankind in dominion over all of the earth and all of the creatures in it. Which renders it an abomination that the working men and women of this city today are subject to the capricious whims of greedy apostates wielding the cudgel of the almighty dollar. By ceding their power, those who labor have become like slaves of old—nay, even worse than slaves: they have become no better than beasts of burden in service to the wealthy who are systematically destroying the poor."

The city's "Irish Thunderbolt," Father Peter Yorke, stood on a large wooden platform in front of the Ferry Building preaching about the evils of capitalism. The audience, made up of strikers, students, and assorted union members, was thoroughly captivated. Dove watched his fellow art student, Nora, succumb to the cleric's rhetorical spell, her face transformed with the radiance of a bride, despite her dour dress.

The priest continued his rant. "And so, it is fitting that all of those who abhor such exploitation, rise up. Rise up and say to your masters of industry and monopoly—no more! For better pay and better working conditions, we will fight! For our children and their future, we will fight! To ensure our inheritance as equal children of God, we will fight! To achieve our very own Eden right here on earth, We ... will ... fight!"

Nora swooned in cadence with the cleric's rising tirade, screaming as loudly as any man in the crowd. At the crescendo she raised her arms in raucous clapping interspersed with ear-splitting whistles, which Dove had never seen a female accomplish with any success. This was a strong woman in thrall to her beliefs. She was mesmerizing.

It doesn't hurt that Father Yorke's a good-looking dark Irishman, Dove thought irritably. *Half his female parishioners are probably in love with him.* The cleric's crowd-pleasing idealism along with his unavailability no doubt added to his appeal.

"Isn't he spectacular, David?" Nora gushed. "Through him we can envision a world where there's no poverty, no bigotry—simply peace and equality and happiness for everybody. I'd give anything to achieve that. Wouldn't you?"

Dove mentally stomped on his first reaction, which was to laugh out loud at her naiveté. *What you envision is never going to happen, doll, and even if it did, I'd be bored to death.* But saying none of that, he merely nodded and murmured, "He's inspiring, all right."

"You said you wanted to learn more about the revolution, and I told you it would all become clear once you got involved. I was right, wasn't I?" Beaming, Nora playfully tapped Dove's arm with the few flyers they had yet to hand out promoting the upcoming art exhibit. As usual, she wore a plain, dark dress, as if to say, "Who I am is of no significance—it's my ideas that are the most important." She had a natural prettiness about her but did nothing to show it off; he found that strangely appealing.

As they'd walked amongst the crowd earlier, he'd deftly gotten her to talk about the different members of the group she was so enamored of, including the sadly departed Lena Mendelssohn. Lena, she'd explained, had been brought into the Incendiaries by Lexi, who'd gone to art school with her years before.

"Where was that?" he'd asked.

Nora frowned. "I don't know. Does it matter? At any rate, I don't think she was a true believer in our cause; she seemed to tag along as a courtesy to him. It's quite sad. He's been a wreck since we all learned she'd been killed."

"Was he sweet on her? I thought he was … you know …"

"Queer? Pretty obvious, don't you think?" Unlike most men, Lexi's very emotional. He has a big heart, even for those who aren't worth his time."

"You didn't like her, I take it."

"Oh, it's not that. Lena was a fine enough person. Kind of like Renata, in some ways, but much smarter. She was just not that dedicated, I guess you'd say."

The Twisted Road

Dove earned his salary that evening, gleaning information about the other members of the group while feigning an interest in the rabble rousers on stage. He used his sketchbook as a diversion while he probed; how could he not be sincere if he was moved to draw such noteworthy speakers?

Designed to bolster the flagging spirits of the laundry workers, metal tradesmen and telephone operators who had joined the streetcar operators in their walkout, the rally lasted nearly three hours. Several speakers strutted on stage and pumped up the crowd with diatribes similar in tone to Father Yorke's. The last one, however, was an exception, and made the ordeal almost worthwhile. John Cutler, who apparently handled member relations for the local carmen's union, wouldn't win any prizes in the looks department, but he was intelligent, soft-spoken, and articulate.

"We're fighting for simple things," he said. "Fair pay. Dignity. A safe neighborhood in which to raise our children. A government that looks out for those of us who sometimes need a helping hand. Like my sister, who died from rickets when I was twelve because we didn't have enough healthy food to eat. That isn't so much to ask." All in all, it was a perfectly delivered pitch on behalf of the working man.

"Oh, my," Nora said once he'd concluded. "He's a lot more impressive than I thought he'd be. I had written him off as a wolf in sheep's clothing."

"What do you mean?"

"Well, Renata and Lexi met with him a while back to see about making posters to support the strike, and Lena went with them. Renata said Mr. Cutler was boring as mashed potatoes and didn't seem all that interested in them, but he really took a shine to Lena. Renata wasn't too happy about that, as you can imagine. Come to think of it, maybe that's why Lexi brought the two of them along, so maybe one of them could sweet-talk him. And it must have worked, because next thing you know, he's put the Incendiaries in charge of signs and posters for these rallies and even paid for the materials." Nora turned somber. "Maybe Lena did something good after all, before ... before, whatever happened to her, happened."

Dove nodded. "Do you think she saw Mr. Cutler after that meeting?"

"I know she did at least once, to bring him our artwork." Suddenly Nora's eyes grew wide. "Oh, I wonder if he knows what happened to her? None of us have heard anything and there wasn't much in the newspaper about it."

Sometimes that's a good thing. "Well, I wouldn't want to be the one to bring it up," Dove warned. "I can't imagine he'd want it to come out that he spent time with a single young woman who was murdered, especially if he was married. He might take it out on you, and that would be the end of your contract."

Nora seemed to ponder that. "You may be right. Best to let sleeping dogs lie."

After Cutler sat down, the final speaker was Alice Lynch, president of the San Francisco Telephone Operators, whose employer had burdened them with heavier workloads and shorter lunch breaks. The women were hoping to be recognized as a union by the International Brotherhood of Electrical Workers, but so far, the IBEW, while sympathetic to their cause, hadn't offered them safe haven. The fact that they were all women made it an uphill climb, but there was no call for the nasty invectives some in the crowd began throwing the speaker's way. One shouted insult led to another, until Miss Lynch was effectively drowned out.

Dove was on the verge of throttling one or two of the disruptors but knew it wouldn't help his investigation if he became the story.

Nora had no such constraints. "Let her speak!" she yelled back, and other women in the crowd echoed her. But by then, a few more aggressive crowd members had surged toward the speaker and Miss Lynch prudently exited stage left.

Tearful with rage, Nora looked to Dove as if he had some sort of power over the male of the species. "I know some men don't think women ought to be working, but why do they have to shout us down? Why can't they just listen to another point of view?"

Dove found himself becoming angry, too. He'd grown up around working women of all types, including his own mother. But she'd had no union to help her and was absent a good part of his childhood. He remembered the anger he'd felt at her near abandonment of him, but it now occurred to him that his resentment was misplaced. He shouldn't have blamed his mother for not being at home; the fault lay with a system that didn't enable her to be at home.

"I don't know," he said in answer to Nora's question. "But if you ask me, they're damn fools." And he meant it.

Nora, apparently pleased with his response, rummaged around in the bag she'd brought and pulled out a yellow scarf. It matched the one she was wearing. She held it on both ends and wrapped it around his neck, tying it proprietarily as a wife might fasten her husband's neckerchief.

Dove grinned. "Does this mean we're engaged?" he asked.

"No, something far more important. It means *you're* engaged—in the important work of the revolution. Welcome to the Incendiaries."

Dove bowed in mock solemnity. "I'm honored. Let me buy you a drink to celebrate."

She smiled and looped her arm in his. They set off and he realized he was looking forward to spending more time with her, which surprised him more than anything.

Chapter Twenty-Seven

Details

Happily, Cordelia didn't have to wait long for Freddie's photographs. He'd printed out several from the scene of the riot and had them delivered to her within two days. They showed clearly that Jimmy Walsh had been shot, and from what direction, but after showing them to three firearms and ballistic experts, Cordelia was no closer to proving Emmett's innocence than she had been before she began. Frank Mendes, who ran the gun shop on Front Street, summed it up. "That poor boy was shot from a higher elevation and the shooter was to the right of him. But I can't tell you how far away the shooter was or how high—the picture just isn't clear enough to tell what impact the bullet had on the entry wound."

Cordelia bit back her disappointment; she'd figured it was a long shot but would have kicked herself if she hadn't tried. She returned to the jail to give Emmett the bad news but tried to soften the blow.

"I'm not giving up," she told him vehemently, "so don't lose hope. Now, I want to go over what happened one more time, and this time I want you to go slowly, and picture everything you remember—and I mean *everything*. I know it went by fast, and I know you got knocked in the head during part of it. But it's critical that you use all five of your senses to recall what happened. That means what you saw, touched, smelled, heard, even tasted."

Emmett sat on his bunk, his hands clasped, staring at the floor. He was breathing heavily and one of his legs was quivering, his foot rapidly tapping the floor. After a moment he looked up. "It's no use, Miz Hammersmith. I can't remember any more than I told you. You may as well walk away."

Cordelia had been standing, ready to record his recollection, but when she heard those words, she tossed her notebook on the bed, stalked over and got down to Emmett's level. The poor fellow was cracking under the weight of his predicament. "Look at me," she said. When he hesitated, she repeated in no uncertain terms, "*Look* at me."

Emmett raised his eyes, the very poster child for pity.

"Did you shoot Jimmy Walsh in the head?"

"No, ma'am. No, I did not."

"Then you are going to fight for your freedom. You want to get out of here, don't you?"

"You know I do. I'm gonna die if I stay in here much longer."

"All right, then. Let's take it from the top. It's almost eight in the morning. Six cars are about to roll out of the barn. Each car has a guard, one of whom is you. Which car were you on?"

"The second one."

"And who else was in the car?"

"Well, me and the driver, and a couple of other Farleymen—those were the strike breakers—who had clubs and were trying to keep people from climbing on board."

"So, the car barn opens and what do you see?"

Emmett shook his head. "It was somethin' awful. They'd put up some barbed wire to protect us from all the strikers overnight, but they'd moved some of it away to let the cars through, and the strikers started to swarm around us like a hive of angry bees."

"All right, they're coming toward you. What was going through your mind?"

"I don't mind telling you, I about peed in my pants, I was so scared of that mob."

"Is that when you first shot your gun?"

"Yes, but in the air. I thought it would scare them, but it didn't, and they kept coming toward us."

"Were there any women?"

"One or two who ran alongside the men. There were others, but mostly they seemed to be in the back, closer to the street, yelling and screaming at us, hateful things, like we were taking food out of their babies' mouths and how we were all gonna burn in hell." He took a moment, as if conjuring the vision. "But right in front of me, climbing up, I remember a man in a red shirt, and … and I just remembered there was another man and two women, and they had yellow bandanas around their necks, and I thought just for a second, *Why do they all have matching bandanas?* And then…"

Cordelia wrote quickly as he spoke. "Then what?"

"Then the three of them rushed toward me, along with so many others. I started using my rifle to fend them off, like I told you. Then I saw one of the women with the bandana had a brick in her hand and her arm was behind her, ready to throw."

"Did she say anything?"

Emmett paused again. "I just remember her screaming, but ... then someone behind me yelled, "Hey Emmett!" and I looked over my shoulder, thinking it was another guard come to help us, but it was another striker. He had dark hair and I remember thinking, *Why'd you call my name? I don't know you.*

"Then why would he know your name? Are you sure you'd never seen him before?"

Emmett squinted, as if to push the memories to the front of his brain. "No, I didn't know him at all. All I remember is, I turned and just then I heard the first two chimes of the big clock on the car barn — 'Bong' ... 'Bong'— before something hit me, *wham*, on the side of the head. And I guess I blacked out. I must have fallen down because when I came to, the car was completely jammed and all I saw was arms and legs and men bashing each other with their fists and whatever else they'd brought along, and some were falling off the car and others were climbing right back on, all the time yelling and screaming. I was gettin' shoved and kicked and nobody seemed to care—I was just a lump of something to get out of the way. They weren't people anymore—they were animals."

Cordelia shuddered. *What must it be like to live through something like that? Like a foot soldier in the heat of a grisly battle.* "Go on," she managed.

"Well, everything and everybody was a jumbled mess, and I was pretty woozy. I think I even upchucked on the floor because I remember that Godawful sour smell, and I saw that I had puked on someone's shoes. I thought, *I'm so sorry I messed up your shoes.* Which was a dumb thing to think, but I wasn't real clear-headed. It took a while—several minutes, maybe—but my head got better, and I realized I had dropped my rifle, so I started looking for it."

"It wasn't right at your feet?"

"No. I thought maybe someone had kicked it, so I started to crawl around, hoping it didn't get too beat up by the mob because it was my father's last rifle before he died and I—" Emmett's voice cracked. "And I didn't want to mess it up. I finally found it at the other end of the car, propped near the back steps. There was that same man who I think had called my name. He looked like he was gonna climb on board and he had his hand on the gun like he was gonna to take it, but then he backed up and laughed. Maybe I imagined it, but I think he said, 'Sorry,' and I knew it was the same voice I'd heard before I got hit."

"Do you think you could pick him out of a group of people now?"

Emmett wiped his palms on his knees. "Maybe, I don't know. I was still a mite dizzy and he ran off so quick. Right after that, I heard the sirens and people began to scatter. I was just happy I'd found my daddy's gun, and I was holding it when the police showed up."

He stopped talking, no doubt worn out from recalling his ordeal. Cordelia hated making him relive it, but if she couldn't sell his version to the appellate judge, then he was going to face more nightmares than he ever dreamed possible.

She closed her notebook and rose. "I'm sorry you had to go through that again, Emmett, but you've at least given me a little more to work with. I'll see what I can do with it."

On her way home, Cordelia pondered the hate and malice that had spewed forth that day. Both sides of the streetcar strike had valid points, but it seemed that being reasonable had no place in how the game was played. If the goals were noble—better working conditions versus a company trying to make enough profit to stay afloat—why did both sides have to resort to violence? It made no sense, but then, she wasn't fighting for her job and her way of life. God forbid it should ever come to that, but if it did, she had to admit, she might turn violent, too.

Chapter Twenty-Eight

More Questions Than Answers

Intent on spending an evening at home sorting out the details of Sybil's murder investigation, Jonathan was taken aback to see Lord Burnham, whom he barely recognized, pacing in front of his entry gate.

The transformation of the man was as remarkable as it was disturbing. Gone was the dapper, international power broker intent on blackmailing Jonathan into mitigating his financial woes. The fact that the Royal Commonwealth Assurance Company was tottering under the weight of so many insurance claims seemed to have lost all relevance.

In his place was a peevish, disheveled graybeard obsessed with avenging the daughter he'd never bothered to acknowledge in life. While his cane had seemed an affectation before, it now appeared to be keeping the old nutter upright. But his obvious frailty was no match for his righteous anger.

"What do you know?" Burnham asked abruptly as Jonathan reached his steps. "What is the latest?"

Jonathan took a moment to gather his patience. It was unfortunate that Burnham knew where he lived, but that couldn't be helped. At the moment, it was imperative to get him off the street in case he became belligerent. "Not much to report, but I can fill you in if you'd like to step inside."

Burnham nodded and worked his way up the steps and into Jonathan's front parlor. "Tell me everything," he said, "and yes, I will have a drink."

Jonathan had to smile. Despite Burnham's sorry state, he was, at his core, an elitist who felt entitled to the niceties offered by those he considered at his level or below, which included just about everybody. Jonathan poured each of them a scotch and motioned for his visitor to have a seat. Burnham took the drink with a shaky hand and knocked it back immediately. "Thank God you can afford the good stuff," he muttered.

Jonathan poured him another. "The police are nearly at a standstill," he began "According to my source (*which happened to be Cordelia's officer friend*), the investigation into Lena Mendelssohn's murder has stalled. No one has been able to find a lead on where she'd lived or where she'd come from. They've gone so far as to send feelers to the Austrian consulate to see if a lady matching Sybil's description had been reported missing. As you can imagine, nothing has come back and they're waiting until 'further developments' lead them in a particular direction."

"Of course, they're not going to find anything related to Lena Mendelssohn," Burnham grumbled. "She's completely made up."

"You and I know that," said Jonathan, "but perhaps we ought to let the authorities know they're barking up the wrong tree. It's Sybil West they should be investigating."

"Goddammit it, no! I'll not have my daughter's name bandied about by every Tom, Dick and Harry wondering what would lead such a beautiful young woman to be slaughtered in a bordello like that. I can't bear the thought of it." He paused to wipe his eyes before looking intently at Jonathan. "And you don't want that either, do you? You don't, by Jove, which is why you haven't told the authorities her real name. Who knows what rocks they may turn over, what?"

"I can't dispute that," Jonathan replied, taking a contemplative sip of his whiskey. He thought about what drove Burnham to so feverishly look for answers. Was it guilt? If so, he was in good company. Jonathan very much wanted to find out who had killed Sybil, not only for her sake, but to absolve himself (and his brother) of having had anything to do with it.

"Well, we're agreed, then, but that don't let you off the hook. I expect you to find some answers, and I don't care how you do it, as long as you keep her name out of it."

Jonathan bristled at the old man's command. "I am 'on the hook' as you put it, of my own volition, not because of any obligation to you. It so happens, however, that I may have a lead on your daughter's roommate."

Burnham perked up at the news. "That's capital! Who is she? Where does she live? How did you find her?"

"None of those details need concern you; just know that I will be in touch after I meet with her. Are you still at Vista Bellissima?"

"No, I've taken lodgings near the wharf; got to save my blunt until this nasty business is concluded." He fished a slip of paper from his vest upon which he'd written his latest address. "Don't share this; as far as anyone knows, I am 'conducting business' elsewhere and will be in touch with them soon."

Burnham was obviously lying to his associates, but at this point, it wasn't Jonathan's concern. He took the paper and rose, signaling the end of the conversation. "Now if you'll excuse me, I really must get back to work. I do have other obligations beyond finding the person who killed your daughter."

Reluctantly, Burnham finished his second drink and awkwardly stood up, using his cane for support. Jonathan helped him out the door and back onto the street. "Would you like me to call you a cab?" he asked.

"Hardly. I'm not so feeble that I can't find my own conveyance. But mark my word—you will find out who's responsible for Sybil's death, and soon, or it's on your head."

Jonathan could have argued the point but didn't. Only when he lay in bed several hours later did he consider that in some ways Burnham was right. While sorely tempted to turn over all the information he was privy to and wash his hands of the affair, Jonathan knew by doing so he'd ignite a full-blown public scandal that wouldn't do Jonathan, his brother, or Lord Burnham any good. He couldn't wrap his head around the idea that Malcolm was involved even indirectly in Sybil's demise; fortunately, so far there was no evidence whatsoever that he was. But that wouldn't stop the authorities—and the newspapers—from barreling down that perilous road. Nothing was going to bring Sybil back, so why wreak such havoc simply for a fishing expedition?

But it gnawed at him mercilessly that a young woman should be murdered for no reason. There *was* a reason, somewhere; he just had to find it. Perhaps meeting with the "Birdie" he'd now identified as Betsy Foster would yield some answers. It was a good sign that she was willing to talk with him; why would she risk it if she didn't feel some good would come of it? Assuming there was a mystery lover, had Betsy been willing to share him with Sybil? Was Betsy in danger like Sybil had been, or was she merely hiding from her own wrongheaded and perhaps deadly decisions? Those were all questions that demanded answers, and the sooner, the better.

"The Hammer" had been busy on her own case, Jonathan noted happily at the start of their case management meeting the following morning.

"I've hit another wall on my appeal, and I need your help," Cordelia announced, looking pointedly at him. "On the table you'll see the photographs of Jimmy Walsh both before and after he was shot. It's obvious that he was hit from the right side and, according to my experts, from a higher elevation. I was hoping to show that the angle of entry was too high or from a different direction than the car on which Emmett Barnes was serving as guard, but those same experts couldn't pin that down. So, I went back to Emmett and gathered a few more facts that he was able to recall. What you have here is a timeline based on his latest account." She handed out copies which read:

7:50 — Streetcars leave car barn - Emmett is on board car #2

7:50-8:00 — Strikers swarm car and Emmett shoots into the air to ward them off, then uses gun to push strikers off the car

8:00 — Clock tower on outside of the car barn strikes the hour. Emmett hears two 'Bongs.' Someone behind him yells 'Hey Emmett!' and he turns. He's then struck on the head with a brick, falling down inside the car and blacking out

8:10 (or so) — Emmett regains consciousness in the middle of a brawl inside the car. He begins crawling to look for his rifle

8:15 (or so) — Emmett finds rifle at rear of car, near the back entrance; sees the man who called his name; hears police siren and everyone scatters."

Oliver raised his hand. "Where was Jimmy Walsh at the time the cars rolled out?"

"In the crowd, but not that close to the streetcar. If he'd been shot at close range, his head wound would have looked much different." She passed around a diagram showing the car barn and its relation to the buildings around it and the street. "Freddie Coleman, the photographer, was at the corner, here, about twenty feet or so away from Jimmy. He said there were armed men on the buildings next to the car barn, but they were shooting to protect the strikers, not the railroad. Jimmy started running and that's when he was shot."

"Possibility of friendly fire, then," Dove said.

"Yes!" Cordelia was all smiles. "That's what Freddie said."

"Except that the authorities concluded it was indeed Emmett's rifle whose shot killed Walsh." Jonathan perused the timeline. "It appears that you have a precise time—according to Emmett Barnes, at least—that he fell, and was therefore unable to shoot his gun. That time was after two peals of the eight a.m. clock tower bell. When he awoke some minutes later, he claims that he had lost his gun. Admittedly, that sounds rather suspect, but assume for the moment he is telling the truth. The timeline does allow for several minutes—not many, but presumably enough—in which someone could have taken his gun and shot Jimmy Walsh. If you can show that Jimmy Walsh was shot *after* the striking of the clock, but before Emmett Barnes had a chance to regain consciousness and position himself once more to shoot, that might be enough to present new evidence and inject reasonable doubt into the mind of the appellate judge."

"The good news is, you don't have to prove *who* killed Jimmy Walsh, just that it wasn't likely Emmett Barnes," said Oliver.

"That's true," Jonathan said, "which is where the notion of 'friendly fire' might come in handy as an alternative theory. Perhaps an overzealous striker took up Jimmy's rifle and his aim went wild."

"Or even another strike breaker," Cordelia suggested.

Dove, doodling as always, straightened in his chair. "You're gonna need corroboration that Emmett dropped after the first two bells, as well as proof that Jimmy wasn't killed until shortly after the bells stopped ringing. Would the photographer be able to help with that?"

"I don't know," Cordelia admitted, sounding slightly deflated. "Maybe he can tell what time he took the various photographs. He would be a good witness."

"Regarding witnesses, what about those who were around Emmett during the course of the riot, both the strike breakers and those who swarmed the car?" asked Jonathan. "Were they interviewed?"

Cordelia thought for a moment. "I don't remember reading any testimony from those in the car. They might have been passed over altogether."

"If we could find out who they were, maybe one or more of them could verify Emmett's version of events," Oliver said. "It's worth doing a little legwork to find out."

"You're right." Cordelia sifted through the notes she'd taken at her last interview with Emmett. "Emmett didn't say too much about those who rushed him, only that one had a red shirt on, and three others were wearing yellow bandanas. Oh, wait, there was another fellow who called out to Emmett as if he knew him, but Emmett had never seen him before. He thought that was odd, so it stuck in his head."

"What were they wearing, again?" Dove asked.

"One in a red shirt, and—" she checked her notes to make sure. "And three had bandanas. Oh, and he said one woman had a brick in her hand, ready to throw. He didn't see her throw it because of the man who called his name, and he turned his head. That's when he got hit."

"Well, I'll be damned."

The group turned to Dove, who didn't look happy. "What is it?" Jonathan asked.

"I might know who beaned him."

Chapter Twenty-Nine

Storming the Barricade

"You know who hit Emmett Barnes with the brick?" Cordelia thrummed with excitement. This could be the break she'd been looking for!

Dove shrugged. "So, I've gotten inside the Incendiaries, that student group, and from what I can tell, there are less than ten members, male and female. So far, I'd say the female with the guts to do such a thing is Nora Taggert. After she and I went to that union rally, she said I'd earned the symbol of the group, which is the yellow bandana. I don't know for sure that she's the one who threw the brick, but it's possible. None of the other ladies seem to have the stomach for such a thing, but of course I could be wrong."

Oliver echoed Cordelia's enthusiasm. "She could corroborate Emmett's story that he was hit."

"And admit that she assaulted him?" said Jonathan. "That's hardly likely."

Cordelia's elation took a nosedive, but she rallied. "But she could be deposed, couldn't she? What if Emmett identified her from a line up?"

"And what if he failed to do so?" Her boss was painfully logical. "Unless you have some corroborating evidence that she attended the event, she could easily deny ever having been there and you'd have no cause to put her under oath. On the other hand, if you had proof that she'd been part of the riot, you would have a much stronger case for deposing her. She would no doubt be a hostile witness, but you still might be able to get her to admit what she'd done."

"What if Emmett promised not to press charges?" Cordelia offered. "Then there'd be no downside to her confessing her role in it."

"Possibly," Jonathan said. "It's worth exploring."

"I'll dig a little deeper, see what else I can find out," Dove said.

Oliver raised his hand again, which wasn't necessary, but the gesture was respectful, which Cordelia appreciated. "Yes?" she replied.

"Emmett said that the girl was with some others, right? Maybe you can work them against each other. With enough pressure, the weaker vessel may crack."

Cordelia clapped with delight. "Oliver, you are brilliant...and ruthless, which is even better!"

"My, what a cutthroat band I've assembled," Jonathan said. "Oliver, what say you? Should we hog tie the witness until she confesses?"

With a grin, Oliver chimed in with, "Or subject her to a nonstop date with Dove until she begs for mercy and cops to it."

Dove, Cordelia noticed, wasn't joining in the fun. *Why not?*

"What am I to do with all of you?" Jonathan admonished lightly. "Seriously, though, Cordelia, I believe your most solid avenue of inquiry would be to find physical evidence—such as the time stamp on the photographs Fred Coleman took, if they exist—to show conclusively that Mr. Walsh was shot during the time when Mr. Barnes was incapacitated. Another fact you might confirm is whether or not Mr. Barnes had a visible wound from being hit. Hopefully the arresting officer, if he was thorough, will have notes that reflect Emmett's physical appearance at the time. Often it is the sequence of circumstantial evidence, slight thought each piece may be, that decides guilt or innocence—or in this case, convinces an appellate judge that the courts should take another look at the case."

With that, her boss ended the meeting and Cordelia, once again invigorated, returned to her office to set up another meeting with Freddie, her concern about Dove quickly forgotten. *Maybe I can pull this off, after all,* she mused. *Wouldn't that be something?*

—∙✧∙—

After the meeting, Dove followed Jonathan to his office. "May I talk to you for a minute?"

"Of course." Jonathan beckoned his investigator to a chair. "What have you learned that you don't want the others to know about?"

"Why would you say that?"

"Otherwise, you would have brought it up to the group. Am I correct?"

"Half-right, maybe. It's not that—or rather, I'm not sure, so I thought I would run it by you first. I learned something from Nora that you might find interesting."

"I'm all ears."

"Apparently, that fellow Lexi—whom I've only seen during class, by the way—had known Lena from prior art courses. He was the one to bring her into the group, although Nora seems to feel she was a half-hearted recruit at best."

Jonathan pondered the news. "To my knowledge, the class with Rosa Hooper was the first and only class Lena, or rather Sybil, took while she was here, which means they had to have known each other elsewhere."

"I thought the same thing, but Nora had no idea where they'd met before. I thought … maybe there's more to Sybil's story—more than you know, or …" He looked directly at Jonathan. "… more than the rest of us know. And maybe it has something to do with your life before coming here. This fellow could be a link to that."

Jonathan regarded Dove for a long moment. *This man is not only bright, but intuitive. But can I trust him with my family's messy history? No, not yet.* "Or perhaps we're overthinking it and he's merely an artist with a wide circle of friends."

It was apparent Dove was disappointed in Jonathan's response, but he chose to let it go. "Yeah, it may be nothing," he agreed, "but I'll keep my eyes and ears open just the same." He rose to go but Jonathan stopped him.

"I meant to tell all of you that I received word through an intermediary to meet our evasive renter Betsy at the Japanese Tea Garden on Tuesday. It sounds like she's quite nervous about her safety in the wake of Sybil's murder. Hopefully, I can calm her fears and learn something about Sybil's actions in the process."

Dove smiled for the first time that morning. "Now we're talking. Do you need back up?"

Jonathan chuckled. "I appreciate the offer, but I don't think that will be necessary; I'm *fairly* certain I can handle a stroll in the park."

—⋅✧⋅✦⋅✧⋅—

To his secret delight, Dove found that his artistic skills weren't half bad. His class that afternoon consisted of sketching a scene in which Judith, dressed as a buxom, larger-than-life peasant woman wearing a yellow headscarf, brandished a broom against a well-appointed mustachioed businessman sporting a top hat and carrying a briefcase. The evil capitalist, Dove learned afterward, was played by Judith's real-life lover, Arnaud.

The depiction didn't make sense. Why would a farmer's wife be confronting a rich city nabob instead of the landowner? And why would the gent be wearing a top hat—strictly donned for formal occasions these days—while going to work? Professor Bass, who had designed the tableau, obviously cared more about symbols than he did real life—which, come to think of it, pretty much summed up his ideology.

About halfway through the session, Bass tapped on a nearby easel to capture everyone's attention. "*Mesdames et Monsieurs*, I am happy to report that tomorrow afternoon our own Lexi will be meeting with our potential patron, Mr. Jonathan Perris, Esquire, to evaluate the effectiveness of our exhibit in convincing the public that our cause is just. I am sure he will be suitably impressed. Please have your pieces in my office by tomorrow morning for consideration. We have minds to change. Carry on."

After enduring an extended shoulder massage from the good professor as he praised "David's" work—the man did have strong fingers—Dove joined the rest of the group after class at the campus watering hole to discuss the exhibit and other topics, such as how to save the world from greed and inequity.

"By the way, where's Lexi?" he asked during a break in the conversation. "Haven't seen him today."

"Oh, he not officially enrolled at the Institute," Renata explained. "Professor Bass lets him audit the class when he can. He delivers for a flower shop on Green Street—'Beautiful Blooms' I think it's called. He's really talented but I've never ever seen him paint any flowers."

"That's because he's concerned with more important things," Nora pointed out, "like the future of mankind."

"Well, we all have to pay our rent," Dove said.

The fellow named Oscar scowled at him. "Speaking of rent, what do *you* do, David?"

"Oh, a little of this and a little of that."

Despite Dove's grin, Oscar wasn't satisfied. "No, really. How do you pay your bills?"

Dove stared him down. "I run errands for people. I'm part of the serving class. What about you?"

Nora raised her eyebrows. "Why, Oscar lives off a trust fund, don't you, Oscar?" She turned to Dove. "His rich papa wanted him to 'find himself' and gave him the money to do it."

Ouch. Obviously, Nora had little respect for her fellow revolutionary. There was an awkward silence as the two other males, Petro and Simon, looked sheepishly at each other. Although Petro was thin and Simon was hefty, they were probably cut from the same cloth as Oscar: poverty and the woes of the working class were abstract concepts to them–not facts they lived with every day. *The men and women who really feel the pinch are too busy working to protest about it,* he thought. *Now there's some irony for you.*

Dove couldn't help himself. "Ah, I see. You're a rich kid who feels bad that you've got more than the average Joe, so you want everybody to have the same as you—is that about it?"

Scowling into his beer, Oscar mumbled, "Something like that."

Dove obnoxiously stroked his chin. "Hmm. Well, maybe instead, you could give your money away so that you're in the same boat as all those poor folks you feel sorry for. You're all for equality, right? How about that?"

Poor Oscar had no answer, so he collected his sketchbook and stood up. "I've got to get going. You coming, Renata?"

Renata looked from Oscar to the rest of the group and clearly decided she'd have more fun staying right where she was. "No thanks. See you tomorrow, though."

If looks could kill, I'd be floating in the bay right now, Dove thought. *Oh, what the hell.* He scooted closer to Renata and put his arm on the back of her chair. "We're going to figure out—collectively, that is—how to spend your money," he said to his angry cohort. "You'll feel so much better once it's not weighing you down."

The group tittered, but Oscar wasn't amused. He bumped into a chair on the way out of the bar and sent it sailing across the room.

"Temper, temper!" Dove called out.

The rest of the Incendiaries chatted for an hour longer, discussing their contributions to the art show the "bourgeois attorney" might sponsor.

"I think it's commendable that Mr. Perris is thinking about supporting our efforts," Lucy said. A tall, big-boned girl, she rarely spoke, as if reluctant to call attention to her Amazonian stature. "As Professor Bass said, he'll bring our cause to a new audience—maybe one with enough money to further the revolution."

"Not to mention, he's very handsome," Renata said.

"There are other considerations besides looks," Nora said pettishly.

Renata had been drinking wine all evening and no one had ordered food. She took another sip, looking at Dove over the rim of her glass. "I'm not so sure about that," she said coyly.

Eventually Petro and Simon called it a night, and offered, at Dove's suggestion, to escort Lucy and Renata home. Dove and Nora found themselves alone, and to her credit, she didn't infer anything regarding Dove's intentions. Instead, she asked, "Why did you poke fun at Oscar like that?" Her amused look told Dove she admired his audacity.

He shrugged. "It's easy to talk a good game, but true commitment means backing your beliefs with bold action. Don't you agree?"

"Of course," she said. "We've already proved that."

"In what way?"

She leaned forward conspiratorially. "Bloody Tuesday," she said. "We were there."

Dove feigned shock. "You're joking. I wish I'd been there. What did you do?"

"Well, it was crazy, as you can imagine. Renata and Simon stayed in the street, but Lucy, Petro and I, and Oscar and even Lexi—let's just say, we stormed the barricades."

"And Lena?"

Nora brushed the idea away. "I told you she wasn't serious. She wasn't even there."

"But you. What courage. You must have gotten there first thing."

"Oh, we did," she said with excitement. "We were there right when they opened the doors and the cars started rolling out. It was glorious—a pure battle between good and evil."

"I heard it was a madhouse, with the scabs fighting the strikers, like hand-to-hand combat."

Her hands expressing her enthusiasm, Nora's eyes lit up with the memory. "That's exactly what it was! They had armed guards on every car, but we threw everything we had at them. I even ... well, let's just say we threw them off their game."

"But one of the guards did kill somebody."

"No, *two* union men were gunned down, but they only caught one of the murderers ... I hope they hang him in the public square."

"You're talking about that guy Emmett Barnes, right? I heard he's appealing the case. And I'm not sure you know this, but the attorney who might help us with the art show? His firm is defending the thug. Can you believe it?" Dove watched Nora's reaction to his next words. "I hear Emmett is saying someone hit him with a brick and knocked him down, so he couldn't have done what everybody says he did."

Nora's face lost its color. "What do you mean? Where'd you hear this?"

"In my line of work, I meet a lot of people, and one of them is familiar with the case. Don't ask me how, but I believe him. He says that one of the firm's legal eagles is identifying everyone who was there that day and is going to prove that the guard's version of events really did happen."

In a telltale sign of nerves, Nora pressed her lips together. Dove wondered briefly if she'd ever been kissed, but quickly realized that was probably the very *last* thing on her mind at the moment. She was too busy rationalizing her point of view.

"But … but even if he was hit, that doesn't mean he couldn't have gotten back up and started shooting," she said.

Shrugging, Dove took his time drinking the last of his beer. "I don't know about that. My friend says they're pinning down the timeline pretty well using photographs and such, and that whoever hit Barnes could be in big trouble."

"That's never going to happen," she said with more bravado than she probably felt. "Too many people, too much confusion. Like you said, it was a madhouse."

"You're probably right." Dove pulled out his wallet to pay for the drinks. "But honestly? It would be a dirty deal if that guard got sent up the river for something he didn't do, even if he's on the wrong side. I mean, we want justice for everybody, right? Not just those we agree with."

Nora swallowed before she spoke. "Oh, he did it all right. I'm sure of it."

"Maybe you ought to tell that to the attorney and swear it under oath. That should put the poor sap away for a long time, maybe forever." Having planted the seed, Dove rose from the table. "Come on, I'll see you home."

"There's no need."

"No, I insist," he said.

Nora lived on Russian Hill in a highbrow neighborhood, which seemed odd, given the intensity of her politics. Come to think of it, her circumstances weren't that much different than Oscar's, and yet she disparaged him for his posturing. Was she even aware that she was the pot calling the kettle black?

He escorted her up the steps to the imposing front door. "What do your parents think of you being an Incendiary?" he asked.

She chuckled softly. "My parents have no idea what I do. They think I'm just a flighty art student, like Renata, hoping to meet a potential husband."

Dove looked around. Her home was substantial, large enough to require servants. "But ... they seem to have given you a lot of freedom, which is unusual for someone in your ... social class."

She leaned toward him, putting her hand on his arm. "Honestly, I am ashamed of all this—it is the bane of my existence. I care nothing for the trappings of the class I was born into, but I use my position to further the cause. My parents may be bourgeois, but my life is my own. I have a studio in the back and I come and go as I please."

Dove leaned forward and kissed Nora lightly on the cheek. "I don't think I've ever met anyone quite like you, Nora Taggert," he said. "You are an exceptional young lady."

"I'll take that as a compliment," she said, stepping back. "I'll see you at school. Goodnight."

After dropping Nora off, Dove opted to walk a few blocks before catching a cab. The night was chilly, as usual, but it cleared his head and encouraged a brisk pace. Dove used the time to mentally review what he'd learned. One was that even though she was smart, Nora couldn't see that in society's eyes she was no better than Oscar—a spoiled rich kid willing to destroy a system that she had benefited mightily from.

She was also more interested in hero worship, as with Father Yorke, than pursuing a flesh and blood relationship. Dove could usually tell if a woman was interested in him or someone else in the group, even if she wasn't obvious about it. Despite her affinity towards him, Nora wasn't keen on forging any kind of romantic relationship. Did that bother him? A little, he had to admit. He found her intensity attractive in the way one is drawn to an exotic, untamed creature.

The third conclusion he'd drawn was the most unsettling of all. Nora knew damn well that she'd incapacitated Emmett Barnes but had convinced herself that he should go down on principle. The question was, how far down that road was she willing to travel? Did the cause of revolution really justify sending an innocent man to prison, or worse yet, hanging him? If she really thought that and wasn't willing to budge, could he get one of the men in the group to turn? It sounded as though Petro had been by Nora's side during the melee, so he'd start with him. But he'd work on every one of them if that's what it took to get one to tell the truth.

As he waited for sleep, Dove chewed on the disturbing idea that poor, dead Sybil West was connected to the Incendiaries. It wasn't beyond the pale to think that one of the members, either male or female, at least knew something about her murder.

The group was also involved in Bloody Tuesday, and possibly played a role in the killing that convicted Emmett Barnes. What were the chances that those two crimes just happened to be connected? In his experience, coincidence was rare as snow on the Fourth of July. What's more, Jonathan Perris was no doubt thinking the same thing. *He's probably wracking his brain trying to come up with a theory that connects the two crimes without placing him smack dab in the middle. Good luck with that.*

Then a name popped into Dove's head that he'd forgotten all about: John Cutler. Cutler was also connected to the group and to Sybil, whom he knew as Lena, and, by virtue of his union ties, to the riot. He was worth checking out as well. Maybe every damn one of them would turn out to be innocent ... or maybe one of them had slit Lena's throat.

Chapter Thirty

Timing is Everything

Freddie Coleman was on a photo shoot, but his wife gave Cordelia the location and she met him out at Land's End, where he was photographing a model cavorting on the sand. The wind gusted mercilessly, and the frigid air made a mockery of the "Fun in the Sun" theme. Cordelia had a lot of sympathy for the young woman who had to force herself to stop shivering long enough for the exposure to stay in focus.

Cordelia waited until the model ran into a cabana nearby to change before approaching the photographer.

"Hard to depict someone enjoying the beach in weather like this," she mused.

"I told her it was insanity, but she wanted to show off her legs, so what are you gonna do? She's payin' for it." He was chewing his usual Black Jack.

"Well, she is very pretty."

"What? I suppose so." He continued to fiddle with his camera for the next shot. "How's it goin', doll? You have any luck with the photos?"

Cordelia waggled her hand. "So. So. I couldn't get any experts to say definitively that the angle was higher than the car to the street, so we're now looking at the timeline of all of it."

"What do you mean?"

"You said you were there first thing when the cars rolled out. That was just before eight a.m. Emmett Barnes was on the second car and he says he heard the first two rings of the eight o'clock hour before someone knocked him out with a brick. By the time he came to, he'd lost his rifle and found it at the back of the car. It's conceivable that while he was unconscious, someone grabbed his gun and took a shot. So, I'm looking to see if there's any way the chronology of the photos you took could back that up."

"Lemme think," Freddie said. "I do remember the clock chiming and to my recollection, I turned to shoot in Jimmy's direction, and he was still alive after the last bell. Problem is, I'm not sure how long after the end of the chimes that he started running and was shot. I can re-check the sequence and see if there's anything that pegs the time on the shots I—hey, I just remembered something."

"Tell me you remember seeing someone shoot Jimmy Walsh and it wasn't Emmett Barnes."

"Not quite," he said, grinning. "But I did catch a shot or two of Dick Marlboro."

"Who's he?"

"I think you saw him the day the verdict was read. Remember the guy recording sound? He recorded on Bloody Tuesday, too. I stopped and got a shot of him. You might even hear my voice on there. And maybe he caught the chimes, too. I know I took his picture before the ones I took of Jimmy. That'll show up on the film strip."

Cordelia was humming again. "Where can I find this fellow?"

"He works for the *Chronicle*. They're still at Market and Kearny."

Turning to leave, she caught herself. She had made a promise.

"You work for *The Examiner* and if I explain what I need to Mr. Marlboro, he'll be in on your scoop," she said.

Freddie shrugged. "Hey, didn't all us newspapers come together for a good cause after the quake?"

"Yeah, that lasted all of one edition; then you were at each other's throats again going after the story."

He chuckled. "True. But if we can get an innocent man out of jail, it's worth it."

Cordelia spontaneously rose on her toes and gave Freddie a kiss on the cheek. "You're the best, Freddie. Let me know what you find out after checking the sequence and I'll see what Dick Marlboro has to say. Maybe when we put it together it will all make sense."

"Gotta make more sense than takin' sun bathing pictures out here."

It was mid-afternoon by the time Cordelia made it back downtown. She headed straight to Market Street and the *San Francisco Chronicle*, which was located in the Flatiron building, one of her favorite landmarks. When the Flatiron opened in 1889, Cordelia was only ten years old, and she had never seen anything so grand. It was ten stories high with a huge clock tower and was billed as the city's first "skyscraper." The quake and fire had damaged it, but reconstruction was underway and the owner, M.H. de Young, had re-started publishing the newspaper from there almost immediately.

Hoping she'd find Dick Marlboro still at work, Cordelia approached the lobby's security guard, handed him her business card, and asked for directions to Mr. Marlboro's office. "He has information that may have bearing on an important case," she explained, hoping the man would be impressed. He wasn't.

"Listen, girlie. I don't care if you're gonna have a tea party with Mr. Marlboro on the rooftop garden, you ain't going up unless he says you can."

Cordelia bit back a caustic retort. *Would you be singing the same tune if Jonathan Perris entered the building?* "Well, then would you please contact him and let him know I'd like to meet with him."

The guard perused her with bleary eyes a moment longer before reaching for the phone and dialing. "Yeah, some broad says she's a lawyer and needs some information from ya." He looked at Cordelia, who was giving him her most lethal stare. "Yeah, she's good lookin', but I can't vouch for her attitude. She's a bit high and mighty for my taste."

Do not engage, she warned herself. *Keep your eye on the biscuits.*

Luckily Marlboro was located on the third floor. Since Cordelia didn't care for elevators, she opted to walk up the three flights of stairs. His office was at the end of the hall, identified by the tinny, non-human sounds emanating from behind the door.

She knocked loudly and Marlboro greeted her without delay. He was probably around Cordelia's age, thin as a whippet and tall, with light wispy hair that would probably be gone by the age of thirty-five. His dark blue eyes and mouth were expressive, however, and transformed him from forgettable to noticeable. Right now, he was bestowing a beautiful smile upon her, showing straight white teeth.

"Come in, come in," he said, gesturing for her to precede him. She entered a room that was more studio than office, whose walls were covered with thick, padded blankets. On one side, a floor-to-ceiling cabinet full of cubbyholes held short, fat, shiny-looking cylinders, each carefully labeled. A phonograph sat on a stand, its speaker horn flaring out like a big brass tuba.

Marlboro noticed her perusal. "I'm persona non grata on this floor, you understand. This is as sound-proofed as I can make it. I'm Dick, by the way."

She imagined this man could charm most anybody if he set his mind to it. He had that endearing quality of earnest scientist about him.

"I'm Cordelia Hammersmith, of Jonathan Perris and Associates." She handed him a card. "Thank you for agreeing to see me. I was afraid your guard dog wouldn't let me through."

He dismissed her concern. "Oh, don't mind Harry. He's very protective of all of us. Sometimes crazy people show up, mad about a story they've read, or insisting that we cover some news that really isn't worth covering. But you seem sane enough. What can I help you with?"

"I understand from Fred Coleman of the *Examiner* that you recorded sound at the Bloody Tuesday riots. As your paper may have reported, our firm is representing Emmett Barnes in his appeal for the murder of Jim Walsh. I'm hoping you can help us prove his innocence."

Dick listened attentively as she explained her theory of the case and how important it was to show an accurate timeline that accounted for Emmett Barnes's version of events.

"Mr. Coleman says he took some photos of you while you were recording sound," she continued. "So, if you happened to record the tolling of the eight o'clock hour while he was taking those photos, he could show, based on the sequence of shots, that Jim Walsh was still alive during the time that Mr. Barnes says he was incapacitated."

Dick seemed pleasantly surprised that someone would find a use for the technology he was trying with limited success to introduce into the news gathering business. "You're saying this might help vindicate your client?"

"That's exactly what I'm saying."

"Well, let's see what we've got." Turning to the display cabinet, he searched the labels until he found the cylinder he was looking for. After placing it on the phonograph, he cranked up the spring-loaded machine. "I was there early, along with Freddie, and I remember we were chatting as the cars were beginning to roll out."

He placed the stylus at the start of the wax-covered cylinder and after a second or two, a cacophony of sound spilled out of the horn. The quality wasn't very good, but you could distinctly hear Dick Marlboro speaking. *I am standing here at the corner of Turk and Fillmore Streets. The crowd has grown ever larger over the last half hour. Each striker or union supporter seems to be armed with some type of weapon, from shovels and bricks and rocks to baseball bats and planks of wood. Some are even carrying guns. They're out to stop the strikebreakers at any cost.*

Cordelia could make out crowd noises in the background and then Freddie Coleman's voice saying, *Hey, Dick, smile for the camera!* and after a moment, Dick replying, *Send me a copy!* A few minutes later came the grinding sound of what was probably the large car barn door sliding open. The crowd noise grew louder and more frenzied, with Dick reporting, *The streetcars, driven by Farleymen, are being protected by armed guards. So far, the guards have only shot into the air, but the strikers are paying no attention to them. They're swarming toward the cars, trying to climb aboard and remove the strike breakers and the guards themselves from doing what they've been hired to do.* And behind his voice, Cordelia could hear it: the faint gong of the car barn's clock tower: *One ... two .... three ... four ...* until the stroke of eight.

"You've got it—you've got it!" she cried. "Mr. Marlboro, you may have just saved an innocent man's life!"

The reporter grinned back, probably just tickled that someone appreciated his work. "Wouldn't that be something! So, what happens next?"

"First of all, I'd love to take that cylinder into our firm's possession as evidence, but I'm scared to death that something might happen to it. It's just made of wax, right? If it melted…."

"It's carnauba, so it's stable to around a hundred and eighty degrees. Still, if it got damaged in any way, you'd lose the sound quality completely. I've transcribed what's on it, as I have all the cylinders, but I didn't get into precise detail as to ambient sounds, such as the clock chiming."

Cordelia thought for a moment. "Tell you what. Do you know someone—besides yourself, of course—who would be considered an expert in sound recording? Better yet, do you know two others? I could call upon them to listen to the recording and attest to what's on it. We won't tell them in advance what to listen for, just that they should write down absolutely everything they hear. That way, even if something were to happen to it in the meantime, we'd have evidence from two reliable, objective sources that it existed at one time."

"Yes, I know a couple of engineers who would fill the bill. What else?"

"We have to match the recording to Fred Coleman's photo sequence and then we'll be off and running. Whatever you do, keep that cylinder safe until we can arrange the deposition."

"Yes, ma'am," Dick said. "Oh, and Miss Hammersmith? Would you like to have lunch sometime and … and perhaps discuss the case in more detail?"

Cordelia was tempted; she found him to be an amiable sort. But there was too much to do. "I'd enjoy that, but I can't discuss anything more than we already have. And one more thing … would you mind keeping this under your hat until the case has been handed to the appeals judge? I wouldn't want to run the risk of injecting prejudice of any kind into the process." She gave him the warmest smile she could muster.

His eyes were so bright, they almost twinkled. "Perhaps after your case is over, then. I'll let you know as soon as I've talked to my colleagues."

Cordelia left the *Chronicle* building feeling more optimistic than she had since taking on the case. But her ebullience lasted just until she'd mentally catalogued all the elements of the case and realized one major component was missing. She had no corroboration that Emmett Barnes had been hit and when precisely that had happened. Was the word of a convicted murderer worth anything? She didn't think so, and shifted her worry to whether or not Dove would be able to find someone to back up Emmett's story—someone who might run afoul of the law if they admitted what they'd done.

Nora Taggert, the young woman who most likely threw the brick, was probably the most difficult, yet most valuable witness Cordelia could put on the stand. Perhaps she would have a better chance than Dove of convincing Nora to tell the truth. Maybe, woman to woman, she could appeal to Nora's idealism, which should include equal justice for all, regardless of where they stand politically. Instinct told her it wasn't going to be easy, but she had to try.

Chapter Thirty-One

A Hostile Witness

It took an hour to track Dove down to get Nora's home address. He gave it to her but warned her not to blow his cover.

"For heaven's sakes, I'm not an idiot," she reminded him with a huff. Checking her watch, she estimated there was just enough time to get to Russian Hill before intruding on the dinner hour.

At Nora Taggert's impressive residence, a maid showed Cordelia into the foyer, where Mrs. Taggert, a pigeon-breasted, self-satisfied matron, greeted her. The woman's bonhomie lasted as long as it took Cordelia to explain that she was an attorney and wished to ask Nora some questions on behalf of a client. Nora was quickly summoned.

"What is this all about, Nora?" her mother asked. "Is there something going on that we're not aware of? You know how your father is about such things. He likes to stay informed."

Nora, as slender as her mother was solid, knew precisely how to diffuse the situation. "Oh Mother, don't be silly. I was expecting Miss…"

"Hammersmith," said Cordelia.

"Yes. Miss Hammersmith. One of my fellow students at the Institute has had a bit of a dust-up with the faculty and asked me to share my perspective on the situation—anonymously, of course. As a sort of background." She turned to Cordelia. "Isn't that about the size of it?"

Cordelia had to marvel at the young woman's improvisation. "That's one way to put it," she said.

"I take it you want to speak in private, even though it's—what do they call it? Off the record? Why don't we use my studio?" Without waiting for an answer, she turned, expecting Cordelia to follow.

"Well, if you're sure," her mother offered, looking bewildered.

"Yes, yes, it's quite all right," Nora assured over her shoulder, and Mrs. Taggert seemed relieved there was nothing for her to worry about.

Once in the studio, Nora shut the door and offered Cordelia a seat. "You are quite striking, you know. Have you ever sat for a portrait?"

Cordelia chose not to sit. "Miss Taggert, I have the distinct feeling that you know why I'm here."

"I think I do," she said. "My friend David heard that someone in your law firm has been working on that murderer's appeal. I'm assuming that's you."

"Guilty as charged," Cordelia said.

"What I don't understand is how you know I was there."

Lord, has she not figured out that "David" is not who she believes him to be? Far be it from me to destroy her delusion. "We have interviewed many people who were there that day," she lied. "Your name cropped up."

Nora frowned. "Who else have you talked to?"

"I'm afraid that's privileged information. But what I can tell you is that you were seen throwing the brick that hit my client, and your testimony can set him free."

Nora frowned. "But why would I want to do that? He shot an innocent man in the head, and he should hang for it."

I can be as brazen as you, Cordelia decided. "Because you know that once you hit him, he dropped, and while he was down—we have proof of this—Mr. Walsh was shot."

"Are you asking me to admit that I attacked someone? That seems beyond foolish."

"Under these circumstances, I can assure you that my client would consider it an accident and not press charges. But I hope you'd want to testify for no other reason than because it's the right thing to do. You believe in doing what's right, don't you?"

Nora gazed at Cordelia for a moment before answering. "Is it the right thing to make workers toil for twelve hours a day for mere pennies in wages? For women to work in dangerous conditions with no breaks? For children to starve because their parents can't earn enough to feed them?"

Cordelia chose her words carefully. "No, none of those things are right. But my client isn't responsible for all of the ills in the world. He was just doing a job, and someone—we don't yet know who—set him up to take the fall for a crime he did not commit."

Nora paused a moment longer before giving Cordelia a sad smile. "I don't really know what happened that day. There was so much chaos and confusion. Maybe what I threw hit Mr. Barnes, but maybe it didn't. And even if it did, maybe he shot that poor striker anyway. It wouldn't be right to let a guilty man go free, and you just don't know for certain, do you?"

Cordelia began a slow burn. *How does Dove put up with this woman?* Instead of admitting the young activist was right, she said, "So, you refuse to cooperate, even though an innocent man will suffer because of it?"

"Innocent in *your* eyes, because you want it to be so," Nora replied with a shrug. "Sometimes things don't work out the way we'd like them to. Wouldn't you say that's true?" She sounded almost wistful. "And sometimes the truth is a bitter pill to swallow."

Keeping a lid on her frustration, Cordelia fell back on the scare tactics of her profession. "You will be deposed, Miss Taggert, and it will be a matter of public record that you assaulted a young man. I hope you—and your family—can live with that."

"I believe I can, Miss Hammersmith." She rose, signaling the end of the conversation. " Thank you for stopping by."

That went well, Cordelia thought morosely on her way home. *Maybe I should have left it to Dove after all.*

Chapter Thirty-Two

The Elusive Lexi

Jonathan returned to the Art Institute and found Professor Bass, who directed him to the room where he could examine the paintings for the art show. "I would join you, but I have a dreary introductory class to lead," Bass grumbled. "Teaching so often gets in the way of the really important things, but it's the price one must pay, I suppose."

Yes, in order to earn a living, you pompous ass. "I'm sure I'll be fine in Lexi's hands," Jonathan replied, immediately regretting his choice of words.

The portly pedagogue snickered. "And lovely hands they are."

Jonathan moved on to the nearby conference room, bare except for the works, mainly poster-sized, that had been set up on freestanding and tabletop easels. Nearly all of them were mediocre, even to the untrained eye, but a few held real promise.

Primarily cast in bold hues of red, yellow, and blue, they all followed a predictable theme: in one, a giant man in overalls stood poised with a sledgehammer above his head, ready to break the metaphorical chains of his labor … in another, a bomb blew the fat cats of capitalism (symbolized by their top hats and monocles) to smithereens. *Dove's contribution, no doubt*, Jonathan mused.

A particularly striking example portrayed a beautiful young woman looking heavenward, but the image she revered was a large red ball painted with the letters 'IWW,' which Jonathan knew stood for the "Industrial Workers of the World," a newly formed radical labor union. Only one, an abstract rendition of a flame, was noteworthy for its stark simplicity.

The exhibit culminated in a large painting depicting a prototypical working family with an iron-fisted father, defiant mother and smiling child. They'd reached an allegorical mountaintop upon which they'd planted a flag printed with the slogan "Justice, Equality, Freedom."

"Which one moves you?" said a cultured voice from behind Jonathan. He turned to see his guide, the enigmatic Lexi, standing just inside the room wearing a bemused expression. The handsome young artist held two beer steins. His hands looked capable, but unused to manual labor. On his left hand he wore a heavy-looking ring.

"In my profession, that is known as a leading question," Jonathan said.

"I suppose it is." Lexi handed one of the steins to Jonathan. "I took you for a beer rather than wine drinker; I hope that's all right."

In answer, Jonathan lifted his stein in a mock toast and took a drink. He turned back to the paintings. "I noticed that none of the works are signed; since there's obviously a range of …"

"'Ability'?' 'Talent'? Yes, you can say it. It is plain to see. But the point is, we are part of a movement in which the individual gives way to the collective. No one need rise to the top, and no one need sink to the bottom."

"From each according to his ability, to each according to his need."

"Ah," Lexi said. "If not a believer, you are at the very least a student of political history."

Lexi spoke the King's English, but had the faintest of accents, which perhaps only native Englishmen would notice. Jonathan could not quite place it. "Where are you from, may I ask?"

Lexi raised his brows. "You don't think I'm English?"

"No, I don't."

The man hesitated, then shrugged. "Moldavia. Near Balti. Do you know of it?"

Jonathan frowned at a wisp of memory. "Vaguely. What is your given name?"

"Alexei Morozov … in certain circles, at least. To others I'm 'Alex Morrow.'" His arm swept across the room. "And here, I am merely 'Lexi.'" He noted Jonathan's expression. "You seem bothered by that."

"I wouldn't use that term. But I do find it odd that someone as dedicated to their cause as you seem to be, feels the need to be circumspect about who they are. Why not announce your beliefs to the world and try openly to win people to your side?"

Lexi shook his head in obvious pique. "Because the Proletariat is *woefully* ignorant. Workers simply don't know what's good for them. They must be persuaded by artifice, encompassing both patronage and fear, and one must adjust the approach depending on the audience and the desired outcome." He looked squarely at Jonathan. "Surely you understand this, having played many roles in your life." He leaned in for emphasis. "Admit it—sometimes it's a relief not to reveal who you really are."

He's a perceptive devil – I'll give him that, Jonathan thought. He gestured to the works. "Despite your wish to remain anonymous, I would venture that yours are the more sophisticated creations. You are talented. You're older than the rest of the group, and by all accounts you are a natural leader. You're a long way from your native land. How did you end up here?"

After a flicker of discomfort, Lexi visibly relaxed. "That is a story for the ages," he said lightly. "Like yours, perhaps. However, now I think we have much more important matters to discuss."

Lexi was not flirting; in fact, there was nothing in his manner to suggest he had "peculiar inclinations" at all. The two men were relatively close in age, height and build, and most likely intellect. Lexi was speaking not as a supplicant hoping for a handout, but as an equal.

Jonathan was impressed. He wanted to keep the man talking, especially about the members of the group. "All right, then. All artifice aside, why I should spend my money on your group and not, say, the Suffragettes or the Women's Christian Temperance Union?"

Lexi laughed at that. "Because while you believe halfheartedly in a woman's right to vote, you do not want to be harangued by the leaders of that movement." He raised his own glass of beer. "And you certainly don't want to give up this."

"Then sell me," Jonathan pressed. "Let me hear your pitch."

Lexi shook his head. "It would be a waste of time. Because the truth is, you don't want to hear about the revolution or the benefits of sponsoring a show—any of it. You, in fact, are here under false pretenses."

Jonathan paused; he'd never heard of such a sales approach before. "I'm not sure what you mean."

"It's simple, isn't it? You're not interested in supporting our cause. You, Mr. Perris, want to know what I know about the members of the Incendiaries. But more than anything, you want to know what I can tell you about Sybil West."

My God, he knows Sybil from before. What else does he know? Jonathan stifled the urge to grab the smug socialist by the lapels and shake the information out of him. Instead, he played dumb to see where it took them. "'Sybil West'? Who is she and why is it important that I know her?"

"This could take some time." Lexi pointed to Jonathan's stein. "Would you like another beer? The campus tavern is just around the corner."

"I don't need another beer," Jonathan snapped. "I need you to tell me the truth."

Lexi's eyes flashed. "Then, Mr. Perris, I demand the same courtesy from you. Let us quit dancing around reality like this. You were often seen in the company of one Lena Mendelssohn, who tragically lost her life less than a month ago." His voice wavered between anger and drollery. "Somehow you have convinced the authorities that you are not responsible and to your credit, you have been trying to figure out what happened to her. Your trail has led you here. Everyone at the Institute knew her as Lena, but I knew her long before she ever came here."

Lexi wandered amongst the paintings as if to comfort himself. Then he paused, looking at Jonathan. "Even before she was the paramour of your *esteemed* brother." His eyes grew moist. "Sybil was a remarkable young woman, one with enormous potential. When I heard she'd been murdered, I too wanted to kill. And you were at the top of the list."

Who is this man? Sybil must have known him during what Burnham called her "bohemian" phase. Was he just a friend, or more than that? He sounds almost jealous of her relationship with Malcolm. Does he suspect foul play on my brother's part? "If you now believe that I am innocent of that crime—which I am—then what do you think happened to her?"

Lexi stopped at the image of the young woman; it was clear he had painted her. "I am an atheist, but I wish to God I knew. She ... she was unpredictable. She did things on a whim. Took chances she shouldn't have. When she wrote to me that she was coming to San Francisco to set her cap for you, I tried to dissuade her. 'One feckless bourgeois lover should have taught you something,' I told her. 'Pick a worthy member of the Proletariat next time.'"

"Someone like you," Jonathan said.

Lexi chuckled without mirth. "As you may have noticed, my proclivities do not run along traditional lines. Still, I cared for her, very much. Which is why I helped her and kept her confidence. I encouraged her to join our little group, however, and had hoped that over time she would feel safe enough to reveal her true self and commit to our cause. But someone took her before that could happen." Anguish seeped from his last words.

It was a lot to absorb, and there were still so many holes in the narrative. Jonathan pressed on. "If you knew the woman you call Sybil so well, what can you tell me about what happened between her and my brother? I understand she was caught in a compromising position. Who else was she seeing when she was with him? Perhaps there's a link between that time and this."

Lexi brushed aside his inquiry. "Because of our ... appetites ... we didn't always travel in the same circles." He looked at Jonathan in defiance. "Sorry, I can't list every man she bedded."

Oh, to be in the ring with this cretin right now, Jonathan thought. *Queensberry rules be damned.* "If her death wasn't random, then it has to be someone she was involved with here. What do you know of John Cutler? I have heard he worked with her on one of your projects."

Lexi rubbed his chin, which was already showing the stubble of a beard. "I suppose he is worth looking into. She did accompany Nora and me once when we talked to him about promoting his next few rallies. She delivered our posters to him. It's possible there was more to it, but I can't be sure."

Jonathan scanned the room once more before taking his leave. "You can tell your besotted professor that I am still evaluating my support of your project, but I'll have to talk to the others in the group to get a feel for their 'enthusiasm.'"

"Oh, I'm sure you will," Lexi said. "Good luck, and please, let me know what you find out. I'd sincerely like to know."

"No doubt you would," Jonathan parried. "But I think I'll wait until you see fit to answer my earlier question."

"Which was?"

"Who is the real Alexei Morozov, and what are you doing here?"

Lexi stared at him, his eyes conveying an emotion just beyond Jonathan's understanding. In that moment he could sense the glimmer of the dreaded *cadou,* weak but unmistakable. *Why?* He wanted to shout. *Why now?*

The feeling passed and Jonathan, suppressing a shudder, left the building without a word.

Chapter Thirty-Three

A Tragic Loss

Peter Windridge, known by his fellow students as the more European-sounding "Petro," worked part time at the loading dock of a shipping company owned by his uncle. He was underweight and awkward, but tolerated by his co-workers. Dove "just happened" to catch him during his Saturday lunch break.

"Looks like you've got enough there to feed an army," Dove remarked as he walked up.

Petro looked more befuddled than suspicious. "What are you doing here?"

"Simon told me you worked here, and I wanted to ask your advice about something."

"Really?" It was obvious Petro wasn't used to being sought after in any way.

"Yeah. Mind if I join you?"

Petro indicated the curb next to him and offered to share his repast. "My mother's eternally afraid I'm going to starve," he said, explaining the stack of sandwiches, fruit and pastries. "I tell her our cook doesn't need to pack so much, but she insists. So, I usually hand out whatever I don't eat before I get home."

"Hmmm," Dove said. "You might convince her that she's overdone it if you bring home what you haven't eaten."

"I could," Petro said thoughtfully, "but there are so many who really don't have enough to eat. It seems selfish to keep so much when I can share what I have with others."

Now here's someone I can work with, Dove thought. He helped himself to a ham sandwich bulging with cheese and pickles. It was delicious.

"Thanks for this," he said.

"So, you needed my advice?" Petro prompted.

"Yeah, I, uh, heard something through a contact of mine and I don't know if I should share it or not. It's not exactly public knowledge, but not sharing it could maybe get some people in trouble…" He looked straight at Petro. "People like you."

"Me?" The young man looked genuinely shocked. "What on earth have *I* done?"

"Well …you see, this gent I know works for that Jonathan Perris fellow, the one who's thinking about bankrolling part of our art exhibit. Frankly, I think he feels guilty."

"How so?"

"Because his firm is handling the appeal of that guy convicted of shooting the striker on Bloody Tuesday. My friend is pretty confident they're going to get the guy off because they've figured out that somebody hit him with a brick and knocked him out during the time the striker was shot."

Petro had stopped eating. "How … how could they know such a thing?"

Dove shrugged. "Photographs and timelines and talking to people and such. So, they know he was hit, and once they confirm that with witness testimony, he'll get a new trial and probably be able to show enough reasonable doubt to get off. I mean, it really does sound like he didn't do it."

"Well … what if no one testifies?"

Let the lies begin. "So, here's the deal. Nora told me the other night that you and some others were there. My source at the law firm says he's getting testimony that pins the dirty deed on you."

"What?! That's a lie! Nora threw the brick! She—"

Dove held up his hands in surrender. "Hey, I don't know who's singing. Could be her, could be someone else. But I just think somebody needs to speak up who knows the truth."

"Yes, but … wouldn't whoever speaks up be admitting they broke the law?"

"I don't think so. The fact is, lots of people were out there throwing things, on both sides. Nobody's talking about pressing charges. I guess the firm is just trying to show their client couldn't have shot that poor striker because he was conked on the head when it happened."

Petro thought a moment. "So ... you're saying if they can prove he was hit, then they can prove he's innocent. Nobody needs to know who shot the gun, though, right? Just that it wasn't the guard."

"That's what my friend's saying, yeah." He shrugged. "If it were me, I think I'd have to say something. I'd have to be brave and step forward and tell them what I know..." He paused for effect. "... even if I knew who actually did the shooting. Because otherwise it's just not right. I mean, we're all fighting for justice, aren't we?"

It took a few more pensive moments, but Petro finally made a decision. "Who would I have to speak to?"

"Whoa. You're willing to step up? That's gutsy."

It was Petro's turn to shrug. "Yeah, well, if someone is going to tell what happened, it ought to be the truth. I was there throwing stuff, but Nora threw the brick that hit him. I saw her do it, I saw him drop, and ... and I saw some other things, too."

"I dunno. If Nora isn't the one my guy says is talking, she might be pretty mad at you for spilling the beans."

At that, Petro straightened up. Apparently used to being a pawn and not a king, he was beginning to relish his newfound role. "I've got to do what's right, no matter what anybody else thinks."

"You're damn straight," Dove said. "So, what else have you got in that basket of yours?"

Dove and Petro spent the next half hour talking about subjects both shallow and deep. The young man had found Lena to be "beautiful, but not real warm." He hoped one day to meet someone he could build a life with, but he knew he had to make something of himself—apart from his family's money—first.

His sympathy for the workers' cause was genuine, and he wanted to help in any way he could, even though he personally felt powerless.

"Maybe someday you'll be in a position to help a lot of people," Dove told him. "And that'll start with saving an innocent man from a lifetime in prison or worse."

After making arrangements for Petro to meet his "friend" (Oliver, back at the office) for a deposition on Monday morning, Dove suggested the young man keep his intentions to himself. "Not sure who you can trust these days," Dove said, aiming for a subtle but unmistakable tone of caution. "At least if *you* testify, you'll know the truth will be on record."

"Damn straight," Petro echoed, grinning. "Here, take another slice of pie for the road."

When Peter's shift was over, he felt confident enough to have a beer with his fellow shipyard workers—something he'd never had the courage to do before. Because they lived the kind of life he had only theorized about, his camaraderie with them was both surprising and intoxicating. It lasted until after dark, at which time he decided to break his long-standing rule not to take a scab-driven streetcar. He hopped on board to return to his parents' home, not knowing that it was the strike-breaking motorman's third day on the job.

The new driver, apparently filled with more cockiness than experience, began barreling down Powell Street. As the speed of the car increased, so did Peter's anxiety; he had never liked racing and clung to the outside post, his hands starting to slide with sweat.

At the bottom of the hill was a sharp right-hand turn. The scab took it much too fast, causing Peter and an older woman to be thrown out of the car. The woman survived with the eventual loss of a leg, but Peter, who was ready to step up and do the right thing, bashed his head against a streetlamp and died instantly. His basket, empty once more, landed in the bushes. Several days later, a little girl found it and used it to carry the meat pies that her sister made and sold on the street.

Chapter Thirty-Four

Down at the Union Hall

Once she learned that Peter Windridge would be coming in to testify about the brick-throwing incident, Cordelia was over the moon. Her failure to move Nora wouldn't matter once Windridge identified the young woman as the culprit who bashed Emmett Barnes in the head. *Too bad for you, Miss Taggert,* she thought, with just a hint of smugness.

Thus, the disappointment she felt Monday morning when the young man didn't show for his deposition was intense, eclipsed only by the tragic news that their star witness was dead.

"Oh, my land and stars!" Althea exclaimed as she read the *Bulletin's* headline. "'Ongoing Streetcar Strike Claims Two More Victims Over the Weekend—One Loses Leg While Another's Skull is Crushed in Powell Street Crash.' It goes on to say 'Peter Windridge, nephew of prominent shipping magnate Nathan Windridge, was thrown from a speeding streetcar that took the corner too fast.' That poor, poor boy," she said, crossing herself.

"Let me see that," Cordelia said, practically snatching the newspaper from Althea's hand. She quickly read the article and barely stopped herself from screaming out loud. Not only had an apparently very nice young man been senselessly killed, but his loss might mean the end of Emmett Barnes's chances as well.

"The rottenest of luck," Jonathan said quietly as he took the newspaper. She knew instinctively that he understood. It was all right to feel the loss on more than one level—it didn't mean she was heartless.

Dove, Cordelia could tell, was shaken by the news. As usual, he cloaked his emotion with temper followed by pragmatism. "Goddamn it, he didn't deserve that. He had a lot of heart, that kid." He picked up on Cordelia's dismay. "He's not the only one who was there."

"Yes, but he's the only one who was willing to testify."

"So far," Dove said. "I'll keep at it. One of them will break, I promise."

Cordelia looked at him with tender reproach. "Don't go making promises you can't keep, Dovey."

"You wait and see," he said, but without his customary bravado.

He rose to leave and Jonathan cautioned him. "I'd steer clear of the fellow we talked about. Lexi's full name is Alexei Morozov, by the way, and he knows that Lena Mendelssohn was Sybil West. He's aware of my social connection to her, and he may also have deduced that you work for this firm. If he shares that information with the group, your cover may already be destroyed. I don't trust him."

Dove nodded, gathered his coat and left the boardroom, slamming his hand against the wall on the way out.

"Will he be all right?" Jonathan asked once Dove had left.

Cordelia nodded. "He feels responsible; he's a protector at heart. But he won't waste time moaning about it; he's already plotting how to get one of the other Incendiaries to turn."

"Good man," Jonathan murmured.

Cordelia was about to retreat to her office when Jonathan stopped her. "As difficult as this morning has been, I need your help. I've set up a meeting with John Cutler from the Carmen's Union under the pretense of helping us understand the union's position vis a vis Emmett Barnes's appeal. As lead counsel on the case, you should be there. In truth, I'm hoping we can learn something from him as it relates to Sybil."

"What does he have to do with her?"

"Dove thinks he may have been one of Sybil's lovers, and it's quite possible he could be the mystery man from Aunt Susie's, although to my knowledge he doesn't have an English accent." Jonathan smiled with self-deprecation. "Unfortunately, my judgment of people has been sorely lacking of late, and your input will be invaluable."

Cordelia was caught unaware. So focused on managing her own shortcomings, it hadn't occurred to her that her boss might be feeling the same frustration. He always seemed so sure of himself. "Yes, of course," she said.

At the appointed time they arrived at the Carmen's Local 205 union hall, located on Battery Street. A group of agitated union members had gathered in the front of the building, and their numbers were growing. Their shouts pierced the air.

"We need our strike pay!"

"When are you going to cut a deal with United!"

"More people are getting killed on account of those no-nothing scabs!"

"We can't keep doing this! We need support from leadership…"

"… or else we'll throw you bums out!"

A man trying to get the unruly crowd under control stood on a box to better get everyone's attention. *I can relate to that*, Cordelia thought. Based on the sketch Dove shared at their last meeting, she could tell he was John Cutler, the very man they were supposed to meet.

"That's Mr. Cutler," she informed Jonathan.

"I know. I'm sure he wasn't planning on this particular distraction." He motioned for her to step out of the fray. "Let's see how it plays out."

Cutler looked overwrought as he motioned for the crowd to quiet down. "We are doing all we can," he shouted. "Remember, most of you voted for this strike. We have to hold firm, or we won't get what we want."

"We want you off your fat asses. We want you to do something!" A particularly belligerent striker yelled his frustration and received affirmation from his cohorts.

The crowd, which had swelled in the last several minutes, began to surge toward Cutler, who was defenseless against them. Some of the strikers had sticks and rocks; one projectile flew and missed Cutler's head by mere inches.

After ducking, he called out, "We're on the same side—there's no need for violence!"

Unfortunately, by that point many, if not most, weren't listening, and Jonathan moved forward to help protect Cutler from the mob. "Stay here," he told Cordelia.

"Not in your life," she shot back, and hurried up to the makeshift podium where Cutler had frozen like a hare sensing a predator. "What are you doing?" she cried out to the men amassed in front of her. "Your wives and daughters would be ashamed to see you like this! You need to tell leadership what you want clearly and soberly—you can't beat them up to get your way!"

The fact that she was female, along with her frank appeal to their better natures, caused enough of them to pause long enough for Jonathan to run interference for Cutler as he retreated toward the entrance to the union hall.

Cordelia hurled one last "Go home to your families—you'll win in the end!" before she quickly followed the two men into the building.

Cutler locked the door behind her, pausing to catch his breath. He looked at them, finally realizing who they were. "Your timing was excellent."

Jonathan glared at Cordelia, no doubt for her insubordination, but affected an air of nonchalance as he turned to Cutler. "We did have an appointment."

The man smiled for the first time. "Right you are."

His accent was decidedly not English.

They followed Cutler to his small, airless office located in the back of the hall. The room had just enough space for a scarred desk, a filing cabinet and two small chairs upon which Cordelia and Jonathan were invited to sit. A picture of the man, his passably pretty wife and a young boy was the only decoration.

Dove had captured the essence of John Cutler: he appeared to be the very definition of bland, with fine, mousey hair, a doughy face, and a body that one would not write home about. Yet Dove had also said that the man's speech was the most stirring of all those he'd listened to during the recent union rally. Apparently, the man's heartfelt words combined with his ability to come across as "Everyman" had left a strong impression on the audience.

Jonathan reminded Cutler of who they were and more importantly, whom they represented. He prefaced the interview with an apology. "We're sorry to have intruded upon your day—although, as you say, our timing was fortunate. We're grateful you've agreed to talk to us, especially since one might consider us adversaries. We assure you we are not. We're simply trying to put this entire tragedy into context from the perspective of the union."

"Well, you certainly got an earful about where the members stand today," Cutler pointed out.

"I can see their plight," Cordelia said, "especially as the strike drags on. It must be very difficult to hold the line when families are running out of resources."

"Indeed," Jonathan said. "And we may perhaps be adding insult to injury here, but not from the usual side of the coin. You may not be aware of it, but United Railroads is not funding Mr. Barnes's appeal. We know a young man was shot to death, but our client continues to profess his innocence, and we feel he may not have gotten the best defense possible. Having said that, we want to fully understand the emotions flowing on both sides of the issue. The brouhaha outside certainly was an eye opener; on the other hand, your members must be happy that the gentlemen of the jury held Emmett Barnes accountable for what happened on Bloody Tuesday."

Cutler's voice held a measure of disgust. "Two members of Local 205 lost their lives that day and dozens of others were hurt. Just because a sliver of justice has been served, doesn't mean we have cause to celebrate."

Seeing that Jonathan was re-calculating his approach, Cordelia stepped in. "You don't sound like you're happy about this strike, Mr. Cutler."

"Happy? I think it was a terrible idea; so did our union president. But somehow the membership got riled up about it and voted to walk out against leadership's wishes."

"How does that happen?" Jonathan sounded genuinely curious. "Does it just bubble up from within the ranks?"

"Sometimes, but more often than not someone from the outside comes in and stirs the pot. It may be subtle, it may take a while. But eventually there's a tipping point and the damage is done."

"You're talking about an agitator," Cordelia suggested.

"Yes, although that term isn't one we like to use in a union shop."

"But isn't that a desirable trait? It takes a strong communicator to motivate a group, to sway them to a particular point of view." Jonathan smiled. "I understand you fall into that category, Mr. Cutler, based on reports of a persuasive speech you made at a recent rally." His tone was laudatory, no doubt so Cutler wouldn't take offense.

The man surprised them both by refuting the compliment. "Do you want to know something? I've never given such an effective speech in my life, and I doubt I ever will again."

Cordelia frowned. "Why do you say that?"

"Because someone else wrote that speech, and she's no longer with us."

Cordelia tried not to focus on Jonathan's reaction. He seemed to freeze in the act of speaking, as if waiting for something to happen. "Who was she?" she asked innocently.

Cutler leaned back in his chair. "Her name was Lena, and she was an art student, but if you ask me, her true calling was the written word. She came to see me along with two others from the Art Institute. I'd seen the young man—Alex ... Alex Morrow, I believe—hanging around the union hall but didn't think too much of it. Students can afford to be idealistic, can't they? Not like us working folk. Nonetheless, I give their little group credit for wanting to do something other than simply jabber about wanting a better system. Alex offered to help us promote a series of rallies to keep everyone's spirits up—not just the carmen, but the others who had struck in solidarity, like the laundry and metal workers."

"The woman," Jonathan said without inflection. "What was she like?"

"Beautiful, no doubt about it." He looked chagrined. "My wife wouldn't have been happy to know I worked with her. But she knew the union cause backwards and forwards. Better yet, she knew just how to bring it down to a level the working man and woman could understand and be inspired by. She even had me talk about my supposed sister, who had rickets." He shook his head. "I don't even have a sister, but Lena knew it would grab the audience, and it did. Not everybody can do that— I certainly can't, not on my own. She offered to write the speech for me if I subsidized their art project. I took her up on it and now I'm sorry I did, because I'll never live up to the standard she set."

"What happened to her?" Cordelia asked.

Cutler paused, fiddling with some papers on his desk; he seemed to be getting his emotions under control. "She ... I understand she met a bad end. We were going to work on another speech, but she never showed up. I found out later that she died, that in fact she may have been murdered."

Jonathan remained quiet so Cordelia expressed the appropriate response. "Oh, I'm so sorry! Do they know who did it?"

"Not that I've heard, but, as I said, she was beautiful, so it wouldn't surprise me if it were a love triangle of some sort. The young man Alex seemed to feel quite proprietary about her."

Jonathan finally spoke. "You mean they were good friends?"

"Oh, more than just friends, at least it seemed that way to me. Their rapport annoyed the other student who came along. I don't remember her name, but she didn't seem thrilled with his behavior."

"Because she was jealous?" Cordelia asked.

Cutler shrugged. "Perhaps. I don't profess to know what goes on inside women's heads, but my guess would be she felt in competition with Lena for some reason."

Unlike men, who are never competitive, Cordelia thought with irritation. "Why would that be?" she asked.

Cutler shook his head slowly. "I have no idea. What I do know is that Alex and Lena were on the same page, focused on the cause and eager to help support the strike."

"How do you think it's going?" Jonathan asked.

"The strike? Don't quote me, but I think it's doomed. It may take a while, but any public sympathy as a result of those deaths on Bloody Tuesday has all but dissipated. People need streetcars to get to work, and they deserve cars that are run by professionals, not Farleymen. And the carmen need to work, too. Our strike fund is already dwindling, and our president had to send out a notice that pay would be cut by fifteen percent. That's what they were protesting just now, and I can't blame them. I don't know what's going to happen, but I fear all the pretty speeches in the world aren't going to clean up this sorry mess."

Jonathan took the opportunity to rise and thank Cutler for his honesty and clear-eyed analysis of the situation. "We truly appreciate your perspective on what is a sad situation for all concerned."

Cordelia waited until they were out of earshot before asking, "Well? What do you think?"

Jonathan didn't answer right away, but when he did, it was odd. "This morning I thought we had two separate cases to solve, but now, I think there may be only one."

Chapter Thirty-Five

A Walk in the Park

Even though he'd been in San Francisco for nearly a year, Jonathan had never had a reason to visit the Japanese Tea Garden in Golden Gate Park. The moment he stepped through the gate, however, he realized what he'd been missing. What stood before him was a singular place—a refuge of serenity in the midst of a boisterous and often chaotic city.

The garden had been established thirteen years earlier as a "Japanese Village" for an international exhibition. It had been bankrolled by an Australian who wanted to introduce Japanese culture and its art (of which he was a dealer, naturally) to the west. Now managed by the city, the park had survived the ravages of the year before and offered a convenient haven for those wishing to leave their stress behind, if only for a little while.

Arriving just after the garden opened, Jonathan took a moment to read the placards about the symbolism of the space. Apparently, the long, winding path meticulously lined with cherry, maple, and pine trees was designed to lure the visitor away from the cares of the world and prepare him for the ritual of the tea ceremony, which took place in the modest-looking tea house at the center of the garden. Rocks, flowers, and most importantly, water, all worked together to create a harmonious, tranquil whole.

Growing up, Jonathan had spent precious little time amongst trees and flowers, so to be in a place such as this filled him with both uncertainty and longing. He knew that bad things often happened to people in rural or wooded areas. God knows he had defended enough perpetrators in those cases. And yet ... the fresh air and earthy scents were both cleansing and invigorating. One got the sense that the earth, if left to its natural state, would constantly renew itself, just as humans can do if they truly want to. Wasn't he a perfect example of that?

Over the years he'd gotten to the point where he could recognize roses and poppies, and even lilacs by their scent. But that—and

The Twisted Road

pulling weeds—was the extent of his gardening expertise. He added "broad knowledge of flora and fauna" to the list of topics he should spend more time mastering. Unlike Marquess of Queensbury rules or art appreciation, he thought he'd actually enjoy learning to distinguish one tree or bush from another.

Jonathan checked his pocket watch and realized it was time to meet Miss Foster. He made his way to the Drum Bridge, imported from Japan as part of the original garden. The bridge tricked the eye, but in a most exquisite way. It was a very steep, rounded wooden structure built over a calm pool to resemble half a drum that, when reflected in the water, formed a complete circle, like a full moon. One had to slow down to walk across the somewhat treacherous steps which apparently helped prepare one's mind for the tea ceremony which lay beyond. In fact, as a nearby sign read, crossing the bridge might just enable one to leave their sins behind.

Much easier said than done.

He had just reached the bottom of the structure when he saw the woman he immediately knew to be Betsy Foster reaching the apex of the bridge. She was petite and had the long, dark curly hair described by the madam at Aunt Susie's.

He waved his hand to acknowledge the young woman, but her reaction was completely unexpected. She looked terrified and called out "Behind you!" but before he could react, he felt a solid blow to the back of his head.

Instantly, all went black.

Chapter Thirty-Six

Recovery

The persistent buzzing in Jonathan's head, which he attributed to an enormous honeycomb whose occupants had been disturbed and therefore enraged, slowly began to recede. Perhaps he had walked away from the melittological maelstrom; perhaps he'd gone inside a house, into a quieter space, where the swarm of bees could not follow.

Nevertheless, he was grateful for whatever had lessened the noise and the rhythmic pounding that had accompanied it. He was even more grateful the blow hadn't triggered his unpredictable *cadou*.

Soon after his head quieted down, he was able to open his eyes. The room he found himself in appeared blurry at first, but soon sharpened enough for him to distinguish a female slumped uncomfortably in a chair at his bedside. He squinted. It was Cordelia, whose luscious hair, normally pinned ruthlessly in place, had become unruly, several strands shading her face as she dozed.

Her presence sent an unfamiliar sensation through him, one of both pleasure and comfort. He couldn't remember the last time someone had cared enough about his welfare to sit in a chair by him long enough to fall asleep. It embarrassed him to feel such vulnerability.

"Miss Hammersmith—Cordelia—what are you doing here?" he asked. She didn't respond so he repeated his question with more vigor, even though it hurt his head to do so.

His voice startled her awake and it took her a moment to get her bearings. She instinctively reached for her hair to try to straighten it, but apparently gave up the ghost and simply pulled it out of her way.

"What does it look like?" she answered peevishly. "Once again, I find myself pulled from my work to deal with the scrapes my employer gets into. I should start charging overtime."

Jonathan held back the smile; he was beginning to love her cheeky attitude. "May I remind you, you are a salaried employee, which means you are not paid by the hour. You must take up any grievances you have with being overworked during your next review."

Cordelia sent him a blistering look, yet he sensed behind it a wave of relief that she was valiantly trying to disguise. He wished they could continue their banter, but circumstances dictated otherwise.

"What happened to me?" he asked.

"Dove said you went to the Drum Bridge to meet Betsy Foster—without telling the rest of us, by the way. Did you at least speak with her?"

Jonathan tried to recall the meeting, but nothing came to mind. "I don't think I did."

She sighed. "Well, at some point, you were clobbered on the head, probably with a stout piece of wood. Fortunately, some visitors found you shortly thereafter and summoned an ambulance, which brought you here."

"How long have I been in here?"

Cordelia checked her pendant watch. "About twenty-four hours, give or take."

"Bloody hell. I think I remember seeing Betsy on the bridge, but then everything went black. Did she let you know I'd been hurt?"

"Not exactly." The look on Cordelia's face told him precisely what he did not want to hear.

"No," he said.

She nodded in counterpoint. "She was found outside the gate of the Garden, bludgeoned just like you. But her head wasn't as hard. They pronounced her dead at the scene."

"My God," he said, turning his face to the wall. *That poor, poor girl. First Sybil and now Betsy? What have I done?*

Cordelia's voice was gentle. "She asked to meet with you, remember?"

Jonathan turned back, his earlier delight replaced by an overwhelming sense of failure. "I was supposed to help her," he said bitterly, "and look what happened. My advice to you would be to leave. You take your life in your hands around me."

"Don't be ridiculous," Cordelia shot back. "You had no—"

At that moment a young woman entered the room, knocking timidly on the door as she did so. "Oh, I'm sorry, I thought you were alone."

Jonathan recognized Ines Barreto. "Please, Miss Barreto. Come in."

She looked terribly distressed. "I don't want to intrude."

"You aren't intruding in the least," Cordelia said, standing up and offering her chair to Ines. "I can wait outside if you like."

"No," Jonathan said. "Miss Barreto is—*was* a friend of Betsy Foster. I'd like you to stay."

Cordelia nodded and sat in the room's remaining chair.

"Miss Barreto, my colleague Miss Hammersmith just told me about what happened to Betsy. I am so very sorry."

"Thank you, but Mr. Perris, It's so awful—I'm just relieved at least you are still alive! I had no idea something like this would happen. I knew she was scared, but I thought it was in her head, you know? I thought you might be able to talk to her, to get her to see reason. But she was right all along—someone *was* out to hurt her. If only I had believed her. If only—"

Jonathan reached for her hand, which was red and chapped along with her ragged fingers. "Miss Barreto, none of what happened is your fault. You did the right thing. I truly meant to help Betsy, and I would have, if … if things had turned out differently."

"But how did it happen?" Ines cried. "She was so careful. She—"

"I think someone paid the messenger boy she used to see the note. I know I can't turn back the clock, but if you'll work with us, Miss Hammersmith and I will do our very best to make sure Betsy receives justice."

Ines looked perplexed. "But what can I do?"

"You can tell us everything you remember about what happened once Betsy decided not to move in with you. Don't leave any detail out, even if you mentioned it to me the last time we spoke. It might trigger another memory or detail that answers the questions we have —and there are many of those." He glanced at Cordelia, who had anticipated his request and taken out her notebook. She was brilliant at using Munson's shorthand. "If you don't mind," he added, "Miss

Hammersmith will take notes, in case we need to refer to any part of what you remember. Now, when we spoke the last time, you said that you and Betsy worked together and had talked about moving in together. Why precisely did that not happen?"

"She met someone at the Union Hall."

"I wasn't aware that the telephone operators had a hall," he said.

"No, it was the Carmen's Local. Her cousin was a member and she'd stop by to see him sometimes."

"Did she tell you the name of the man she'd met?" Cordelia asked.

"She called him 'Lev,' but I had the feeling that was a nickname. When I asked what his real name was, she said she didn't want to share it because her cousin and the rest of her family would be 'madder than hell' —that's the way she put it. She said that even though he tried to hide it, he was a foreigner. I don't know what she meant by that. You could tell it caused her a lot of heartache to be so secretive."

Progress, Jonathan thought. "So, you never met him in person?"

"No, but Betsy couldn't stop singing his praises. She said he was 'tall, dark and handsome,' which didn't mean much because she was so small herself. But there's no question she was under his spell. It changed everything between us."

Cordelia wrote as fast as Ines could talk. "How so?" she asked without looking up.

"We had planned to move in together in part because Betsy's stepfather was a ... a—"

"Wife-beater?" Jonathan supplied.

Ines nodded. "I hate to say it, but yes. She hated the man. Betsy wanted so much for her mother to leave him, but her mom wouldn't think of it. So, she thought maybe if *she* was out of the house, it would cause less tension. We were all set to look for a place when she announced that she had made other plans that involved Lev. Later I learned she had gotten a place on Fulton Avenue, but she never gave me the address. She never even asked if I wanted to move in with her. Instead, she found another roommate."

"That must have hurt," Jonathan said.

"It did, for a while. Especially since her roommate turned out to be a stranger."

Cordelia frowned. "That seems odd, when you were willing and able to move in with her."

"I know, but she did whatever Lev told her to do. The woman had been a friend of his. Betsy said she was helping the lady out as a favor to her new man, but she didn't mention the roommate by name and didn't seem to know anything about her."

Ines went on to fill in as many details as she could about Betsy's descent into hell. The last thing she described was the panicked message she'd received declaring that she was going into hiding because something terrible had happened to her roommate—she wouldn't tell Ines what—and she wasn't sure she could trust anyone besides Ines.

"Did you wonder if maybe Betsy herself had done something wrong?" Jonathan asked.

"It never crossed my mind," Ines said with more force than she'd displayed since she'd entered the hospital room. "Betsy was a sweet person. If anything, she was *too* nice—too nice to her boyfriend, too nice to a roommate she didn't even know, too—" her voice quivered. "Too nice to let me help her in any real way."

Cordelia now reached out to Ines. "I think that's a sign of how much she cared for you; she felt you might be in danger if you got too close to her. She was protecting you."

Chewing on a fingernail, Ines contemplated Cordelia's words. "Maybe that's right, but it's not working out that way. A policeman has already been by asking questions; I think Betsy's mother gave him my name."

Jonathan glanced at Cordelia. "What did you tell him?"

"Pretty much what I told you—about her secret boyfriend and the strange roommate and all. But it's too little too late, isn't it?" She stood up. "I have to go now. My family has a ranch near Petaluma, and we work it every summer. I just wanted to stop by and apologize before I went."

"Thank you for that," said Jonathan. "And thank you for trusting us with your recollections. As I said, Miss Hammersmith and I will do all we can to find out who did this terrible thing."

Ines nodded and gave her Petaluma address to Cordelia. "In case you learn anything."

Cordelia scanned her notes and caught Ines just as she was headed out. "One last thing: do you happen to know which cousin introduced Betsy to Lev? We might be able to learn more about the mysterious boyfriend from him."

Ines shook her head. "That's impossible, I'm sad to say."

"Why?" Jonathan asked.

"Her cousin was Jimmy Walsh."

Her cousin? No wonder the Doyles were in mourning. "You're talking about the young man who was killed on Bloody Tuesday?"

Ines nodded. "It's so sad. I met him once. He was really nice. Protective, you know? They caught the man who did it, but that won't bring Jimmy back."

When the door shut, Jonathan and Cordelia looked at each other.

"Do you think it's possible that Jimmy Walsh really was targeted that day?" Cordelia asked.

"Entirely," he said, "but I don't think Emmett Barnes killed him."

Chapter Thirty-Seven

Absent Without Leave

Jonathan began to pull the hospital sheet aside in order to get up but stopped himself in time. He couldn't very well get dressed in front of Cordelia.

She caught his intention, however, and asked in a most officious tone, "What do you think you're doing?"

Had he really thought her forthrightness endearing? "As soon as you walk out that door, I am going to get dressed and pay another visit to Alexei Morozov, who knew Sybil before she came here and I'm guessing is our mysterious 'Lev.' I fear he has much more to answer for than I imagined."

"Absolutely not. May I remind you that someone—perhaps even that 'Lev' person himself—just tried to kill you? You are in no condition to——"

Her tirade was cut short by the arrival of Dove, who wore an overcoat from whose pockets he removed two bottles of beer. "Oh, I thought you'd left," he said to Cordelia. "I would have brought one for you, too."

"She was just leaving," Jonathan said firmly.

Cordelia gathered her things and once more fussed with her hair. "Well, only because Dove's here to make sure you don't escape. You've been hurt and you need to rest."

"And you need to worry less. Now go home and get some sleep; you look a fright."

Far from being insulted, Cordelia seemed to relish the badinage. "No thanks to you," she sniffed. "And you might want to check a mirror yourself: you look like a vagrant who forgot how to use a comb and a razor." Just before leaving, she turned to Dove. "Look after him, will you? He's obviously not capable of doing it himself." And with that she was gone.

"Maybe absence will make the heart grow fonder," Dove mused.

The Twisted Road

Jonathan chuckled, but the gesture cost him. The back of his head was beginning to throb again, although nowhere near as intensely as before. Sometime before Cordelia arrived (how long had she been there?), he remembered waking up and the nurse asking him if he could swallow a pill. Not quite sure where he was, he balked, and she reassured him it was a form of willow bark "like your mama probably gave you when you were little and got hurt." He'd wanted to laugh at the thought of his mother ever considering such a thing, but he was in no position to do anything except nod and take the pill, hoping that sleep would follow. Now its effects were wearing off.

Dove handed Jonathan a bottle. "Thought you might need some hair of the dog."

"You are too kind," Jonathan said, taking a swig. "I think I'll live. Unfortunately, I can't say the same for Miss Foster."

"What a nasty business. You get a chance to learn anything from her before you were hit?"

Jonathan shook his head, albeit slowly. "Her friend Ines Barreto was just here, however. It turns out Betsy's nickname for her gentleman caller was none other than 'Lev.' And she met him through her cousin, a union man, now deceased, by the name of Jimmy Walsh."

"You're kidding."

"I wish I were. She said Betsy described Lev as dark and handsome, and a 'foreigner.' Apparently, Betsy was afraid to share Lev's real name because she knew her family—especially Jimmy—wouldn't like him."

"A motive to get rid of Jimmy, perhaps?"

"Perhaps. I—"

The door opened and Jonathan's nurse came in, wheeling a small cart. Despite her sterile white uniform, she was a pretty young thing, but Jonathan imagined she could be just as bossy as his diminutive colleague. Without making eye contact, both he and Dove discreetly placed their bottles out of sight.

"And how are we doing this morning, Mr. Perris?" she chirped, but when she glanced at Dove, she frowned. "I'm sorry. I'm afraid we'll have to take a break from visitors for a while. We'd like to catch up on our rest."

Why do nurses always talk as if they're part of the person being cared for? It makes no sense. "Oh, my friend here was just filling me in on some news before he leaves. I was wondering ... might you have another of those pills you gave me earlier?"

"The acetylsalicylic acid, you mean?"

"Yes, that's the one."

"Well, I'm glad our stomach tolerated it." She took a small bottle off her cart, shook two tablets out and gave them to Jonathan, followed by a cup of water. He downed them immediately, which caused her to smile. "It truly is a miracle drug, isn't it? Now I trust your friend, Mr.—"

"Rebane," Dove said, treating her to one of his trademark smiles. "At your service."

Apparently, she wasn't impressed. "Well, I trust Mr. Rebane here understands how important it is that we rest so he'll be leaving shortly." Alas, she sounded far older and more authoritative than she looked.

"Of course," he said, his smile not quite so radiant.

Both men watched the young nurse skillfully wheel her cart out the door. As soon as they were alone, Jonathan swept back his covers and swung his legs over the bed. Without asking, Dove went to the small cupboard against the wall, pulled out Jonathan's clothes and handed them over. In a matter of moments Jonathan was ready to go; he could already feel the medicine beginning to work. *Thank God for small favors.* Pulling a sheet from the chart at the foot of the bed, he dashed off a note, which read:

> *Dear Miss Winchell (which I ascertained from the name on your uniform),*
>
> *I am sorry, but an important meeting has come up which I must attend.*
>
> *Thank you for all of your tender care. I shall return as soon as possible to sign myself out properly as well as pick up more of those miracle pills.*

Yours affectionately,
Jonathan Perris

"I take it you want to pay another visit to Lexi?" Dove asked.

"Immediately, if not sooner."

Dove opened the door and checked the hallway; it was apparently clear. "Then let's go." They left the hospital by a side door. "I'm not sure where we'll find the worm this time of day. Renata from the group said he worked at a flower shop on Green Street, but I checked, and they never heard of him. They said a man who matches his description buys flowers now and again, but that's it."

As they walked, Jonathan straightened his tie and ran his fingers through his hair. "That doesn't surprise me. I'm more than convinced he isn't who he purports to be."

"I'll second that. Beginning with who he likes to sleep with. He's got one woman on a string, maybe two, yet at the art school he acts like a fairy."

"And how does he live? He's earning money from somebody or else he's being supported. Perhaps Dr. Bass can tell us what we need to know."

"You're not going to push me into that poof's clutches again, are you?" Dove grimaced. "He gives predators a bad name."

"I don't know, you two seemed to have such a rapport." Jonathan grinned.

The two men had had just turned onto the main street from behind the hospital when they came face to face with Detective Hennessey. Although it was only mid-morning, the hefty lawman's suit was already crumpled, as if he'd spent all night working.

"What in the hell are you doing out of the hospital?" Hennessey squawked. "I was just coming to see if you'd woken up yet."

Jonathan pasted on a smile. "Detective. It's nice to see you again."

"No, it ain't and you know it. But at least you saved me the nightmare of going into that hospital. Those places give me the willies." He paused to light a cheroot and took a drag, which seemed to calm him down.

Jonathan and Dove continued their walk, forcing the detective to follow. "What can we do for you?" Jonathan inquired.

"You can come down to the precinct and give me a statement about what the hell happened to you at the Japanese Tea Garden and how it connects to the murder of Miss Betsy Foster. And while you're at it, you can tell me everything you know about a certain man named Lev."

Dove played dumb. "Lev?"

Rolling his eyes, Hennessey addressed Jonathan. "You think I don't know how much you and your right arm here—" He gestured to Dove— "have been sniffing around looking for anything on that Lena Mendelssohn case? I don't know what her murder has to do with this current mess ... yet ... but I do know you're connected somehow. Hell, I just finished questioning that young lady Ines Barreto, and she hightails it over to you. Something's fishy, even if you did get bashed in the head."

"Thank you for that, at least," Jonathan said, all attempts at joviality gone. "I hope you aren't still blaming me for what happened to Miss Mendelssohn."

"His alibi is airtight, as I recall," Dove added.

"I don't need reminding from the Peanut Gallery where the evidence stands—or doesn't—in that case. I'm sayin' you know more than you're lettin' on and that's called 'obstruction of justice.' So, to keep your own sweet selves from getting in a heap of trouble, why don't you fill me in right now?" They'd walked halfway down the block, and he gestured to a bench. Taking out his notebook, he licked the tip of his pencil and cocked his head, waiting.

Hennessey was right, of course. Jonathan should just lay out everything he knew and wash his hands of *all* of it. But after a lifetime of trading the commodity known as information, he knew how valuable it was and wasn't eager to part with much of it unless it was absolutely necessary. He didn't think, for example, that the detective had put two and two together in terms of Betsy telling Ines that something terrible had happened to her roommate. It was probably only a matter of time before they made the connection, but it seemed the authorities were still operating under the assumption that

Lena Mendelssohn, not Sybil West, had been murdered. Jonathan glanced at Dove, who raised his eyebrows, as if to say *You gonna come clean this time around? I'll follow your lead.*

Jonathan wanted very much to keep Sybil's name out of the record, but he knew he had to toss the detective a bone. So, why not put Alexei Morozov in the crosshairs? The man certainly deserved it.

Jonathan sat next to Hennessey on the bench while Dove, embodying his usual six-foot thrum of energy, stood nearby. "For the record, I have no idea who hit me in the Garden," he began, "But yes, I do happen to know the man you're speaking of. Not well, mind you, but enough to know that his real name is Alexei Morozov, although I believe he also goes by the name Alex Morrow. Both Mr. Rebane and I met him through a professor at the San Francisco Art Institute."

"Who—the lady that paints the tiny pictures?"

"Rosa Hooper," Dove supplied.

"Yeah, that one."

"No," said Jonathan. "A Professor Quincy Bass. He sponsors a group of politically active art students called the Incendiaries. Apparently, Mr. Morozov is one of their leaders."

"What do you know about him?"

"Not too much," Jonathan hedged. "He's several years older than the rest of the group, he's not a full-time student, and he doesn't seem to have a job—at least one that he'll admit to. I talked to him about an art exhibit they're planning; they want to raise money for their cause."

"Which is what, exactly?"

"They don't like the way the country operates," said Dove. "They think capitalists are a bunch of greedy pigs—which, let's face it, a lot of them are. But they want everything equal, meaning nobody's rich and nobody's poor. They want workers to revolt and start a revolution to make it happen."

"They sound like that fellow, Debs, who ran for president, that Socialist guy."

"Eugene Debs, yes," Jonathan confirmed. "A lot of people liked what he had to say, apparently. I think he won about three percent of the vote in your last election."

"Sounds about right; the Reds would vote for him. The man's got a snowball's chance in hell of ever getting elected, though. But you're saying this Alexei character carries water for him? Is he a Commie?"

Jonathan shrugged. "I don't know who he works for; I just know he is very much on the side of the union in the streetcar strike."

"And how does he fit in with Betsy Foster?"

"Ines said he met Betsy at the carmen's union hall, even though he doesn't work the streetcars. They struck up a … 'friendship' … but kept it secret."

"Friendship, my ass," Hennessey muttered. "You got anything else for me?"

Not that I want to share with you "Ah, no. That's it."

"How about you?" Hennessey asked Dove, who'd been feeding a squirrel tiny pieces of bread that he'd apparently found in his pocket. Jonathan wondered how long the bread had been in there.

Dove looked at Jonathan before returning his gaze to the detective. "Uh, nope."

Hennessey sighed, put away his notebook and rose. "Well, I've got something for you, then. Another of the 'Hello Girls' who worked with Betsy is married to a streetcar driver and said she ran into Betsy a while back. Betsy was with her so-called boyfriend who the girl recognized from the union hall. Said his name was Alex and that he's a part time art student who likes talking up the union members about the raw deal they're getting. We tracked him down and he's now in custody downtown. Who knows—he may have somethin' to do with the death of your former lady love, too. Maybe we got an artsy serial killer on our hands."

"If you knew all that, why'd you give us the Third Degree?" Dove sounded a bit put out.

Hennessey sent him an evil rendition of a grin. "Because I can, boyo. Because I can." He turned back to Jonathan, all business. "Based on what we've learned from Miss Barreto, we're gonna keep this guy Morrow as long as we can and, if we can swing it, at least charge him with the murder of Betsy Foster. Too bad we don't have any eyewitnesses, or we'd nail him for assaulting you, too. But here's the kick in the pants: When we asked him if he's got representation, he said yes, he did."

"Who is it?" Jonathan asked. "Maybe I know him."

Hennessey smirked. "Yeah, I think you might. Because it's you."

Chapter Thirty-Eight

Good and Bad News

After leaving Jonathan in Dove's hands, Cordelia did go home to change clothes and make herself less of a "fright." She was torn between profound irritation at her employer's high-handedness and intense relief that he seemed to be on the mend. *My God, he can be infuriating.* He was going about his business in an ill-conceived and reckless manner, and it had landed him in trouble more than once. He was an undeniably intelligent man—why did he take such chances?

Having no power to affect that particular situation, she focused on what she could control. She had promised to give Emmett Barnes an update on his appeal and headed to the jail to meet with him. The case wasn't nearly as dire as she'd thought when she'd first learned of Emmett's less than perfect character traits. Between the photographer, the sound recorder, the engineers, and the ballistics experts, she'd at least been able to establish a theory that reflected Emmett's version of events. She'd even gotten several booking photographs from Paul Nuncio showing Emmett Barnes with a gash on the side of his temple. Assuming he was hit before the clock finished chiming, she could now present evidence that Jimmy Walsh was struck shortly *after* the bell stopped ringing. There was indeed time—albeit not much—when someone else could have picked up Emmett's rifle and shot Walsh.

To render the theory credible, however, they had to find a witness who would testify that he or she had seen Emmett get knocked out by the brick. Nora was being stubborn, poor Petro was dead, and Dove had not yet reported any progress with the rest of the Incendiaries. In this case, no news was not good news; Dove would have been quick to brag if he'd lined up another witness.

One thing she now knew: Alex Morrow was somehow involved. He was there on Bloody Tuesday because according to what Nora told Dove, Morrow had "stormed the barricades" along with her and others. As a striking carman, Jimmy Walsh was there, too. Jimmy apparently didn't like Alex, and didn't want him near Betsy. Betsy knew that, which is why she kept her relationship a secret. The question was, would Alex take the opportunity to eliminate such an obstacle, even if he was on the same side of the union conflict? From all reports, he seemed like a user, so it was entirely possible. But how callous could one person be? Such a man would be without morals, probably even vicious if cornered. Her boss was in no condition to go against such an adversary, but maybe Dove could somehow get Alex to incriminate himself.

Fat chance.

A victory doesn't always require grabbing the brass ring. Just getting a judge to consider Emmett Barnes's side of the story reasonable enough to call for a retrial would be a major accomplishment. She reminded herself that she didn't have to name the real murderer; she just had to show that it likely wasn't Emmett Barnes.

A question kept nipping at her, however. *If Alex Morrow killed Jimmy Walsh because he stood between him and Betsy, why kill Betsy, too?*

She found Emmett lying on his cot staring at the ceiling. When Cordelia and the guard approached, her client scarcely took notice.

"See, he's in one of them dark holes," the guard muttered. In a louder voice he barked through the bars, "Stand up, ya sorry bastard —'scuse my French, ma'am."

Emmett reluctantly rose but sat back down as soon as the guard left them.

"Good morning, Emmett. How are you?"

"It is a good morning? I wouldn't know," he said. "You got any news for me, Miz Hammersmith, other than the date I'm gonna be sent up the river? At least I'll get outta this place."

"Emmett, your enthusiasm knows no bounds," she said, sitting on the cell's chair and pulling out her notebook. "As a matter of fact, I've come to tell you we're making progress."

"That's not funny."

"No, really. We've established a timeline of the period you were knocked unconscious and compared that to when Mr. Walsh was shot. We're working on corroborating your claim that you were knocked out and once we do that, I believe a judge will be hard pressed not to grant a new trial based on new evidence, and—"

"Wait. You're saying there's a chance they might spring me?" Emmett had perked up like a wilted flower after a summer rain.

"Now, let's not get ahead of ourselves," she cautioned. "I make no guarantees, but I truly believe you have a shot at beating this thing."

Emmett's transformation was a thing of beauty. His smile took over his large, round face, making him more cherub than thug. She could see how a woman might eventually find something endearing about his simple, earnest demeanor. He popped up from the cot and began pacing the cell. "I can't wait to tell Betsy," he gushed. "Maybe after she sees I'm innocent, she'll give me another chance."

Betsy? No, please don't let it be what I think it is. Cordelia schooled her features. "Um, who is Betsy, Emmett? You've never mentioned her."

"Sure, I have. She's the girl I've been telling you about. Betsy—well, she likes to be called 'Elizabeth,' but she's such a little thing, she'll always be 'Betsy' to me."

Cordelia swallowed. "What's her last name, may I ask?"

"Foster. I told you, Jimmy Walsh was her cousin, on her mama's side." He rubbed his hands together. "Once she knows I didn't kill him and have gone through the fires of hell for no good reason, she might come around after all."

I have to tell him, Cordelia thought. *It would be cruel for him to learn about it from somebody else.* "About Betsy," she began.

Emmett looked at her quizzically. "What about her?"

"Why don't you have a seat?" Cordelia gestured to his cot.

Now he looked truly puzzled, and as the wheels seemed to turn in his head, he frowned. "What do you know about Betsy? Does she hate me?" His eyes grew wide as he contemplated a worse possibility. "Has she up and gotten herself *married*?"

"It's worse than that, Emmett. She … she was killed yesterday morning."

"What?!"

"She was near the Japanese Tea Garden, and—"

Emmett's head was shaking rapidly now. "No, it can't be."

"I'm afraid it's true. It so happens she was about to meet my employer regarding another case, and someone attacked both of them, wounding Mr. Perris but killing her."

"What other case?"

"I'm afraid I can't go into it now, but oddly enough, there may be some connection to your appeal."

"Who was it?" he demanded.

"We don't know for sure, but we suspect it may be the same young man you heard she was seeing."

"What's his name?" he asked coldly.

"He goes by the name 'Alex Morrow,'" she said. "Do you know him?"

Emmett shook his head, but the look in his eyes was ominous.

"I warn you, we have no proof yet. We are also considering the remote possibility that he was the one to pick up your gun and shoot Jimmy Walsh. A witness has come forward to say that Jimmy had introduced Alex to Betsy, but didn't approve of the man, which is why she kept their relationship a secret."

Emmett looked shell-shocked. "I can't believe it."

Cordelia reached out to comfort him, but it was a paltry gesture. "I am so sorry, but I want you to know we are working very hard to not only get you out of here, but find out who attacked your friend—"

Emmett swiped her hand away. "My friend? My *friend*? I loved her!"

"I know. And I know it doesn't have much meaning for you now, but we really are working on your—and her—behalf." She got up to leave, knowing that sometimes, grief is the only visitor one can deal with at a time. She left Emmett staring at the wall; he was swaying and muttering something over and over; only later did she realize what it was.

"Gotta get out of here," he'd chanted. "Gotta get out."

Chapter Thirty-Nine

Another Dubious Client

"For Heaven's sakes, you cannot represent that man!" Cordelia had returned to the office and encountered Dove and Jonathan sitting in the kitchen, each nursing a glass of whiskey. When Dove relayed what had transpired with Detective Hennessey, she practically shouted her objection.

"Why, counselor?" Jonathan asked calmly.

"Number One—" She counted her fingers for emphasis—"you shouldn't even be out of the hospital much less planning to defend a man we all know to be a murderer." She glared at Dove. "When I left, I thought I was leaving our employer in good, safe hands, but you … you thought nothing of his weakened condition and just took off with him, like two little boys playing hooky. He could have fallen, or blacked out, or—"

Jonathan's voice remained even. "But I didn't. Please continue."

His cool-headedness made her want to smack him, but she refrained. Barely. "Number two: all evidence points to Alex Morrow or Alexei Morozov or whoever the hell he is, being the mystery man, the 'Lev,' at Aunt Susie's. Since the two women who shared him and that room are *dead*, that makes it pretty damn obvious he was involved in those crimes."

"It does appear that way, however—"

She barreled on. "And Number three, I feel it in my bones that he is the man who picked up Emmett Barnes's gun. He was at the riot, Jimmy Walsh didn't like him, and he knew Emmett Barnes, at least indirectly. So, it would be a total conflict of interest for us to represent both the defendant and the probable killer!"

"How can you be so sure about all that??" Dove asked.

"Betsy Foster was the girl that Emmett Barnes was sweet on, and it's highly likely Alex knew that. Emmett said that a man he didn't recognize called out to him just before he got hit with the brick. Later, when Emmett came to, that same man had his hand on Emmett's gun

The Twisted Road

at the back of the car. At the time, Emmett thought he was going to steal it, but what if he was just returning it after shooting Jimmy Walsh? What better way for Morrow to rid himself of two obstacles than to kill one of them and pin the crime on the other?" She paced in front of the blackboard, a kind of frazzled energy racing through her. Inhaling deeply, she let her breath out slowly. It usually helped to calm her.

"May I speak?" Jonathan asked.

Still using her special breathing technique, Cordelia nodded. She noticed that Dove was suppressing a smile and wanted to smack him, too.

"All of your points are valid," Jonathan began. "Let me answer them in reverse order. Alex Morrow has not been arrested for the crime of shooting Jim Walsh. Moreover, as you already know, you are not required to find Mr. Walsh's killer, only to show the strong possibility that Emmett Barnes didn't do it. You can certainly state that you believe Alex Morrow is the killer, but if you make that allegation, you must provide evidence to support it. I have not agreed to defend him against that charge, so I see no conflict of interest there."

He swallowed the last of his drink. "As to what happened to Sybil West and Betsy Foster, I see this as an opportunity to find the answers we've been searching for. Morrow is indeed the nexus among all the major players in this drama—Sybil, Betsy, and even perhaps Jim Walsh. I need to know how all the pieces fit together, and if I can establish a relationship with the man, I might be able to do that."

"And what if he cops to one crime, but not the one you're defending him against?" Dove asked.

"Yes," Cordelia pressed, "What happens then? As his counsel, you're honor-bound to keep whatever he says between the two of you. Are you willing to defend a man you know is a killer—one who maybe killed someone you cared about—and someone who was more than willing to have you go down for the crime?"

Jonathan paused before answering. "I honestly don't know." He rose and spread his arms. "As to your first objection, you can see that I am, if not hale and hearty, at least on the mend. I plan to stop by the hospital and pick up some more of that aspirin, I think they call it. I've never had occasion to use it before, and I must say, it's top notch."

"And after you go to the hospital?" Cordelia asked with a scowl.

"You know where I'm going. I'm sorry, but I must."

Cordelia's arguments had hit their mark. Could Jonathan defend a man innocent of one crime but guilty of another? *Of course, I can*, he thought morosely. *I defended that prick Horace Baxter, and I already knew he was guilty!* Even though a clear motive hadn't yet emerged, Jonathan was fairly certain that Morrow had killed at least one of the women, if not both; for his own peace of mind, he had to know what had happened and, more importantly, *why*. But Cordelia had a point: what *would* he do if Morrow convincingly professed his innocence when it came to the women, but smugly took credit for shooting Walsh? It would be relatively easy to put on a defense that led the jury to convict him of a crime he hadn't committed. Hadn't Paul Nuncio accused the United Railroads attorney of doing just that with Emmett Barnes? But could Jonathan do the same? God help him, he wasn't sure.

He made his way to the precinct where Morrow was being held—ironically the same one that had hosted Jonathan himself not so long before.

The sergeant on duty raised his eyebrows at Jonathan's entrance. "Can't get enough of us, eh?"

Jonathan's smile was perfunctory. "I'm here to see Alex Morrow."

"You his lawyer?"

"That remains to be seen; in the meantime, you may check with Detective Hennessey regarding permission for my visit."

The sergeant harrumphed, but motioned for him to head back, where a guard took him to the cell block. The accused was sitting in his cell, calmly reading the newspaper. He looked up at Jonathan with a knowing smile. "I knew you'd come. Aren't I clever?"

Jonathan signaled for the guard to leave them and leaned against one of the walls. "Undoubtedly. I take it you want to gloat to me about your accomplishments knowing that attorney-client privilege will protect you."

"You obviously think I'm guilty."

"Are you?"

"I would hope you'd know by now." Morrow shook his head in disappointment. "In truth, you know nothing."

Jonathan could feel his own ire starting to build. "I know that Sybil and Betsy are dead. I know they didn't deserve what happened to them. I know you were the common denominator, and I think I see now how it might have unfolded."

Morrow smirked, but there was an edge to his nonchalance. "Oh, you do, do you? Please tell me what you believe I did."

"All right ... *Alexei*. Or should I call you 'Alex' ... or 'Lexi,' or maybe even 'Lev'? I confess it's difficult to keep your multiple personas straight."

Morrow countered easily. "Whatever you wish, 'Barrister Perris.' Then again, perhaps you prefer the moniker 'Bonnie Jonnie.'"

A frisson of *cadou* sped through Jonathan, much as it had the first time they'd spoken. He sensed a small flicker of light bounce at the corner of his eye. *God, no.* His tone sharpened. "Where did you hear that name?"

"I know that and much more about you, *brat*. I know about your father; I know about your mother. I know about the first half of your life which you would rather relegate to the dustbin."

Jonathan felt his equilibrium tilt. "Why do you know so much about me?"

"It's a long story ... and about as old as you are. Tell me, did you think it mere happenstance that Sybil followed you here and I was here as well?"

"I assumed you were in league with her."

Morrow tsk tsked. "Hardly. As I told you, I was not in favor of her foolish plan. I thought attorneys were trained to base their analysis on facts and not assumptions."

Jonathan's reasoning had been off from the beginning. It seemed the *cadou* was not only fickle but at times it conspired against him. He regarded Morrow for several moments before asking point blank, "Who are you?"

Morrow smiled. "I wear many hats. I am a scout. A recruiter. At times a *provocateur*, an instigator, an agitator. Some would call me a 'pot stirrer.' And yes, I'm an artist. But perhaps overall, I am an apostle of those who believe the world can do much better for its inhabitants. Sadly, there are many places I could go to do the work I do. If you had settled in, say, Chicago, that's where Sybil would have found me."

"So, you've been following me." The realization chilled Jonathan to his marrow. "It makes no sense. Why?"

The cocky prisoner Jonathan had first encountered was now subdued. "I am all those things I've told you, but I am also part of a mission that is much more complicated in scope. It requires information I was hoping you had, but I sense you do not. I long to talk to you about that and many other things, but I cannot—the stakes are too high. Someday, perhaps, you will understand. You probably won't agree, but at least you'll understand."

Morrow shifted mood again, this time with a grin. "At the moment, however, I would like to focus on getting out of this jail cell. I shouldn't be incarcerated, but you obviously disagree. As I recall, you were about to tell me what I've supposedly done."

Jonathan began to pace the cell. "As much as you profess to know about me," he began, "I think I know a bit about you as well, at least as it pertains to Sybil."

Morrow crossed his legs and leaned back in his chair. "I am breathless with anticipation."

"Sybil was bright, but she was not a revolutionary at heart. She rarely discussed politics with me, and one witness has said she often made fun of your little group."

Morrow's frown indicated Jonathan had hit a nerve. *Good.* "She wanted the life that her father and so many others had. Who could blame her? It wasn't her fault she'd been born outside the marriage bed. She was intrigued by you, yes, but in the end, she wanted more.

She wanted my brother and the life he could give her. Eventually she knew she had to choose, and she chose him." He paused before adding, "And that made you angry."

Morrow nodded, his lips pursed. "Yes … so far, you are right. After all our work, she could have had the best of both worlds. But she chose to limit herself."

Jonathan put the pieces together in his mind. "Of course. Here you had been a Pygmalion of sorts—you're no doubt familiar with the sculptor of Greek legend— and you created this woman who could be your eyes and ears at the highest levels of government and industry, who would help you spread your ideology from within. And then the beautiful Galatea rebelled. She told you she didn't want you anymore."

"She was a fool," Morrow muttered.

"So, what did you do?"

"What do you think I did? I destroyed her little fantasy. I showed her how easily she would be dismissed, that he would never accept someone of a lesser class in the end."

"And you did this by … wait … I was told she cheated on my brother with someone and was caught. She didn't know who had betrayed her, but it was you!"

Alex sent him another catbird smile. "Bravo. I knew she still had feelings for me, and I asked for one more night between us." He shrugged. "She found it difficult to say no. She obliged."

"And you arranged to have the two of you discovered."

He nodded. "There is nothing simpler than to prey upon a man's sense of ownership, whether it comes to land, capital, or sex. But here is a strange fact: a man will fight for his land or capital. No matter how he came by it, he will kill to retain it. But if a man believes his partner is disloyal, if he believes his ownership has been usurped willingly, then he will most likely rid himself of that particular 'property' in a heartbeat." Morrow sighed. "It's a shame, really. If you were more enlightened, you would see that there is sybaritic pleasure to be found in any and all combinations of human interaction."

"As Professor Bass would attest."

"As he most assuredly would."

"But if such things as a faithful partner mattered so little to you, why would you destroy her happiness because of a decision she made that didn't include you?"

Morrow looked surprised at Jonathan's bewilderment. "Don't you see it yet? The relationship is not the point: the *revolution* is the point. Sybil backed out of her commitment to the cause."

"So, she had to be punished."

"If that's the way you prefer to describe it, then yes."

"So, you failed with Sybil. Is that why you went after Betsy?"

Morrow's eyes turned cold. "My only failure with Sybil is that now she is dead and perhaps I could have done something to prevent it."

The *cadou* had become a low-level hum inside of Jonathan, as if he and Morrow were connected in some way. They had both failed Sybil, that was certain. Jonathan felt his concentration begin to slip. "But why Betsy?"

"Ah, Betsy. 'Elizabeth,' actually. She said the name made her feel taller and more serious. She was a delightful girl. Over time she would have become a true asset to the cause." His tone became wistful. "She reminded me of someone …someone beautiful, but whom I must stay away from, at least in the short term."

An image of Cordelia flashed across Jonathan's brain, but he rejected it immediately. Miss Hammersmith had nothing to do with this wretch except a burning desire to see him convicted of murder. "I have no time to play Twenty Questions with you," he said. "The point is, if you were so fond of Betsy, why did you kill her?"

In an instant, Alex turned sour. "I don't know how many times I have to tell you: I killed neither Sybil nor Betsy."

"But you are the common thread," Jonathan argued. "Both women had relationships with you. My God, man, you even had them living in the same apartment!"

"I know it looks incriminating. Yes, I knew Sybil from before—I have admitted as much. But so what? As for Betsy, there is no tangible proof I had anything to do with her other than having met her through her cousin, who happens to be dead. You and I both know that Ines Barreto's testimony is hearsay and therefore weak. There are no eyewitnesses to what happened to either woman, and even if there were, they would exonerate, not incriminate me. Because I … did … not … kill … them."

Chapter Forty

The Interview Continues

Jonathan's expression gave nothing away, but he was confounded by Morrow's protestation of innocence. Was he that good an actor or was he telling the truth? "How then do you explain what happened to them?"

Morrow himself now looked chagrined. "I don't know. I took great pains to keep my ... intimacies ... with the two women separate. Sybil was aware of my proclivities, but accepted them, albeit grudgingly. I knew she would not deign to 'compare notes' with Betsy. I also knew that while Sybil understood and supported our struggle, she saw me as merely an insurance policy against heartbreak."

"You sound as if you were made for each other," Jonathan said. "Both cold and calculating."

"You judge us too harshly," Morrow replied. "Believe it or not, part of me hoped the two of you *would* grow closer, for her sake. If that had happened, however, history would no doubt have repeated itself—she would have chosen you over the cause. We would once more have parted company, probably for good, and my 'dance' would have required far less intricate steps. But it has crossed my mind that somehow Betsy learned the true nature of my relationship with Sybil and killed her in a fit of jealousy. We all used Aunt Susie's for our ... entertainment ... so it's possible."

Jonathan wasn't buying it. "Even if she did do such a thing—it's just as likely you killed her out of pique."

"And I attacked you as well?"

"You said yourself I don't have whatever information you were looking for. There is no love lost between us. Perhaps that was to be your solution to whatever role you think I play in your revolutionary drama."

Morrow bristled at Jonathan's suggestion. "I assure you, if I had wanted to kill you, I could have done it long before now. We are not thugs; our road is long, with many twists and turns. Our goals, while ambitious, involve much more subtlety. Besides, it would never cross my mind to hurt you. We are linked, you see. Each of us is a pawn on a rather large chessboard."

"But you're losing too many players, aren't you? If you think Betsy killed Sybil, then what happened to Betsy?"

"I do not know," he said icily, "but I strongly suspect the trail leads to your fellow countryman, Lord Burnham."

"Lord Burnham? What do you know about him?"

"Far more than you. I have been aware of the good baron for as long as I knew Sybil. Her natural father is a narcissistic, greedy, sycophantic capitalist who, as you well know, is not above blackmailing when it suits him."

"I can only imagine what he thinks about you."

"Oh, he has no idea who I am. I was one of the faceless 'bohemians' he let Sybil get involved with, thinking that writing a check was all a father needed to do."

Morrow sounded resentful; perhaps his own father had acted the same way. But Jonathan wasn't following his logic. "What does he have to do with Betsy's death?"

"I am thinking he found out they were roommates and assumed that Betsy killed his daughter out of jealousy. Perhaps he even found proof of it. So, it would be a simple case of revenge."

"And assaulting me?"

To keep you from interfering."

Jonathan considered the possibility but came up short. "I'm sorry, that does not comport with the man I know."

"Have you seen him lately? I've kept him in my sights, and he appears … well, he's not the cocksure bourgeois he used to be."

The man had a point. Perhaps Burnham *was* capable of something as heinous as killing a young woman in cold blood. "I must agree with you there. But have you no other theories? What about someone in the Incendiaries?"

With a wave, Morrow dismissed the idea. "That group is but a means to an end—a way for me to move more freely among the workers without having to do the work myself. Betsy was not part of that aspect of my life; I had bigger plans for her. The only other possibility is Betsy's would-be suitor—the brute your colleague is trying to free on appeal."

"So, you knew him."

"I knew who he was. Such a Neanderthal could have sought revenge because she chose me over him."

"The retribution you propose is difficult to carry out when one is in jail," Jonathan noted caustically.

"I know that, but you would be surprised at what one's supporters will do to help those whose cause they believe in."

Interesting. Jonathan dug deeper. "Would I? I'm glad you mentioned Emmett Barnes. It may interest you to know that Miss Hammersmith is building a case that will exonerate him ... and possibly point the finger at you."

Shifting immediately into his homosexual persona, Morrow used an exaggerated facial expressions to feign surprise. "What? Oh, my goodness! Whatever can you be talking about?"

"What—are you tired now of being honest? Ines Barreto established that Jim Walsh didn't like you—that's why Betsy kept her relationship with you a secret."

Morrow's face clouded over. "You're right, he didn't like me. He despised me, in fact, once he saw Betsy's interest in me. He never asked about my background, but I could tell he considered me, God forbid, *foreign*. Of course, he didn't like that sop Emmett Barnes, either. Perhaps he wanted Betsy for himself."

"We'll never know that, will we, since both he and that unfortunate girl are dead. But that 'sop' as you call Mr. Barnes, may as well be, since he's in jail for a crime I don't believe he committed. He was hit in the head with a brick—probably by a member of your own merry band. It turns out there was enough time for you to take his weapon and eliminate one of your encumbrances when it came to Betsy Foster."

"Now you're simply talking through your hat." All verbal affectation gone, the "other" Alexei Morozov had returned.

Time to stretch the truth a bit. "No. I'm talking about an eyewitness. In this case, my colleague has one."

Morrow frowned, processing what Jonathan had said. Then he smiled. "No, she doesn't. I know all about David, the newest member of our little band. I understand the poor man's been trying to worm his way into their confidence, but I haven't bothered to expose him because, frankly, I wanted to see what he came up with regarding Sybil. However, I can assure you, those who were there on Bloody Tuesday wouldn't expose me in any way; they are too loyal to the cause, and by extension, to me. If I could name an Achilles heel, it would have been Petro. But the gods intervened in his case, didn't they? Sorry to say that poor fellow won't be testifying to anything on this side of the veil."

Jonathan smiled back and blatantly lied. "Not him."

"Then who?"

"Now why would I tell you that, when leaving you in this dank little cell, to contemplate which of those you trust might have your fate in their hands, will drive you just slightly more deranged than you already are?"

The prisoner stared at Jonathan for a moment. "You are ruthless, aren't you? Under that polished facade you are capable of almost anything. Do you want to know something perverse? It energizes me … because it reminds me of me. So, are you going to take my case?"

Jonathan rose and called for the guard. "I haven't decided. Enjoy your solitude, comrade."

As Jonathan left the cell, Morrow called after him. "What about bail? Can you at least get me out of here?"

"I do know the answer to that. No. Unequivocally, no."

Morrow chuckled. "I figured as much."

Returning to the office, Jonathan was awash in contradictory thoughts. On the one hand, he was now nearly convinced that Morrow had murdered Walsh. When Jonathan brought the possibility up, the man had focused not on his innocence, but on who might betray him. Yet the motive was weak. Why go to such lengths simply to eliminate a disgruntled relative and a rival you had already bested?

But what if Morrow determined that killing a striker would further his political cause? The public had seemed to rally around the union, for a time, at least, after what many considered a cold-blooded murder. Perhaps Morrow was so lacking in conscience that he figured the benefits of taking Jim Walsh's life outweighed the cost. By God, if he was found guilty of that crime—and if Dove could convince one or more witnesses to come forward, he likely would be—then he should hang.

But the murders of Sybil West and Betsy Foster were another matter entirely. Jonathan hated to admit it, but Morrow sounded innocent. He had proven to be a superb impersonator, but what if in the case of those poor women he turned out to be right? That would put Jonathan back at square one, where he decidedly did *not* want to be.

And what about the strange connection that Morrow insisted he had with Jonathan? What nefarious plot did he hope to drag Jonathan into? He couldn't dwell on that—not when three murders had yet to be explained.

Chapter Forty-One

A Demand and A Request

Long after Jonathan had left for the jail, Cordelia still found it difficult to concentrate. She'd had no concrete update from Dove, only that he was headed to the Art Institute to see who else he could "persuade" to testify. She knew he would do everything in his power to bring her the testimony she needed, but she also knew it was a long shot. What upset her even more was the terrible position Jonathan was poised to put her in. If he decided to represent Alex Morrow, would she be able to put up with it? She didn't think so. How could one defend a person one knew to be a murderer?

As she fretted in her office, she looked up to see Althea standing in the doorway with a note in her hand. She was about to hand it over when they both heard a man's voice shouting, "Perris! Goddammit, where are you!"

Since the two women were the only ones in the building, Cordelia joined Althea to confront the intruder in the foyer.

A middle-aged man with a relatively fit build and uncombed salt-and-pepper hair was pacing in front of Althea's desk with a cane. His clothing was of high quality, but in need of a good pressing.

Either he's in a hurry or down on his luck, Cordelia thought. *Best be careful.* "May I help you, sir?"

"I'm looking for Jonathan Perris and I've not heard from him in several days. I demand to know what progress he's made in the hunt for Sybil's killer."

Who was this man? Jonathan had expressly asked them not to reveal Lena's real name. Better play dumb. "Sybil?"

"What? He didn't tell you Lena's real name? That's rich. Hiding the truth from his own staff. Then you have no idea who I am, I'll wager."

"No sir, we don't. Now, if you don't mind—" Althea began.

"I'm Lord George Burnham, damn you, and I do mind!"

Cordelia tried to placate him. "Sir, we do in fact know that Lena's real name was Sybil West, but I'm sorry, Mr. Perris has not mentioned you."

Lord Burnham—if that was his real name—looked fit to be tied. "So that's the game he's playing, is it? Keeping his own team in the dark about the whole sorry mess he got himself embroiled in. What a coward. Well, you tell that high and mighty barrister that I'll let the whole wretched, screaming cat out of the bag on both sides of the Pond if he doesn't come up with something soon, consequences be damned."

"Where can he reach you, sir?" Althea asked.

"He knows where. Just tell him to show me his progress—or by God he'll rue the day he ever crossed me."

"If it's any consolation, Mr. Perris is at the jail right now," Althea said. "He's interviewing a man who might be involved in Miss West's murder and that of another young woman."

No! Cordelia thought. *Don't give the man anything. We don't know who he is!* She reached out to caution Althea, but the woman was focused on Burnham.

"The Devil you say. Who is it?"

"An art student named Alex Morrow. Supposedly he was friends with Sybil from before. That's all we know at this point."

"Well, it's a start," the man grumbled. "When he gets back, you tell your employer I want answers, or so help me, I will give his story to every newspaper in town—and none of you will survive the torrent of bad publicity that will come from it."

"You've made your position more than clear, Mr. Burnham," Cordelia said, refusing to use his title. She opened the outer door and stood resolutely by it. "Good day to you."

When the man left, the two women looked at each other in shock. "I need to make some tea," Althea said, and headed back to the kitchen. After locking the front door, Cordelia followed.

"Althea, I don't think you should have told—"

Althea held up her hand. "I know. I'm sorry, but I felt we had to give him *something*. If ever there was a man in pain, it was him. I thought he was going to go off his rocker and start attacking us!"

"It'll probably be all right. Maybe it'll be enough to calm him down."

"I wish that were true, but I don't think so. Whatever he's got hanging over Mr. P's head sounds bad if he's this upset about it."

"I agree. It sounds like it relates to something that happened back in England, but that could be any number of things. He tried a lot of cases."

I know. Mr. P's like a piece of baklava, only not quite as syrupy. He's got many layers to him, but at his core he's a good man. I figure he'll let us know what we need to know, when we need to know it."

"I suppose you're right," Cordelia said, although inside she wasn't nearly so sanguine about it. She'd known from the start that he was holding something back; otherwise, he would have told the police everything from the beginning. But what was it, and why hadn't he shared it with them? Was it a matter of trust, or was something darker at play? She was about to head back to her office when they heard Oliver Bean call out, "Anybody around?"

Heaving a sigh, Althea poured another cup of tea. "Now, that boy's as sweet as plum pudding," she confided. "Too bad he's late for everything." She poked her head out of the kitchen. "In here, Mr. Bean."

Ten minutes later, Althea knocked on Cordelia's door.

"Come in."

Looking exasperated, Althea held a note in her hand. "So sorry," she said. "I was about to give you this when that Burnham fellow showed up. It's from Sergeant Jansome down at the precinct."

Cordelia opened it and read:

Emmett Barnes is goin' stark ravin' mad in here—went after the guard on duty and we had to smack him to get him to calm down. Anything you can do for him? I feel sorry for the bugger.

Rolly.

"What's it say?" Althea asked.

"He says Emmett's pretty down in the dumps."

"Well, who wouldn't be, stuck in a cell all day for something you didn't do? But I don't know what you can do about it."

"Me neither but thank you." Cordelia tried to concentrate once more on the appeal, but it failed to hold her interest. *My God, that poor fellow,* she thought. *First, he's accused of a murder he didn't commit, then the love of his life is murdered and he's helpless to do anything about it. And to top it all off, he can't stand small spaces. Could anyone have worse luck?*

She had built a credible timeline using the evidence she'd gathered. All that remained was corroborating testimony from an eyewitness that Emmett had been hit by a brick. Hopefully Dove could collect that from one of the other Incendiaries. But maybe, in the meantime, it would be enough for the judge to set bail. Cordelia knew she wouldn't have enough clout on her own to convince him, but according to Jonathan, someone existed who very well could.

Before she could talk herself out of it, she gathered her reticule, coat and hat and left the office. It was finally time to meet the incomparable Alma de Bretteville.

Cordelia debated with herself all the way to the Marina District. She loathed the saying, "It's not what you know, but who you know," even though she understood it to be true. From the time she could understand such things, she'd vowed never to rely on mere connections to get ahead. And for the most part she'd adhered to that philosophy. She'd gotten into law school through merit and finished with high marks thanks to an ungodly amount of dedication and hard work. She'd even gotten her job with Jonathan Perris on her own.

But connections *did* make the world go round, and sometimes they were necessary to right a wrong. Jonathan Perris had gotten a foothold here in the city thanks to his relationships with socially prominent people, but he worked tirelessly for every client who retained him, and the word had spread that he was an exceptional lawyer. One might even make the case that had Jonathan not met the Firestones, they would not have hired him to defend Dr. Tom Justice, and if they hadn't hired him, who knew where Tom might be today? So, in that sense, connections weren't a bad thing at all.

The Twisted Road

But so often connections were the sum and substance of how people got ahead. They were let into exclusive clubs, or admitted to prestigious schools or given prominent jobs, all because of who they knew. But wasn't it presumptuous at best to foist herself upon a woman based solely on a mutual acquaintance? Yes, it was, she admitted. It shamed her to even consider it. But, to borrow another phrase, "Desperate times call for desperate measures." If this woman could convince the appeals judge that Emmett Barnes deserved to be out on bail while his appeal was adjudicated, it might save the poor man's sanity, and that was worth a lot. By the time she reached the right cable car stop, she had made her decision and donned the armor of her justification.

Cordelia had done her homework. Alma Emma Charlotte Corday le Normand de Bretteville, the twenty-six-year-old paramour of one of the richest men in the Golden City, lived in a tiny house on Francisco Street with her parents and several siblings. Cordelia didn't have to knock on the door, because the front room of their home served as a bakery. The delectable smells of danish pastry (the butter! the cinnamon! the raisins!) assaulted her will power with such ferocity that she capitulated within minutes and ordered a peach turnover as she asked after Alma, explaining that she worked for Alma's "good friend," the attorney Jonathan Perris.

"Oh, you're in luck," said her mother. "My daughter's just home now changing for some gathering she's attending with her gentleman caller." She called down the short hallway. "Alma dear, someone here to see you."

I can see where Alma gets her beauty, Cordelia thought. Mathilde de Bretteville was a lovely woman, despite having a passel of kids and running a business.

In a few moments, Alma appeared, pinning her dramatically plumed hat in place as she entered the parlor store. She wore a deep blue walking dress that impressively showed off her six-foot figure. "Oh, I know you," she exclaimed. "You're the cagey lady lawyer who's gonna get that guard off on appeal. I told Jonathan that, and there's a fur coat hanging in the balance for me, so you'd better come through." Grinning, she put a dollar down for a chocolate confection. Her mother started to make change, but Alma stayed her hand. "That's

A.B.'s tip." She motioned Cordelia to join her outside. "Keep me company while I wait for my ride," she said.

Cordelia followed her out to the front step. "I'm sorry to bother you, Miss de Bretteville—"

"Call me Alma," the young woman said. "What do you need?"

"Well, I—"

"Spit it out," she said. "I ain't got much time before my chariot gets here."

Cordelia swallowed. "My client, Emmett Barnes, is innocent. I am sure of it. And I have the facts—or nearly all of them—to prove it. But he's going nuts in that cell and I'm afraid he's going to do something stupid enough to have them put him away for cause. The judge has the power to let him make bail while the appeal process plays out. I was hoping …"

The statuesque beauty waggled her perfectly shaped eyebrows. "Hoping I might whisper something in his ear to get him to consider lettin' your man out?"

Cordelia was shocked. Surely Alma didn't think she was implying …"Oh, please, I'm not insinuating that you might—"

Alma let loose a full-throated laugh. "I'm just funnin' ya. I worked with his wife to get supplies out to folks after the big fire last year. She's got an eye for art like I do, so we stay in touch. I can pass the word along if you like. As long as you're sure he's innocent—I don't want to let any varmints out once we've put them in the pen. Enough of them running around as it is."

"Thank you, Miss—I mean, Alma. Thank you so much. I promise you, my client did not kill Jim Walsh. I'm just looking to give him some hope while we prove it in court."

A well-appointed carriage pulled up. "Consider it done," Alma said, climbing into the conveyance. "I'll send word when I've tickled his ear."

As she watched the carriage pull away, Cordelia could only stand and marvel. *My God, no wonder Jonathan and Mr. Spreckles and everybody else seems to be in love with her—she's electrifying!*

Feeling satisfied with what she'd accomplished, despite using a connection to do it, Cordelia treated herself to the peach turnover on the way home. Her thoughts drifted, however, and she was reminded of the strange visitor she and Althea had encountered that morning. What could possibly cause such an uproar that Jonathan wouldn't tell his own staff about it? She pondered the possibilities as she licked the pastry crumbs off her fingers.

Chapter Forty-Two

Bad Ideas

Peter Windridge was given a proper burial by his well-to-do family, but the send-off he would have enjoyed most came as the Incendiaries gathered after the funeral at the Art Institute's student tavern to celebrate his life.

Dove was the first to arrive, soon joined by the now-smaller cadre. Simon wore an expensive wool jacket that strained against his belly. He'd been closest to Petro and was the most emotional. Oscar, dressed in fine mourning attire, was serious and polite, no doubt feeling the circumstances warranted a truce between Dove and him.

Despite her somber hat and walking dress, Renata found it difficult to maintain a sad demeanor, and Lucy, who no matter what she wore, could not mask her large frame, assumed her usual role as church mouse. Nora hadn't dressed specifically for the occasion; her garb was usually drab and matched the mood of the group. No one commented on the fact that "Lexi" hadn't shown up; Dove wasn't sure if anyone besides him knew why.

"To Petro, who was kind and good and way too decent for this world," Simon said, raising his stein. His voice broke as he added, "We need more like him."

Everyone responded with a chorus of "Here! Here!" except Lucy.

"I'm not so sure," the normally reticent Amazon said in a small voice. "The revolution doesn't need more sweet people. It needs more warriors. It needs men and women with courage—who aren't afraid to do the hard thing to reach their goal."

She was right; no revolution ever succeeded by overwhelming the enemy with nice guys.

"I'm going to miss his smile," Renata said wistfully.

"I think in his own way, Petro *was* brave," Oscar said. "I mean, he really believed in helping those who didn't have what he had. And even though he was gentle by nature, he was there on Bloody Tuesday and for sure he would have fought to protect those he loved."

Throughout the discussion, Nora had been silent, but at last she spoke. "I know how we can honor Petro, but it will take the kind of courage you talked about, Lucy. Enormous courage and strength and commitment."

Judging by his frown, Oscar wasn't used to putting money where his mouth was. "What do you have in mind?" he asked warily.

"The way I see it, Petro set a fine example of why the workers—the *real* workers, not the scabs brought in to pretend to run the cars—need to win. The more that riders are 'inconvenienced,' the more accidents that happen, the more people are hurt, the more the bourgeoisie will have to take notice. The nice little society ladies like my mother won't want to ride the cars for fear of falling off and breaking their skulls. Hansom cabs are expensive; that means less money for fripperies. They'll start to clamor for the strike to be over, and United Railroads will have to capitulate."

"What are you suggesting?" Dove asked.

"A night of destruction," Nora proposed, her eyes taking on a peculiar brightness. "The Farleymen are now housed around the city; only a few guards protect the cars at the Turk Street barn, and they probably won't show up until after we're gone. I say we sneak in and wreck the place. Bring paint. Bring knives to slash the seats. Bring tools to loosen the gears; bring oil to spread on the tracks. Bring dung to smear on everything. And bring weapons for protection. You never know if we'll meet some resistance. We go in as a unit, work quickly and leave before they know what happened, or else fight our way out."

Renata was looking more horrified by the second. "But … but why do something that will probably cause even more people to get hurt? Won't that put the carmen in a bad light? Won't people hate the strikers more than they already do?"

"On the surface, yes," Nora explained. "They'll cry and moan about it. The papers will be full of their whining. But in the end, capitalists will always do what's necessary to keep themselves safe and at the top of the pecking order. They'll complain, but they'll consider it a cost of doing business and give in to the union. That victory will make the workers stronger. Over time, workers everywhere will grow more powerful, and they'll bring about the death of capitalism and the beginning of our socialist utopia. And that is what we're all striving for, isn't it?"

Simon looked like he'd rather be any place but in that tavern. "Yes, but ... but we're just a few students. What can we really do?"

Nora sounded like she was losing patience. "Look, the kind of changes I'm talking about don't happen right away, with one poster or one speech or one strike. But every poster, every speech and every strike builds one upon the other until eventually our contribution helps to generate the change we want to see. The struggle calls upon each of us to do our part. We must each do *something*, no matter how small, to contribute to the cause. The question is, do any of you have the courage to act instead of simply regurgitate slogans?"

Like Renata, Dove was appalled ... yet he was fascinated, too. He had to admire Nora's attitude. She sounded loony, and she took no prisoners, but isn't that how real reforms often happen? It's too bad the grand statement she wanted to make made no sense; how can causing more death and destruction bring about a utopia? The world could use more action-oriented women like her, but why not work within the system to improve it instead of tearing it apart?

Oscar remained skeptical. "What does Lexi say about all this, anyway? And does anybody even know where he is?"

"I'm afraid we won't be seeing much more of Lexi," Nora said solemnly. "He sent word he's in jail. They're saying he may have killed two women, including his old friend Lena." She pulled a handkerchief from her pocket and dabbed her eyes.

"No," Lucy said adamantly. "I can't imagine he did such a thing."

"He didn't even like women that much," said Renata.

Nora shook her head. "I don't know what to believe. I thought I knew him, but now I'm not so sure. The point is, we can't count on him anymore. We're going to have to go it alone."

"I agree," Lucy said, sitting up straighter, her soft voice rising. "We must carry on for Lexi and Petro's sake. So ... do you have any thoughts on when we might do this?"

Dove tamped down his surprise. *Lucy sounds downright inspired; Who would have thought?*

The Twisted Road

In response to Lucy's question, Nora broke into a wide smile. "Yes. I have the perfect date, in fact. Next Friday evening. Ten o'clock."

"But that's the night of the exhibit," Simon pointed out.

"Precisely. You may not have noticed, but Professor Bass has made that event all about him. None of our work is signed, so it's not like anybody who shows up is going to know who we are and how we fit in. We're all just part of the Collective, remember? But imagine all those fat cats buying our work to show how much they care about the downtrodden…how much they love the idea of workers being paid a fair wage and children going to school instead of factories. And what better way to show how feckless they are than by turning around and destroying the symbol of their capitalist greed—the streetcars."

Simon didn't look convinced but said nothing.

Good. Dove could work with that kind of hesitation. After assuring Nora that he would bring the necessary items ("I have access to everything we need."), he offered to buy Oscar and Simon a drink down in the flats. "Sorry, ladies, but us gents have our own way of mourning our fellow comrades. We'll send Petro off in fine style."

Renata pouted, Lucy looked relieved, and Nora waved them on, too busy planning her next act of rebellion, no doubt. He'd bet money that when the time came to put up or shut up, neither Renata nor Lucy would show up. But Simon and Oscar were another kettle of fish. They might show simply to prove they had Nora's kind of rocks.

Dove kept up the repartee extolling Petro's virtues until they reached the bottom of Nob Hill before changing his tactic. "So, what do you think of Nora's plan, gentlemen? Are you up for causing some outrageous property damage for which you could do serious jail time, all in the name of a dead friend, an accused murderer, and a so-called revolution?"

Oscar and Simon glanced at each other and paused; they both seemed to be feeling their way on shaky ground.

"Why? Aren't you?" Simon asked.

Oscar, the more intelligent of the two, had been staring at Dove. "You … you know something, don't you."

May as well get it over with. "Yeah, I know something. I know if you go anywhere near that car barn on Friday night, you're going to be arrested, tried, convicted and sent to prison for a whole host of crimes, up to and possibly including accessory to murder."

"What?" Simon cried. "What are you talking about?"

"I'm talking about what happened on Bloody Tuesday."

Oscar took a menacing step forward. "I knew there was something off about you. You aren't one of us. You never have been. Question is, who in the hell are you?"

Good question, Oscar. Since Dove was no longer an official member of law enforcement, a bit of truth-stretching was called for. "Let's just say I'm the long arm of the law and I'm talking about the killing of the union member Jimmy Walsh."

Oscar scoffed at that. "What makes you think we were even there?"

"Save it for acting school," Dove said. "We have eyewitness testimony"— *from Nora, although she'd never cop to it*— "that you were both there and you know Nora threw the brick that hit the guard and that he went down." *Time to go out on a limb.* "You also know that your sainted Lexi—known by his Soviet handlers as Alexei Morozov, by the way—picked up the rifle and fired it."

Oscar continued to parry. "I think you're fishing. Why would he shoot a member of the union? He was on their side."

Dove shook his head. "Beats me. Maybe he's a double agent. Maybe he's a lousy shot and missed his real target. Or maybe it had nothing to do with the strike at all. The point is, Petro was there, saw it all, and was ready to testify about what happened. Fate stepped in for that poor kid, but you two have the opportunity to make it right."

Neither young man countered with Nora-like platitudes, which probably meant they were both nervous as hell.

Oscar was leery but listening. "How could we do that?"

"It goes without saying that you stay the hell away from Turk Street on Friday. The place will be crawling with cops"— (*maybe, possibly, probably not*) —"just dying to arrest some violence-prone punks like you. And who knows? Bullets might start flying and someone could get plugged who shouldn't and they'd chalk it up to the heat of the moment. On the other hand, if you cooperate, tell the authorities exactly what and who you saw, there's no need for your records to show you were anything but bystanders on Bloody Tuesday. No one's going to press charges against you, guaranteed. I'm sure your maters and paters would much rather remain ignorant of your misdeeds than read about you in the paper. Wouldn't you agree?"

They'd stopped by a streetlamp and Dove could swear Simon was turning a sickly shade of green. But the boy still had a bit of the hero in him; maybe he was emulating Petro.

"What about Nora?" Simon asked. "We can't just leave her there alone."

"Don't worry about her," Dove said. "I'm going to meet her as planned and make sure she doesn't dig an even deeper hole for herself than she already has. If she doesn't show, however, I'll know one of you tipped her off and we'll add obstruction of justice to your rap sheet. Do we understand each other?" Dove looked pointedly at both of them, waiting for their nods of understanding.

He got what he needed.

"Excellent. Now, what do you say we go get that drink? I'm buying."

—◆◆◆—

Alma de Bretteville had made good on her promise and got the judge to grant Emmett Barnes' bail. The law prohibited Cordelia from posting it, so Emmett's family had scraped together the required one hundred dollars and Emmett had gone home to await the results of the appeal.

Despite the reprieve, however, the young man hadn't emerged from his profound despair over Betsy's death. According to his mother, he was holed up in his old bedroom, sinking lower and lower each day. Cordelia decided to pay him a visit in the hope of cheering him up.

Emmett and his brothers lived with their widowed mother in a small apartment near the Embarcadero. Three years earlier Mrs. Barnes had moved her family from a farm south of the city that had not produced enough for them to live on. The plan was for Emmett and his brothers to find work while she took in laundry and mending to make ends meet. It was a never-ending source of torture for Emmett that his troubles had caused them additional hardship. Perhaps Cordelia could convince him that his melancholy was a burden, too.

When Cordelia arrived, Mrs. Barnes greeted her warmly, wiping her work-roughened hands on her faded apron and beckoning her in. "Thank you for getting Emmett out on bail, Miz Hammersmith. He's in the back, moping as usual. I hope you can talk some sense into him."

She followed the woman's directions to a small bedroom into which three pallets had been crammed. Emmett sat on one of them, much as he had while incarcerated. He acknowledged her greeting with a mumble.

She decided a non-nonsense approach was in order. "You know, Emmett, you were pretty adamant about wanting to get out of your prison cell, so I went the extra mile and arranged for the judge to review your case and recommend bail. But it looks like you've just exchanged one prison for another."

"I'm sorry, Miz Hammersmith. I can't get over the fact that my Betsy's gone."

She was never your Betsy, Cordelia thought, but refrained from stating the obvious. "So, how are you spending your time, now that you're *free*?"

"I've been thinkin'," he said.

"About what?"

"About the man you said might have killed her. That Alex Morrow rotter."

"What about him?"

Emmett gazed at the wall. A crucifix hung on it, a solitary decoration, if one could even call it that. "I've been wondering why he did it."

Cordelia spoke calmly and carefully; she could tell he was having a hard time keeping his emotions in check. "There is circumstantial evidence, but keep in mind we don't know for sure that he's the one.

The police are gathering all the facts they can. In our system, one is innocent until proven guilty."

"Like me," he said dolefully.

"And sometimes, in our system, appeals are necessary to right a wrong, as in your case."

Emmett looked up, his eyes full of entreaty. "But he's locked up, right? I mean, so he can't do it to anybody else?"

Dammit. She could lie, but it wasn't in her nature to do it. Sooner or later, he'd find out. "I'm afraid you weren't the only defendant who was able to post bail this week, Emmett."

"You mean that monster is out walking around?"

"I wouldn't call him a monster, but … yes. Or perhaps he's home like you, wondering who could have done such a thing."

Emmett had sat up for their conversation, but now he stood. "I want to thank you for all you've done for me, Miz Hammersmith," he said formally, as if they were ending their professional relationship.

Cordelia felt uneasy but tried to shake it off with levity. "You're not firing me, are you? We're not through yet; we've got to get your conviction thrown out."

"I know," he said, smiling for the first time. "But I think I'll take your advice and get some fresh air."

"Good. Maybe your mother will put you to work." As Cordelia left, Emmett was putting on his coat and buttoning it with care. She turned to admonish him not to do anything stupid but refrained from doing so. The last thing that poor young man needed was advice he'd probably heard a thousand times.

She left shortly afterward, hoping she'd lifted his spirits somewhat. But as the day drew to a close, she thought about the trouble Emmett had gotten into so many times before and regretted not speaking up. *For once I kept my mouth shut, and I shouldn't have.* She couldn't wait to see the appeals process play out so Emmett Barnes could get his life back and begin to heal.

Chapter Forty-Three

Ignition

"You should be in bed." Jonathan heard Cordelia's quiet admonition from the doorway as he wrote on the large slate in the boardroom. Dusk had descended upon the city, and he wondered briefly why she was still in the office.

"I agree," he said with a backward glance. "I'm trying to clear some of my thoughts in order to sleep."

"I know the feeling." Cordelia stepped inside and perused the board. "Still no word on who posted Alex Morrow's bail?"

"No, they've remained anonymous. The question is why?"

"Perhaps the murderer had an accomplice."

He paused to gaze at her fully. "It's possible. But my sense tells me Morrow's innocent when it comes to the women."

"But not Jimmy Walsh. And yet you're still thinking about defending him." He could hear the exasperation in Cordelia's voice and couldn't fault her for it.

She read the names he'd written: "'Professor Bass' ... 'John Cutler' ... 'Rosa Hooper.' I've never met the professor, but from Dove's description, he sounds like the type who might become enraged over Alex Morrow's infidelities. John Cutler, on the other hand, doesn't seem like he'd risk his marriage and family over an infatuation. And for heaven's sake, Rosa Hooper? How does an art instructor figure into all this?"

Jonathan shared her skepticism. "I don't know—she was jealous of Sybil's talent, perhaps? I admit I'm grasping at straws here, but I can't assume a detail is unimportant when it might prove to be the key that solves the case."

"You're right," Cordelia said. "But we aren't going to solve anything if we keep going around in circles without taking a break."

Jonathan smiled ruefully, wincing at the throb that had resumed in his head. Although the *cadou* had receded, remnants of the concussion remained. Apparently, those miracles pills only lasted so many hours before the pain came back. "That sounds like something I would say to you."

"Yes, it does, which tells me you aren't completely recovered—that, and the fact that you still haven't shut the door on defending Mr. Morrow." She took the chalk out of Jonathan's hand and slipped her arm through his to guide him out of the room. "Since Dove is doing all he can to secure the testimony I need, the least I can do is nag you into going home and getting some rest."

"I will on one condition," he said.

Cordelia looked askance at him. "Which is…"

"That we share a cab to our respective domiciles. No public transportation tonight."

Cordelia shot him a weary smile. "Agreed."

I'll take my victories, paltry though they might be, he mused as they left the building.

—⸱✧⸱—

By rights he shouldn't even be attending the event, Jonathan thought on Friday as he shaved in advance of the exhibition. He'd contacted Bass and begged off sponsoring the show because of the "conflict of interest" he felt in possibly defending Bass's favorite student and playmate. "I simply don't think I could be objective at this time," he'd lamented.

Anyone with a semblance of a brain could see what a pitiful excuse it was.

Bass was surprisingly gracious, however, about a mark like Jonathan Perris slipping through his grasp. "It's quite all right," the professor had assured him. "I completely understand. Fortuitously, we've had a new sponsor step up who has been considerably more than generous. I would love to introduce you to him at the exhibition. You will be coming, won't you?"

Jonathan had agreed, reluctantly, but his spirits lifted somewhat when Cordelia confronted him in his office, insisting that she accompany him.

"I can't depend on Dove—especially tonight—so who else is going to keep you from heading down another dangerous path?" She stood resolute, almost daring him to refuse.

"Such self-sacrifice," he'd replied in the driest of tones. He knew she was hoping to glean something more about Alex Morrow to aid in her appeal; he would have expected no less from her. Nonetheless, since Dove was busy trying to head off vandalism at the car barn, he was glad to have her company. Even though the headaches were now intermittent, it would still be helpful to have someone as sharp as she along to help assess the players, many of whom he assumed would be attending the show.

But a new sponsor? The characters in this play seemed to be multiplying.

Jonathan finished dressing and took a cab to pick up Cordelia at her boarding house. It seemed his associate had called a truce between them because she had no further exhortations when she joined him in the conveyance. She wore a simple evening dress of pale green satin with black trim that featured no waistline and therefore made the most of her petite stature. A black lacy shawl covered her decolletage. Cordelia would never be tall, never statuesque, but one would be a fool to ever consider her a "mere" female.

She was straightforward and focused on their mission. "What are you looking for tonight?"

"I wish I knew. I trust that if we are vigilant, we might ascertain who Alex Morrow works for, and that will help both of our cases."

"Well, we know with a virtual certainty that he killed Jim Walsh; whether we can prove it is another matter."

"A formidable task," Jonathan agreed. And in a rare bout of complete openness he added, "I'm glad you're joining me tonight. You have insights that I may not, and I value your opinion."

"I will do my best." She smiled at him before turning to gaze out the carriage window.

The exhibition of student revolutionary art dubbed "Ignition" was held in an empty warehouse along the Embarcadero near the Ferry Building; Professor Bass had no doubt deemed it a more atmospheric location than the Art Institute. The pieces had been set up on tables around the large space, leaving room in the middle for refreshments which consisted of beer, plain bread and hunks of cheese. A sign on the table read, "This is what sustains the working man."

It seemed that Jonathan's withdrawal from sponsorship had not impacted attendance. Several notable Committee of Fifty members and their subordinates were there, probably to shore up their credibility in terms of caring for the city's labor force. Capital was abundant and flowing in all directions, but if the workers stopped constructing the frames and riveting the steel, the Golden City would come to a screeching halt.

"These posters aren't very good," Cordelia murmured to Jonathan as they perused the students' work. "I'm no expert, but there's nothing the least bit subtle about any of them."

"I think they've determined that the most effective communication clobbers one over the head."

Cordelia was about to respond when Professor Bass, dressed in a garish red jacket with a yellow ascot, walked up. "Ah, Mr. Perris—so good of you to join us this evening!" Turning to Cordelia he added, "and this is your lovely wife, I take it?"

Cordelia didn't flinch but extended her hand and quickly set the record straight. "Ah, no. I'm Cordelia Hammersmith, an attorney in Mr. Perris's law firm, Mr.—"

"I am remiss," Jonathan interjected. "Cordelia, this is Professor Quincy Bass, the mentor of these student revolutionaries and the creator behind this most enthralling exhibit."

"Oh, you are too kind," Bass said. "I am gratified by the turnout. We've already had several financial commitments from local captains of industry who are concerned about the gap between the rich and the poor, who see that our world can be infinitely more productive if we all share equally in the spoils. Many of them are no doubt feeling the weight of their exploitation and seek to atone for their transgressions. Speaking of which, here comes one of our newest benefactors, the man I was telling you about over the phone."

And he gestured to none other than Lord George Burnham.

Chapter Forty-Four

Confrontation

*B*urnham? Jonathan and Cordelia glanced at each other, eyes wide in disbelief. She'd told him about Burnham's outburst at the office and how Althea had placated him with the fact that a suspect named Alex Morrow was an art student. Obviously, Burnham had ingratiated himself with Bass in order to get closer to the man he thought had killed his daughter. *This cannot be good.*

The tiny sparks of light that sometimes accompanied the *cadou* began to flicker again. *It's my headache*, he told himself. *Nothing more.*

But he knew better.

Burnham had almost reached them, an unholy gleam in his eye, when Professor Bass stepped in with introductions.

"Lord Burnham, may I present a countryman of yours who is a fellow aficionado of the struggle for social and economic justice," he said. "Mr. Perris is—"

"An old friend of mine, to be sure," Lord Burnham rejoined. "We go way back, don't we, old man?" His expression was defiant, as if he dared Jonathan to call him out.

"We do indeed." Jonathan was willing to go along, at least for the moment. "You must have received good news since the last time we met, my lord. Back then you seemed to be in a bit of the doldrums."

"Yes, you appear quite *relaxed* compared to the other evening when you stopped by our offices," Cordelia added. "I hope you are feeling better?"

Burnham did in fact look nearly as polished as he did the day of the Cliff House lunch. Only the deadness in his eyes revealed the truth. "Yes, quite," he said, ignoring Cordelia's oblique reference to his tantrum. "I have developed, shall we say, a new lease on life—or perhaps more succinctly, a new reason for living. It is quite invigorating ... to have a purpose."

Bass, Jonathan could tell, had no inkling of Lord Burnham's hidden agenda. How much had Burnham promised to donate to the cause? Would Bass be surprised to learn that the baron's source of wealth was about to collapse? Doubtful. Burnham, it seemed, had but one lodestone and his name was Alex Morrow.

The same Alex Morrow whom Bass had just beckoned over to their group.

As Burnham turned to watch his quarry, Cordelia murmured to Jonathan, "The hatred in Burnham's eyes is chilling. You don't think he would do anything foolish, do you?"

"Unfortunately, I do." Jonathan couldn't tell her that the sparks in his peripheral vision were becoming more pronounced and the flashes had begun, as if he were seeing individual frames of a moving image, too far apart to form a coherent sequence, but getting closer. At this point he could only tell it was two individuals in conflict. He bloody well hated the *cadou* but was powerless to stop it now.

As soon as Morrow reached them, he was taken under the proprietary arm of the professor.

"Ah, so this is the artistic revolutionary you were telling me about, eh, Professor?" Burnham locked eyes with his adversary and extended his hand. "Alex Morrow, I presume?"

"Lexi, darling, I'd like you to meet Lord Burnham, who has so generously agreed to sponsor our upcoming endeavors. I imagine you and he will find much to talk about over the coming weeks."

"I'm sure we will," Morrow said flatly, his hand gripping Burnham's.

Too absorbed in himself, Bass did not seem to pick up the undercurrents between the two men. "Well, now that I have brought you two together, I must leave you to greet our other attendees. You never know when an individual might *truly* feel the pull of our movement—" He looked pointedly at Jonathan —"and want to join our cause like the good baron here."

Once Bass was out of earshot, Cordelia dispensed with all niceties, fearlessly heading straight to the heart of the matter. "Mr. Morrow, I'm Cordelia Hammersmith. You probably already know that I am representing Emmett Barnes in the matter of Jim Walsh's murder. I am very close to being able to prove without a doubt that my client was wrongly convicted and that someone else pulled the trigger. I know you were recently arrested for another crime. May I ask who posted bail for you?"

Alex Morrow smiled slowly. "Your forthrightness arouses me, Miss Hammersmith—yes, I know who you are. I would love to tease you by withholding that information, but alas, I don't possess it myself."

"So, the good Professor didn't spring for it?" Jonathan asked.

"I thought perhaps he had, but he needed all of his spare cash for this affair, or so he said." He gestured to the paltry refreshments being served. "There must be a premium on Farmer's cheese this week."

"Then who—" Jonathan glanced at Burnham and the man's expression solved the mystery.

Morrow followed Jonathan's gaze. "You?" he said to Burnham.

Burnham put his own cards upon the table. "Your days are numbered, you bastard; I want full access to you as they draw down."

"You think to frighten me?" Morrow's tone was glacial. You, who have so much more to answer for than I do?"

"Yes, I mean to frighten you," Burnham shot back. "And I have nothing to answer for except that which might befall *you*. But that will happen on my terms, not yours."

These two want to kill each other, and one of them is going to succeed, Jonathan thought wildly. *I must do something to stop it.* "Gentlemen, you sound like a couple of bulls pawing the ground, ready to lock horns. Can we not sit down somewhere private and discuss your differences rationally? Perhaps the truth lies somewhere in between."

"There is no 'in between' when it comes to murder," Burnham snapped. "My daughter died at your hand, Morrow, and you are going to pay for it."

"You have been listening to the wrong people," Morrow countered, his voice growing more agitated. "But then, you've never been much for making the right decisions, have you? You refused to claim your daughter and then thought you could buy her affection by throwing money her way. But all you did was stoke her desire for the privileged, bourgeois life you lead. Talk about dangling a carrot in front of a hare! Her one shot at happiness would have been finding love and purpose with me, but your corruption of her ideals ran too deep. My God, what an asset to the cause she could have been if only someone hadn't taken her life. And then you made your *next* bad decision by killing Betsy Foster—"

"What? You think *I* killed that woman? I didn't even know her!" Burnham's face had turned red in disbelief.

"Of course, you didn't, but knowing her was beside the point, because it was all about revenge. But against who—Betsy, for what she did to Sybil? Or me, because I cared for Betsy? And I won't even get into the sordid mess you've made of your livelihood. I'm surprised you could even afford to bail me out! You are a pathetic bundle of bad decisions, *Lord* Burnham. You disgust me."

"Why you greasy little—" Burnham lunged toward Morrow and Jonathan stepped between them, forcing them apart. Although they'd been standing some distance from the other attendees, a few of the guests were beginning to notice their fireworks.

"Let's take this outside. Now," said Jonathan.

Burnham stepped back and straightened his jacket. "Gladly," he said before heading for the exit.

Morrow, with a glare at Jonathan, followed suit.

Jonathan smoothly reached for Cordelia's arm and leaned in to speak softly. "This could get ugly; are you sure you wouldn't rather remain inside?"

"You're doing it again, protecting me," she reminded him. "I think you all need me to keep it civil."

He nodded and by the time they turned to follow the two combatants, the men had left the building. Jonathan and Cordelia quickened their pace; once they reached the outside, Burnham and Morrow were half a block away, close to the wharf, walking quickly but closely together. Despite his now aching head, Jonathan focused through the shroud of the evening fog. The adversaries looked strange.

Cordelia picked up on it, too. "Something's not right," she said.

They drew closer and as the two men passed beneath a streetlamp, Jonathan could see that Burnham was holding a pistol to Morrow's side.

"Burnham, no!" he called out, running toward them. "That's not the way."

Burnham stopped abruptly and turned toward Jonathan. "What do you know of 'the way'?" His voice was a study in agony. "Have you ever hated so much you were willing to kill for it? Have you? It eats at you, devours everything else but your need to make it go away."

"I *have* been where you are, Burnham. And I'm still telling you, what you're doing is wrong. Let the law decide—"

"The *law*? That thing you can bend and twist until it does what you want it to?" Burnham laughed and Morrow took advantage of that moment to try and wrest the gun away from the older man. The two struggled for what seemed an eternity, locked together and turning in circles as one tried to gain the upper hand in a deadly *pas de deux*. Then two shots rang out in quick succession.

"My God!" Cordelia cried out as Burnham crumpled to the ground.

Chapter Forty-Five

A Painful Interruption

Secure in the knowledge that the boys would stay away, Dove's strategy was to meet Nora at the car barn and talk her out of her foolhardy action by playing her against her compatriots. He'd explain that Simon and Oscar had not only thrown in the towel but were ready to tell what happened on Bloody Tuesday under oath. She was an intelligent young woman with a lot to offer the world; was she willing to go down for destruction of private property, as well as assault? Faced with such a choice, she would be crazy not to cooperate.

He'd gone over his plan with Jonathan, who'd agreed with his reasoning, and with Cordelia, who hadn't.

"She's not going to bend, even to you, Dovey; she is one tough cookie."

"If all else fails, I'm bigger," he replied with a grin, but Cordie wasn't impressed.

"We'll see," she'd said.

At ten o'clock on the night of the exhibit, with carpet bag in hand, Dove made his way to the meeting point in front of the car barn. It was quiet as a churchyard. The strike between the carmen's union and United Railroads had been going on for more than two months, and fatigue had set in on both sides. The daily pickets still showed up, and streetcars were often sabotaged on the road with greased tracks or cut trees blocking their path, but by and large, everyone went to their respective corners at night. The barbed wire that had originally protected the yard and its resident scabs was nearly all gone, a simple chain link fence taking its place. As Nora predicted, even the guard shack was unoccupied. No doubt the shift started near midnight to save a little money.

There was a crescent moon, so in between the street lamps, the light was scarce. A man stood in the shadows by the gate, talking to a young kid before pointing across the street and shooing him away. As he drew closer, Dove realized it wasn't a man at all, but Nora. She was dressed in men's clothing, covered by a workman's jacket, her hair tucked under a cap. She carried what looked like a newsboy's canvas bag, probably filled with the tools with which to commit her crimes. On some level she hadn't believed he would bring what she needed.

"Where is everybody else?" he asked innocently.

"I don't know. I figured most of them would back out anyway." She pointed to his bag. "But if you've brought what I asked for, you and I can do what needs to be done."

"Here you go," he said, handing it over.

Nora opened it and looked inside. It was empty. "What is this, some kind of a joke?"

Knowing she couldn't clearly see his face, Dove used his tone of voice to convey his message. "You know it's not a joke, and neither is what you're planning." He reached out to her in the darkness. "Nora, this is wrong and, in your heart, you know it's wrong."

"I know nothing of the kind," she hissed, shrugging him off and backing away. She'd reached the dim pool of light given off by the nearest lamp and he could see her fury. "Are you playing a game with all this, or are you just a coward?"

"I am someone who knows the law and the penalty for breaking it. You stepped over the line on Bloody Tuesday when you assaulted that guard with a brick, and if you go through with what you had in mind tonight, you'll be in far worse trouble. If you just—"

"Just what?" she shot back acidly. "Stay on the sidelines? Go to meetings and listen to more theories about the ideal state of the working man? Let the men make the decisions and take the action? I don't think so." She was pacing as she vented, but abruptly stopped, apparently putting two and two together. "How stupid am I? You don't just *know* someone in the law firm—you work for them, don't you? My God, you probably work directly with that Cordelia what's her name—"

"Hammersmith," Dove said. "And yes, I do. We are trying to save the life of an innocent man, and you can help us do that."

Despite the shadows, Dove could see how disappointed she was in him. Her face was pinched with bitterness. "I told her that I wouldn't help her then, and I'm telling you the same thing now, so go to hell,

Mr. 'I just want to learn more about the revolution.' You make me sick."

Dove didn't typically cajole a perp into giving himself up; his style was to simply get the job done. But Nora was different, so he tried again. "I don't blame you for being angry," he said patiently, and I'm sorry for misleading you. But the stakes are very high here and I'm just trying to get you to see reason." He gestured to her satchel. "I can't just walk away and let you go through with it." He reached for the bag, but she deftly stepped away, pulling a knife from her pocket and brandishing it.

"But you're going to have to. Walk away, that is, unless you want to get hurt."

My God, Nora's really going for it. Dove sensed for the first time that Cordelia was right about the young woman's stubbornness. *In fact, she's gone round the bend.*

He began the process of disorienting her, talking to her in a constant patter as he slowly began to circle her, bobbing and weaving, leaning in and retreating. Nora lunged at him in turn, and it crossed his mind that anyone watching them from afar might think they were performing some strange ritual or maybe a dance of the macabre. He'd turned her around several times and at last saw her begin to falter. *That's my girl.* He stepped in to disarm her when someone shrieked from over his left shoulder. He turned to see Lucy—sweet, quiet Lucy—pointing a gun straight at him, her arm shaking, no doubt out of fear.

That wasn't the worst of it, of course.

The worst was that Nora took the opportunity to sink her knife deep into Dove's chest.

"No, no, no, no, no!" Lucy cried as Dove staggered back. "Nora, what have you done?!"

"Me? *You're* the one who's at fault. I was just getting ready to turn my weapon over when you screamed and made me stab him. Here, give me your gun before you shoot one of us by mistake."

"That would not be a good idea, Lucy," Dove said haltingly. He was having trouble breathing, but he figured if she gave all the power to Nora, breathing would be the least of his problems.

"I don't know what to do!" Lucy cried, the derringer beginning to wobble dangerously. Nora took advantage of her indecision and calmly took the weapon before dispassionately yanking the knife out of Dove's chest. She pointed the gun at Dove to forestall any heroic moves on his part, then turned back to Lucy.

"I'd leave right now if I were you, and forget you ever showed up." She gestured to Dove, who wasn't going anywhere. "Don't even bother about him. He's a traitor and deserves to bleed out. No one will know you were responsible."

Lucy's anxious gaze swiveled between Nora and Dove, who had painfully maneuvered himself onto the ground. Slowly taking off his coat, he'd pressed it against his wound. Nora had missed his heart and major arteries, but it hurt like a son of a bitch, and he could still bleed to death if he didn't get help soon.

"Can't I come with you?" Lucy begged. She sounded like a three-year-old who wanted to intrude on her parents' night out.

"No, you can't, sorry," Nora said. "You're on your own." And with those comforting words, she took off around the corner.

Lucy, still unsure of her next move, looked at Dove and wrung her hands.

"Lucy, sweetheart, are you wearing a petticoat by any chance? If you are, would you mind if I borrowed it? I need to stop myself from bleeding to death and if you help me, I'll swear you had nothing to do with any of this."

She hesitated a moment longer, then apparently decided to err on the side of saving another human being. "Yes. Oh, my goodness, yes." She quickly divested herself of her undergarment and kneeled down to help him, even taking the initiative of ripping it so that he could use it as a makeshift bandage.

"That's good thinking," Dove managed. Sensing he was going to faint fairly soon, he touched Lucy's arm and explained how she needed to find a policeman or ambulance or someone who could get the help he needed as soon as possible. "I need you to save my life, Lucy," he said. "And I know you have the courage to do it."

"But what about you? I can't leave you."

"You can and you must. I need help and you're the only one who can get it for me. I'm counting on you."

She looked at him for an excruciatingly long moment (for him, at least) and then nodded. "All right, but promise you'll stay alive until I get back," she cried.

"I promise," he said, and she took off. "Just don't let me down, sweetheart," he muttered, and fought to keep his eyes from rolling back into his head.

Chapter Forty-Six

A Deadly Struggle

Free of Burnham at last, Morrow scrambled to his feet and backed away. "I swear, I didn't pull the trigger. I didn't pull it. You saw what happened. He tried to kill me. It was self-defense. You saw what happened."

"Yes, we saw everything. You need to calm down now," Cordelia told him in a voice no doubt intended to have a soothing effect but falling short because she was shaking all over. Burnham was still alive but bleeding heavily. The pistol, a British Bulldog, lay on the ground where it had dropped.

Jonathan slipped it into his pocket and lifted Burnham's head onto his lap, taking his own coat and putting it around the baron who was obviously going into shock. It was cold and damp by the dock.

"I'm sorry—I don't have a slip I can take off to staunch the bleeding," she said. "My shawl, maybe, but—"

"Morrow, take off your shirt. We need it," Jonathan ordered.

No doubt in shock himself, Morrow did as he was told for once, putting his jacket back on over his bare chest. "You saw what happened," he repeated. "You saw what happened."

"Alex, I want you and Cordelia to go back into the warehouse and alert the professor or better yet, someone who doesn't have their head up their arse, to call an ambulance." He looked up at Cordelia. "See that he doesn't run, all right?"

She nodded and turned to Morrow. "Come with me to get help or you'll be charged with a lot more than just leaving the scene of a crime."

They took off and Jonathan looked down at Burnham, who was gazing at him with rheumy eyes that knew the end was near. "He was right—I should have loved her more," he rasped. "I should have told her what she meant to me."

"Listen to me, George. I meant to tell you. I was able to visit the place where Sybil was living and you know what I found? The locket.

You know the one you bought her when she was fifteen, the one you said she didn't like? Well, she did like it, because she kept it all these years. Took it with her wherever she went. She loved you in her own way; you can feel good about that."

"Really?" he said, lightly touching Jonathan's arm. "You aren't just humoring an old man, are you, old man?" He smiled feebly at his joke.

"No, I'm being completely honest. I will show it to you, but you must get better for me to do that. You understand?"

Burnham nodded and closed his eyes. His chest hardly moved, and Jonathan knew from experience that this stage did not last long if something wasn't done to stabilize him.

Save for the water gently lapping at the pier, it was eerily quiet in those few moments alone on the wharf. The only human sound was Burnham's faint and labored breathing. Jonathan looked down the street toward the warehouse and sighed with relief as he saw Cordelia and Morrow returning.

However, about halfway down the street a young boy—at least that's what he seemed to be—stopped Cordelia. He looked vaguely familiar. She pointed at Jonathan as if to say she didn't have time, but the boy must have caught her attention because she paused long enough to listen.

As he watched them, the flickering sparks began anew in Jonathan's head, and the flashing images grew sharper. Usually, the *cadou* petered out once the event had happened; this was new.

Cordelia hurried up to him. "An ambulance should be here any minute," she said. "How's he doing?"

"He's alive, but by a thread. What did that boy want?"

Cordelia took a deep breath. "Please listen before you react. He had a message from Nora, of all people, telling me that Dove has been hurt at the car barn and that I need to come right away, that he's calling for me."

"My God, what happened to him?"

"I don't know, but it sounds bad. The kid said Nora was frantic and kept telling him there was no time to waste."

The sparks in Jonathan's head were exploding now, and the images, which he had originally assumed were two men, assumed a slightly different shape. One seemed to be a man, in workmen's clothing, and the other, in pale green—*Oh my God.*

"Cordelia, you have to wait and let me go with you. Trust me on this. As soon as the ambulance gets here, we'll head right over, I promise."

"No," she said firmly, standing up now. "I know you want to protect me, and I appreciate it, I really do, but you can't keep doing this. You don't own me. Follow me if you can, when you can, but I have to go *now*."

The *cadou* was in full force now, the images flickering and melding together to show the two he'd assumed were men were really Nora and Cordelia, locked in a battle of some sort, perhaps physical—he couldn't tell. Nor could he describe to Cordelia what was going on—she'd think he was a complete nutter. He rubbed his temples to calm the turbulence inside his brain.

Desperate to stop her, he called out, "What if your position depended on you staying here?"

"Then I quit," she called back, and took off.

Cordelia must have put the fear of God into the self-proclaimed atheist Alex Morrow because he dutifully followed her back to where Jonathan sat with Burnham.

"He's not going to make it," Morrow said.

"You don't know that," Jonathan snapped. He checked his watch; it was just past ten thirty. He should be with Cordelia, not here, but there was nothing at the moment he could do about it except request some help from a God he didn't know very well. He certainly couldn't leave Burnham alone with Morrow, and none of the "concerned captains of industry" had bothered to come out and offer to help.

His mind kept returning to the young messenger. Where had he seen him? It took several moments, but he finally hit upon it. "Did you see the boy talking to Cordelia?"

"Yes. Why?"

"What color hair did he have?"

"Bright red, like a flame," he said. "Fate won't smile on him. He won't have access to women like you or me. He—"

"Good God, man, will you shut up? I think I know who killed Betsy Foster and bashed my head ... and she may very well have killed Sybil, too."

Morrow studied him for the longest moment and Jonathan had the eerie sensation of gazing into a mirror, where puzzlement morphed into a horrified awareness. "It can't be," Morrow said, swallowing. "Nora wouldn't ..." His voice trailed off.

"She would, and she did. I'm sure of it." He frowned at the agitator. "And you are, too."

Morrow shook his head, admonishing himself. "Why didn't I see it earlier? I should have seen it." The self-possessed Alexei Morozov was gone; in his place was a man now unsure of the game he was playing—a man no longer in control.

Jonathan had no time to pull out whatever truth might be in him. "If the ambulance doesn't come in the next minute, we are headed to Turk Street anyway. Cordelia may have walked right into a trap."

"I'm not going."

"You bloody well are. I need you to talk to your acolyte and get her to change course."

"It's too late. You know it's too late. You have the *cadou*. You see what's happening."

"Damn you, it is not too late!" Jonathan grabbed Morrow by his lapels. "If you want me to defend you against the murder of Betsy Foster—if you want to keep your *teeth*, then you'll do as I say."

Sirens announced the arrival of the ambulance. Jonathan looked down to give Burnham the news, but it was too late. The baron was dead.

Jonathan helped lay his body in the wagon and once again checked his pocket watch. Cordelia had a twelve-minute start on them.

It was time to move.

Chapter Forty-Seven

Admission

Cordelia arrived at the car barn a little before eleven, but it was dark and desolate. Where was the night watchman? And where, for that matter, was Nora? She'd expected to see an ambulance at least, loading Dove. Maybe he was already on his way to a hospital. Oh, she could strangle him for not wanting back-up and thinking he could handle Nora on his own!

"You won't find your precious David." Cordelia turned to see Nora, dressed as a man, wearing a workman's coat and a tattered hat. But the most disturbing aspect of her attire was the small gun she held, pointed at Cordelia and ready to shoot.

Stay calm. Be reasoned. She ignored Nora's weapon. "So, where is he? The boy said he'd been hurt, that he was calling for me. You were frantic about it, the boy said."

Nora walked closer. "Oh, I was frantic, all right. After I stabbed him, I left him to bleed out, but he had some unexpected help. A policeman came by and picked him up a short while ago. God knows where he is right now. Maybe he didn't make it in time. Maybe the traitor is dead."

Cordelia had grown cold inside, which had nothing to do with the temperature of the night. This young woman was insane. "Why did you ask me to come here, then?"

Nora gestured around the empty yard. "As you can see, all my so-called comrades have deserted me, and I need some help of my own."

"To do what?"

"Why, I'm going to make a statement. Or, rather *we're* going to make a statement. We're going to completely trash the streetcars involved in this wretched strike, and you're going to die a martyr to the cause."

"Me? Why me? What have *I* done?"

"You're the perfect story for the *Bulletin* or the *Call*. Even the *Chronicle*. They'll all pick it up: 'Lady Lawyer Representing Union

Killer has Change of Heart—Destroys Symbols of Worker Oppression but Killed in the Process.' Can't you just see it?" Nora's expression abruptly changed. She was all business now. "Inside. Let's go."

She marched Cordelia into the cavernous barn itself, lit only by an anemic kerosene lamp. The cars, perhaps twenty of them, were parked end to end, reaching back into the darkness, resting after being driven hard by Farleymen who didn't know what they were doing. Many of the cars' windows were broken or completely punched out—the result, no doubt, of countless rocks and bricks thrown in anger at the scab drivers and disloyal passengers. Which car would be the next to run over a child or throw its passengers into the street?

Nora motioned for Cordelia to enter the first car. "We'll start here."

I have to keep her talking, If she's talking, she's not destroying. "Nora, do you know who killed Lena Mendelssohn?"

Nora looked at her in disbelief. "Have you still not figured it out?"

"No. I haven't. None of us have. Why don't you tell me? All this time I've thought it was Alex Morrow, but he has denied it. Repeatedly. Vehemently. And it occurs to me, based on what's happened here tonight, that, well, maybe we've been looking at the wrong people throughout this ordeal. Tell me. I'd really like to know … was it you?"

Nora tapped the side of her head. "Never let it be said that a woman can't reason her way out of a paper bag as well as any man."

"What about Betsy Foster?"

"What about her?"

"Did you eliminate her, too?"

"I like the word 'elimination.' It sounds practical. Professional. Yes, you can say that I eliminated her."

Nora was walking up and down the narrow aisle of the car, waving the gun—a derringer, by the looks of it—as she spoke. She was strangely animated, as if her nerves were losing their tether. Maybe her mind was reacting to the stress she was obviously under. She seemed to be entering a world apart from the one she was living in, which was not a good thing when she carried a loaded gun. But

Cordelia needed time. Time to think of something. Time for Jonathan to get there. *Keep her talking.*

"Why did you kill them?" she asked. "When you found out that Alex was ... interested in women as well as men, were you jealous of them? Did you want Alex Morrow for yourself?"

Nora's face was cast in shadow but the disdain in her voice was clear. "Of course, that's what you and every other bourgeois would think—that I carried a torch for him. I couldn't care less about who he diddles. Don't you see? It's so much more than that. From the moment I discovered his real name, I knew he embodied the essence of our movement. Alexei Morozov comes from the homeland of the revolution. He learned at the knee of Trotsky, for God's sake! He was on the front lines in Moscow just two short years ago. He—"

"Wait – I thought that uprising failed."

"You are misinformed. It did not fail, it was merely the Great Rehearsal. Lexi was born to lead us, to form us into a highly effective revolutionary force." She looked dismissively at the firearm she was carrying. "Not with guns, although those may be needed later."

"With what, then?"

"With words and images that grip the people, showing them the evils of our current society and convincing them to join our fight. Lexi was a man of both words and action—what he did on Bloody Tuesday proved that. To actually kill someone in order to rally public support in our favor is true dedication, don't you think?"

"But he had a personal reason for killing Jimmy Walsh."

"What do you mean?"

"I mean your sainted revolutionary lusted after Betsy Foster and Jimmy Walsh was her cousin. He knew Lexi was no good."

Nora brandished the pistol, her voice unsteady. "You're lying. You're just trying to turn us against each other. The truth is, we had momentum, until ..."

"...until Lena showed up?"

"Yes. Lexi's connection to her was strong. Too strong. It had to be severed."

"And Betsy?"

"She was nothing. I don't know why he even bothered with her. I tried to be clever and pin Lena's murder on her – they were roommates, after all. But the police were too stupid, and I realized she had to go, too. They were both distractions to our mission."

"And yet you were fine with him being arrested for Betsy's murder— a murder that you committed. That doesn't seem very loyal to me."

"But it was a perfect misdirection, don't you see?" Nora shrugged. "They had no evidence to speak of; he would have been released eventually."

"And then you would have had him all to yourself, which is what you wanted."

Nora's eyes blazed. "I wanted him for the revolution!" she screamed.

Jonathan and Morrow caught the first hansom cab they could find and, thanks to the promise of a hefty tip, Jonathan convinced the driver to fly down Market to Turk Street as if his life depended on it … because the *cadou* had told him Cordelia's life might very well hang in the balance. If the cabbie maintained his current pace, they'd reach the car barn within fifteen minutes; Jonathan could only hope Cordelia had found a slow horse.

As he silently urged the driver on, he felt the baron's revolver in his pocket and pulled it out.

"What are you doing with that?" Morrow sounded anxious.

"I'm going to empty it. It's done enough damage for one night, wouldn't you say?"

The Bulldog's cylinder carried five rounds. He took out four cartridges—apparently Burnham had been spoiling for a fight.

But something stuck with him. "Wait … how many shots did you hear when the gun went off?"

"Two," Alex said immediately. "I wondered how he could fire off two shots so quickly when we were both grappling with it."

"I heard two, also." He showed Morrow the four remaining cartridges. "Then how can this be?"

"An echo, perhaps?"

No, that was no echo. Then what was it? What had his vision left out?

The *cadou*. He remembered Morrow's words—he'd known what Jonathan was going through. "How did you learn about my supposed 'gift'?"

Morrow had been looking out the cab's window but turned at the question. "I've only rarely considered it an advantage. What about you?"

"Wait. Are you saying you also have it?"

The young man gazed at him. "How do you suppose I knew what was in the letter from the investigators you hired?"

"How do you—" The flicker of light and the humming inside his head were stronger than ever before. The sense of "pre-knowing" overtook him, the images piling one on top of the other—Cordelia and Nora and Morrow and ... and someone else. Had to be Burnham. God, he was losing perspective. Morrow was trying to distract him. "You're lying," he said coldly.

"Am I, *frate*? I told you we were linked. I've been looking for her, too."

Jonathan's retort was interrupted by the cabbie calling down to them. "There's yer car barn across the street. Ya wanna get off here or have me turn around?"

"Here is fine." Jonathan hopped down and quickly paid the man. He and Morrow ran across to find the stygian car yard completely deserted.

Morrow started to talk, but Jonathan signaled for him to stop. In the silence he could barely make out the sound of voices coming from inside the barn itself. The door was slightly ajar, and a weak light shone through. *Thank God I'm not too late; keep her talking, Cordelia.*

"Do precisely what I tell you to do," he instructed Morrow. "Wait just inside the door while I assess the situation. Do not leave, or I swear I will hunt you down myself."

Morrow nodded and they slipped inside. Jonathan spied Cordelia sitting in the first car while Nora paced back and forth in front of her, waving a small gun.

Nora sounded like she was rambling. Jonathan couldn't risk taking her out while she was moving, so he called out from the shadows. "Nora, it's Jonathan Perris. It's time to give it up. No good is going to come of this."

Nora stopped immediately and grabbed Cordelia's arm, pulling her in front and pointing the gun at her head. Because of Cordelia's small stature, there was a small area of Nora's shoulder left exposed. Perhaps it would be enough. It had better be enough.

Nora peered into the darkness. "Show yourself or I swear I'll put a hole in your pretty attorney's head."

Never, in all the terrifying moments that had made up his younger life, had Jonathan ever felt as shaken as he did now. Before, his powers of calculated reasoning had prevailed, enabling him to tamp down his fears and solve the problem at hand. But now, another person's life was at stake, and not just anyone's —Cordelia's.

He stepped into the dim light, hands raised. "You can see me now," he said. "Please, put down your gun and let's talk about this."

Nora's voice echoed in the gloom of the cavernous barn. "I'm not sure what you want to talk about. I've already explained why I had to get rid of the women, and how I'm going to get rid of this one. You understand the cause is greater than any of us, don't you? The revolution must take place. It must—"

"You are a disgrace to the revolution!" Alex yelled from the darkness.

Nora turned at the sound, giving Jonathan the seconds he needed to reach into his boot and pull out his knife. *Don't move, Cordelia. Please don't move.*

And he sent the blade sailing through the air.

Chapter Forty-Eight

The Reckoning

My God, how did he do that? Cordelia thought with a raging mixture of shock and relief. She wanted to run to Jonathan, but it was not the time or place.

"This isn't the end of it, you know," Nora said moments later as Cordelia wrapped her wounded shoulder with strips from Nora's own work shirt. Jonathan's blade had rendered her gun hand useless, and Cordelia had quickly grabbed the derringer as it fell.

Her energy slipping away in the aftermath of the struggle, Cordelia had very little patience for the deranged young woman. "Really," she replied drily. "You admitted to killing two young women in cold blood, you stabbed a third person, and you were about to cause thousands of dollars' worth of damage to a barn full of streetcars." They began walking out of the barn to wait for the police. "What do you think is going to happen to you?"

Nora nonchalantly lifted her good shoulder. "I imagine my parents will hire a very good lawyer who will say that I accidentally stabbed your rat of an investigator—who was holding up fine when the ambulance came for him, by the way—and that there's no direct evidence linking me to the murders of the two women. He'll paint me as a poor, misunderstood young woman who didn't know what she was saying when she confessed to the crimes. Eventually my father will bribe the judge, who will give me a few years in a women's prison or better yet, an asylum, where I'll convert as many fellow inmates as I can to the revolution. I'll continue to do my part."

Jonathan, who had gently removed the knife from Nora's shoulder, wiped it off before replacing it in his boot. "Are you all right?" he murmured to Cordelia. At her nod, he turned to the young revolutionary. "I'm glad you've outlined your defense. I will personally see to it that the authorities are aware of your plan to circumvent the justice system through feigned insanity."

Morrow had been pacing angrily outside but now walked up, furious with his disciple. He stopped to confront her. "You are no better than the bourgeois class you intend to hide behind. How dare you kill two women I cared for and blame it on the revolution! I hope you decay in a prison cell, or better yet, swing from the gallows for what you did."

"As if you have any room to talk," Nora scoffed. "You murdered an innocent man for the cause—but not really. The truth is you didn't like him. And you sat back while another innocent stooge went to prison for it."

Morrow smiled. "I have two words for you: Prove—"

In the next second a shot rang out from a roof top and tore a hole in the top of Alex Morrow's head, killing him instantly.

"Get down, get down!" Jonathan yelled, pushing both women to the ground and covering them as well as he could. Cordelia landed on her back and looked up into the night sky. By the light of a quarter moon, she could just see the silhouette of a man on a roof, lowering what she knew was his father's Winchester.

"Don't do it!" she cried, but it was too late. Emmett Barnes had taken his pistol—the one his bosses wouldn't let him bring to his job because it might be too dangerous—and emptied a single bullet into his own tormented skull.

Chapter Forty-Nine

Recompense and Recuperation

What Emmett hadn't considered when he took matters into his own hands was the loss of *him*. That is what caused his mother and siblings almost unbearable pain.

But sorrow doesn't help pay the bills and on top of their misfortune they were liable for the full one-hundred dollar bail amount, since technically, Emmett hadn't shown up for his appeal. Suicide makes it difficult to keep appointments.

Cordelia had known grief and disappointment and the pressure of having to make ends meet even when the only step that seemed worth taking was curling up into a ball and finding oblivion through sleep. She felt responsible for what the Barnes family was now going through and was determined to at least lessen their financial burden by paying off the bail they'd posted. The money represented most of her savings, but that was nothing—at least she still had her job. During her visit she hoped to pay her respects as well as the debt.

"Hello, Mrs. Barnes," Cordelia said when the older woman answered the door. Looking frail and dressed in black crepe, she matched the limp black ribbon attached haphazardly to the faded door frame.

"Yes?" Mrs. Barnes's tone was flat, which didn't bode well.

"May I come in? I have an update for you as well as something I think will help you and your family."

Mrs. Barnes said nothing, but stepped aside and opened the door wider so that Cordelia could enter. The parlor seemed even smaller and more threadbare than the first time she'd been there. The one mirror in the room was covered in crepe as well. Melancholy had moved in.

"I take it your other sons are working?" Cordelia asked.

The woman shrugged. "Gotta keep movin' forward, no matter what."

"Yes, I totally understand. I wanted to let you know how sorry I am for how things turned out. If it's any consolation, the conviction of Emmett for the murder of Jim Walsh has been overturned. An eyewitness stepped forward and confirmed that Emmett had been unconscious during the period when another man took up his rifle and shot Mr. Walsh. Emmett was not guilty of that crime, and the record now reflects that."

"Well, he was guilty of something else," she said acerbically.

"I know. He should not have done what he did. But in his mind, he was avenging the woman he loved, and that, while misplaced, was understandable, if not admirable."

Mrs. Barnes shook her head. "It ain't never admirable to take another person's life, no matter what they done, except in war, and even that's questionable."

The woman took no pleasure in platitudes; she faced the truth without flinching. What strength she possessed! "I also came to give you something." Cordelia pulled an envelope out of her purse and handed it over. "Here is money to pay off the bail you owe. At least that will be one less thing to worry about."

The woman looked puzzled and didn't take what was offered. "It's already been paid," she said.

Cordelia frowned. "By whom?"

"By that Englishman, that Mr. Perris. Ain't he your boss? Well, he came by and gave us the money yesterday. He also let us know all the work you did for Emmett was something called "pro bono," whatever that is, so we don't have to pay that back, neither."

"Ah, I see. We ... must have gotten our signals crossed."

"Must have," she said. "Well, I've got mendin' to do, so if it's all the same to you ..."

"Yes ... yes, certainly. I'll say goodbye, then. And once again, I am so sorry for what happened."

As Cordelia turned to leave, Mrs. Barnes touched her arm. "Listen, ma'am," she said, her voice softening just a little. "I can tell you feel guilty for helping get Emmett out of jail. You think if you'd kept him behind bars, things wouldn't have turned out the way they did. Maybe that's true, maybe not. But you got no power to divine that. Only God does. You did what you thought was best for Emmett and for that you ought to be proud. He's the one who listened to the Devil and did the Devil's work, not you. So don't waste your time fretting about us. We'll be fine. You just keep on going, helping those you think you can help. And the Good Lord will see what's in your heart."

As she walked back to the street corner to catch a cab (she wouldn't be taking a streetcar anytime soon), Cordelia tried hard to keep her tears from flowing. They wouldn't obey, so she rustled around in her reticule to find a handkerchief. Emmett Barnes's mother was far wiser than her appearance and manner would suggest.

Like most single people in the Golden City, Dove lived in a boarding house and his landlady wasn't equipped to care for him. Fortunately, Jonathan's flat off Alamo Square had three bedrooms plus a servant's quarters, so he insisted that Dove convalesce there. Jonathan's housekeeper Vesta agreed to come in every day to look after Dove while his body healed. A middle-aged Samoan of ample proportions, she was strong enough to bathe and dress him, as well as tend to his wound.

"And don't you worry none, Mister Perris, if he gets outta line, I'll knock him upside the head."

Jonathan grinned at that one. "You have my permission to do whatever is necessary to ensure Mr. Rebane's complete cooperation." Dove, he noticed, looked a wee bit fearful.

Now, however, the entire staff of Jonathan Perris and Associates was gathered around Dove's bed to wish him well.

"I can't believe that young woman was so vicious," Oliver Bean said. "She was willing to commit virtually any crime without batting an eyelash."

Jonathan offered a possible rationale. "One might say she embodies the saying 'The end justifies the means.' She so fervently believed in her ideals that it seems there was no line she wouldn't cross."

"I should have picked up on it earlier," Dove lamented. If I'd been paying better attention, maybe we could have avoided the whole nasty mess."

"I doubt it," Cordelia said. "You weren't going to stop her; she was on a mission."

"How did she find out about Alex Marlow's philandering with the opposite sex, I'd like to know," Althea pondered. "There's a lesson in there for young men who get the wandering eye." She made eye contact with the three single men in the room.

Dove responded with the look of a fallen angel. "I have no idea what you're talking about."

"You tell 'em, Althea," said Cordelia. "Look, that girl was clever. She had her parents wrapped around her finger and the freedom to go wherever she pleased. She was just on the wrong path. My guess is she was so enamored of Alex Morrow as a revolutionary leader that she stalked him and discovered his various 'appetites,' shall we say."

"I'd agree," Jonathan said, "much like George Burnham and Emmett Barnes stalked him, but for very different reasons."

"What will happen with Nora's case, do you think, Jonathan?" This from Dove, whom Jonathan knew had enjoyed and appreciated the spirited young woman.

"I've heard her father has retained a top-notch lawyer to represent her…"

"…exactly as she predicted," Cordelia added. "I hope she's wrong about the rest of it, but I'm not going to hold my breath. At least she and the rest of the incendiaries are alive, well, except for Alex Morrow. That poor fellow traveled halfway around the world to promote his ideology and died for his efforts."

"I don't know if anyone here knows about karma," Oliver said, "but I have made a study of it, and I believe Alex Morrow is a perfect example of it."

"What's karma?" Althea asked.

"It's complicated," Dove said, "but suffice to say, 'What goes around comes around.' In Alex Morrow's case, the bad energy he spread amongst so many people came back to bite him in the end."

Jonathan glanced at Cordelia but said nothing.

"I suppose I should pray for that man's soul, but I really care more about poor Emmett Barnes," Althea said. "He didn't deserve what happened to him—not one bit."

Sensing that Cordelia was going to ask some difficult questions, Jonathan preempted her. "It seems like I'm always thanking you all for getting me out of trouble, but I must thank you again for sticking by me when I wasn't as straightforward with you as I should have been throughout this ordeal."

"Oh, Mr. P., no need to—"

"No, no, Althea, hear me out, please. The truth is, I didn't want the story about Miss West, whom I knew as Lena Mendelssohn, to become widespread." He paused, taking a fortifying breath. "My brother, you see, is the Duke of Strickland. Such titles mean nothing here, which delights me, but in England the peerage is quite political and extremely powerful. It turns out Sybil West was my brother's mistress."

Noting the shocked looks on everyone's faces, he quickly added, "Not while she and I were together, mind you. My brother and I are not close, and I knew nothing of his personal life. Apparently, he had broken it off with her and she'd come here specifically to seek revenge for his callous treatment. I was the pawn in that particular scheme and the story would have been rich fodder for the newspapers both here and abroad."

"We would have kept it under our hats," Althea said confidently.

Jonathan reached over to touch her hand. "I believe you, but the police would not have, and therein lay the problem."

"What role did George Burnham play in all this?" Cordelia asked. "He seemed ready to shout the story from the rooftops."

"He was Sybil's natural father and threatened to expose all if I didn't use my influence to save his insurance company, which is faltering under the payouts from last year's fire."

"Land sakes, he'd betray his own daughter? What kind of self-respecting man would do that?" Althea looked disgusted.

"None that you would associate with, I hope. Needless to say, I refused to do his bidding. I'm not sure Burnham would have gone through with it, but Sybil was killed before he had to make that decision. Investigating Sybil West instead of the fictional Lena Mendelssohn would have eventually led to the whole sordid tale coming out. I simply did not want to put my family, nor you, nor, if I'm honest, myself through the meat grinder that is the popular press. The public is hardly qualified to criticize the misadventures of others."

"Let he who is without sin…" Oliver intoned.

"Leave the rest of us alone so we can party," Dove finished. He turned to Althea. "Did I hear you've brought a bundt cake to help celebrate my incarceration—er, my convalescence?"

"Indeed, I have. It's got a special rum frosting to mark the occasion. And what's more important, I brought beer."

"Bundt cake and beer—the quickest way to a man's heart," Dove announced.

And the party began.

Chapter Fifty

A Matter of Trust

The tombstone was simple. It read:

> *Here lies Lord George Burnham,*
> *a baron of England,*
> *successful businessman and loyal*
> *subject of*
> *His Majesty King Edward VII*
> *along with his beloved daughter Sybil*
> *Now an eternal family*

"Why didn't you put in the dates of their births and deaths?" Cordelia asked. She had accompanied Jonathan to the quaint cemetery high on a hill overlooking San Francisco Bay. It was a bucolic setting, close to the city, but far enough away to leave the chaos behind. Since Burnham had no immediate family to claim his or Sybil's remains, Jonathan had paid to have them interred together and made sure Sybil was wearing her father's necklace when they closed her coffin. The place reminded him in a small way of coastal England, which he thought Burnham would have liked. He'd bought a large bouquet of vibrantly colored flowers, including poppies, roses and lilacs, to lay upon the grave.

"I thought it might spur too many curious types to look into his and Sybil's story. I sense he would have wanted his English bonafides made known, as well as his true relation to Sybil. That's all anybody else needs to know, don't you think?"

"You are very careful about information others need to know," she said.

He saw a bench nearby and motioned her to sit next to him. Of all his staff, she was the one whom he felt should have a deeper explanation, if only because she would continue to dig for one. "I meant what I said the other day. I truly appreciate how everyone, especially you, gave me the benefit of the doubt, even when you didn't have all the facts at hand."

Surprisingly, Cordelia's censure was mild. "I sensed from the beginning that you weren't telling us the whole story; I just wondered why you didn't confide in us."

He nodded. "We work in a profession in which both the suppression and dissemination of information is crucial. I don't take either of those steps lightly. On top of that, I have a terribly complicated background, which at times I can't even bear to think about, much less share with others."

"But we are a team, as you've pointed out to me more than once," she countered. "Why not fill us in so we can have a clearer picture of what the issues are, of what we're dealing with?"

"You're right, of course. Old habits die hard. And frankly, it wasn't so much to keep you in the dark as to keep you and others from getting too close to trouble and the possibility of getting hurt. I didn't know who my enemies were and that makes it difficult to protect you against them."

Setting her jaw, Cordelia turned to him. "When are you going to learn that protection is a two-way street? There will be times—my goodness, there already *have* been times—when you need protection, too. We can't operate at our best around each other without trust."

Jonathan leaned forward and clasped his hands. It was difficult to even look at her. "I am not a very good student of 'trust,' I'm afraid. It may take me a while to learn it."

Cordelia took a breath as she looked out over the bay. He followed her gaze. The day was crisp, but sunny, and the sky was a crystalline blue, plumped up with cotton-candy clouds. It was the kind of day that made one look around and give thanks for the beauty of the natural world. Being in a cemetery added a poignant quality to that gratitude. He gestured to their surroundings. "A reminder that we are all mortal, is it not?" he mused. "We should make the most of the time we have."

"I agree and having people you can count on adds immeasurably to it." She turned back to him. "I don't believe I thanked you for coming to my rescue that night. I'm sorry I didn't listen to you when you told me to wait, but I had to go. You know that." She placed her hand on her heart. "But in here, I knew that I could count on you—that if you could possibly make it in time, you would. And you did." Taking a breath, she continued, "I hope you know you can count on me ... even as it pertains to information you are still reluctant to share."

Jonathan frowned. "To what are you referring?"

"It's 'to whom.' The other day at Dove's party you failed to explain Alex Morrow. Ever since his death, in fact, you haven't said his name once. Why is that?"

"You, Miss Hammersmith, are at times too perceptive for your own good," Jonathan said with a half-smile. "I haven't mentioned Mr. Morrow because I haven't yet figured out all the ways he impacted this tragedy. When I do, I promise you shall be the first to know."

She looked at him with those luminous dark eyes. "It's Cordelia, and I will hold you to it."

"You mean you've decided not to quit after all?" He grinned as he said it, but her smile was more deliberate.

"Not yet."

"Duly noted," he said, an unfamiliar feeling he could only describe as joy spreading through him. "I'm fortunate to have you in my corner."

That night, sustained with a glass of whiskey, Jonathan relaxed before the fire, a letter in hand from the ex-prostitute Francine. She was doing well with her treatment and had begun to train as a midwife, of all things. "Thank you, Mr. Perris, for giving me a second chance at life," she'd said. "I'm forever grateful."

He laid the letter aside and contemplated the harrowing events he'd just lived through. He had much to be grateful for as well: his freedom, for one thing ... a thriving practice, a warm, comfortable home, more than enough food to eat. He employed a team of professionals whom he felt he could also classify as friends—perhaps one day (although the concept was still difficult to embrace) *trusted* friends.

But a major stumbling block remained.

Jonathan hadn't mentioned Alex Morrow at Dove's gathering for one cowardly reason: he feared the *cadou* would return. He'd seen multiple visions the night at the car barn, but the connection he'd felt with the murderous agitator had been the most intense of all. Needing to learn more, he'd used the vague term "distant relation" with the police to secure Morrow's personal effects; from those he'd discovered that the man had rented a room on Fillmore. The place happened to be a short walk from Jonathan's own flat, and he'd paid an additional month's rent on it just so he could take his time going through what Morrow had left behind. *He could have broken in here at any time*, he rationalized. *Surely that's how he knew about the letter regarding the search for my mother.* Even as he said it, he knew it wasn't true.

Jonathan needed time and the right mindset to apply the logic that had served him so well for so long; he couldn't afford to be muddled by his unwanted inheritance.

"We are linked," Morrow had said.

Frate. In his mother's tongue, it meant "brother."

He swallowed the rest of his drink. "Why didn't you tell me, Esmé?" he said aloud, bitterness infusing his words. "You sent me a half-brother but now he's dead." And he threw his empty glass across the darkened room.

Historical Note

Corruption at all levels of government is nothing new. San Francisco suffered mightily from it as far back as its gold-fueled expansion in the latter nineteenth century. Case in point: the city's grandiose City Hall, which opened in 1899 as a symbol of the city's 'Paris of the West" status, took twenty-seven years to construct and ran more than 400% over budget. It was so shoddily built that its impressive dome—not to mention the rest of the structure—collapsed during the 1906 earthquake and had to be completely demolished. It was only seven years old.

So, it's no wonder that the city's administration, including its board of supervisors, fell prey to corruption charges during San Francisco's reconstruction. As depicted in *The Twisted Road*, the streetcar strike that began with the "Bloody Tuesday" riot of May 7, 1907, was rooted in large-scale bribery and extortion. Over the course of the conflict, thirty-one innocent lives were lost through shootings and streetcar accidents (twenty-five of which were passengers). More than a thousand additional passengers were injured. James Walsh was indeed a victim, although his murder is pure fiction on my part. The strike dragged on until November, when the workers finally capitulated. The Carmen's Union Local 25 was dissolved in February 1908.

The Twisted Road takes place during what is called the Progressive Era in the United States (1896-1917). As industrialization swept the country, so did corruption (as we've seen) and a widening disparity between rich and poor. Political and social activists rose up to counter unfettered capitalism; many of them offered socialism, with its belief in equality of outcome, as the cure.

Some things never change.

Thank You!

Thank you so much for reading **The Twisted Road**!

Readers like you are powerful, and you would be doing me a great favor by posting an objective review on Amazon, Goodreads, or other platforms based on the e-reader you use. In today's publishing world, those reviews are "golden" to authors like me.

Sharing your thoughts with others (including me!) on social media would be wonderful as well. You'll find me on X (Twitter), Facebook, and Pinterest.

Please don't forget to stop by my website (abmichaels.com) to learn more about my work, including short stories and other bonus material.

If you haven't done so already, I'd love to have you sign up for my mailing list so you can receive periodic updates. As a thank you, I'll send you a free eCopy of my novella *Affair at the Majestic*, in which attorney Jonathan Perris and company defends a sultry young woman accused of adultery despite a mountain of evidence against her. The story serves as a bridge between "The Golden City" historical series and my newest series "Barrister Perris."

Click HERE to join and get your free eBook.

Keep reading for a preview of *The Art of Love*, Book One in "The Golden City" historical fiction series.

Bonus Material

Here's a preview of *The Art of Love* (Book One of **"The Golden City"** historical fiction series):

CHAPTER ONE
May 1896
The Klondike

"Finally," August Wolff muttered as he heard the first groan of breaking ice along the Fortymile's frozen bed. The sun had worked hard that day. Now, in the late afternoon, the sharp blue of the sky was giving way to a muddy dusk and the cold was once again seeping through his worn leather gloves and flannel shirt. But change was coming and he welcomed it.

He walked by Shorty Calhoun's stake; the old prospector was half-heartedly sifting through his tailing pile.

"Won't be long now," Gus remarked.

"Yessir," Shorty said. "Cain't come too soon for these old bones." The old man grinned, his remaining teeth yellowed by the tobacco chew he habitually stored in the pouch of his cheek. He spat on the ground. "How's your take? Hit pay dirt?"

Gus gave his standard reply to the daily question. "Not yet. You'll be the first to know."

Shorty completed the verbal ritual. "Same goes." He turned to the rucksack lying next to him. "Listen now, I made somethin' for the young'un." He pulled out a burlap bag and handed it to Gus. "Her first birthday and all."

"Thank you kindly," Gus said, taking the bag. He hefted it. "Feels heavy."

"Just some painted blocks is all." Shorty went back to his sifting. "You best get back to your pretty little family. They'll be waitin' on you."

The Golden City

Gus nodded and continued on toward the camp, slinging the bag over one shoulder and his shovel over the other. Shorty was like so many miners he'd met over the past few years: kept to himself most of the time, but had a soft spot a mile wide. Gus had invited the old man to dinner a time or two, but Mattie'd felt uncomfortable around him, so he'd stopped. Maybe she'd change her tune about Shorty once she saw the gift he'd made for little Annabelle.

He trudged up the last hill to the main section of Forty Mile, the mining town where he, Mattie, and Annabelle lived. With the beginning of the spring thaw, the streets, if you could call them that, had turned to a murky, grayish-brown slush. Raised wooden sidewalks fronted the trading posts and saloons, but you were on your own once you crossed to the other side. Mattie complained almost daily about her perpetually dirty hems; back in Seattle she'd been a seamstress, so it made sense she'd worry about such things.

Still, the town wasn't so bad. Porter Wilson had sold Gus his claim on a little crick upriver and opened a restaurant just last fall. Hell, there was even an opera house, though the season only ran from June through August.

Gus stopped in Fannie Beringer's general store to pick up the porcelain doll with blonde ringlets he'd put a deposit on the week before. "You're in luck," Fannie had told him. "Just got this in from Billy Fortuna. His little gal told him to sell it so he could get a new pickax. Ain't that sweet?"

Now, Gus pulled out his pouch and measured out the gold dust he needed to pay the balance. Fannie threw in some scraps of leftover cloth along with the doll. "On the house," she said. "Little something for the poppet." Fannie knew Mattie could sew a set of clothes for the doll that would keep little Annabelle occupied for hours. At least Gus hoped that would happen.

A few blocks later he turned up the street someone had jokingly named "Nob Hill." Along the road were several log houses—really no more than shacks, truth be told. Gus was lucky to have gotten one the year before, but Maggie hadn't been impressed. He remembered the look she'd given him when she first saw it. "Flour sacks for curtains?" She hadn't been smiling.

He could hear Annabelle's cries three houses away. His little blonde girl was as pretty as her mama; the only things she seemed to have inherited from him were her dark eyes and the tiny cleft in her chin. Unfortunately, her nature seemed to mirror Mattie's as well. Gus was big and he was strong. The roughness of life in the Yukon goldfields suited him fine. Mattie, and now Annabelle, well, they were a different story altogether. But they would adjust. Eventually.

He set his shovel and packages outside the door, pausing to crack the thin layer of ice that had formed on the basin of water that Maggie had put there. Picking up the sliver of lye soap next to it, he lathered up as best he could, splashing water along the back of his neck and up his arms before grabbing the towel left on a nearby hook. *A woman's touch*, he thought with satisfaction as he dried off, a reminder that despite the surroundings, they were all civilized human beings. He'd needed the prompt more than once.

"Is there a little Annabelly in here?" he announced as he entered the small front room that served as both kitchen and parlor. Annabelle stopped fussing as soon as she heard his deep voice.

"Dada!" she cried, waving her hands in the age-old sign language of children that said *Pick me up!* Gus put down the two presents he'd brought in and scooped his sweet-smelling baby daughter into his arms. He bussed her neck loudly, causing Annie to squeal with delight. Then, he leaned over to kiss Mattie, but she gave him her cheek and turned abruptly, wiping her hands quickly with the towel she had tucked into her apron.

"Sit yourself down for supper," she said.

Gus sighed and sat down with Annabelle on his lap. After two years of marriage, he could sense Mattie's shifting moods even when she tried to hide them. Unlike him, she wasn't good at keeping her emotions locked up. She was easy to read, and generally Gus liked that about her; it took a lot of time-wasting guesswork out of their relationship. The problem was, when it was bad, you couldn't dance around it for very long. But maybe, on account of it being Annabelle's birthday, she'd keep it to herself for a little while—at least long enough to enjoy the party. "So, did you invite Marybeth and the kids over to celebrate?"

"No, it's just us," Mattie said. She put a bowl of rabbit stew in front of him, along with a plate of sourdough bread. Wiping her hands again, she settled into her chair, then jumped up to get him a glass of water. She sat down again, but was up once more, gesturing to him to give her the baby. Annabelle strained to go back into Gus's arms, but Mattie held her tight.

"Aren't you gonna join me?" Gus asked.

"No. Annie and I already ate." She handed Annabelle a wooden duck and walked back and forth, jiggling the baby to keep her distracted.

Gus began to eat his dinner. The stew wasn't particularly good, but it was filling, and that was the main thing. He tore off a piece of bread, closed his eyes, and savored the taste; there was nothing in the world like sourdough. A moment later he opened his eyes; his wife was still pacing.

"You're as jumpy as a frog, Mattie. What's eatin' you?"

Mattie took a moment before answering. "Annabelle and I have got to go," she finally said.

The stew sank like a lump in his stomach. "What do you mean, 'gotta go'? Where to?"

"Seattle," she said. She sat down and bounced Annabelle on her lap a little too forcefully.

"Here, give her to me." Gus took the baby, giving himself time to marshal his thoughts. "I told you we had one or two more years here before this plays out," he said.

"Yeah, I know, but it's not working, Gus. It's not the life I thought it would be. I don't know. It's just…"

It was Gus's turn to stand. "Just what, Mattie? Just too cold? Just too hard?" He roamed around the small confines of the cabin, using his protective instinct with Annabelle to keep his temper in check. He told himself, *Mattie's only nineteen; she was just a girl when we got married*. It didn't help much. "You knew what you were getting into. I told you what it would be like before we left. You said—"

"I know what I said," Mattie snapped. "And I tried. I truly did. But having a baby out here was too hard, and knowing your ways, I'd be having another one before too long. Annabelle coughs all the time. I think she's got the croup. And there's nothing but ice to play with."

"Now there's where you're wrong." Taking a small blue-checkered quilt from Annabelle's crib, Gus spread it on the floor and placed his daughter on it. He got Shorty's sack and knelt in front of the baby. "Happy birthday, little Annabelly," he crooned, showing her Shorty's sack. "See what Uncle Shorty made for you." He reached into the bag and drew out a small block, painted with letters and numbers, parts of a tree and parts of a house on each of the six sides. He drew out the others, twelve in all. Annabelle immediately picked one up and put it in her mouth. She then flung it away and picked up another, happy for the moment with her new toy. "You see?" he said to Mattie, hating his wheedling tone.

"Annabelle's going to walk any day now, Gus. Just look at this place." Mattie gestured around the small room. "Where is she gonna go once winter hits and it's too cold to step outside for more than a minute before freezing to death? What if one of us leaves the door open and she wanders out? And why wouldn't she? There's nothing to do here!"

Annabelle had tired of throwing blocks and began to crawl off her blanket. The wooden floor was cold and wet in spots where Gus's boots had tread. He put Annabelle back on the quilt, reached for the present, and handed it to her. "See what Daddy brought you," he said softly. He helped her unwrap the package to reveal the blonde-haired doll. It was dressed in a faded blue gingham dress and its eyes, which had once opened and shut, stared permanently straight ahead. He sat back down to watch his daughter.

Mattie let out a sob. "Where did you get that?" she demanded.

Gus frowned. "Fannie sold it to me. Why?"

"That's little Janey Fortuna's doll, isn't it?"

"Well…"

Mattie stood. "It is! Jesu, Gus! Billy's so down on his luck he has to sell his own daughter's most favorite thing in all the world? What is it with you miners? You get the gold fever and you're willing to sacrifice most anything, even your families, to strike it rich. And how many of you have done that, huh? The Fortunas up on Preacher

Crick? Bob and Marybeth on Butte? The Millfords up on Deadwood? At least they're hanging it up, finally. Heading back down. What about Shorty? You going to keep on going 'til you look like that old man? How long will it be before you have to sell Annabelle's doll to the next miner with more brawn than brains? Tell me!" Mattie ran out of steam and slumped back down in her chair.

Had Gus really thought he liked his wife's openness? It felt like she'd taken a knife and sliced right down to the center of him. "I guess the idea of being rich someday doesn't have the appeal it once did," he said.

Mattie sounded weary. "I think I could have stuck it out, but it's no place for little ones." She looked at Gus, tears pooling. "You know I'm right."

Hell and damnation, she *was* right. Despite her assurances when they'd married, he'd feared she wouldn't cotton to life in the north. Why would she? She was young and pretty and deserved someone a lot better than him. But he'd traded on his strength and good looks, and the promise of riches down the road. Her ma had died and she had no family, so she'd bought in. But babies, they made a difference. And she was right about that too; given his appetites in that area, he wouldn't be able to keep more from coming.

They remained silent for several minutes, the only sound Annabelle's cooing and chirping as she continued to examine her new prize. She put the porcelain doll's arm in her mouth and Mattie gently reached down and took it out.

"You said the Milfords are heading down?" Gus asked. "When?"

"They've got passage for the beginning of June, soon as the river thaws."

Gus nodded. "Yukon should be pretty much broken up by then. They going to Seattle?"

"Yes. They said I could stay with them until I found work."

"What? You told them you were going before you talked to me?" His tone was sharper than he intended, but hell, this was nobody else's damn business.

"I told them we were *thinking* about having me go ahead of you," Mattie said, wrapping her arms around her middle as if to protect herself. "That's all."

"Well, since you've made your mind up already, I guess that's it," Gus said, his voice clipped. "I'll see about getting you passage with them."

"And you'll follow like I said, right?"

"I don't know, this might be the strike," Gus countered, knowing full well it wasn't panning out any more than the others had. "Tell you what, I'll work the tailings 'til the end of summer, and then come Outside to meet you. And we'll take it from there. Is that all right?"

Mattie smiled and took Gus's hand across the table. "Yes, that's all right. You'll see. Somehow we can make it work."

Gus felt her hand. It was chapped but warm and he thought maybe it *could* work out for them. Somehow. He leaned in to kiss her, but she gently resisted.

"I just finished my monthlies," she said with a hint of apology. "I don't want to take a chance on any more babies, Gus. I just can't." She got up and busied herself with Annabelle. "Come on, little birthday girl. Mama made you a sugar cake. Mama's big girl is one today."

Gus stood looking at his wife and daughter, the full meaning of what she'd told him finally beginning to sink in. The family he'd created was going away, and if he want to keep them, he'd have to give up a dream he'd had for a very, very long time. It didn't seem right, and it didn't seem fair. But right now there was nothing he could do about it.

End of Preview

The World of A.B. Michaels
"THE GOLDEN CITY"
Historical Fiction Series

The tempestuous, fast-changing world of turn-of-the-twentieth century San Francisco forms the backdrop of the series, "The Golden City."

Despite its sandy, fog-enshrouded terrain, San Francisco lies next to one of the world's greatest natural harbors. Yet it took the promise of gold in 1849 to turn "Yerba Buena" from a sleepy coastal village to a metropolis rivaling the most celebrated cities around the globe. Unforgettable characters from all walks of life struggle to find purpose and meaning (and occasionally love) in this award-winning series.

Novels in the series include: *The Art of Love*, *The Depth of Beauty*, *The Promise*, *The Price of Compassion*, *Josephine's Daughter* and *The Madness of Mrs. Whittaker*. Brief descriptions are listed below.

All books in the series are stand-alone reads and can be purchased on my website (abmichaels.com) at a discount or in three-volume discounted Book Bundles. They are also available at many on-line book retailers.

THE ART OF LOVE
(Book One of "The Golden City")

At the end of the Gilded Age, the "Golden City" of San Francisco offers everything a man could want —except the answers August Wolff desperately needs to find.

After digging a fortune in gold from the frozen fields of the Klondike, Gus head south, hoping to start over and put the baffling disappearance of his wife and daughter behind him. The turn of the century brings him even more success, but the distractions of a city some call the new Sodom and Gomorrah can't fill the gaping hole in his life.

Amelia Starling is a wildly talented artist caught in the straightjacket of Old New York society. Making a heart-breaking decision, she moves to San Francisco to further her career, all while living with the pain of a sacrifice no woman should ever have to make.

Brought together by the city's flourishing art scene, Gus and Lia forge a rare connection. But the past, shrouded in mystery, prevents the two of them from moving forward as one. Unwilling to face society's scorn, Lia leaves the city and vows to begin again in Europe.

Gus can't bear to let her go, but unless he can set his ghosts to rest, he and Lia have no future together.

THE DEPTH OF BEAUTY
(Book Two of "The Golden City")

In turn of the century San Francisco, Will Firestone is right at home among society's shallow elite. But the handsome, wealthy bachelor senses there must be something more. When business draws him into the heart of the Golden City's controversial Chinatown, he discovers a mysterious yet thoroughly enticing new world. With the help of an exotic young mother and a gifted teenage orphan, Will begins to examine his own values, learning through love and loss that true beauty takes many forms, and is anything but superficial.

Mandy Culpepper has seen a lot of tragedy in her young life, but her spirit is undimmed, even after being forced to leave the only home she has ever known. As she matures into a beautiful young woman, she is determined to remain true to herself, regardless of what society has in store for her. Will she find the soul-deep happiness that has so far eluded her?

THE PROMISE
(Book Three of "The Golden City")

A catastrophic earthquake has decimated much of San Francisco, leaving thousands without food, water or shelter. Patrolling the streets to help those in need, Army corporal Ben Tilson meets a young woman named Charlotte who touches his heart, making him think of a future with her in it. In the heat of the moment he makes a promise to her family that even he realizes will be almost impossible to keep.

Because on the heels of the earthquake, a much worse disaster looms: a fire that threatens to consume everything and everyone in its path.

It will take everything Ben's got to make it back to the woman he loves—and even that may not be enough.

THE PRICE OF COMPASSION
(Book Four of "The Golden City")

April 18, 1906. San Francisco has just been shattered by a massive earthquake and is in the throes of an even more deadly fire. During the chaos, gifted surgeon Tom Justice makes a life-changing decision that wreaks havoc on his body, mind, and spirit. Leaving the woman he loves, he embarks on a quest to regain his sanity and self-worth. Yet just when he finds some answers, he's arrested for murder—a crime he may very well be guilty of. The facts of the case are troubling; they'll have you asking the question: "Is he guilty?" Or even worse…"What would I have done?"

JOSEPHINE'S DAUGHTER
(Book Five of "The Golden City")

Set amidst the backdrop of the Gilded Age and beyond, ***Josephine's Daughter*** explores many social and medical issues facing women of that era—issues that resonate today. Independence, reproductive rights, sexual assault, birth control, childbirth, and parenting are all put to the test in *Josephine's Daughter.*

In the late nineteenth century, wealthy and headstrong Kit Firestone chafes under the strictures of the Golden City's high society, especially the interference of her charming but overbearing mother, Josephine. Kit's secret rebellion leads to potentially catastrophic results and keeps her from finding happiness.

When her brother nearly dies from a dangerous infection, Kit defies convention and becomes a working nurse. Through her troubled romance with a young doctor and a series of dramatic events, including a natural disaster and her mother's own critical illness, Kit begins to understand who her mother truly is and what their relationship is all about. She may not get the chance to appreciate their bond, however, because, through no fault of her own, a madman has Kit in his crosshairs.

THE MADNESS OF MRS. WHITTAKER
(Book Six of "The Golden City")

Book Six of The Golden City series, *The Madness of Mrs. Whittaker* explores two major forces of early twentieth century America: the religious movement called Spiritualism and treatment of the mentally ill.

While reluctantly exploring the possibility of contacting her dead husband through a spirit medium, a young widow is pronounced insane and committed to an asylum against her will. As she struggles to escape the nightmare she's been thrust into, she is stripped of everything she holds dear, including her identity and her reason to live. The fight to reclaim what is rightfully hers will test every aspect of her being, up to and including her sanity. Is she up to the task, or has her grip on reality already slipped away?

A "GOLDEN CITY/BARRISTER PERRIS" Novella:
Affair at the Majestic

My novella **Affair at the Majestic** serves as a bridge between "The Golden City" and the "Barrister Perris" historical mystery series.

English attorney Jonathan Perris is new to San Francisco and has just concluded his first big case, the murder trial of Dr. Tom Justice (See *The Price of Compassion*, Book Four of "The Golden City" series). Having hired his two law clerks as associates, Perris is ready to take on new clients. Enter Minerva Jo Letterman, a beautiful young woman whose husband is suing her for divorce, claiming adultery. She insists she's innocent, with a sob story that seems preposterous in light of the evidence against her. Lead attorney Cordelia Hammersmith takes on the challenge, but soon has second thoughts. Is the scrumptious Mrs. Letterman guilty or innocent? You decide.

As a thank you for joining my email list to get periodic updates about my work, I'll send you a *free* eCopy of *Affair at the Majestic.*

"BARRISTER PERRIS"
Historical Mystery Series

At the dawn of a new century, San Francisco is a phoenix, rising from the ashes of a massive earthquake and fire, brimming with more than its share of energy, opportunity and legal machinations. English trial attorney Jonathan Perris emigrates to "The Golden City" and opens a small law practice, hoping to forge a productive life far from

London's intrigue. With the help of his quirky American colleagues Cordelia Hammersmith, Oliver Bean and Dove Rebane, "Barrister Perris" takes on cases other lawyers won't touch. He's more than up for the challenge, but a major obstacle continues to haunt him: the unsettling past he's trying to forget.

Each book is a stand-alone read and can be purchased on my website (abmichaels.com) at a *discount*. They are also available at many on-line retail book sites.

Novels in the series include *The Twisted Road* and *Smoke*, now from Historium Press.

SMOKE
(Book Two of "Barrister Perris")
COMING IN 2026

San Francisco
September 7, 1907

The popular but controversial restaurant known as the Cliff House has mysteriously gone up in flames, crashing into the ocean off Land's End. When rumors start flying that it was arson, the manager hires attorney Jonathan Perris to save his reputation by finding out who lit the match. Meanwhile, Jonathan's associate Oliver Bean reluctantly agrees to investigate the death of Wallace Portman, a financier who lost his fortune on a stock scheme gone bad. All signs point to suicide, but Gwen Portman insists her father was murdered.

The cases appear completely unrelated, but Jonathan and his colleagues uncover evidence that points to a possible link involving corruption, illegal drugs and the horrors of addiction. Exposing the truth leads to violence that touches virtually every member of the firm. Will they survive to smoke out the guilty party?

"SINNER'S GROVE SUSPENSE"
Contemporary Romantic Suspense Series

"Sinner's Grove Suspense" is a contemporary series featuring descendants of characters from "The Golden City."

At the turn of the twentieth century, a wealthy businessman bought a unique parcel of land north of San Francisco, nestled in the redwoods and commanding a spectacular view of the Pacific Ocean. After meeting the love of his life, the two of them turned the site into an artists' retreat that gained worldwide fame for nearly half a century before closing its doors. Now the retreat is about to re-open, and the descendants and friends charged with making it happen are learning why the locals call the area "Sinner's Grove."

All books in the series are stand-alone reads and can be purchased on my website (abmichaels.com) at a *discount* or in three-volume discounted Book Bundles. They are also available at many on-line book retailers.

SINNER'S GROVE
(Book One of "Sinner's Grove Suspense")

A startling discovery when she was fourteen left San Francisco artist Jenna Bergstrom estranged from her family; unforeseen tragedy only sharpened her loneliness. But now her ailing grandfather needs her expertise to re-open the family's once-famous artists' retreat on the California coast. The problem? She'll have to face architect Brit Maguire, the ex-love of her life.

Seven years ago, Maguire spent a magical time with the woman of his dreams, only to have her disappear from his life completely. Now she's back, helping with the biggest historic renovation of Brit's career. No matter how deep his feelings still run, Brit can't afford the distraction of Jenna Bergstrom, because something is going terribly wrong with the project at Sinner's Grove.

THE LAIR
(Book Two of "Sinner's Grove Suspense")

After her father dies in a boating incident, innkeeper Daniela Dunn must travel from Northern California's Sinner's Grove back to Verona, Italy and her childhood home, an estate called the Panther's

Lair. It's a mansion full of frightful memories and deeply buried secrets, where appearances are deceiving and the price of honesty is death. As Dani is drawn further into her family's intrigues, she has an unlikely ally in handsome Marin County investigator Gabriele de la Torre. He says he's come along merely to support her, but his actions show he has an agenda all his own.

Gabe de la Torre needs to settle old family debts before starting fresh with the woman he feels could be The One. But once Dani finds out whom he's beholden to, all bets might be off. When a mystery woman reveals that Dani's father may have been murdered, the stakes rise dramatically and Gabe realizes they're now players in a dangerous game. Protecting Dani becomes his top priority, even as she strives to figure out whom she can trust: her relatives, Gabe, or even herself.

THE JADE HUNTERS
(Book Three of "Sinner's Grove Suspense")

Award-winning jewelry designer Regina Firestone is proud to exhibit her famous grandmother's multi-million dollar "bauble" collection at the grand re-opening of The Grove Center for American Art.

The fact that she's considering modeling the jewels in the nude like her grandmother did infuriates photographer Walker Banks, an owner of The Grove who's in charge of the exhibit. Their spat takes a back seat, however, when Reggie discovers that one of the most compelling pieces in the collection is not at all what it seems. Tracking down the truth will take the couple into the dark heart of a quest that's lasted more than a century—one in which destroying human lives—including Reggie's and Walker's—means nothing in the pursuit of a twisted sense of justice.

Thanks again for reading my books
—see you soon with my latest novel!

Acknowledgments

Writing is both a solitary and a collaborative pursuit, and I have the best collaborators around. My editor, Andrea Robinson, has perfected the art of making such comments as "Do you think he might want to..." Or "I'm wondering if..." She knows a *lot* of gentle suggestions, because her drafts often come back more red than black! Her input always makes my story better—much better.

Tara Mayberry at Teaberry Creative must have known me in a former life, because she quickly tunes in to my vision when it comes to covers. She's done it again with *The Twisted Road*, giving it just the right blend of historical verisimilitude and dramatic tension, which is what a good historical mystery cover should convey.

And as always, undying thanks goes to my husband Mike, who handles so many of the little details of both publishing and daily living; Whatever the ask, he gets it done. How'd I get so lucky?

About the Author

A native of California, A.B. Michaels holds masters' degrees in history (UCLA) and broadcasting (San Francisco State University). After working for many years as a promotional writer and editor, she decided it was time to focus on writing the kind of fiction she likes to read.

    A.B. and her husband live in Boise, Idaho. On any given day you might see them on the golf course, the bocce court, or walking their gray-haired "puppy," Teddy. More than likely, however, you'll find her hard at work on her next book.

https://abmichaels.com

www.historiumpress.com

www.ingramcontent.com/pod-product-compliance
Lightning Source LLC
LaVergne TN
LVHW040040080526
838202LV00045B/3415